His hair was relatively long, but even so, Chris could see patches of scalp. She pinched a small number of hairs between her gloved fingers and pulled. They came out with less effort than it would take to pick an onion. She shifted position so she could get a better look at the man's face, a self-imposed penance to fix in her mind the life that had been cut off through the chain of events she had started.

A phone call to Michael . . .

A conversation that lasted less than ten minutes the day her father reappeared.

Such a small event. And as a result, five people were dead.

Five.

Three was horrible, but five was . . .

Her mind suddenly rebelled against adding this one and the Druid Hills body to her tab. Because if she accepted these, she'd be acknowledging that there might be more.

No.

There *mustn't* be more. These *can't* belong to us.

She reached down and took hold of the cadaver's right arm, intending to fold it across the chest so she could see the hands better. But the body was in rigor and resisted, as though even in death the victim was holding a grudge.

Unable to move the arm, she bent closer.

And found . . .

THE
JUDAS
ViRUS

DAVID BEST

BERKLEY BOOKS, NEW YORK

THE JUDAS VIRUS

A Berkley Book / published by arrangement with the author

PRINTING HISTORY
Berkley edition / November 2003

Copyright © 2003 by Don Donaldson.
Excerpt from *Retribution* by Jilliane Hoffman copyright © 2004 by Jilliane Hoffman.
Cover design by Marc Cohen.
Cover photograph by Pure/Nonstock/Photonica.
Interior text design by Julie Rogers.

ISBN: 0-425-19298-9

BERKLEY®
Berkley Books are published by The Berkley Publishing Group,
a division of Penguin Group (USA) Inc.,
375 Hudson Street, New York, New York 10014.
BERKLEY and the "B" design
are trademarks belonging to Penguin Group (USA) Inc.

PRINTED IN THE UNITED STATES OF AMERICA

10 9 8 7 6 5 4 3 2 1

ACKNOWLEDGMENTS

This book couldn't have been written without the generous help of Dr. Santiago Vera, who provided me with the necessary technical background in liver transplantation. Nor could it have gone forward without the contributions of Dr. Bryan Simmons, who helped me understand what's involved in being both a practicing infectious disease specialist and the infection control officer of a major hospital. I'm also grateful to Dr. Clyde Hart and Dr. Walid Heneine of the CDC for taking the time to discuss retroviruses in general and pig retroviruses in particular with me. I received an excellent overview of the potential dangers of transplanting animal organs into people and the regulatory role of the FDA in this endeavor from Dr. Michele Pearson and Dr. Louisa Chapman of the CDC.

When I needed information on patent law, my old friend from graduate school and a truly exceptional woman, Dr. Claudia Adkison, stepped right up to help. The hospitality and assistance I received from Patrick and Julie Burnett during my short stay in Atlanta were outstanding and far beyond anything I expected. Any evidence in this book that I have a working knowledge of safety procedures with regard to infectious agents is due to conversations I had with Don Bailey. My road was additionally smoothed by discussions with Melissa Crouch, Dr. Valery Kukekov, Dr. Dennis Steindler, Dr. Dianna Johnson, Dr. Renate Rosenthal, Dr. Michael Heard, Dr. Kevin Newman, Dr. Howard Horn, Dr. Bill Armstrong, Laura Reed, Dennis Paden, and Lucinda Williams. If I've made any mistakes of fact, they are solely my own.

PROLOGUE

KAZAKHSTAN

This shouldn't be happening, TR thought as the truck hit a big pothole in the ruined highway. *I'm not supposed to be here.*

The truck dropped into another hole, throwing him against a crate. He struggled to his feet and banged on the cab window with his fist. "Watch where the hell you're going."

He could hear the two members of the French team in the cab laugh at him. Then the truck hit another hole, probably on purpose.

Laugh it up boys, TR thought. *Soon, things won't be so funny.*

How he hated those two. They called him Le Boucher, the butcher, because they thought his mouse dissection technique was too aggressive and careless—their way of diminishing him. As though *they* were so damned superior. Well, it wouldn't be long now and it'd be *their* turn.

But this was not the plan. By now, *he* should have been in Tselinograd with Bill Lansden, his leader. He wasn't there because Lansden's wife had been in a bad car wreck back in the States and Lansden had to depart early with the truck, leaving

TR to finish packing the equipment and take it and himself out
with the French.

And after nine weeks, was he ever glad to be going. He
looked out the back of the truck at the endless prairie, unbroken by any living thing except green wheat, stretching end-
lessly to the horizon. It was a hellhole even without the
epidemic they'd all come to fight.

What a fiasco. Fly eight thousand miles, bring in a ton of
medical equipment and supplies, only to discover that a
French team had arrived for the same purpose the day before.

The damn Kazakhstanis had sent out pleas to the U.S. and
France and didn't tell either country about the other.

The two teams had combined forces and had traced the
strange illness that had killed fourteen of the villagers to a microbe carried by the local mice, which had overrun the place
after a big snowstorm had buried a bumper wheat crop the
previous year. The snow hadn't melted until spring, giving the
furry little monsters more food than they could consume. So
they'd done what all animals do under those circumstances;
they'd created a population explosion, which had led to infes-
tation of even the wheat thatch on the village roofs.

The two teams had determined that the disease organism
was expelled from infected animals in their urine. Invariably,
some of this urine made its way through the thatch into the
villager's homes, and when the floors were swept, microbe-
laden dust was inhaled by the home's occupants. That much
they'd established for sure. But they didn't have the equipment to determine much about the bug except that it was completely destroyed in infected individuals within an hour after
death, and it was a virus belonging to the hanta genus. To
learn more would require sophisticated equipment neither
team had brought.

The truck banged into another pothole, bouncing TR into
the air and jarring his spine so hard when he came down that
his teeth clicked.

Jesus, doesn't this thing have any springs on it?

The two teams had agreed to publish the results of their
work together. And when the French had proposed that *they*
take all the blood samples and do the molecular biology work,
that dope Lansden had agreed. He'd paid no attention when
TR suggested dividing the samples and giving *each* team a

set—too much trouble, Lansden had said. His position on this was crazy. So TR had taken charge. And for all their insulting behavior and their attempt to dominate the study, he'd decided that the French should go home empty-handed.

The truck suddenly slammed to a stop. Three men dressed in camouflage fatigues, all of them armed with machine guns, materialized out of the wheat twenty yards back.

TR leaped up and looked over the cab, where he saw a jeep containing more armed men blocking the road. They'd apparently been hiding in the ravine to the right.

The ones behind the truck began screaming at TR in Russian and motioning for him to get out. He jumped to the pavement and was spun around so he was facing the field flanking the road. A foot in his back sent him sprawling onto the shoulder. He tried to get up, but was held on his knees by a gun behind his ear. As he realized that this was the traditional Russian method of execution, the contents of his stomach turned rancid.

The men from the jeep pulled the Frenchmen out of the truck and forced them to their knees beside TR.

"You don't understand," TR whined. "I'm not with these other men. I'm—"

The guy with the gun at TR's head shouted at him and pressed the pistol harder against his skull. To his right there was a gunshot and the Frenchman who'd been driving the truck let out a faint grunt as though he'd been hit in the gut. In his peripheral vision, TR saw the man fall face forward into the wheat.

Then, beside him, not three feet away, another shot sent a bloody aerosol and pieces of the remaining Frenchman's skull flying before he, too, crumpled onto his face.

An instant from his own death, TR rolled onto his back and yelled, "Nicolai Butuzov! Nicolai Butuzov! Amerikanski! Amerikanski!" Expecting to be shot in the face, TR raised his arms as if they could protect him.

A burly guy dressed like the others, but wearing a military beret had been inspecting the contents of the truck. He turned now and barked an order in Russian. He left the truck and walked over to TR. In heavily accented English, he said, "How do you know Nicolai Butuzov?"

TR had suspected from the start that the name his contact

had used was probably an alias, but shouting it had done the trick. "I'm the one who hired you, for Christ's sake."

The burly Russian gave another order and the assassin looming over TR stepped back. The Russian extended a hand to help him up. "Why didn't you say so earlier?"

CHAPTER 1

CHRIS COLLINS CAUGHT Jamie Mallon, one of the hospital's circulating nurses, just leaving the OR.

"Hi Jamie, do you have a minute?"

"Sure. What's up?"

"Last week you worked with Dr. Blake on a laminectomy. Did Dr. Doyle, the cardiovascular guy, come into the OR at any time during the procedure?"

Chris was working a hunch. In the last two weeks, three patients in the hospital had developed strep A infections in their surgical wounds. One case would have raised her eyebrows, three was an epidemic. As the hospital's medical director of infection control, it was her job to contain this thing. Since strep was an organism carried by people and not by contaminated water or instruments, and was most often transmitted into wounds during surgery, she had concentrated her attention on the OR personnel in each case.

Dr. Tom Doyle had been the surgeon of record on two of the three cases, but not the third. Interestingly, the OR log sheets had shown that the laminectomy case Chris had asked Mallon about had been done in OR #4, which was right next to the room where Doyle had performed a triple bypass that had become infected. And the two surgeries had been done on the same day at the same time, a fact too intriguing to ignore.

"Dr. Doyle . . . ," Mallon said, thinking back. "Was he listed in the log?"

One of Mallon's responsibilities as circulating nurse was to keep a list of everyone who entered the OR during a procedure.

"No."

Mallon's brow furrowed and her eyes flashed. "Are you suggesting I didn't do my job properly?"

"Not at all. It's just that I know sometimes things get hectic in there and you're trying to do three things at once and sometimes, very rarely, a little thing like keeping the personnel log kind of gets neglected."

Seeing that Chris was so understanding, Mallon let her defenses down. "The laminectomy," she said, once again examining her memory. Then she hit on something. "He *was* there . . . for just a minute. Stopped in to tell Dr. Blake that he had to drop out of the fishing trip they had planned."

In Chris's mind, this pretty much sealed the deal. Doyle was the carrier. The pager in her pocket began to vibrate. She touched Mallon's shoulder in a show of appreciation, thanked her, then looked at the number on the pager: her office. She headed for the nearest house phone.

"Paula, this is Dr. Collins."

"Your father's here to see you."

My father?

She hadn't heard from him in twenty-nine years, not since he'd left her mother for another woman.

My father, here? "I'll be there shortly."

She hung up and stood for a moment, her mind grappling with what she'd just heard. It *couldn't* be. Paula must have misunderstood. Then she began to remember what it had been like for her and her mother struggling financially without her father. And how she'd felt growing up: inadequate and somehow at fault for making him leave. How even now, with her mother dead, she faced life alone, unable to trust any man enough to let them get too close, unwilling to ever put herself in a position to be left again. Even knowing where these feelings came from, she hadn't been able to shed them. The truth will set you free? Not always, brother.

No, that wasn't him waiting for her. He'd ignored her for nearly three decades. Why would he crawl out of hiding now? And after what he'd done, he wouldn't *dare* show himself.

In addition to her duties as medical director of infection control for Good Samaritan, Chris was part of a three-member private infectious disease practice housed in the physicians office building next door. The call she'd just taken had come from there. So even with the new crossover between the two buildings on the third floor, she faced a fairly long walk.

Though she would have bet that the man waiting for her was *not* her father, the anger she'd resurrected in thinking about him was a wind at her back, propelling her through the halls even more briskly than usual. Upon reaching the entrance to the main office, she took a moment to gather herself, then went in.

Almost all their practice came from being called in by other physicians to manage infections acquired by patients already in the hospital. So it wasn't the kind of situation where there was always a full waiting room, which is why they only had a couple of chairs, mostly for drug reps who dropped in. Thus, when Chris walked through the door, there was only one man there. He stood expectantly and they stared awkwardly at each other.

He was wearing black slacks and an eggshell-colored sport coat over a black turtleneck. His brown hair, receding in front, hung to his shoulders in back. Round wire-rimmed glasses and a neatly trimmed salt-and-pepper mustache and goatee completed the impression that he was either a creative-type guy or wished to look like one. Chris had only two pictures of her father: a fuzzy full-length snapshot taken when he was twenty and a better head shot made around fifteen years ago. This man bore some resemblance to her father, but she still found it hard to accept that this was him. Beyond her general disbelief, she remembered him as being a lot bigger. But of course everything seems bigger to a six-year-old than to an adult. And she clearly wasn't seeing him at his best, for there was no doubt in her mind that he was seriously ill. His skin had a distinctive yellow-green hue and the waistband of his turtleneck rested on a potbelly probably caused by fluid accumulating in his peritoneal cavity. A classic case of liver failure.

He spoke first. "Hello, Chris. You've grown into a beautiful woman. And all this . . ." He gestured to the offices. "You should be very proud of yourself."

Not wishing to play this scene out in front of the practice's secretary, Chris said, "Let's talk in my office."

He followed her there and she shut the door. In part because she really did need proof of who he was, but also appreciating the subtext in the comment, she said, "I'm going to need some identification."

He flashed a shocked expression, then nodding in resignation, he reached for his wallet, from which he produced a driver's license that he handed to her.

The name on the license was Wayne Collins. It *was* him. She returned the license, then showed him her back as she crossed the room. She stepped behind her desk and sat down. "Why did you do it?"

"Leave?"

"What *else* would I mean?" she replied, her brows knitted, a chain reaction boiling in her green eyes.

She hadn't invited him to sit, but moving carefully, like a cat doing something it knows is forbidden, he put himself in the only visitor's chair. He leaned forward, his hands dangling limply from the armrests, his gaze directed at the mahogany panel on the front of her desk. His tongue snaked out and caressed both corners of his mouth. Then he looked up.

"It's hard to explain . . . I don't really understand it myself. I just felt . . . smothered. It's not that I didn't love you. A part of me did, but another part couldn't accept all the responsibility. And your mother and I . . . we just were so different from each other."

"Did you ever hear of child support?" Chris snapped. "We could have used a hand."

"I've barely been able to support myself. I had a novel published about fifteen years ago. *Billy Runyan* it was called." He raised his eyebrows in hope. "Did you know?"

"Afraid I missed it."

Her father snorted. "You and the rest of the world. I've written three others, all unpublished, so I guess I'm a misfit there too. I've been able to eke out a living by writing assembly instructions for furniture and toys. Put nut A on bolt B . . .

that's me. But you . . . Chrissy, you've accomplished so much despite what I did."

"That's the way I look at it, too."

"I'm sure you don't think I have any right to feel like I'm part of your accomplishment, but I do. I have to because you're the only element in my whole miserable life that has amounted to anything. You never knew it, but I was at your medical school graduation, feeling as proud as any of the other fathers."

"Why didn't you let me know you were there?"

"I didn't want to ruin your big day."

"Maybe if you'd have written or called or come to see me a couple of times while I was growing up, you wouldn't have had that to worry about."

"I've considered that more times than I can count. It's hard to think that your tombstone, if you can afford one, should read, 'Here lies an alcoholic who abandoned his family and pissed his life away.'"

This made Chris even angrier. *She* was the injured party here. She was the one entitled to throw the spears, but now with his self-pitying whining he was trying to deprive her of even that. Infuriating as this was, his obviously grave condition kept her from retaliating.

"Is that what destroyed your liver—alcoholism?"

"They trained you well."

"It's pretty obvious."

"My doctors tell me I need a transplant. I've got medical insurance that'll pay for it, but only at the program in Kansas City. The waiting list there for my blood type is twenty-eight months. And they say I probably won't last that long."

"Won't they move you up if you suddenly take a bad turn?"

"They would if I didn't have a history of alcoholism. They're very strict in their program and require six months of sobriety before I'd be eligible for special placement. And I've only been clean for ninety days. I'm doing the twelve steps with AA, but three months doesn't cut it. To complicate matters, you know how in cirrhotic livers the blood flow backs up and produces varicose veins in your esophagus . . . Well mine are huge and ten weeks ago I had one burst. The blood just gushed out. So much that I went into shock. If I hadn't gone down in a public place I'd be dead now. But paramedics got to me in time.

"My docs say it could happen again at any moment. If it does, and I can't get to a phone or no one sees what's happening, I'm done. Even if I get prompt attention, next time I could have brain damage . . . I mean beyond what you probably think I have already. There *are* other transplant centers that aren't quite so rigid about the alcoholism, but I don't have a hundred and fifty thousand dollars to give them for their services."

"If you came here to ask me for the money so you could go to a different program, I couldn't help you if I wanted to. I'm still paying off my student loans and I had to hock my soul to buy into this practice." Even as she spoke, Chris became upset with herself for going into such details with him about her finances.

"No, I didn't think you'd be able to do *that*," Wayne said. He paused, apparently searching for words.

Suddenly, Chris got an ugly premonition. Surely he wasn't going to ask her . . .

"I know I have no right to expect you to help me," Wayne said. "And I wouldn't have come except I don't want to die with the sorry legacy I've built for myself. I need time to balance the scales, to find some way to make up for a lifetime of self-absorption that did nothing for anyone else. So forgive me for what I'm about to say, but I read somewhere that it's possible for a living person to give a part of their liver to another, and within a few months the part the donor contributed grows back, so they're as good as new, except for maybe a little scar."

Oh my God, Chris thought. *That is why he came. He wants a piece of my liver. This is just a visit to his parts warehouse.* Her anger toward him surged to new levels for putting her in this position.

"Of course the blood type of the donor and the recipient have to be appropriate," her father said. "I'm type O and I remember that you are, too."

"After your history with me, you have the nerve to ask for this?"

"Believe me, I didn't want to come. But I couldn't think of any other solution."

"What about the woman you left us for? What's *her* blood type?"

"That only lasted a few years. I don't even know where she is."

Chris was so filled with disgust she couldn't stand to look at him another second. "I've got a very busy day scheduled and I'm already running late. I can't talk any more just now." She pulled a sheet of paper from the box on her desk, wrote her address and phone number on it, and got up and handed it to him. "Come to my apartment tonight at seven o'clock. And don't expect dinner."

He rose, took the paper, and put it in an inside pocket of his jacket. "I'm sorry for doing this to you." Then he left.

With him gone, Chris wondered why the hell she'd given him her address and agreed to meet with him again. There was no way she was giving him part of her liver. Undergo major surgery and let somebody hack out a piece of her so a louse of a man could . . .

Live.

Damn it. That's what we're talking about here. The man's life is at stake. How could she just ignore that?

Feeling the needle on her stress gauge creeping into the red zone, she closed her eyes and began the meditation exercise she learned from a Chinese classmate when she was a medical student. Within a few seconds, her pulse and respiration slowed and her blood pressure edged downward. In just a few minutes she was once again fit for duty.

On the way out she stopped at the secretary's desk.

"Hope I'm not being out of line," Paula said, "but your father doesn't look well."

"Just one of his many problems. I need to talk with Tom Doyle, the cardiovascular surgeon, ASAP. When you get him on the line, page me, would you please? I'll be making rounds."

Ten minutes later, in the ICU, Chris was writing an order for fluconazole to combat a cryptococcal lung infection in a woman who caught the bug from the droppings of her newly purchased parrot. Just as Chris scribbled her name on the order and closed the chart, her pager sent her again to a house phone, where she learned that Paula had Doyle on the line.

"I'm at six-eight-two-three," Chris said. "Ask him to call me here."

In seconds, he did.

"Tom, thanks for getting back to me so quickly. Would you have a few minutes today to talk about those two patients of yours with strep infections?"

"Are you free now?" Doyle asked.

"Yes. Where are you?"

"The CCU."

"Let's meet in my office in five minutes."

If Chris had merely wanted to discuss her management of one of Doyle's patients in her role as a private infectious disease consultant on a case, she would have just met him in the coronary care unit. But implicating him as a strep carrier was not something to do publicly.

Five minutes gave her time to check on one more patient, a retired fireman whose respiratory infection was so extensive his ventilator had blown a hole in one of his weakened lungs. She found his chart in the hands of Charles Hickman, an effusive young pulmonary physician who hadn't lost enough patients yet to whittle away at his boundless optimism and good humor.

When he saw her, he grinned and showed her the plot of the fireman's temperature since Chris had added amphotericin B to the antibiotics he was being given.

"You could ski down that slope," Hickman said, referring to the plot's precipitous drop to normal. He pointed at Chris. "You da *man*."

With more important things on her mind, she let the opportunity pass to remind Hickman that she was actually the other sex sometimes found in the practice of medicine. Instead, she just said, "Keep that up and I'm going to think you're surprised. How's he sound?"

"Better," Hickman said. "See for yourself."

She slipped on a gown and mask and donned gloves from the isolation cart outside the fireman's room. Listening to his lungs with the isolation stethoscope, she noted a distinct improvement in the man's chest sounds. Returning to the hall, she wrote a short note to that effect in his chart.

"Well, it's been real," she said to Hickman.

"Going so soon? What is it—my breath, my personality, my wife?"

"All of the above," Chris said, wiggling her fingers over her shoulder at him.

On the way back to her office, a small voice began telling Chris that any woman who would refuse to help her dying father, regardless of what he had done to her, was cold and callous and possibly deserved being abandoned when she was a child. She had always been impressed by the enormity of death. The passing of life from any creature was not a casual event no matter how many times it had occurred in the history of the earth, for the aggregate passing of billions in the past didn't lessen the impact on the next one to die. And wouldn't her refusal to help him be doing the same thing to him he had done to her?

Worse, the voice said. *You lived.*

And she was a doctor, for God's sake . . . Her whole life was dedicated to *helping* the sick.

WITH ALL THE weight he carried, Tom Doyle looked as though he'd soon be needing a bypass himself. Whenever Chris saw him, she was reminded that every pound of fat needs two hundred miles of blood vessels to support it. It was no wonder he had the flushed complexion of a hypertensive.

"Hello, Tom. Let's go in the conference room."

"It's my understanding that there have been three cases of strep infection. And only two of those are mine," Doyle said, following her. "So who's the common denominator?"

"Have a seat. Can I get you some coffee?"

"I'm fine," Doyle said, sitting at one of the wooden chairs around the mahogany conference table.

Chris sat opposite him. "Tom, how have you been feeling lately?"

"Overworked and fat," he replied, scratching his head. "You know who I think it is . . . Bill Gooch, the anesthesiologist. He's always farting in the OR. And I once heard of a guy who had a rectal strep colonization contaminating his OR by farting them into the air."

"My question about how you've been feeling wasn't a social inquiry. Have you or anyone in your family had a sore throat lately?"

"Wait a minute," Doyle said, catching on. "You think it's me?"

"The strep case that isn't yours . . . you went in that OR while the surgery was taking place to speak to Dale Blake about a fishing trip. Do you remember that?"

"Who said so?"

Not wanting to create any trouble for Jamie Mallon, Chris said, "Then you *didn't* go in there?"

"I might have."

"Tom, *you're* the common denominator. Have you had a fever lately, or any little skin eruptions?"

Doyle scratched his head. "No, nothing like that."

It actually wasn't necessary for a strep carrier to exhibit any symptoms, so Doyle could have harbored a colony in his nose or his rectum without any signs. On the other hand . . . "Would you wait here for just a sec? I'll be right back."

Chris made a quick trip to her office and returned with a pair of rubber gloves and a swab and saline kit. "Would you mind if I took a sample from your scalp?"

"Of course not. But it's not me. You're mistaken."

Chris donned the gloves and swabbed a scaly patch on Doyle's scalp. "I'll send this right down to the lab. We should have the results by late tomorrow. In the meantime, you don't have a case scheduled today or tomorrow do you?"

"I have one early in the morning."

It was within Chris's authority to suspend Doyle's OR privileges until the strep problem was solved. But without the lab results for confirmation of her hunch, she was reluctant to play that card.

"Under the circumstances, do you feel comfortable operating?"

"It's not me," Doyle said. His hand headed for his scalp, but he caught himself and put it back on the table. "You'll see. It's somebody else."

"But what if it is you?"

There was a brief trapped-animal look in his eyes, then the fight went out of him and he flipped his hand in the air. "All right. I'll postpone my next case until we hear from the lab."

When he left, Chris sat at the big table all by herself and wrestled once more with the problem of her father. Finally, needing to get moving, she roused herself and headed back to the hospital to drop off the swab and continue her rounds.

She returned to her office a little after four o'clock, having considered and reconsidered all the arguments in favor of giving her father what he wanted. But she just couldn't do it. If that meant she was cold and heartless, that's what she'd have to be.

A few minutes later, while perusing the weekly morbidity and mortality report from the CDC, where, before her infectious disease fellowship, she'd spent two years as an Epidemic Intelligence Service (EIS) officer, she was struck by a sudden thought. Maybe there was something she could do for her father.

She flipped through her Rolodex, found the number for Michael Boyer, and called it.

"This is Dr. Collins at Good Samaritan. Is Dr. Boyer available? No? Would you page him please and have him call me? It's very important that I speak to him today."

Boyer quickly returned her call and they spoke for nearly ten minutes. Hearing her suggestion, he expressed strong interest in the idea and then made a proposal himself that took her by surprise. By the end of the conversation, she had set up an interview for her father which, if it went well, would not only give him a chance to live, but would make him famous.

CHAPTER 2

CHRIS PICKED UP the hardcover novel and looked at the author's name: Wayne Collins. The only book her father had ever published. His picture on the back was the head shot she'd mentally referenced when he'd shown up in her office. She'd found the book by accident many years ago browsing in a secondhand bookshop in Boston. It was a rags-to-riches story set during the Depression about a boy growing up in rural Kansas in a family so poor their suffering drove the father to commit suicide. Possessed of a gritty determination and unschooled intelligence, the oldest son became the family breadwinner, supporting them with money he made running a street-corner shell game in Kansas City. With what little he could put aside, he bought a calf and raised it on land the family didn't own. From the sale of that animal he earned enough to buy two more calves. Eventually, the boy became head of the biggest meat-packing operation in the state.

Chris had read the book a dozen times looking for clues about why her father had abandoned her, so that the book, which looked practically new when she'd bought it, was now battered and worn from being thrown across the room in anger on many occasions.

The buzzer at the front entrance sounded. She carried the book to the intercom and asked who it was.

"Wayne Collins."

The formal way he identified himself struck Chris as odd. But then what could he have said . . . *It's Daddy?*

She pressed the button that released the security door in the lobby and hastened to her study, where she dropped the book behind a row of novels with medical themes. She returned to the living room and waited for her father to arrive.

After what seemed like an inordinately long time, she heard three light taps on the door. She opened it and there he was, wearing the same clothes as before. There was an awkward moment as they sized each other up, Chris wondering how he was going to greet her and how she should respond. Finally she just stepped back and said, "Come in," not calling him by name because it seemed odd to do so.

"Hello, Chris," Wayne said, stepping in. "Hope my visit earlier, at your office, didn't upset your routine."

"Why should it?" she said, shutting the door. "I don't see or hear from you for nearly three decades and then you just show up one day and tell me you're dying . . . Sure, that's an event that wouldn't affect anyone's day."

"I'll just put that on the list of everything else I'm sorry for."

There he goes again, Chris thought, *the old self-deprecation ploy.*

"I brought you something." He raised his right hand and offered her a small flat package in a floral gift wrapping.

Chris took it without enthusiasm and appraised him with cool detachment.

"Open it."

Chris removed the paper and discovered a spanking-new copy of *Billy Runyan,* Wayne's only published novel.

"There's a dedication inside," he urged.

Chris turned to the title page and read in a neat hand:

To Chrissy,

Who, like Billy Runyan, became a success despite the actions of a spineless father. Whatever else you might think of me, please believe that I do love you.

Your wayward father,
Wayne Collins

Well, there was the thread she'd been looking for in the book and missed—the spineless father. Pretty obvious now. But did he really expect her to believe he loved her? And what was with the date after his signature? "Why is this inscription dated seven years ago?"

"I wrote it the day before you graduated and had it with me at the ceremony. I was going to give it to you then, but I lost my nerve."

Chris was taken aback by this. So her father had expressed his love for her in this dedication long before he knew he needed a new liver. *If* he was telling the truth, which she greatly doubted. She looked at the dedication again, as though she could somehow detect the age of the ink. Then, feeling extremely suspicious of him, she closed the book and mumbled her thanks. More as a gambit to delay their coming conversation than out of any wish to be a good host, she said, "Could I get you something to drink?" She was about to offer him a glass of wine but caught herself. "I can make coffee, or there's Coke, or tea . . ."

"I just ate, so I don't need anything."

After another awkward pause, Chris gestured self-consciously to a pair of overstuffed chairs by the fireplace. "Let's sit over there."

"Your apartment is nice," Wayne said. "You have good taste."

Chris immediately wondered what he meant by that. Was he suggesting that if she could afford this place, she could find the money to help him? "Everything was chosen carefully," she said. "With an eye toward economy."

Well, for the love of— She'd done it again. Defended herself to him. What was wrong with her?

When they were seated, Wayne said, "You have your

mother's red hair and green eyes, and you're petite like she was."

Chris fumbled through her mind for a response.

Not getting one, Wayne went on. "Have you ever worn your hair long, or has it always been short like that?"

"Mostly short."

"It suits you."

An ice age followed, during which neither of them knew what to say. The tension for Chris was unbearable and her hands became so cold they hurt. She felt a frigid drop of perspiration fall from her right armpit and hit her side under her blouse. Then, suddenly, she became angry at being nervous. This was her *home*. He had no right to come in here and cause her this kind of discomfort. And there was no need to feel guilty about her decision. She should just tell him and get it over with. "I can't be a donor for you," she blurted out. "I've thought about it and I can't."

A tide of hopelessness moved across Wayne's jaundiced eyes. "Well," he said, "I don't blame you. It was a lot to ask."

Affected by his obvious disappointment, Chris quickly moved on to tell him the rest of what she'd planned to say. "But I made a phone call today and you may have another option."

Wayne moved to the front of his chair. "What would that be?"

"You'll have to pass an interview. It's not a sure thing that you'll be accepted."

"Into what? Some kind of clinical trial for a new drug?"

"A different kind of transplant." She hesitated, looking for a way to phrase it that wouldn't make the whole idea sound so *desperate*. But there was no other way to put it. "There's a group at Monteagle Hospital here who are looking for the right candidate to receive a liver from a genetically altered strain of pigs they've developed."

"Pigs?" Wayne said, hardly believing he'd heard her correctly. "You want to put a pig organ in me? Is that all I am to you . . . someone to experiment on?"

"It's the only way I could think of to help you."

"Pigs . . . a pig organ. They can do that? And it'll work?"

"They think so or they wouldn't try. But you'd be the first human they've ever worked with. They've had success transplanting pig livers to other primates, but you have to understand that the technique is entirely experimental. There'd be no guarantees."

"Why pigs?"

"Their organs are anatomically similar to humans and they're the right size. And since we already use pigs for food, it doesn't create an ethical problem."

"How is this possible? Won't my immune system reject the organ immediately because it's not human?"

"They've altered the donor animals so their cells don't contain the surface markers that create the worst mismatch. And they have several animal lines that mimic the various human blood types. The leader of the Monteagle team told me that the livers from their animals are as compatible as any human liver a person might receive from an unrelated donor of the same blood type, which is about the only tissue-matching requirement used for livers."

Wayne got up and began to pace. "A pig liver . . . It sounds bizarre."

"It is bizarre at this point. But that's only because it's never been done. A few years from now, it could be routine."

"Or some factor they didn't anticipate could go wrong and I'll die."

"That's certainly a possibility."

Hands in his pockets, eyes on the beige carpet, Wayne resumed his prisoner's stroll, his tongue making sucking sounds against his teeth. On his third trip over the same course, he turned and looked at Chris. "I don't see that I have much choice. When's the interview?"

"Three-thirty tomorrow. Meet me in my office at three and we'll drive over there together."

"Despite what I said earlier, I do appreciate you setting this up. It just took me by surprise."

"I hope it works." Chris got out of her chair and moved toward the door. "Now, it's been a long day."

"I understand." Wayne walked quickly to the door, which Chris opened for him. Before leaving, he paused and touched her arm. "It's been great seeing you."

Chris wasn't sure what she'd have done if he'd tried to kiss her, but fortunately, he didn't. When he was gone, she felt the tension flow out of her. It had gone as well as it could, but the experience had drained her. She picked up the book Wayne had brought her and reread the dedication, wanting to believe it had indeed been written as dated. Then she sat down with the book, turned to the first paragraph, and began reading.

She finished the book at twelve-thirty, disappointed once again. Even with the spineless-father theme pointed out to her, she found that the story contained little relevance to her own situation. Just one more instance where dear old Dad failed to deliver.

With a full day facing her tomorrow, she showered and crawled into bed, where she thought briefly about the significant potential problem with pig transplants she hadn't mentioned to her father, mostly because she wasn't up on the latest developments. No matter. Michael Boyer, the head of the transplant team, would certainly brief him.

But *she* couldn't wait for that. Tomorrow, Boyer would want her response to the favor he'd requested when she'd called him about Wayne. And she didn't want to be making her decision just using information he'd given her. She wanted some hard data to examine. So first thing in the morning, she'd dive into the literature.

LITTLE CHRISSY STOOD *frozen at the corner, watching the crossing guard urgently motioning her forward. But her legs wouldn't move. Across the street old Mrs. Lipinski was looking real mad. She hated Mrs. Lipinski and that terrible old closet, but if she didn't go to her, there'd be trouble.*

Chrissy looked back at the little white house next to her school, hoping to see the red truck or, even better, her father himself. She didn't understand why he no longer lived at home, but was sure that she'd done something so terrible he didn't want to be around her anymore. It had been a year since he'd left and moved into the white house with another woman that her mother had called a slug or slut once on the phone talking to Aunt Ellen. Chrissy hadn't seen her father since the day he left and she missed him terribly.

Even though her mother had told her never to stop there, once after school, when Mrs. Lipinski was late coming to the corner, she had knocked on the door of the white house, but no one was home. So she hadn't even seen the woman who was a slug.

The crossing guard blew her whistle at Chrissy and began motioning to her more wildly. Mrs. Lipinski too was now doing the same thing. Helpless to resist, Chrissy obeyed.

When she reached the other side, Mrs. Lipinski grabbed her by the shoulders. "Child, what's the matter with you? You think I like standing here while you daydream?"

Mrs. Lipinski's breath smelled like cabbage and when she was upset like this, spit flew out of her mouth.

"Now come on." She grabbed Chrissy by the hand, jerked her around, and pulled her toward the old house with the squeaky floors and the dreaded closet.

Going up the front steps a few minutes later, Chrissy's feet barely touched the cement. Inside, as she did every day, Mrs. Lipinski said, "Do you have to pee?"

"No."

She took Chrissy through the parlor and opened the closet door, where a chrome kitchen chair sat surrounded by old water-stained cardboard boxes in which they lived. Chrissy didn't want to go inside, but if she didn't, Mrs. Lipinski would poison her dog, Buddy. And would do it, too, if she told her mother about the closet.

So, in she went. For Buddy's sake.

Mrs. Lipinski shut the door and turned the key in the lock. Darkness . . . Heavy . . . Musty . . .

Meditation, Mrs. Lipinski called it. Said it was good each day to sit quietly and think about all the bad things you had done or thought about doing, and concentrate on being a better person.

As usual, in less than a minute, Chrissy heard Mrs. Lipinski's car start. The engine revved, then faded as the car backed out of the driveway. It would return in two hours, just before Chrissy's mom came from work and took her home.

Only two hours. That wasn't so bad. Or it wouldn't have been if it wasn't for them.

It never took very long. By the time Chrissy counted to a hundred she could feel the first silverfish crawling like a tickling feather up her leg. Then they came by the scores, exploring her . . . so many and so curious she couldn't brush them all away.

They didn't bite, so she just let them have their way, holding in the scream that pushed at the back of her throat as they traveled over her skin. Today, for some reason, it seemed more horrible than usual, their feet more probing, their numbers larger.

She kept her sanity during this time by putting her eye against a hole drilled a long time ago in the closet for a phone line that was no longer there. Through this opening, Chrissy could see her father's little white house and she would look at it and imagine him inside.

Today, when she looked, there was her father's red pickup in his driveway, the first time she'd ever seen it since he left.

He was there.

Just across the street.

So close.

She never spoke while in the closet. What was the point? But today, with her father so near and the silverfish so numerous, she moaned, "Daddy . . . Help me. Please . . . Save me."

In her bed, Chris, still asleep, hugged her pillow, the events of so long ago recurring with vivid clarity in the dream she had not had for nearly eight years.

Still lost in slumber, her lips moved against her pillow. "Daddy . . . Save me."

CHAPTER 3

THE NEXT DAY, Chris spent the morning on her computer trying to determine what was currently known about the potential threat for infection that transplanted pig organs posed to human recipients. The basic problem was that during their evolution, pigs had been infected with a unique class of viruses known as retroviruses, which had inserted their genes into the chromosomes of the pig's reproductive cells, so that the virus was now passed to every member of every litter of pigs from the moment of conception. The consequence was that most every pig cell in the world carried up to fifty copies of the complete genetic sequence of a virus that routinely caused those cells to shed infectious particles. The virus didn't seem to harm the pig, but what would it do in a human? That's what Chris wanted to know.

The question was extremely important because history is replete with examples of viruses that were relatively harmless in animal hosts, but produced devastating effects in humans. The most notorious was the flu virus of 1918, which killed more than 20 million people after mutating from a virus that evolved in pigs. Moreover, the necessity of giving her father immunosuppressive drugs so he wouldn't reject the transplant could allow a pig virus that his body wouldn't normally tolerate to become established in him. There, it could flourish and possibly mutate into a more human-adapted form, which would allow it to infect people with normal immune systems.

These were issues that would interest Chris even if her father were not potentially in line to be the world's first recipient of an indwelling pig liver. But she had another reason as well.

When she'd called Michael Boyer to discuss the possibility of getting Wayne into the program, Michael had told her that the infectious disease member of the team had recently dropped out and they needed a replacement. Then he'd asked her to take his place.

It wasn't something she wanted to do. She had enough responsibilities already. When she'd said this to Boyer, he'd responded with a low blow.

"Chris, you realize that if you were a member of the team, you'd not only have a vote on whether we accept your father, but your presence could have a lot of influence in how the others feel about him."

"That's blackmail."

"I prefer to think of it as a cooperative venture with a mutual benefit to both of us."

"Like I said, blackmail."

The first pertinent information Chris found in her search was disturbing. A group of researchers in England had found that when pig kidney cells were cultured in the same dish with several types of human cells, the latter became infected with the pig retrovirus, proving that at least those human cells possessed surface characteristics the virus could exploit to gain entrance. She soon found an additional paper from a German group establishing that human cells could also be infected from the cells that line pig blood vessels.

This certainly wasn't good news. Chris leaned back in her chair and mulled over what she'd just learned. Surely Michael Boyer knew about these papers, yet he was still ready to proceed with a transplant.

Of course, cells in a dish and cells in an entire organism were not the same thing. Maybe there was newer data relative to that point.

Moving on through the databases, she quickly found a study that showed no evidence of pig virus infection in ten people who had received insulin-producing pig cells to treat their diabetes. Another paper reached the same conclusion for two people with kidney failure who had briefly had their bloodstream connected to a pig kidney.

Then she found an even larger study that looked for evidence of pig virus in the blood of 160 people who had been exposed to pig cells or tissues up to twelve years earlier. In addition to the two kinds of exposure covered in the previous papers, this one included individuals whose blood had been allowed to pass for a time through a pig spleen, and others who had received temporary pig skin grafts. More significantly for Chris, the study also reported on people with liver failure whose blood had been run through a device composed of pig liver cells enclosed in a semipermeable membrane. There was even one patient whose blood had been allowed to course through an entire intact pig liver.

Bottom line: Once again, there was no evidence in any of those people that they had been infected with the pig virus. This included thirty-six patients who had received drugs to suppress their immune systems.

This was good. So in all likelihood, there was no viral danger in proceeding. But even as she shut off her computer, the skeptic in Chris whispered, *But no one has yet been transplanted with a whole, internal pig organ. That kind of exposure could be very different from what's already been done. And the pig virus is a retrovirus, a group that readily mutates. Look at HIV. If it weren't for its mutability, we might already have a vaccine against it.*

There was a knock at the door and Paula, the office secretary, leaned in. "This just arrived for you."

Paula came in and handed Chris a thick manila envelope bearing Michael Boyer's return address at Monteagle Hospital.

"Thanks. I was hoping that would get here this morning."

Inside was the investigational new drug application Boyer's team had filed with the FDA for permission to perform pig liver transplants. Chris spent the next thirty-five minutes reading it.

From the contents it was obvious the FDA was very concerned that transplanting animal organs into people might unleash a plague that would decimate the human population. Practically the entire application dealt with this issue, covering every conceivable facet of the procedure, from maintenance and screening of donor animals to the lifelong clinical surveillance of donor and recipient, including a provision for archiving tissue samples of both upon their death from any cause.

Boy. Was *this* more responsibility than she wanted. But could she really say no? She'd already cut off one possible avenue to her father's survival. Didn't she owe him this?

The part of her still angered over being abandoned quickly chimed in, *You don't owe him anything.*

There was another knock at the door. This time it was Dale McCarthy, one of her partners in the practice.

"Hey kid, I need a favor."

Though they were nearly the same age, he always called her "kid." McCarthy was one of the most open, likeable people she'd ever known, but he was also the worst dressed, favoring polka-dot bow ties, shirts a size too big, and suits with wrinkled pants held up by garish suspenders you could see every time he reached for the pager clipped to the elastic waistband. But he was a great infectious disease man.

"Don't tell me," Chris said. "You can't take the new patient rotation today."

"God, I love working with understanding people," McCarthy said. "Diane's car broke down in Talking Rock and she has no way to get home. There's no telling how long it'll take me to get this straightened out. And Jerry's off today."

"How many new cases do we have?"

"Three. I could come back tonight and do them, but I don't want their care to be delayed because of my personal problems."

"Okay, I'll handle it."

"I knew we did the right thing when we brought you in."

"Needed someone with a low threshold for a sad story, did you?"

"That was certainly at the top of *my* list. Paula has the skinny on the new cases. I'll see you later. Thanks."

Chris saw the three new patients before lunch and made

rounds afterward of the cases already in her care, pushing herself so she'd finish before meeting her father.

At eight minutes till three, she called the micro lab to check on the results of the sample she'd taken from Tom Doyle's scalp. She learned that blood agar cultures had supported the growth of a beta hemolytic bug, indicating strep A, just as she had expected. Though it was just a formality to fully close out her investigation, she told them to proceed with tests to compare the Doyle strain with the bug found in the three infected patients. Barely three minutes after that, she had Doyle on the line.

"Tom, it's official. You're the carrier."

"I'll be damned."

"You need to treat yourself right away with a course of penicillin and see a dermatologist."

"How long before I can operate again?"

"Three days after you start treatment."

"A little forced vacation, huh? I'm not happy about this, but I'm with the program. You *will* keep this to yourself . . ."

"I'll have to put your name in my report, but that's a limited-access document and I'm certainly not going to talk about it."

WAYNE SHOWED UP in Chris's office precisely at three wearing a conservative blue suit, white shirt, and tie, but he hadn't cut his hair, so the suit didn't work.

"Do I look okay?" he asked.

"I'm sure the effort you exerted will be noticed." She told Paula where she was going and she and Wayne headed for the parking lot.

Monteagle Hospital was north of Buckhead on so-called Pill Hill, where it towered over St. Joseph and Northside Hospitals, its golden facade reflecting a benevolent light on the sick and weary. Determined to be one of the world's leading medical centers, Monteagle was underwriting the entire cost of the pig liver transplant program, mostly, Chris believed, for the publicity any success would bring.

They reported to the general surgery waiting room and identified themselves to the woman behind the reception desk. Recognizing their names, she immediately summoned a nurse, who took them to an empty examining room, where

Wayne sat on the examination table and Chris took the only chair.

A few minutes later, the door opened and Michael Boyer swept in. "Hello, Chris. You're looking great as usual."

"And you're as full of baloney as always," Chris said, trying not to look pleased at his compliment.

Boyer gave her a 350-watt grin. He was blond and stocky, and even in his scrubs looked more like a professional wrestler than a surgeon. "And this must be Wayne."

Boyer offered his hand and they exchanged a brisk handshake.

"Wayne, has Chris explained the situation here?"

"You've developed a strain of pigs whose livers are as compatible for transplantation as human livers and you're looking for a suitable recipient."

"And how do you feel about going through life with a pig organ in your abdomen?"

"You said the magic word. Life. If that's what it takes for me to live—and right now, that appears to be the case—bring it on."

"As I understand it, your own liver was damaged by alcoholism. Are you still drinking?"

"No. I've been clean for over three months. I joined AA in Kansas City. You can call them and they'll tell you I haven't had a drink since I started with them."

"Do you do drugs?"

"Never."

"Would you mind taking off your jacket? I'd like to check your blood pressure and a few other things."

Boyer gave Wayne a short physical, then said, "Wayne, I want you to fully understand what you'd be getting into if you should be chosen for our program. First, there can be no guarantees that this will save your life. I strongly believe it will. But that doesn't change the reality that you will be the first person ever to undergo this procedure. And first attempts at dramatic new treatments often do not end well.

"Second, there is a very small risk that you might acquire a hitherto unknown disease from the transplant. This possibility arises because pig cells are known to carry a certain type of virus that cannot be eliminated from the transplant. It causes no harm to the pigs and the best evidence says that there is some barrier in the human body that prevents this virus from establishing itself in human tissues."

"Even in people who are taking drugs to keep their immune system from rejecting a transplant?" Wayne asked.

"Even there. So most scientists believe this virus poses no threat to recipients of pig tissues. There have in fact been hundreds of people whose blood has been exposed to pig cells and no one has acquired any disease from this experience. But the possibility is one the medical and scientific community feel must be acknowledged to the point that you would have to agree to certain requirements should you be chosen."

"Like what?"

"Of course, you must never drink again. You must agree to practice safe sex with any future partner and inform them of your situation. You must inform us of any serious or unexplained illness that you acquire at any time during the rest of your life. You must always keep us informed of your current address and phone number. You will have to return to this center annually for the rest of your life for a routine physical and blood work. You will have to allow a complete autopsy upon your death for any reason. And finally, you must agree to never donate tissue, organs, or any other bodily fluid for use in humans. In return for all this, we will underwrite the total cost of the transplant and the cost of all immunosuppressive drugs, which you will have to take for the rest of your life and which currently would cost approximately a thousand dollars a month. We will also pay all travel expenses incurred when you return for your annual physical.

"One further note on the drugs you'll be taking to prevent transplant rejection. You should understand that these drugs would be necessary even if you were receiving a human liver. Because of the special nature of our donor animals, the amount of immune suppression you will need will be no different than for a human liver. In either case, these drugs can make you susceptible to opportunistic infections. This shouldn't be a major problem, but it's something to consider. So, what do you think? Have I frightened you off?"

"I never thought this would be risk free. It still sounds preferable to my current situation."

"Good. Now I need for you to step into the waiting room

and fill out a medical history. Ask Teri at the reception desk for the form."

When Wayne was gone, Michael looked at Chris, who was now standing. "I was under the impression your father left you and your mother when you were a kid. So this surprises me."

"Me, too. He just showed up in my office yesterday and informed me he was dying." At this point, she almost told him about Wayne wanting a part of her liver, but not wanting him to think badly of her for refusing, she left it alone.

"That form he's working on is pretty extensive," Boyer said. "Let's go down to the cafeteria for some coffee."

It was long past lunchtime and the staff at the cafeteria had brought out a lovely display of pastries for those with no willpower. Chris admired them briefly, then caught up to Boyer at the cashier, where he paid for both coffees.

When they were seated, Boyer said, "Do you think he's still drinking?"

"I've only seen him twice, yesterday afternoon and later that evening, and I didn't smell anything on his breath either time. What do you think? Is he a viable candidate?"

"He could be. It depends . . ."

"On?"

"The complete physical I'm scheduling for him tomorrow, for one thing, and what AA in Kansas City tells me about him for another. There's also the issue of how the vote will go if I decide to present him to the rest of the group, which brings me to the question I asked you yesterday. Will you join us?"

"It doesn't make any sense. The infectious disease member should be Monteagle's director of infection control. Otherwise, if something happens, the two of us would be butting heads over territory."

"Just now we don't have a director. Want the job? I'll bet we can offer you more money than you're making now."

The thought of working in the same hospital with Michael was tempting, but that would just make it all the harder to keep their mutual attraction for each other under control. That was also a major reason why she didn't want to be part of the transplant team. If only she wasn't so drawn to him . . . To her female friends it was crazy: Date guys you like as buddies, avoid those who make your hormones surge. But her friends hadn't attended the Wayne Collins school of pack and run.

"Thanks for the offer," Chris said. "But I'm happy where I am."

"So join the team until we find a director. We've got to have infectious disease expertise on board before we proceed. And as I mentioned yesterday, that would give you a vote as to whether your father is our man."

"How many on the team?"

"Six."

"What if there's a tie vote?"

"I get to decide."

"What if I say yes and the vote goes against him?"

"You stay on the team until we get a new director."

Chris sat quietly, thinking.

"Even if the team wanted to proceed with your father, we can't do it without you."

"Are you that worried about the danger? You think the studies showing no viral infection in people exposed to pig cells could be wrong?"

"No. Why would I want to proceed if I thought that? The FDA requires someone with your skills on the team. Frankly, I don't understand your reluctance here."

"Because of my father?"

Boyer shrugged in agreement.

Damn it. She didn't want to join. Why did it have to come to this?

"Tell me again. What are the chances for my father if he's accepted?"

"I honestly believe it's going to work. And soon, no one will ever have to die of liver failure because no organ could be found in time."

Of course, he *would* put that extra spin on it.

"All right," she said, throwing up her hands. "I'm in."

CHAPTER 4

"FRENCH LAUNCH DEEP Space Infrared Telescope"—
TR's gut lurched at the first word of the article's headline.
It had been twelve years since the two Frenchmen had
been assassinated beside him in Kazakhstan, but he still
couldn't bear to see or hear anything that reminded him of
them. His story had always been that the last time he saw
them was when they'd dropped him and his equipment off
at the warehouse in Tselinograd. In truth, he'd really been
taken there by the Russian hijackers.

Though he had never been questioned in person by anyone
about the French team's disappearance and had only spoken
by phone once and sent one letter to Kazakhstan authorities
about it, for months after he'd returned to the States, he'd
lived in fear that one day there would be a knock at the door
and he'd be arrested for his role in their murders. Five months
after his return he'd had a nervous breakdown and spent eight
weeks in a mental hospital, a fact he'd been able to keep from
his present employers. With the help of the drug BuSpar, he
had now largely put the Kazakhstan affair behind him, until a
headline in a paper or a story on TV would overwhelm the
drug and it would all come flooding back.

In TR's view, the Frenchmen were responsible for their own deaths. If they hadn't treated him with such disdain and tried to take all the blood samples, he never would have had to hire the Russians. So put the blame where it belongs. But of course, the police would never see it his way.

Set off by the headline, TR continued to muse over the situation. Twelve years with no knock on the door, and a few days ago, a mutual acquaintance had told him that Bill Lansden, the other guy with him in Kazakhstan, had recently had a stroke that left him with an aphasia, so his brain could no longer handle language. Apparently he was now unable to make much sense when he spoke or wrote anything.

Nice guy, Lansden. Too bad about that stroke. But it did mean that the one man in this country with personal knowledge that TR was the other member of the U.S. team in Kazakhstan couldn't tell anybody. From that perspective, it'd be great if Lansden never recovered. Probably should go over to the hospital and see just how bad he is. Uh-oh. Time for that transplant team meeting.

"MR. COLLINS WOULD like to make a statement to you all before we vote," Michael Boyer said. "Wayne, the floor is yours."

Boyer took his seat at the head of the long conference table as Wayne rose from his chair on Boyer's immediate right. Like most people with a failing liver, Wayne had experienced a reversal of his sleep cycle, so he was always wide awake at night and drowsy during the day. Usually by now, he needed a nap. But not this morning. He was too nervous and adrenaline was churning all his motors. He looked at Chris, who was seated across from him, for a little sign of encouragement, but her expression remained neutral. Nothing he could do now but plunge in.

"I'm sure at least a few of you have reservations about accepting me into the program." The almost imperceptible nod of agreement he saw on the face of Sidney Knox, the immunologist member of the team, made Wayne's heart drop into his shoes, but he was determined not to let it show.

"I'm an alcoholic. I can't take a drink and stop there. I know that. But I can successfully fight the urge to take the first drink. I can say that because I've done it for three months. I

hope you can appreciate what that means. It's not like someone giving up french fries or ice cream. Alcohol beckons me
every minute of every day. But I have resisted. That has to
mean something. And I will continue to resist because I don't
want to be remembered as just another drunk.

"You all have accomplished lives. You can point to patients who are alive because of you or count the papers you've
written that brought new knowledge into the world. You have
people who love you, lives you've enriched. I had one novel
published many years ago that sold so poorly my editor
wouldn't even read anything else from me. I've done nothing
to earn love or even grudging respect. If I died tomorrow, it
would be an event of total inconsequence. And that hurts, and
frightens me.

"I wish I could bargain with you and show you why it
would make sense to save me, why the world would be better
off with me in it. But I can produce no evidence to support
that position. All I can say is if you give me this chance, I *will*
find some way to be worthy of it. I simply *must*. Thank you
all for listening."

"Does anyone have questions for Mr. Collins?" Boyer
asked, rising. He scanned the gathering. "No?" He looked at
Wayne. "Would you wait outside please?"

When Wayne was safely on the other side of the door,
Boyer turned to Chris. "Is there anything you'd like to add to
what your father said?"

"I think he presented the situation pretty clearly."

"Then the matter is open for discussion."

Sidney Knox was the first to reply. He was a slightly built
man like Wayne, but with an effeminate face. "Dr. Collins,
please don't take this personally, but I find this whole situation extremely inappropriate. How can we have an open exchange of views when the candidate's daughter is sitting right
here?"

Chris had to think fast for a reply. Despite the circumstances, she wanted her father to have this chance, and if her
presence on the team shaded the votes of any of the other
members in his favor, good. "I assure you, Dr. Knox, I won't
take any of what's said in this room personally. I want you all
to feel free to say exactly what's on your mind. And when
we're finished, I'll leave it all right here."

"Very well. What assurance do we have that Mr. Collins won't destroy the transplant the same way he ruined his own liver?"

Boyer looked at Robin Victor, one of the best psychiatric guys in the city. "Robin, can you respond to that?"

Victor had an egg-shaped head topped by a comb-over. Chris had only seen him a few times before, but on each occasion, as today, there was a ruddy glow on his high cheekbones and his full lips looked as though he'd just been eating fresh cherries.

"We generally consider three factors to predict whether a man or woman will be able to remain sober once they decide to do so," Victor said. Tapping the extended index finger of one hand with that on the other, he began listing the factors. "Are they employed? Do they have an address? And is there a supportive family?

"Though Mr. Collins is a freelance writer and is not on the regular payroll of any company, he has supported himself for years in this manner. So I give him a yes on that one. He has lived at the same address in Kansas City for two and a half years, giving him another yes there. As for family support . . ." He looked at Chris. "It's my understanding that you've been estranged from your father for many years."

"That's true," Chris said.

"And has your relationship changed any in the last few days?"

Chris hesitated. It hadn't, but she was concerned that if she simply said that, it might hurt her father's chances with the team. Better to leave it open-ended. "I'd have to say that's an issue still unresolved."

"It sounds as if there's hope there," Victor said. "But regardless of what happens in the future in that regard, Mr. Collins has two of the three predictors of sobriety.

"I spent two hours talking with him yesterday and I was impressed with his motivation and sincerity to stay sober and make up for the behavior he's exhibited most of his life. In my opinion, what he said to the committee was not an act and I believe he can be trusted."

"I agree," Eric Ash said. Ash, the Ph.D. virologist on the team, had run the Monteagle virology lab for nearly five years. He held a doctorate in molecular biology from Cal Tech and looked the part: hair tumbling down one side of his high forehead, wire-rimmed glasses with little lenses, a self-conscious smile that nervously waxed and waned when you spoke to him in casual conversation.

"He seemed quite sincere," Ash continued. "And I'd be very surprised if he let us down."

"Consider what's at stake here," Knox countered. "We're going to look very foolish if you're both wrong. And I just don't feel this is a risk we should take. Let's wait for a better candidate. There's no hurry."

"If I may, I'd like to change the subject." The speaker was William Hessman, the vet responsible for maintaining the program's genetically modified animals. He was a big bald fellow who reminded Chris of Daddy Warbucks from the Little Orphan Annie comics. He tapped the file folder in front of him that contained Wayne's medical history. "I notice that Mr. Collins was seriously ill about a year ago when he lived in New Mexico. Do we know exactly what that was?"

"I checked with the hospital there this morning," Boyer said, "and no diagnosis was ever made. It was some kind of respiratory problem. But as you can see from the report of his chest film, it didn't produce any lasting visible lung damage. And his respiratory function is normal. The thing apparently responded to penicillin, so it was probably pneumonia.

"Aside from his failing liver and the resulting varicose veins in his esophagus, he's in very good shape. No heart problems, kidney function good. From a physical standpoint, he'd be an excellent choice.

"Any further discussion?" No one spoke. "Then I guess we're ready to vote."

Boyer distributed pencils and ballots with yes and no boxes on them.

Everyone marked a ballot, folded it, and handed it back. When he had all of them, Boyer began the tally.

"Accept."

"Reject."

"Accept."

"Accept."

"Accept."

"Accept."

"Gee, who do you think the negative vote might have been," Knox said glumly.

Chris had mixed reactions to the result. Her vote hadn't

been needed. It hadn't been necessary for her to join the team at all. Of course, maybe her presence *had* influenced the other members. No way to know. But whatever alternate scenario might have occurred, *this* was the one she had to deal with.

"There's a note on his physical that his teeth have a couple of cavities," Ash said. "We need to be sure those are taken care of before we start him on immunosuppressives."

"I was planning on that," Boyer said. "But I appreciate the heads-up. Anything else? Okay, thanks, everybody. I'd like to be the one to give Wayne the good news, so please don't say anything to him on your way out."

As the others left, Boyer said to Chris, "Or would you rather tell him?"

"You can do it. I'll watch."

When they walked into the hall, Wayne eagerly came toward them.

Boyer put out his hand. "Wayne, welcome to the program."

They sealed their new relationship with a quick handshake and Wayne said, "When do we do it?"

"You need to see a dentist first. We can't have bugs from a dental cavity taking advantage of you when you're immunosuppressed. I'm sure I can get you in to see somebody tomorrow. Give me a call later and I'll tell you the time and place. So let's admit you on Sunday evening around seven o'clock and we'll give you your new liver Monday morning. That'll give you most of the weekend to get ready. We'll have a little chat after you're admitted and I'll let you know exactly what the schedule is going to be. If you have any questions before then, feel free to call me. Or maybe you have some now?"

"I don't know. I'm still kind of shell-shocked over being accepted."

"Well, you know how to contact me. Chris, thanks. I'll talk to you later."

Then it was just the two of them.

"Do you know what?" Wayne said. "I'm scared."

Seeing him so obviously unnerved and looking so frail, Chris suddenly heard herself say, "There's no need for you to stay by yourself. The sofa in my study opens into a bed. If you want it, it's yours."

Wayne reached out and tugged on the sleeve of her blouse. "You don't know how good that makes me feel."

CHAPTER 5

FROM MONTEAGLE HOSPITAL, Chris and Wayne returned to Good Samaritan, where they parted until Wayne showed up again at her apartment at six-thirty with his suitcase.

"Your room is back here," Chris said, leading Wayne down the hall. In her study, she had already pulled the sofa bed out and dressed it. Wayne was drawn immediately to the French doors leading to the balcony.

"May I?" he asked, his hand on the doorknob.

"If you like."

He opened the door and stepped outside, where Chris had created a small strip of forest with potted hollies and ferns arranged so the plants divided the balcony into a series of little enclosures, one outside each of the apartment's three main rooms. Wayne glanced briefly at the parking lot ten floors below, then looked across the city at the setting sun. "Beautiful view," he said, turning back to Chris, who was standing in the doorway. "And you've really made this little outdoor area pleasant."

"It all suits my needs," Chris said. "Look, I emptied the top two drawers of the chest in here so you could use them. And there's room in the closet for whatever you'd like to hang up. The bathroom is across the hall. There are plenty of towels in the cabinets in there." She reached into the pocket of her slacks and got a key and a plastic card, which she gave him. "The key is to the apartment, the card will open the security door in the lobby. Lose either one when I'm not here and you won't be able to get in."

"I won't lose them."

"Now, I'm sorry to do this on your first night, but I have something scheduled tonight and I have to leave. There's food in the fridge and the little pantry in the kitchen. Use anything you like. I probably won't be back until late."

"I'll be fine."

Chris then hurried from the apartment, went to her car, and drove quickly from the lot in case Wayne was watching from above. There was actually no urgency to all this, because she had made up the story about having plans. If he wasn't there, she would have had a hot bath, watched a movie on pay TV, read awhile, and gone to bed. Now she was so uncomfortable with him, she'd fled her own apartment.

And lied to him.

She thought about Michael Boyer and how if she'd accepted his invitation when she'd called him about Wayne, she'd be having dinner with him. Had she only known. Then she needn't have lied.

Nearly thirty years.

Her father.

And now he was in her apartment. Amazing.

Even that late in the day, the roads were still choked with traffic, and the drivers of those vehicles were as aggressive as ever. Where most visitors to the city believed Atlantans to be rude by nature, Chris had lived there long enough to realize that because of the heavy traffic and chaotic complexity of the expressway system, where if you missed your exit, it might take an hour to get back there, the stakes were simply too high for timidity.

Forty minutes later, without consciously being aware of even having a destination, Chris pulled into the driveway of Jerry and Lynn Kennedy in Decatur. Jerry was the senior partner in her practice and Lynn taught hospital administration at

Emory. Having two young boys, they were always on the go. So she was surprised to see both cars there.

She got out, went up the walk, and rang the bell. Lynn answered wearing an apron over a blouse and skirt that she'd probably worn to work.

"Chris. How nice. Come in."

Despite the two boys, the house was immaculate.

"Have you had dinner?" Lynn asked. "The boys had a soccer game tonight, so we're eating late. Jerry's out back grilling burgers."

"Now that you mention it, I haven't eaten."

"Then of course you'll join us. I'll tell Jerry. Come on."

Chris followed Lynn to a large, brightly lit kitchen. Through the big picture window in the breakfast area, she could see Jerry at the grill and the two boys, still in their soccer uniforms, kicking a ball around the yard.

Lynn went to the back door and opened it. "Honey, Chris is here. Put on a couple more."

Jerry waved at Chris through the window and went back to work.

"Sit down." Lynn motioned to a stool at the counter, where the ingredients for a garden salad were laid out by a big crystal bowl. She picked up some lettuce leaves draining on a paper towel and began shredding them into the bowl. "Jerry told me about your father suddenly reappearing. That must have been a shock."

"And still is," Chris replied. "He's at my apartment right now. I sort of ran out on him."

"Situation too uncomfortable?"

"I've been holding this anger at him inside me my whole life. Now, when I finally see him, he's sick. How can I unload on him now? On the other hand, I can't pretend I'm glad to see him and that all is forgiven. He's a stranger and I'm letting him stay with me. That's not smart."

"Sometimes compassion overrules our intellect. And I wouldn't say that's a bad thing."

"He's been accepted into Michael Boyer's experimental transplant program."

Lynn stopped work. "The pig program?"

"He's going to be the first recipient. They're doing it on

Monday. Boyer used the situation to rope me into temporarily joining the group."

"Your father is going to be a celebrity."

"They're not announcing anything. They don't want a lot of media attention right now."

"Does Jerry know?"

"I haven't told him. But you can. Just keep it in the family."

"Of course."

"He asked me for a part of *my* liver."

"Just appeared out of the blue and asked that? Must have been a rough decision."

"Why do you say that?"

"Well . . . the blood relative angle and all."

"You think I was wrong to refuse him?"

"Honey, no. I'm not saying that."

"This transplant, it's a huge risk. Michael is convinced it'll work, at least that's what he says publicly. But I have to think that if it does work, a part of him will be shocked."

"You don't sound optimistic."

"It's uncharted territory. And if something goes haywire . . ."

"You'll feel responsible because you didn't help him."

This brought Chris to her feet. "You came to that conclusion pretty quickly."

"Isn't that what you were thinking?"

"No . . . Maybe. But you wouldn't have known that if you weren't thinking it too. I'm having enough trouble over this without my friends piling on."

"Honey, I . . ."

Chris headed for the front door. "I'm sorry, but I have to go."

Traffic had eased to where aimless driving around didn't require much attention, allowing Chris to focus on her thoughts.

Shouldn't have snapped at Lynn like that. Unfair of me. They're a nice family. Must be satisfying to have that . . . someone you can count on to be there for you. But don't forget; Jerry's not perfect. He was married before. Left her for Lynn. So can she really rely on him? Will he eventually let her and those boys down? The jury's still out.

Eventually, she found herself cruising down Ponce de Leon, past the old Candler Mansions.

The Candlers...

All that Coca-Cola money...

Built these great houses for their families, now they've moved on...

And others have taken over, repainting, knocking down walls, out with the old, in with the new. Adaptive reuse; apartments and schools... No continuity even among the wealthy. Here today, tomorrow replaced... Everything shifting.

But there *was* one constant in the world. Needing to be a part of that, if even briefly, she headed for the Majestic, a greasy spoon that had been around since the thirties. *Open twenty-four hours a day; there's something you can count on.*

But when she arrived, the place was dark; closed tonight with no explanation.

With that option unavailable, she ate instead at Lettuce Souprise You, a restaurant where the sign painter had used carrots for the two ts in lettuce.

Hoping that if she stayed out late enough, her father would be asleep when she got home, she went to a movie after dinner. And when it was over, she went outside and bought a ticket to a film showing on a different screen.

By the time she put her key in the door to her apartment, it was a quarter to one.

Be asleep. Be in bed, she thought.

Even as the door opened, she heard the TV. But he could be asleep in front of it.

"Hello, Chris," Wayne said, getting up from his chair.

"How'd your evening go?" she said, hiding her disappointment at finding him awake. "Locate everything you needed?"

"I used four of your eggs, some cheese, a few slices of bread, and two scoops of coffee for dinner."

"You don't have to keep inventory like that. Just take what you want."

"The coffee is still hot, if you'd like a cup. We could talk."

"I've got work tomorrow. And it's pretty late."

"Sure, okay. You go to bed. Do you care if I stay up and watch TV? I'll keep the sound low."

"I don't mind."

"I put away all the clean things in the dishwasher and loaded it with what I dirtied. But I didn't run it. Not for just that small load. But I could. Be kind of noisy though with you trying to sleep."

"You did fine. Now I'm—"

"Chris."

"Yes?"

"I notice you don't call me anything. I know it's too much to expect you to call me Dad. But could you just once in a while use my name?"

Chris felt her face blush. "I've called you by name."

"Sorry, but you haven't."

"Well, I'm sure I have. So there's no need for me to say I will."

"I understand."

"I'm going to bed."

"Good night, Chris."

She was fully aware that what he'd said was true. And here was the chance to give him what he wanted. "Good night." She intended to add *Wayne* but it wouldn't come out.

She slept poorly that night, but at least when it was time to dress for work, Wayne had finally gone to bed. Afraid of waking him, she moved as quietly as possible and didn't even bother to brew fresh coffee, for fear the gurgling coffeemaker would bring him into the kitchen.

Seconds from escaping, with the door to the hall already opening, she paused, thought a moment, then eased the door closed and went to the kitchen. There, she tore off a piece of paper toweling and scrawled her father a note with a pen from her handbag:

Don't forget your dental appointment.

She put the note on the table, anchored it with a salt shaker, and got away clean.

One of Chris's priorities for the day was to call Lynn Kennedy and apologize for acting like an ass last night. Important as that was, she decided not to spring on Lynn quite this early. Therefore, when she arrived at the office, she went right to work on an issue that fell jointly under her infection control and quality management responsibilities.

In the existing Good Samaritan protocols, when the surgeon in a given OR was about fifteen minutes from finishing a case, an OR nurse was supposed to call the appropriate staff person and advise them to get the next case ready. That patient was then given a prophylactic antibiotic injection to ward off any bugs that might gain entrance during surgery. The timing of this injection was crucial. If given too early, the antibiotic in the blood would fall below the desired level by the time the procedure began. Two weeks ago, because of an emergency case, a patient who had already received his antibiotics was not taken to the OR until four hours later. Then last week, orderlies took a patient to surgery before the injection had been given, so the patient had no protection.

Chris immediately saw how to fix the problem: Change the protocol so the antibiotic was given *in* the OR and make the anesthesiologist responsible for seeing that it was done. She had booted up her computer, opened her e-mail program, and begun drafting her recommendation when there was a knock at the door and Jerry Kennedy stepped in.

"Hi. Lynn told me what happened last night. She wanted me to apologize to you."

Jerry's sandy hair and mustache were as well groomed as always and he was wearing a Mario Zegna gray suit with a crisp white shirt and a gray mini floral tie. The best single word to describe him was conservative. No striped or colored shirts for Jerry. It wasn't obvious that he was six foot three because he always stood in a slight slouch, a habit Chris suspected he'd adopted so he wouldn't be taller than everybody else.

"I'm the one who should apologize," Chris said. "Lynn didn't do anything wrong. I'm just confused right now."

"I don't wonder, with your father about to become the first patient in Boyer's program. And Lynn said you'd joined them as their infectious disease person."

"Not exactly freely. I was kind of coerced."

"I know they don't want any media attention, but it's bound to happen eventually. This is too big an event to keep under wraps for long."

"I suppose."

"In looking ahead to the time when the press gets hold of

it, it occurs to me that you'll certainly be a prominent part of the story."

Chris now saw that Jerry wasn't just making conversation. He was clearly headed somewhere with this. "Why do you say that?"

"It's loaded with human interest. Father reappears after a three-decade absence, asks his daughter to donate part of her liver to save his life, instead she funnels him into an experimental transplant program in which she's a member of the team."

"So?"

"I'm just concerned about how those facts could be slanted."

"In what way?"

"If, God forbid, things go wrong, it could be said by some muckraking journalist looking to sensationalize events that you were so interested in furthering the goals of the program that you sacrificed your father to it."

Chris was so shocked at this, she was momentarily speechless. Finally, she said, "I'm not a vested member of that team. I wasn't even part of it until two days ago when Michael Boyer talked me into it. And I'm only temporary, until Monteagle gets a new director of infection control. Then I'm gone."

"The accusation will sell papers or magazines or whatever. Your explanation won't."

"So you're saying . . ."

"Drop out now."

"Are you worried about me or the negative press the practice might receive?"

"You foremost. But the other to a degree."

Could this whole situation get any worse? She didn't want to be on that team, but she sure wasn't going to be forced off it, either, because Jerry was worried about how it might affect *his* reputation.

"I can't quit. I told Michael I'd do it until Monteagle found a new director."

"Don't decide now. Just think about it."

Jerry left.

And she did think about it. How could she not? But the more she dwelt on it, the angrier she became at Jerry and his hypothetical. And certainly at her father for precipitating the whole mess. Some of this emotion spilled onto Lynn Kennedy, so Chris lost the desire to call her and patch their rift.

A little after ten o'clock, her father called saying he'd like to prepare dinner for the two of them and wanted to be sure she was available. She told him she already had plans.

Chris managed to avoid him that night and most of the weekend, but Sunday night, it seemed so heartless to send him to the hospital alone, she volunteered to take him.

They spoke very little on the way, but after she'd parked the car and reached for the door handle to get out, Wayne put his hand on her arm.

"Chris, wait. I'd like to talk before going in. After all, it could be our last opportunity."

"Don't be so pessimistic. Michael Boyer is an excellent surgeon."

"I know it's been hard on you having me around. But even though we haven't really connected, I've cherished just being close to you."

"Cherished? Isn't that laying it on a little thick?"

"You don't believe me?"

"You haven't banked a lot of that kind of capital to draw on."

"How about extending me a little credit then."

"Which brings us back to trust. You don't get that as a gift. You have to earn it, by being honorable and strong and reliable year after year; by going to work when you don't feel like it so you can provide for your family; by caring for your wife and child when they're ill; by encouraging your child when she's convinced she's not good enough, or pretty enough, or smart enough. You take her for walks and you teach her things. You check out her boyfriends . . ."

"I wish now I *had* done those things. But it can't all be one way. Daughters have responsibilities too. They have to understand that fathers aren't mythical figures. They have fears and weaknesses and sometimes they make bad decisions. Daughters should be forgiving and understanding and realize that people can and do change. When Dad makes a mistake, daughters don't hold it against him the rest of his life. You don't have to come in with me. Just open the trunk so I can get my bag."

Chris pulled the trunk release lever and Wayne got his suitcase and headed for the hospital's front entrance without looking back.

In her car, Chris closed her eyes, leaned forward, and gently began banging her head on the steering wheel.

CHAPTER 6

CHRIS LOOKED AT her pager and saw Michael Boyer's number on the display. It was 1:35 Monday afternoon. If her father's surgery had begun at 7:30 as scheduled, they should be finished by now. She found a phone and soon heard Michael's voice.

"It's Chris. How'd it go?"

"Couldn't have been better. He'll be sedated for the next twelve hours, so there's no point in going to see him, unless you just want to take a look. He ought to be fully awake, and hopefully responsive, for a morning visit."

"Okay, thanks for the update."

"Usually I'm beat after six hours in the OR, but I feel like I could pedal a bicycle up Mount Everest. Let's do something together tonight to celebrate."

"It's pretty early to be so enthused."

"I just have this feeling that he's going to do *so* well."

Chris wanted very much to accept. Instead, she said, "Let's watch awhile and see how it goes."

"Chris, would you like for me to stop bothering you?"

"You're not bothering me."

"But I'm not getting any encouragement here."

"What is it you want?"

"I can't answer that without knowing you better."

"I'm not trying to be difficult. I just want to be careful."

"I think you're being *too* cautious."

"I'm certainly willing to think about that."

"Chris, time is like a river. I didn't think that up. I read it, but it's true. You can't stand on the bank and expect that things won't be carried downstream. There's a moment when they can be reached and then they're gone."

CHRIS LOOKED AT her father's chart. In the twenty-five hours since his surgery, his temperature had remained within normal limits; no fever, therefore no bacterial infection. And compared to his pre-op values, his blood clotting time—a measure of how effectively his new liver was making clotting factors—was already looking better. So much for her duties as physician. Now she had to be a daughter.

Normally, the ICU is an open ward where all the patients are in a common room so they and their monitors can be observed easily at all times by the nursing staff. Wayne Collins, however, was recovering in the isolation ward Monteagle had built as part of their commitment to Boyer's program.

In this area, behind double doors off the hall on the floor above the primary ICU ward, there was a dedicated nursing station and four private rooms. Just outside the entrance to each room was a small antechamber where all the protective apparel was kept for anyone wishing to enter the main room. In both the antechamber and the private room, the wall facing the nursing station had a large glass panel in it so the patient inside could be seen without entering either area.

Because the occupant of each patient room would be immunosuppressed, it was important that no infectious organisms be allowed to enter. In keeping with FDA concerns about unknown diseases developing in animal organ transplants, it was also necessary to ensure that no microbes be allowed to get *out*. This dual requirement was met by equipping the antechamber with airtight sliding doors and a HEPA filtered ventilation system that could effect a complete change of the antechamber air every thirty seconds. Thus, by the time someone wishing to enter a patient's room had properly suited up, any airborne organisms that had entered the antechamber with the visitor would have been swept into the ventilation system. The same would apply as the visitor left. Observance of the thirty second interval for air exchange after entering from either door was enforced by a timed locking mechanism on the opposite door.

To minimize any contamination passing from the isolation ward to other wards, Wayne had been assigned a dedicated ICU nurse, who, if she needed to leave the area, could call in another nurse from the main ICU ward downstairs.

"He seems to be doing fine," Chris said to the nurse on duty.

"Extremely well," she replied. "I understand he's your father."

"An accident of biology."

"Isn't it always?"

Chris left the nurses station and went into her father's antechamber, where she put on the required protective clothing. The standing routine established by the previous infectious disease member of the team was for all visitors to wear disposable gowns, booties, head cover, gloves, and a full face respirator with HEPA filtering capacity. Chris thought the respirator was overdoing it and that a much simpler N95 nose and mouth mask would have been sufficient, but feeling like a substitute schoolteacher in her role with the team, she was reluctant to change any of the established protocols. So she'd cooperated and gone to see the Monteagle environmental safety officer to be fit tested for a respirator. Unable to obtain an airtight fit with the Wilson model he preferred, the guy had tried a North and that worked.

There were four masks on hooks beside the metal shelves holding the disposable clothing: a large Wilson for Michael, a medium Wilson for the regular nurses, another medium Wilson for the backup nurses assigned to each shift from the main ICU ward in case an extra pair of hands was needed, a third medium Wilson for the phlebotomists assigned to the ward on each shift, and Chris's North. Hers being a different make from the others, the adhesive tape with her name on it was hardly necessary.

She struggled into her mask and pulled the straps tight. Following protocol, she fit-tested it by covering the HEPA filter cartridges on each side with the palms of her hands and inhaling forcefully. Then she exhaled hard. Satisfied that it was airtight, she entered her father's room, where he still had a Swan-Ganz line in his neck to monitor his pulmonary artery pressure, cardiac output, and fluid status. There were also two Jackson-Pratt drains in his abdomen to leach off the fluid that had built up in his peritoneal cavity, and a Foley catheter in his urethra so a close watch could be kept on his kidney function. He was wired to a pulse oximeter and a cardiac monitor.

And he was awake.

Though she wasn't recognizable in all her protective gear, Wayne knew who she was because he'd watched her dress through the glass window in his room.

"So far so good," Chris said.

"You'll have to speak up," he said, weakly. "The mask muffles your voice."

"How do you feel?" she said, putting more effort behind her question.

"Like hell," he said slowly.

"No reason you shouldn't."

"It was good of you to come."

"I'm one of your doctors. I needed to look at your chart."

"And that's the only reason you're here? You could have done that and stayed out with the nurse."

"I . . . thought you could use some emotional support."

"I'm ready," Wayne said. "You can start now."

"Don't push it, Wayne."

"You did it," he said, his face registering a tired expression of surprise.

"Did what?"

"Called me by name."

"It's not that big a deal."

"But it *is* progress, Chris."

"Don't read too much into it."

"You try to be a hard case, but I think it's all a bluff."

"A belief derived no doubt from our close association for, what was it . . . the first six years of my life?"

Wayne closed his eyes. "I don't feel up to this. So maybe you should leave now and let me rest."

Chris hadn't meant for her visit to take this direction, so she stood there trying to think of a way to mitigate her behavior. Unable, or more accurately, unwilling to do so, she left without saying another word.

On the way out, she stopped at the nurses station to mention something about the masks.

"I noticed that the backup respirator doesn't have any filter cartridges in it."

"I took them," the nurse said. "The protocols specify that we're to change the filters in our masks at the beginning of each shift, but there are no fresh ones up here, so I stole those in the backup for mine. The record sheet shows that nobody's used that mask. I put a call in to Central Supply for some filters, so we should be restocked soon."

Having no cartridges in a mask was an obvious concern, but using one for more than a single shift was, in Chris's opinion, no problem at all because they were rated for much longer than that. Continuing in her determination not to alter any procedures the staff had been instructed to follow, Chris simply said, "That's good."

AT 8 P.M., MARY Beth Cummings, the nurse on the second shift, went into Wayne's room and interrupted the TV program he was watching to check his temperature. While he had the digital thermometer in his mouth, she noted that there was no blood in the liquid moving through his abdominal drains and he seemed to be making urine, both good signs. But when she read his temperature, it was a bit high.

"Am I going to live?" Wayne said.

"For a very long time, I think," Mary Beth replied, having no idea what his prognosis might be.

Because he was the hospital's prize patient and she was keenly aware of the FDA concerns about unknown infections from animal transplants, Mary Beth returned to Wayne's room an hour later to see if there had been any change in his temperature.

"What, again?" Wayne said.

"You're just so charming I can't stay away," she said. This time, his temperature was 99.2, up two tenths of a degree from the last reading. And was he developing. . . . ?

"Mr. Collins, may I see your incision?"

"You show me yours and I'll show you mine."

"Don't be naughty."

Mary Beth pulled the covers back and opened his gown to reveal his transplant incision, which angled from side to side under his rib cage like a boomerang with one arm longer than the other, stainless steel staples holding the edges together. The wound appeared typical for a patient at this stage of recovery, and the rest of his skin looked the proper color. Before leaving, she put a stethoscope to his chest and listened to his breathing, which gave her no cause for concern.

But his rising temperature made her uneasy. She thought about paging Michael Boyer, but didn't want to act precipitously, so she decided to wait another hour.

Because she only had one patient to care for, she'd brought her contract law textbook to study. If everything went according to plan, eventually, there'd be a JD to follow the RN after her name. Then there'd be one more champion in the world to fight for all the people who had been damaged by careless, arrogant MDs. It was a day she longed for.

But because of Wayne, she couldn't concentrate on her book. Fifteen minutes dragged into twenty, then thirty. *If his temperature goes up even a tenth of a degree, I'm calling Dr. Boyer,* she thought. *And if it stabilizes, well, I don't know. I'll decide about that when it happens.*

Finally, the hour was up. She returned to Wayne's room, where she instantly saw that her earlier suspicions were correct. Wayne read her reaction in her eyes. "What's wrong?"

"You've got a rash."

"I do? It doesn't itch."

"How do you feel?"

"A little warm now that you mention it."

Without asking, Mary Beth pulled the covers back and opened Wayne's gown. The rash was all over his chest and abdomen. She checked his temperature and found that it had risen to 99.6, up four tenths of a degree.

"THE HOSPITAL PHARMACIST has looked over his meds and doesn't see any potential adverse drug interactions," Chris said to Michael Boyer as they stood outside her father's room.

"Maybe it's a reaction to a single drug," Boyer said.

"His temp was 99.6 when you were first called and it's holding steady." She looked at Mary Beth. "How would you describe his rash now compared to what it was when you alerted Dr. Boyer?"

"It's about the same."

Chris turned back to Boyer. "So whatever it is, it doesn't appear to be getting any worse and he isn't having any respiratory problems. Let's get a diff count and blood culture and watch him over the next hour to see how he does."

"I'm going to stay close," Boyer said. "How about you?"

"I don't want to leave yet. At least not until I see the white cell counts."

"Let's go down to the cafeteria."

"Okay."

Boyer looked at Mary Beth. "Would you please get that blood work underway and let us know when the counts are back. And call us immediately if his situation changes in any way."

Michael and Chris headed for the elevators.

"Damn, I hope this isn't anything serious," Michael said.

"His temp isn't very high and he seems stable," Chris said. "So I wouldn't be too worried."

In the nearly empty cafeteria, they had their choice of tables.

"Seems like coffee down here is the only way I get to see you socially," Michael said.

"And I'm not sure this counts," Chris replied, smiling.

"Well now," Michael said, perking up. "I haven't seen that nice a smile from you in a long time."

Shying away from that line of conversation, Chris said, "Did you know he asked me to give him part of *my* liver?"

"Your father? You couldn't."

"Obviously I agree. But it took me a while to decide that. And I can't help but feel guilty about not helping him."

"You don't understand. There wasn't any decision to make. He's not a large man, but he's too big for you to be a donor. The anatomy of the liver only allows it to be divided into two unequal portions. So when we're dealing with a living donor, we take sixty percent and leave forty. Your sixty percent wouldn't be enough to satisfy his metabolic needs. You'd have to be about the same size to be a donor for him."

"Why didn't I know this?"

"You don't make your living doing liver surgery. So now you can stop feeling guilty."

"It's not that easy. When I turned him down, I thought it was possible. So what you've just told me doesn't help."

"Those are pretty high standards you've set for yourself."

"Believe me, if I could, I'd lower them in a minute."

They were still there twenty minutes later when Michael was paged by Mary Beth. Picking up a nearby house phone on the wall, he learned that the blood counts were back.

They returned to the transplant ward and called up the results on the computer at the nursing station.

"There's no evidence here of any infection," Chris said.

"Then what is it?"

"Let's check his temp again and take another look at that rash."

When they were gowned and gloved and masked, they all trooped into Wayne's room.

"I thought this was a private room," Wayne said. "What's the verdict?"

"Don't have one yet," Michael said. "We wanted to see your rash again and get another temp reading."

While Wayne incubated the thermometer, Chris and Michael leaned close and examined his face, then checked his chest and abdomen.

"Looks the same to me," Chris said.

"I agree."

The nurse retrieved the thermometer and read it aloud. "Ninety-nine point six."

Michael patted Wayne on the shoulder. "Thanks."

"Unh-uh. I'd rather you stayed in here to discuss this."

"Fair enough." He looked at Chris. "Your call."

She turned to Wayne. "The rash still doesn't itch?"

"No."

"I don't see a need to do anything right now, except watch and wait," she said to Michael.

"Okay. Wayne, we're going to leave you alone now. If you start to feel uncomfortable or unusual in any way, call the nurse."

"I haven't felt comfortable or usual in months."

"You know what I mean."

"I do. Thanks for coming back here tonight. Are you going home now?"

"Yes." Michael looked at Mary Beth.

"And I'll page you if there's *any* change," she said.

"Good night Chris," Wayne said. "Thanks to you too . . . for coming back."

"You've been through a lot in the last thirty-six hours," she said. "Try to get some rest."

And so Chris left the hospital without noticing that the backup respirator still had no filter cartridges in it.

THIRTY MINUTES AFTER checking on her father, as Chris walked through her front door, the phone rang. It was Michael.

"I just got a page from the hospital. He's developed a slight cough. It's very minor; intermittent and dry."

"Any other changes?"

"No. Temp is still holding steady."

"There's no point in rushing back there for this. But keep me informed."

Figuring that she'd better stay readily available, Chris turned on the TV and found a movie to watch. She fell asleep in her chair before it was over. The phone never rang again that night.

CHAPTER 7

MICHAEL BOYER WAS still in a state of disbelief as the elevator doors opened and Carter Dewitt, Monteagle's VP for business affairs and finance, got on.

"Hello, Michael," Carter said, punching the button for the fifth floor. "You look kind of disoriented. Nothing wrong, I hope."

Dewitt had thin lips that he usually held pinched into a smirk that made it appear as though he thought everything you were saying was a lie. But the man and the myth were two different things, for Dewitt was actually a nice guy who had just seen too many padded budgets.

"I guess you're aware that we did our first pig transplant on Monday."

"As much as that isolation ward cost the hospital, I genuflected and faced the east to celebrate the occasion."

"Well, the patient is doing incredibly well. We had a bit of a scare early on when he developed a little fever, a rash, and a cough, but it all cleared up without treatment. A successful human transplant normally takes about a week to reach full function. It's only been three days and we're already there with Mr. Collins."

The elevator reached the fifth floor and Boyer got off with Dewitt so he could finish his story.

"Generally, we don't remove the suture clips in a transplant incision for a couple of weeks, but the unsutured wounds from his drains are already so well healed they're nearly invisible. So those clips can probably come out in another day or so."

"Sounds like you picked an ideal candidate."

"We did, didn't we?"

"When will you do another?"

"Too soon to think about that. We need to wait awhile and see how this case plays out . . . Make sure it stays as good as it appears now."

"I do hope your program begins to make money in my lifetime."

Boyer hit Dewitt gently on the shoulder with his closed fist. "Your happiness is all we strive for."

IT WAS MARY Beth's night off at the hospital and it couldn't have come at a better time. Going to law school part-time and working a forty-hour week were taking a toll on her, so that she decided to turn in early.

Exhausted, she slept soundly for six hours, but then woke at 3 A.M., feeling warm and thirsty. On the way to the kitchen, a tickle in her throat made her cough. At the kitchen sink, she filled a glass from the tap and drank deeply. Remembering that she hadn't brushed her teeth before going to bed, she thought about doing it now, but when she reached the bathroom, she shuffled on past and returned to bed. Had she not ignored that small act of dental hygiene, she would have seen in the bathroom mirror that her face was speckled with a rash.

"GINNY, WAKE UP." Dominic Barroso shook his wife by the shoulder.

"What's wrong?" Ginny said, opening her eyes. "Did I oversleep?"

"I don't think you should go in tonight."

"Why not?"

Dominic gave her a hand mirror. "Take a look."

She lifted the mirror and saw that her face was mottled with pink blotches.

Dominic put his big hand on her forehead. "And you feel a little feverish."

Then she coughed. "Oh, you've got something all right," Dominic said.

"These are the same symptoms my patient had night before last," she said, referring to her stint as the third-shift nurse on Monteagle's experimental transplant ward.

"So what was it?"

"Nobody said, but it only lasted that one night. He's fine now. So it couldn't have been much of anything. But I think you're right. I'm scheduled to return to the regular ICU ward tonight, and I wouldn't want to carry anything in there, even if it doesn't cause any more harm than this." She looked at him quizzically. "How'd you know I had a rash? Wasn't the light out? Were you watching me sleep again?"

"You're so beautiful. I can't help it." He stroked his wife's long brown hair. "You should wear it down like this all the time."

Ginny mock-slapped his hand. "Oh, I'm sure that would go over well at the hospital. Hand me the phone, would you?"

Ginny entered the number of her supervisor at Monteagle.

"Val, this is Virginia. I've got a little cough and a rash so I thought I'd better stay home tonight."

"That means I'll have to scramble to get someone to fill in," Val said. "But you've made the right decision. So you probably won't be in tomorrow night either . . ."

"I'm betting I will." She told Val why she thought so, then said, "Dr. Boyer wants to be informed of any illness in the staff caring for Mr. Collins. So he needs to be told about this."

"I'll call him. You take care of yourself."

IT HAD BEEN nearly midnight and Michael Boyer had been asleep when the emergency call came. Now, standing in front of his open locker in the Monteagle surgery dressing room, he was wide awake. A patient who had received a human liver transplant two days ago was leaking bile into his abdominal drains. Tests had confirmed that there was a defective connection between the patient's bile duct and that of the transplant.

It seemed like these things always became evident at some ungodly hour of the night, which Michael actually enjoyed.

The hero riding to the rescue. Not on a white horse, but in a white Porsche. The similarity in the sound of horse and Porsche did not enter into Michael's decision to buy the car, it was just an added bonus.

As Michael was unbuttoning his shirt and thinking about what he had to do, his pager went off. He returned the call on the wall phone next to the locker room door.

"Michael Boyer answering a page."

"Doctor, this is Valerie Pettis. I just had a call from Virginia Barroso, the third-shift nurse who's been taking care of Mr. Collins. She's feeling a bit under the weather tonight and isn't coming to work. But that won't be a problem for you. She's been so bored taking care of just the one patient that she asked to go back to her regular ICU duties. So I'd already scheduled a different nurse to replace her."

"Has this new nurse read and signed the pertinent information form?" He was referring to the document explaining the potential risks that animal organ recipients posed for health care workers.

"It's all taken care of."

"And she's been checked out on our isolation protocols?"

"Yes."

Because Wayne was doing so remarkably well, Michael had already filed Wayne's brief symptoms two nights ago under "things too inconsequential to think about." So, instead of asking for more details on Ginny Barroso's illness, he simply said, "Okay, good job."

CHRIS TURNED TO Michael after examining Wayne's transplant incision. "It looks totally healed. I can barely even see where the clips were and you took them out only yesterday."

"I've never seen anything like it," Michael said. He put his gloved fingers on the faint line that marked the incision, and pressed. "Wayne, does that hurt?"

"No."

He moved along the incision line and pressed in another place. "There?"

"No."

"Or there?"

"No."

Michael looked at Chris. "It's not even tender. Wayne, have you always healed this fast?"

"Other than when they fixed those veins in my esophagus, this is the only real surgery I've ever had. I don't have any frame of reference."

"Surely you've cut yourself from time to time."

"Little cuts, sure. But I don't know what would be considered fast for that." He thought a moment. "I fell off a diving board at a quarry once and cut my knee on some rocks when I was a kid. It took six stitches to close that wound and I don't remember the doctor being impressed with the way I healed then. Want to see something else unusual?"

"What?"

Wayne held out his two thumbs side by side. "Look at the base of each nail where that little white arc should be."

Michael examined the two nails and turned to Chris. "His lunulas are gray. Take a look."

"What are lunulas?" Wayne asked.

"They mark the front edge of the germinal zone that produces the nail."

"I can tell you that they weren't gray before I checked in here."

"Any idea what caused that?" Michael asked Chris. "His nails look healthy."

"You got me. Maybe there's been an invasion and proliferation of pigment cells in that area."

"Wayne, you're just full of surprises," Michael said.

"Here's another one. I want to get out of here. When can I do that?"

"Your illness put you in a very poor nutritional state and while that *is* improving, you're not yet where I'd like to see you. And we still need to closely monitor your immunosuppressant levels, blood chemistry, and liver function."

"Tell me what I should eat, what I should avoid, and I'll do it. And can't all that other stuff be done on an outpatient basis?"

"Let's give it the weekend and then on Monday, we'll see."

After they left Wayne's room, Michael said to Chris, "There's no question that his progress has been remarkable, almost eerie, but I hate to turn him out into the world with no supervision. I don't know what kind of relationship you two are going to have after this, but would you let him stay with you for a little while after I discharge him?"

"I rarely cook for myself. I'm no one to rely on for nutrition."

"I just want him to have some structure around him and whatever emotional support you can provide."

"I might have trouble there, too."

"For a week. Just give him that."

Chris stood silent for a second, grappling with the idea of living with her father for a while longer. Finally, she said, "A week. That's all I'm agreeing to."

SEATED AT HIS computer, Dominic Barroso let out a whoop. He got up, reached for his cane, and hobbled into the bedroom, where Ginny, now fully recovered from whatever had caused her rash and those other symptoms last night, was putting up her hair before leaving for the hospital.

"You know that eighteenth-century silver tea service I listed this week? The high bid is already eleven thousand. And I only paid three for it. This is great. It might have taken a year to sell it in the shop. Online, everything sells so fast."

Dominic had owned a small antique shop until the arthritis in his right knee had destroyed the slippery cartilage cells that lined the articulating surfaces of the joint. Now, when he tried to walk, bone grated directly on bone.

With his mobility severely restricted, he was unable to operate his business the way it should be run. Because of this, he decided to close the shop and sell off the stock through an internet auction house. He'd let his part-time clerk go, but kept Ben, the warehouse man, to pack and ship all purchases. Ben was such a reliable employee that Dominic had only to call him and tell him where to send each item that sold.

The whole operation was so easy to run from home, and the items he listed sold at such good prices, that Dominic quickly saw that even with a bum knee, he could not only stay in the antiques trade, but earn more than when he'd operated the old way.

"And guess what we're going to do with the profits from that tea service—put them on a new car for you so you don't have to drive that old wreck anymore."

Ginny slipped the last pin into her hair and grabbed her

bag. Before leaving, she kissed Dominic on the cheek. "That's very thoughtful. Now, while I'm gone, I want you to think again about that knee replacement we discussed. Our medical insurance will cover it, so the cost is not a concern."

"I know. I just don't want to go through that."

"You'll never play major league baseball if you don't."

Dominic smiled. "And I was so close before my knee gave out."

"Just think about it."

After Ginny left, Dominic reviewed the bids on the other fifteen items he had listed on the auction site, then he worked on his business records for a while. A little before midnight, he went to the thermostat and turned on the air-conditioning.

His first cough came while he was thumbing through the new issue of *Art and Antiques*. He didn't catch on to what was happening until the red blotches appeared on his arms.

The time between Ginny's exposure in the transplant isolation ward and her first symptoms was approximately forty-eight hours. In Dominic's case, it took half that time.

CHAPTER 8

TR SLOWED HIS car so he could watch the tall blonde in the green dress from behind for as long as possible. Her skirt stopped about four inches above her knees, showing off shapely calves and enough of her thighs to make his heart ache. Knowing that with the right man this woman would probably do almost anything sexually—and that he would never be that man—made him hope her face was homely. Sometimes it happens. The inexplicable shuffle of genes occasionally gives a woman a fine body and then abandons her when it comes to her face. But as he passed her and looked in his rearview mirror, he could not find solace in that possibility, for she had cool, elegant features.

And you could bet she was bright too. In his experience, the gorgeous but dumb blonde was a fantasy made up by inadequate men to protect their egos from the unattainable. When women looked like the blonde in the green dress, they always had a quick mind they could use to verbally slice you like a cucumber if you approached them.

But he still wanted her so badly it made his head hurt. He had a lot of headaches from yearning. His car was new, but it wasn't the Jag he wanted and that made his head hurt. He owned his own home in Little Five Points, a bungalow they called it, but he wanted a sprawling estate in Buckhead. And *that* made his head hurt. He wanted to walk up to his gardeners after they'd just planted a large dogwood and say "not there, over *there*." He wanted to fly everywhere first class, and wear designer suits, and drink wine that hadn't been bottled last year.

He was a bird tied to the earth.

His IQ was in the near-genius range. So why couldn't he figure out how to get a dollar from every adult in this country? One dollar is all it would take. Or maybe two. Then he could fly. And that blond bitch he'd just passed wouldn't be so eager to give him a hard time.

In his mirror he saw her leave the covered walkway that ran along the commercial strip's storefronts and go to her car, where she put the purchases she was carrying in the trunk. Then, instead of getting in her car, she headed back to the walkway. On impulse, TR turned left at the first opportunity and drove back toward her car.

The lot was packed, but he found a slot close to where the blonde had parked. He got out and walked to her car, his eyes darting about him. Satisfied that he wasn't being watched, he slipped between the two vehicles separating him from the blonde's car, and moved forward in the narrow space until he reached her left front fender. After another quick look around, he got out his pocketknife and dropped to one knee.

Crouching like that made his headache worse, but the hiss of escaping air as he worked his blade into the side wall of her tire was more than adequate compensation. He quickly made his way around to her remaining tires, then feeling as though he'd struck a blow for men everywhere against sharp-tongued sluts, he returned to his own car.

But now, with each heartbeat, he felt as though a depth charge was going off in his brain. He got behind the wheel and popped open the glove compartment, where he shuffled through the crap in there until he found his pills.

No time to look for water now . . .

He shook two of the tablets into his hand, then threw them into his mouth and chewed them. They tasted horrible; bitter and metallic. But he knew they'd work. They always did. And his headache would go away.

The pills could stop his headaches, but the desires that kicked them off lingered, sometimes for days, producing such a feeling of despair he had often thought he should just end it all.

In the months following the murders of the two Frenchmen, he had been so afraid their assassination would bring the authorities to his door he had put a gun to his head and pulled the trigger. But the bullet had ricocheted off his skull. When the police came and he'd regained consciousness, he told them he'd been the victim of an attempted carjacking. Though they hadn't believed him, the lie had kept the truth from becoming known at work, which would have been impossible for him to bear.

Maybe that old injury helped bring on the headaches. Whatever it was, he could already feel the pills working. But he still wanted that blonde.

WAYNE WAS DISCHARGED from the hospital at 6 P.M. Monday evening. When Chris came to get him, she found Mary Beth Cummings at the nurses station staring at her right hand, lightly stroking her little finger. Seeing Chris, she held her hand up, palm out, and slowly moved her little finger back and forth.

"I can't believe it," she said. "I haven't been able to do that for three years, ever since a glass vase I was washing shattered and cut my hand." She stroked both sides of her little finger with the index finger of her other hand. "And I can feel that . . . not to a normal degree, but the sensation is definitely returning."

Then, realizing she was running on about something Chris was probably not interested in, she said, "Sorry, I'm just excited and surprised that after all this time . . ."

"No need to apologize," Chris said. "I'd be excited, too."

Wayne joined them from his room, fully dressed and carrying the overnight bag he'd brought. He was still thin, but he looked a lot better than when Chris first saw him in her office; his jaundice almost gone and his belly no longer protruding.

"Let's get out of here," he said. Then to Mary Beth, "That's no reflection on you. You've done a fine job and I'll always be grateful."

Mary Beth took hold of a nearby wheelchair and pushed it

over to him. "Now I get to take you for a ride to the front door."

"I can walk."

"Hospital policy," she said firmly.

TEN MINUTES LATER, Chris slid into the driver's seat and started the car.

"I can't believe how much better I'm feeling," Wayne said.

"I'm glad it's working out so well," Chris replied, backing out of her parking space.

"The worst part after the surgery was everybody being so covered up when they came in my room, like I was something to be feared. It does things to your mind."

Neither of them spoke again until they were out of the parking lot and onto the highway. Then Chris said, "When I was talking with Dr. Boyer a few days ago, he said something that surprised me. It wasn't possible for me to give you part of my liver. You needed more tissue than I could supply."

"Why are you telling me this?"

"Just so you'd know."

"Have you eaten yet?"

"No."

"I'm dying for a burger and fries. What do you say?"

"I'm sure that wouldn't be Dr. Boyer's choice for you, but after what you've been through, why not? But starting tomorrow, that kind of meal is off limits. There's a woman in my apartment building that loves to cook, but she's widowed and doesn't have any kids. I've contracted with her to cook for us during the time you'll be staying with me. I don't eat much in the morning, so you'll have to shift for yourself then. I've got plenty of everything on hand. You'll go to her apartment for lunch and she'll make dinner for us in mine."

"So we'll be eating dinner together, you and I?"

"Unless something comes up that prevents me from being there."

"Is that likely to happen?"

"I really can't say."

"Let me do it. You might not believe this, but I'm a great cook myself."

"You'd need to shop for groceries and get them upstairs.

You shouldn't be doing that. It's too much so soon after your surgery."

"There must be a store that delivers."

"I don't know."

"Just let me take care of it. I want to. Don't make an invalid of me."

"All right. We'll do it your way."

THE CRY OF seagulls and the sound of ocean waves caressing a rocky beach filled the room. Dominic Barroso turned from his stomach onto his back, but remained asleep until the loons began calling. He always woke with the first loon call. Maybe because it was so spooky.

He sat up, shifted his legs over the side of the bed, and turned off the tape he used for an alarm clock. When Ginny was working the third shift, he always rose at 8 A.M. so he could have a nice breakfast waiting for her when she got home. They didn't live far from Monteagle, but because of the traffic it would take her an hour to make the trip, just enough time for him to shower, dress, get his joints oiled up, and prepare something nice to eat.

He reached for his cane and got up, as usual, putting most of his weight on his good leg, "good" being a euphemism for the leg not as screwed up as the really bad one.

He hadn't taken more than three steps when he realized that his legs were feeling pretty good today. He took a few more steps. Pretty good, hell. They were feeling great.

THAT SAME MORNING, while Chris was making rounds, her mind kept coming back to what her father's nurse had said about movement and sensation returning in her little finger; nothing for three years, then, while taking care of a patient whose incision heals far faster than normal, she too, experiences an unusual therapeutic event.

Interesting.

The epidemiologist part of her kept pecking at those facts. As a result, a little before eleven o'clock, she factored in her father's odd symptoms the night she and Michael had come back to the hospital. That led her to a possible chain of events so strange she banished it from her thoughts.

She spent the early part of the afternoon reviewing all incidences of hospital-acquired infections for the past two weeks, looking for any patterns she should be aware of. Then the scenario she'd dispatched from her thoughts that morning crept back into them.

After briefly debating with herself about whether she should follow up on this, she reached for the phone.

The woman's name was Mary Beth Cummings. Chris remembered that from seeing it on her name tag. But would the hospital give out her home phone number?

It turned out they would, but reluctantly, and only after Chris explained to three people that she was a member of Michael's transplant team and had been seeing patients there as part of her infectious disease practice for over a year.

Her call to the Cummings home, however, produced only Mary Beth's answering machine. Chris left her name and number and turned her attention to other matters.

At four-fifteen, Mary Beth returned her call.

"Thanks for getting back to me. I'm sure you remember the rash and the other symptoms my father had the night you called Dr. Boyer and we came back to the hospital. Since that night, have you ever had the same symptoms?"

"No. Under the circumstances, I certainly would have mentioned it to Dr. Boyer if I had. Why do you ask? Did anyone else have them?"

"Not that I'm aware of."

"Do you think there's a problem? Your father seems very healthy now."

"There's nothing to be concerned about. I was just curious."

"If that's all then, I have to leave for work."

"Okay. Have a good shift."

So that's it, Chris thought, hanging up. It was a crazy idea. Now she even felt a little foolish for having made the call.

Then the phone rang again.

"This is Dr. Collins."

"Mary Beth here. I just remembered . . . Wednesday night, when Ginny Barroso, the third-shift nurse who'd been taking care of your father, came to relieve me, she told me that starting Thursday, she was going back to work in the regular ICU. When I ran into her on Friday before her shift started, just to make conversation, I asked her how it felt to be back in the regular trenches. She said she didn't know because she'd been sick Thursday. She seemed fine when we spoke on Friday, so she couldn't have been too sick."

This information greatly piqued Chris's interest. "I appreciate you telling me this."

Having established her credibility earlier with the guardians of the Monteagle staff's privacy, they gave Chris Ginny's number without a scuffle.

AT THE BARROSO home, while Ginny slept, Dominic sat at the computer reviewing the bids on his listings. With all the time he spent online, Ginny had been after him for weeks to have a separate phone line installed, but he hadn't taken care of it. So he had no idea someone was trying to contact them.

BUSY . . . CHRIS BROKE the connection with her finger. Too curious to wait until the Barrosos' line was clear, she started thinking about who else might be able to tell her what was wrong with Ginny the night she was ill. Surely Ginny had reported her illness to her supervisor the night she hadn't come to work.

After another round of phone calls, Chris had Valerie Pettis on the line. She identified herself, then asked, "Do you recall the night last week when your regular third-shift nurse taking care of my father didn't come to work because she was ill?"

"I remember."

"Did you discuss with her what was wrong?"

"She said she had a rash and a cough."

"And you didn't tell us about it?"

"I did tell Dr. Boyer."

"You specifically spoke about the rash and the cough?"

"Now that you put it that way, maybe not. As I recall, the conversation shifted quickly to Ginny's replacement and whether she was up to speed on the isolation protocols. Is something wrong?"

"I'm not sure. But thanks for the information."

As Chris was about to try the Barrosos' number again, the phone rang. It was Wayne.

"I'm planning dinner for six o'clock," he said. "You'll be here, won't you?"

Of all the times to be constrained by this, Chris thought. She wanted to be free to pursue the disturbing facts she'd just learned.

"It's going to be wonderful," Wayne said. "Salmon over linguini, new potatoes in a dill sauce."

The dinner seemed so important to him that, despite her own wishes, she said, "I'll be there."

She tried the Barroso number twice more without success before leaving the office. So Ginny's brief illness was still on her mind when she arrived home.

Wayne had not exaggerated his culinary skills and had produced a dinner that deserved the compliments Chris paid him. Their conversation during dinner was polite and civilized and strained. When she wasn't expressing anger at him, it seemed that Chris had nothing else to say. Over the years she had often imagined what it would be like to have a father. Now that she did, she didn't know what to do with him. And she still didn't trust him.

After dinner she helped clean up, then excused herself and headed for the phone in her bedroom. This time when she called the Barrosos, a man answered.

"Ginny Barroso, please."

"I'm sorry, but she's asleep."

"This is Dr. Collins. I'm a member of Dr. Boyer's transplant team at Monteagle Hospital. Ginny took care of one of our patients last week and I heard that on Thursday she called in sick. What was the nature of her illness?"

"She had a rash and a slight fever and was also coughing. She didn't want to give her patients anything, so she stayed home."

"How's she feeling now?"

"Fine."

"Better than usual in any way?"

"I don't understand."

"Has she had any long-term health problems that have recently improved?"

"Not that I can think of."

While Chris was assimilating this information and wondering what else she should ask, the man added, "You should have asked that question about me."

"Why?"

"For years arthritis has been eating away at my knees. Messed up one so bad they said I needed an artificial replacement. Couldn't walk without a cane. But I'm sitting here now looking at my cane on the other side of the room."

"You're saying . . ."

"Didn't use it at all yesterday or today. I don't know what's going on, or how long it'll last, but my knees are better."

"This rash," Chris said, her mind reeling. "Did you get it too?"

"The night after Ginny did."

CHAPTER 9

"MICHAEL, IT'S CHRIS. I think we have a problem."

She told him what she'd learned about Mary Beth, Ginny, and Ginny's husband. "I don't know at this point if it all originated with my father's transplant, but I suspect it did."

"Jesus." Then there was silence on Michael's end of the line.

"Michael, are you still there?"

"I'm just trying to absorb what you've said. How could this have happened? We took precautions."

"Apparently they weren't good enough."

"Let's say it did come from the transplant. How much trouble are we in? I mean, the illness conveyed was very minimal and now they're all feeling fine . . . better than fine."

"That's the case today, but who knows what'll happen down the line. We're in uncharted waters here."

"What do we do now?"

"First, we have to determine the extent of this. All hospital staff will have to be questioned to see who else might have recently experienced the same symptoms. We should set the time frame as the last two weeks. If we find any cases that occurred before the transplant, we'll know it didn't start there.

Since the symptoms were so minor and lasted such a short time, if they occurred at night, they might not have been noticed. I think that's what happened with Mary Beth Cummings. But we'll just have to live with that constraint."

"So maybe we were infected too and just don't know it?"

"I can't say, but it seems possible."

"Then we could be spreading it even now."

"Let's hope not."

"What do we do till we find out, quarantine ourselves?"

"Until we get a handle on this, you shouldn't do any surgery and I'm not going to see any patients. To alter our lives any more than that at this stage would be overreacting."

"What about your father?"

"I'm going to ask him to stay in the house until we learn more. Monteagle doesn't have a medical director of infection control, but the IC office must still be staffed."

"I'm sure it is."

"I'd like to get started tonight canvassing the hospital staff. There's probably no one in the IC office now, but we need to get someone to come in to help us. Can you take care of that?"

"I'll get right on it. Are you going over there now?"

"As soon as I hang up."

"I'll meet you in my office."

"Do you have Eric Ash's home phone number?"

"Why are we calling him?"

"If the evidence points to my father as the index case of the symptoms we're concerned about, I'll be wanting all my father's stored blood samples and the blood of everyone who came in contact with him at the hospital tested for pig retrovirus. And I want to be sure Ash has the necessary reagents on hand. The earlier he knows that, the better."

"Just how open are we going to be about why we're questioning the staff?"

"While we don't know what we're dealing with, we're going to be evasive and vague."

WITH CHRIS STANDING beside him, Michael looked around the conference room to see if everyone was there. Thirty-nine busy hours had passed since Chris had told him that the pig virus in her father's liver had apparently infected several people. It was now time to explain matters to the transplant team and the appropriate members of the administration.

"Something's going on," Eric Ash said in a hushed voice as he joined Chris and Michael.

"What do you mean?" Michael asked.

Ash looked across the room, where John Scott, Monteagle's CEO, was talking to Norman Stewart, the medical director, and Carter Dewitt, VP for financial affairs. "Scott himself called me first thing this morning and asked me about the results on those blood samples. When I told him what I'd found, he said I was to divide all the samples from your father and put half of each one in a separate tube labeled with his name and the date they were drawn. Thirty minutes ago, Carter Dewitt came to my lab and picked them up."

"Dewitt," Michael exclaimed. "What's *he* doing handling blood samples?"

"And I also heard that Scott brought Dominic Barroso, the husband of the infected nurse, in for an arthroscopic knee examination."

"That *is* odd," Michael said. "What did they find?"

"I'd been trying to learn that myself ever since I heard about it, but hadn't been able to get in touch with the orthopod who did it until just a few minutes ago. Before this guy Barroso became infected, he had almost no articular cartilage left in his knee. Now it's completely regenerated."

"That's incredible," Sidney Knox said.

At that moment, the two men they were waiting for, Henry Bechtel, VP for legal affairs, and Chuck Alford, head of public relations, arrived.

"Okay, everyone, we're all here now," Michael announced. "So let's begin."

When the transplant team and everyone else had found seats around the big conference table, he said, "I think most of you are aware that we've experienced something unexpected with our first pig-to-human transplant. I've called this meeting to bring everyone up to date. Shortly after receiving—"

"Dr. Boyer, I'm sorry to interrupt," John Scott, the CEO, said.

Scott was known around the hospital as the great white shark—the *white* part of that appellation coming from his prematurely silver hair and beard; the *shark* part, from his cold black eyes.

"I'd like you to be as accurate as possible in what you tell us," Scott said. "And the phrase 'shortly after' isn't consistent with that wish."

"Of course." Michael briefly consulted the notes he'd brought, then continued. "Our first patient, Mr. Wayne Collins, received his transplant on the morning of the eleventh, a Monday. On Tuesday evening, I was called by the second-shift nurse caring for Mr. Collins and told that he had a slight fever and a rash. Dr. Chris Collins," Michael looked at Chris, "the patient's daughter, who serves our team as its infectious disease specialist, and I returned to the hospital and examined Mr. Collins. We ordered a CBC and a diff count, which came back normal. Because of that and the minor nature of the symptoms, we decided to watch and wait."

TR hated meetings. They never accomplished anything and just gave blowhards the opportunity to hear themselves talk. Because of that, he usually resented every minute he was obliged to spend in one. But today, considering the circumstances, he was interested in this one. If only his blasted headache would clear up.

"Later that evening . . ." Michael looked at Scott to see if that time frame was specific enough. Receiving a nod, he continued. "I was informed by the same nurse that Mr. Collins had developed a slight cough. By the next morning—"

"You did nothing then to treat the cough?" Scott said.

"We judged it too minor a problem to treat."

"Thank you. Please go on."

"By the next morning, the fever, the rash, and the cough were gone. Mr. Collins then began a rapid course of recovery which included a return of normal liver function and a quite remarkable healing of his abdominal transplant incision. He was discharged from the hospital on the evening of the seventeenth, a week after his surgery.

"It subsequently came to my attention that one of the third-shift nurses who cared for Mr. Collins during his stay developed the same symptoms he showed the night Dr. Collins and I returned to the hospital to see him."

Knowing she would soon be given the floor, Chris was getting nervous.

"Through some communication glitch," Michael said, "I did not learn of this until five days later." Michael was not surprised that this brought a quick response from Scott.

"Isn't this just what the FDA was concerned about—the transmission of some unknown animal disease to humans?"

"Yes."

"And didn't you design safeguards to protect the staff?"

Trying not to let his irritation at being treated to like a child show, Michael said, "We did."

"Then how could this have happened?"

"I agree it's an unacceptable failure in our procedures."

"I'd like a detailed report from you by tomorrow morning explaining how this occurred."

"You'll have it. May I continue?"

Scott waved his permission.

"It was Dr. Collins who suspected something was wrong, so I'll let her take it from here."

Hoping Scott wouldn't go after her as he had Michael, Chris stood and told them how she'd learned that Ginny Barroso and her husband had become ill with the same symptoms her father had shown.

"At this point, we canvassed the entire staff of the hospital to determine if anyone else had experienced these symptoms. We found no one. That established Mr. Collins as the index case and pointed to the transmission of some factor from him to Ginny Barroso, and from her, to her husband.

"Suspecting that the transmissible factor might be the retrovirus known to be widely present in pig cells, I asked Dr. Ash," she gestured to Ash, who was sitting across from her, "to test all the stored samples of my father's blood as well as samples from everyone who came in contact with him after his surgery, including Dr. Boyer and myself. Positive results were obtained for the Barrosos, Mary Beth Cummings, and the earlier samples from Mr. Collins. The later Collins samples and those from everyone else were negative.

"The absence of virus in the later Collins samples may mean that since the virus was in his blood longer than any of the others, his immune system destroyed it. Or it may be hiding in cells outside the blood. It's quite likely the virus will soon disappear from the blood in the other three positive cases as well. We have plans to follow that.

"The limited number of positive cases suggests there was a very small window of infectivity. I believe it was during the hours when Mr. Collins had a cough, which would explain why neither Dr. Boyer or myself were infected. Nor was the phlebotomist who drew Mr. Collins's blood the night we were called back to see him. All three of us were in his room before the cough developed. Mary Beth Cummings and Ginny Barroso, of course, were present during that period."

"Dr. Collins . . ."

It was Norman Stewart, the medical director.

"This organism in question is a retrovirus, in the same general category as HIV. But retroviruses don't spread by aerosolized transmission; in coughs or sneezes. Infection requires intimate contact of mucous membranes with contaminated body fluids."

"Apparently our virus isn't aware of that." Realizing this sounded a little rude, Chris added, "What I mean is, rules for the behavior of a given class of organisms develop slowly, reflecting our experience with them. When that experience shows us something new, we change the rules."

Stewart responded. "How do you reconcile the presence of this virus in the blood of the four individuals you discussed when none of the published studies on this question have found evidence this can happen?"

"I'll let Dr. Ash answer that."

Ash rose and said, "I found the virus in Mr. Collins and the others using the PCR technique. Without going into details, I'll just say that this method allows detection of small stretches of the viral genome in test samples. To do this, it uses reagents based on known genetic sequences in the virus. So all it can do is reveal the presence of whatever the known sequence is you looked for. If the rest of the virus is different, the test cannot reveal that. It's entirely possible this virus began as one of the known forms of pig retrovirus, but then changed into something with enough similarity to the original that my reagents were able to detect it. "In other words, it mutated." Something retroviruses are known for."

"What are the possibilities this same mutation could occur in another human recipient of a pig liver?" Scott asked.

"Without knowing where the mutation is or how much of the genome is involved, that's hard to say. But being it was probably a totally random event, I'd say it's very unlikely to happen again."

Chris saw from the look on Scott's face that he found this answer satisfying.

"I gather from everything I've heard that there is presently no danger of the four infected people casually passing the virus to anyone else," Scott said.

With the conversation back on medical rather than technical matters, Chris rose and Ash returned to his seat. "I believe that's true," she said. "And when it disappears from the blood in all those infected, as I think it will, the possibility of transmission will be extremely remote."

"What are the chances the two nurses and the husband could have passed the virus to anyone else during the infectious period?"

"I've considered that. But all three were at home, so it couldn't have happened. Even though the two nurses were well beyond the infectious period and obviously didn't pass the virus to anyone else on the staff during the time we were unaware they were carrying it, I've put them both on leave until we're sure the virus is cleared from their blood."

"Thank you, Dr. Collins," Scott said. "If everyone would just excuse me for a moment." He motioned to Dewitt and Bechtel and they all left their chairs and huddled at the front of the room while everyone else exchanged questioning looks. After less than a minute, the three-man caucus turned to face everyone else and Scott said, "Dr. Boyer, I want those three remaining infected individuals tested daily. And as soon as the results of those tests are known, I want to be informed. Dr. Ash, I assume you have the expertise to do a complete sequence on this new virus . . ."

"I should be able to do that."

"Get started on it right away. Now Mr. Dewitt has a few comments for Dr. Boyer and the other members of his group."

Dewitt cleared his throat and said, "As you may or may not recall, the agreement you all signed when you joined Monteagle as an employee or as a physician with privileges here specified that any patentable discovery produced in connection with your hospital duties becomes the property of Monteagle. As the hospital will soon be entering discussions with several major drug companies to license all rights to the therapeutic effects of the mutated virus, we thought it useful to remind you of the agreement in force. If you have any questions about this, Mr. Bechtel will be happy to remain after the meeting and discuss them with you."

Dewitt scanned the group for any response. Seeing none, he looked at Scott, who said, "Then we're adjourned."

No one from Michael's group went over to Bechtel. They all formed their own huddle at the foot of the long table.

"Why didn't *I* hear anything about any of this before the meeting?" William Hessman, the vet, said.

"Sorry about that, Bill," Michael said. "With you spending most of your time in the animal facility several miles away, that puts you out of the loop. It's one of the reasons I called the meeting. And I wasn't sure how much of the story the rest of you knew."

"What does all this do to the program?" Hessman said.

"I'm not sure," Michael responded. "I need to discuss this with the FDA. And Eric, we need that sequence data so we can figure out exactly what happened. So for now, we're on hold."

"It occurred to me in a very general way that there might be some money to be made from the therapeutic effects of this virus," Sidney Knox said. "Scott certainly didn't waste any time exploiting that."

"It seems premature to me to be trying to sell the rights to this virus," Chris said. "It's so early yet, there's no way to tell what the long-range effects might be. It looks therapeutic now, but where does the virus go when it disappears from the blood—the heart, the brain, the bone marrow?"

"Or nothing could go wrong and the hospital will make a fortune from it," Ash said.

"Or that," Chris agreed.

"I hope you'll keep all of us informed from this point on about the status of the program," Hessmann said.

"I'll try to do better, Bill," Michael said.

The group dispersed, leaving just Michael and Chris behind.

"I'll keep everyone better informed if there still *is* a program," Michael muttered.

"Why do you say that?" Chris asked.

"The pig virus wasn't supposed to do something like this.

Even if it *is* a good thing, it shows that in humans, the virus is unpredictable. So there's bound to be renewed concern about the potential dangers involved in animal-to-human transplants. There's no telling how long debate will rage now over that issue. This could derail the whole program. And if your prediction that even the mutation we've got will turn ugly comes to pass . . ."

Though she tried to suppress it, Chris felt a burst of tenderness for Michael. Seeing him despondent like this over the turn his work had taken weakened the wall she tried to keep between them. She reached out and touched his hand. "It wasn't a prediction," she said gently. "Merely a possibility. And I'm sorry now I said it."

Michael looked down where her hand still rested against his. And with that, the moment passed. Face reddening, she hastily pulled her hand away and folded her arms over her chest. "Just a possibility," she said almost in a whisper as Michael looked hard into her eyes, trying to figure her out. Then he remembered another problem.

"What the hell am I going to tell Scott about how this happened? What did those two nurses do that got them in trouble?"

Something about the way he'd phrased the question made Chris think of the backup respirator with no filters in it she'd seen when she'd visited her father the morning after his surgery. She had no idea how that could have led to the two nurses becoming infected, but it was an irregularity that ought to be investigated.

"Let me do some checking around and see what I can come up with," she said. "Is the isolation ward open?"

"There's no one there, so it's locked," Michael said. He pulled a key ring from the pocket of his white coat, removed a large brass key, and gave it to her. "Hope you find something."

DOWN THE HALL, TR was heading directly for his office to take another pill for his headache. Painful as it was, it didn't keep him from thinking hard about the surprise Scott had pulled on everyone at the meeting. He didn't like the man, but had to admit he had vision and knew how to seize an opportunity.

But Chris Collins had said something interesting. "It seems premature to be trying to sell the rights to this virus." Now *there* was something to think about.

It took the pill about fifteen minutes to work, and when his headache had cleared, TR sat at his desk with his feet up, doodling on a notepad, converting the fantasies spooling through his brain into boxes and arrows and ink-drawn Slinkies, ignoring his duties.

TR's knowledge that Scott had ordered the examination of Dominic Barroso's knee was but a hint of how diligently TR worked the hospital gossip mill and picked the fruits of its grapevine. The amount of personal information he had accumulated on the staff was truly impressive. He knew that Michael Boyer had quit smoking when he was twenty-two, that Chris had graduated from medical school fifth in her class, and that Chuck Alford, the head of public relations, had once been arrested for shoplifting. But he was most interested in financial matters, and he could tell you the current salary to the penny of every Monteagle administrator.

From the dossiers he had accumulated on all the key hospital personnel, he had learned that people who were undergoing a lot of stress and hardship in their lives rarely self-destructed as he almost had after the events in Kazakhstan, but could hide it remarkably well. He'd seen an excellent example of that just this morning. In their recent divorce, the man's wife had taken his home and half his assets and income, so he was now living in a cheap three-room apartment without enough money to satisfy his basic needs, which included lap dances from a girl named Amber and a significant cocaine habit. Yet you couldn't tell any of that from just looking at him.

Feeling as though he'd had a very productive morning, he reached for the phone to call that man.

CHAPTER 10

CHRIS UNLOCKED THE doors to the transplant isolation ward and went inside. She turned on the lights and stood for a moment listening to the whisper of the ventilation system. Then she walked over to her father's anteroom and pressed the button controlling its airtight door. Entering, she saw that the backup respirator was hanging right where she'd last seen it, but it was now completely equipped with a filter cartridge in each socket. She looked on the metal shelves and found a box of North filters and two boxes of filters for the Wilson masks.

She thought back to her conversation with the day nurse the morning the filters had been borrowed from the backup. Filters had been ordered from Central Supply and would soon be there, the nurse had said.

But had they arrived?

She tried to remember. Did the backup have filters in it that night when she and Michael checked on her father's condition following Mary Beth's call reporting his fever? She closed her eyes and attempted to see the masks that night.

No good. They wouldn't come into focus.

But suppose the filters *had* still been missing because no

new ones had been delivered. It wouldn't mean anything. The old ones could be used with perfect safety for many shifts. They didn't *have* to be changed so often.

Even though *she* knew that, her mind wouldn't set the filter issue aside because the nurses didn't know it. What would they have done if there were no replacements available? There must be a log book somewhere up here with filter-replacement records in it.

She left the anteroom and went to the nurses station where she quickly spotted a clipboard holding the records she wanted. The sheet for the nurses respirator was on top.

According to the records, the nurse who'd taken the filters from the backup respirator had made no note of that, but had simply written down the time she'd changed filters and added her initials as though the filters she'd used had come off the shelf.

But there was a note by Mary Beth's entry for her shift that gave Chris a jolt: "Filters from Engineering." And the time noted was *after* she and Michael had gone home that night.

Filters from Engineering. Did they use HEPA filters? She had a horrible feeling that they didn't.

Chris snatched up the phone and had the hospital operator connect her with Engineering. The phone rang five times, and then six, with no answer.

"Come on, come on," Chris mumbled.

On the ninth ring, a man picked up.

"Yeah. Ed Sumner."

"Ed, this is Dr. Collins. May I speak with the shift supervisor?"

"You already are."

"Do you use full face respirators for anything?"

"Sometimes."

"What color are the rims on the filter cartridges?" She asked him this question because HEPA filter cartridges were color coded with purple rims.

"I dunno," Sumner said. "Never thought about the colors."

"Could you check, please?"

"Hold on."

While she waited for the bad news, Chris felt an escalating sense of dread, because if Mary Beth had to get filters from

Engineering, that meant the backup respirator was probably still without them that night.

And if it *was*, Chris felt she should have noticed that when she and Michael came to check on Wayne's fever. Then she could have explained to Mary Beth that it was okay to use the same filters for more than one shift. Transmission of the virus had so far not harmed anyone. But it shouldn't have happened. Ultimately, as the team's infectious disease specialist, she had to bear the responsibility. Even though she'd come on board late, she was supposed to protect everyone. Now, on her watch, a poorly understood animal virus was loose in four people. And if the engineering filters did not have purple rims, she could have easily prevented it.

Please let Engineering have the right ones . . .

"Doctor?"

"I'm here."

"All our filters are yellow."

She mechanically thanked him for his help and hung up.

Yellow.

Damn it.

Mary Beth had become infected by using the wrong filters. But what about Ginny Barroso?

Chris picked up the filter replacement log and looked for Ginny's entry the night she was infected. There . . . filters replaced at the start of her shift.

Replaced with what? Mary Beth must have gotten two extras from Engineering. Or Ginny didn't actually replace the filters. Either way, she must have worked her shift with yellow filters in her mask. Just to be sure, Chris went down to the ICU, hoping to find the nurse who'd worked the isolation ward day shift during her father's stay.

She spotted her almost immediately: a big, dark-haired woman whose nose dominated her face. Chris couldn't remember her name. Brenda, maybe. She walked over to where the woman was adjusting the delivery rate on a patient's IV. When Chris was a couple of steps away, the nurse finished with the IV and turned, giving Chris a glance at her name tag, which was not Brenda.

"Hello, Barbara, how are you?" Chris asked.

"Dr. Collins. I'm all right. It's a lot more work down here than it was taking care of your father. How's he doing?"

"Still better than anyone expected. Do you remember the day we discussed you taking the filters from the backup respirator?"

"Yes."

"You were expecting the new filters to come up from Central Supply at any time. Did they ever arrive that day?"

Barbara thought back. "I don't think they did . . . no, I remember, they brought a couple of boxes the next morning, a few minutes after my shift started."

"So you used some of those when you changed filters."

"I'm sure I did."

"Do you remember anything unusual about the filters you replaced?"

"The rims were yellow, not purple. I thought that was kind of odd, but I just assumed they were from some other maker."

"Thanks. You've been a big help."

"And I didn't even have to lift anything."

Chris wasn't eager to tell Michael what she'd learned, but he needed to know. She passed up the house phone in the ICU and found one in a less public area. Michael returned her page promptly.

"I know how the virus got into those nurses," she said. She told him her story objectively, with no attempt to hide her culpability.

"Amazing," he said when she finished. "So many places where that chain of events could have gone a different way. Good job. Thanks."

"How will you write your report?"

"What do you mean?"

"Whom will you blame?"

"No one. It was just a series of mistakes that got compounded as the day wore on."

"Will Scott see it that way?"

"I have no idea. Do we really care?"

"He does run the hospital."

"So maybe we'll have a difference of opinion. Wouldn't be the first time. And I've got bigger problems than that to worry about. I better get started on my report. Thanks again for figuring it all out."

Chris was not comforted by Michael's charitable view of the account she'd given him. She knew who was at fault.

She arrived home a little after 6 P.M. still thinking about the backup respirator. She expected to find her father busy in the kitchen and dinner nearly ready. But he wasn't there. She saw some strips of well-pounded veal and an uncooked spinach casserole on the counter and there was a big fresh garden salad in the fridge. But the cook was somewhere else.

And the apartment was silent.

Mildly curious, she went down the hall to what was temporarily serving as Wayne's room and knocked on the door.

"Hello. Anyone home?"

No answer.

Fearing that he might be in there in some sort of coma, she opened the door and looked inside. Her eyes went first to the sofa bed, which was neatly made up and didn't have Wayne in it. She flicked on the lights and went inside to see if he was on the floor on the other side of the bed.

He wasn't.

Puzzled, she started for the door, but then saw something on the chest she'd let him use. It was a bottle of Bombay Gin.

Flushed with anger, she grabbed the bottle and took it into the living room, where she pulled an armchair around so it faced the door. Then she sat, the gin bottle in her lap, waiting for her father to return.

At 6:14, she heard the sound of a key in the lock and Wayne came in carrying a small brown paper bag.

"Where have *you* been?" Chris said accusingly.

Obviously confused by her tone of voice, Wayne held up the brown bag. "I needed some fresh garlic."

Chris stood up and stalked over to him. She held the gin in front of his face. "Recognize this?" Without waiting for an answer, she turned and walked away, talking now to the wall. "You know how important it is that you not drink." She turned to face him. "You promised a room full of people that you could be trusted. And they believed you, invested their time and a considerable amount of money in you, and this is how you repay them? You said you had changed. Well, forgive me if I see the same old Wayne, all for himself and to hell with everyone else."

"Look at the cap on the bottle," Wayne said.

"What about it?"

"Is the seal broken?"

She examined the cap. "No."

"So I couldn't have consumed any of the contents."

"Not yet. But you were planning to."

"I bought it so I could look at it every day and see the enemy. It's not good enough to just be strong when there's no alcohol around. I have to be able to resist even when it's easy to take a drink. Have you ever smelled alcohol on my breath since my return? No? So why did you assume the worst when you found an *unopened* bottle in my room?"

When it came to her father, Chris realized that she was two people. One wanted to roast him over an open flame, deaf to all pleas for mercy. The other wanted to love him and believe he loved her. As those dual incarnations grappled with each other to see which would deal with the current situation, a third Chris stepped forward. Cool and objective, this one understood that her reaction to all this was being colored by anger at herself over what she'd just learned at the hospital. She saw now that Wayne *could* be telling the truth.

"You're right," she said. "It was wrong of me to accuse you like that. I'm sorry."

"Apology accepted. Now let me get in the kitchen and put this garlic to use."

THE NEXT MORNING, Dominic and Ginny Barroso and Mary Beth Cummings all reported to the hospital and each gave a blood sample. By late afternoon, Ash had the results: virus absent in the two women, still present in Dominic. Shortly after Chris learned of the results, she got a phone call.

"Dr. Collins, would you hold please for Dr. Scott?"

The Monteagle CEO. What could *he* want? Uh-oh. Michael's report . . . Scott had learned how she'd screwed up and was probably calling to vent all over her.

After a few seconds, he came on the line. "I assume you've heard that the blood of the two nurses was negative for virus today."

"I was informed of that not fifteen minutes ago," Chris replied, thinking this was an odd way for him to begin.

"I want to reinstate the two women and allow them to return to work. But I thought I'd get your views first."

He wanted her opinion. As though she were still in good standing with him. Hadn't he read the report yet? The ques-

tion of reinstatement of the two nurses was one she'd been
thinking about since even before she'd been told of the test results. Despite the possibility that months or years from now
the virus might somehow damage all those who had been infected, there seemed only one reasonable course of action. "I
don't see that we have any good reason not to reinstate them.
And since they were infected as part of their regular duties,
they may have legal recourse if we don't."

"That's what Bechtel said. And I certainly don't want the
hospital involved in a protracted lawsuit over this issue while
we're in negotiations for licensing rights to the virus. I appreciate your sensitivity to that. You're obviously a person who
sees the larger context here."

Uncomfortable with Scott's belief that her decision had
come from a fear of legal action, Chris hastened to correct
him. "Even though I mentioned the possible legal ramifica-
tions of not reinstating them, I was more concerned with treat-
ing those women fairly."

"Of course," Scott said. "As was I. By the way, Dr. Boyer
told me you were the one . . ."

Here it comes, Chris thought.

". . . who figured out how the virus was transmitted. That
was good work. I don't know if you're aware of it, but Monteagle is looking for a medical director of infection control
and I think you'd be an excellent choice. I don't need your decision right now. Think about it. I'll hold the job open while
you do. If you have any questions, call me."

Chris stayed by the phone after hanging up. How could he
want her after she'd let those nurses become infected? Too
puzzled to concentrate on anything else, she called Michael.

"I just talked to Scott and he offered me the infection control job at Monteagle."

"Good. I'm glad."

"Why'd he do it?"

"Why wouldn't he?"

"Those nurses . . . it was my fault."

"No, it wasn't."

"The backup respirator . . ."

"C'mon, no one could have foreseen what was going to
happen from just that."

"Did you put it in your report?"

"No."

"You should have."

"It was irrelevant."

"I don't think so."

"It wasn't a novel. Just a report on the salient facts."

"I don't need you to protect me."

"That never crossed my mind. Believe me, it didn't."

"Well . . . I wish you'd put it in."

"I'm sorry. I probably should have let you see it before I gave it to him. But I was pressed for time and thought I had the facts well in hand."

Though she was upset, Michael's explanation seemed reasonable. "I guess I understand. I'm sorry I came on like that."

"Is there a chance you'd take the job?"

"I don't deserve it."

"Chris, ease up. Not only weren't you responsible for what happened, no one was hurt. No harm, no foul."

A sports cliché. Did he really think that would make her feel better?

But in the next moment, her strong need for absolution made her more receptive. *It's true, no one was harmed. At least not yet. And maybe never. Why carry that burden before I have to?* "I suppose you're right."

"So think about that job. I'd love having you over here."

Chris sat for a moment after hanging up, reflecting on what Michael had said. *Had* he been trying to protect her by submitting an abridged report? If so, then he, too, believed she was culpable. No, he didn't think that. He was right. No harm, no foul.

GINNY BARROSO LOOKED with dismay at her silver-handled brush.

"What's wrong?" Dominic said, pulling on the shirt he was going to wear when they picked up Ginny's new car.

She showed him her brush, which was so packed with strands of her hair he could barely see its bristles.

"How long has *that* been going on?" he asked.

"This is the first I've noticed it."

"Are you using some new kind of shampoo?"

"I'm not doing anything different. How does my scalp look?" She bent her head down so he could see.

"Come in the kitchen. The light is better there."

They went to the kitchen, where Dominic sat Ginny under the hanging light fixture over the breakfast table. There, he prowled diligently through her hair, seeing nothing unusual about her scalp, but pulling many hairs loose even though he was trying to be careful.

"Your scalp looks fine," he said finally. "The hair is just coming out. Could this have something to do with that virus we picked up from the hospital?"

"I suppose it's possible, but no one mentioned that this might happen. And it's not even in our blood anymore. If they thought I was sick, they wouldn't have let me go back to work. How's your hair?"

Dom tested his hair in several places. "It's okay. But I didn't get the virus the same time you did. We should talk to Dr. Boyer about this."

"They'll probably want to examine me. Let's swing by the hospital after we pick up my car."

An hour later, they were flying down the highway with Ginny behind the wheel of a brand-new white Pontiac with a gray interior that smelled so good it almost made her forget her hair was falling out.

Trying not to think about it himself, Dominic kept up a constant flow of chatter about the car's features. "Look, here's a place in the console that stores change by denomination, and another compartment below that for tapes."

About seven miles from the Monteagle exit, Ginny started to feel hot and sweat began to pearl from her forehead. She turned up the air-conditioner.

Though Dominic found the new setting distinctly uncomfortable, he didn't complain.

Five miles from their exit, Ginny cranked the air up another notch.

Three miles later, just as Dominic was about to tell Ginny she was freezing him, a shimmering opalescent cloud bloomed in the center of both her eyes, through which she could see nothing.

"Oh, Dom . . . Something's wrong with my eyes. I can't . . ."

She began cranking her head around so she could see past the obstruction.

"You're weaving," Dom shouted. "Stay in your lane."

Ginny knew she had to get off the road, but they were in the middle lane and there was traffic all around them which she could only see around the edges of the shimmering cloud.

"Dom, I'm going blind. I can only see . . ." Slowly, the cloud expanded, snuffing out even more of her vision.

As the car veered to the right, toward a tour bus, Dominic reached for the wheel, but the sudden movement caused his seat belt to catch, restraining him. With a crunch of metal, the car collided with the side of the bus.

Instinctively, Ginny turned the wheel hard to the left, sending the car too far in the opposite direction so that it was struck by a pickup in the next lane. The impact deployed both airbags in the Barrosos' car. Fused at their front ends, the two vehicles headed for the shoulder and left the road. The pickup bounced over the ground and came to a stop with its driver unharmed. But the Barrosos' car hit a huge cement drainage tile.

With the airbags already depleted, the impact snapped Dominic's head forward, breaking his neck and severing his brainstem. Though still blind, Ginny was otherwise unhurt.

"Dom, are you all right?" She threw off her seat belt and groped for her husband. Then she felt the fire, burning her feet with such pain as she had never known. The flames spread up her legs—excruciating pain.

Unable to think about Dominic, she clawed at the car door, got it open, and threw herself from the vehicle. The fire had now reached her thighs. She beat at the flames, but her hands couldn't feel them.

Such pain . . . the burning . . . so bad . . .

She screamed the whole time she was dying. And with the ambulance less than a minute away, the screams and her life ended.

It was the most awful thing the driver of the pickup had ever witnessed. The woman was screaming about being burned alive and there was nothing he could do to help her. Because there *was* no fire.

AS MARY BETH Cummings reached for the shampoo, she launched into the first few bars of "You Light Up My Life." She didn't need the help of tiled walls to make her voice sound good, for she was an exceptionally gifted singer. She had power and range and just enough of a sawtooth edge on her delivery to make the sound distinctive, all the ingredients that would have given her a real shot at becoming a professional singer. But even as a child, she'd believed she was destined to be a nurse, so that her dolls always looked like victims of some catastrophe, with their heads and limbs swaddled in plaid, flowered, or striped bandages made from any scraps of fabric she could find.

A nurse was all she'd ever wanted to be. Yet here she was, not four years into her dream, enrolled in law school, on her way to joining the ranks of one of the most ridiculed and disliked professions on earth. There probably were nurse jokes out there, but she couldn't have told you one, even if you'd given her an hour to think. But everybody, even Mary Beth, knew a few lawyer jokes. Nurse to lawyer; just one of life's little surprises.

Like picking up the funny virus that fixed her finger. And on Friday, thinking that after she'd given them another blood sample at Monteagle, it'd just be an ordinary day: a class in civil procedure, one on torts, a quick lunch followed by a couple of hours in the library, then dinner and back to the hospital. There'd been no way to anticipate that at lunch she'd be sharing her table with a guy who looked like a model. His name was Tom Fitzpatrick and he was part owner of a chain of Atlanta health clubs. He'd amused her all through lunch with an exaggerated Irish accent, and then while she was practically choking on her sandwich after one particularly funny line about the potato famine, he asked her out. So as Mary Beth shampooed her hair, she had every right to be singing.

She was so lost in thought about Tom Fitzpatrick and her song she didn't notice that the water in the tub wasn't draining, until it began lapping at her ankles. Yet the stopper lever was set on open.

Puzzled, she bent down and put her hand in the water. She groped around the drain and found the problem—a huge clot of hair.

CHAPTER 11

AS HUGH MONROE began the superficial examination of Ginny Barroso's body, his mind was running on several tracks. *He* was the heir apparent to succeed the chief medical examiner, who'd just retired, not those interlopers they'd brought in to interview. He told himself that the other candidates were merely window dressing to make it look like a real search, that everyone realized he was the logical choice. But deep down he knew he had made enemies who could hurt him on this. So it was no time to be demonstrating any inadequacies, like that case he'd done earlier today. What was her name . . . Mary Beth Cummings.

Except for some kind of scalp condition that had caused her to lose her hair, he hadn't found evidence of any significant pathology. So why had she collapsed and died? He didn't know. Of course, the tox results weren't back yet and there might be something instructive in the tissue sections. But still it was disturbing to have seen nothing.

He recorded a small scar on Ginny Barroso's left forearm, and a couple of recent contusions on the outside of her left leg. She'd also broken several fingernails on her right hand, probably as she struggled from the car after the crash. Pretty minimal stuff for an accident that had killed both occupants of the vehicle. He shifted his attention to her scalp, intending to look for signs of head injury.

He had been doing this kind of work so long that his pulse no longer shifted gears when he walked into an autopsy suite, as it had when he was a much younger man. But when he saw that this woman, too, had been losing her hair, the years rolled away.

Two cases in the same day with a scalp condition; one suddenly dead on her apartment steps for no apparent reason, the other dead after an accident that had barely left a mark on her. His interest aroused, he moved faster. Soon, he was in the cadaver's chest, his scalpel severing the major vessels that anchored her heart.

Now the organ was in his hand.

He visually inspected all its glistening surfaces, then focused his attention on the coronary arteries, which encircled the organ like serpents. Running a gloved finger along the right coronary, he found it utterly normal in appearance and resilience. But while his finger was traveling along a major branch of the left coronary, he encountered a suspicious firmness. He picked up his scalpel, made a cut across the vessel, and let the remaining blood drain out. Then he parted the cut edges and peeked inside.

"Well, hello, my dear."

"DR. MONROE, THERE are some people here to see you; Drs. Collins, Boyer, and Ash. It concerns . . ." She checked her notes. "The Cummings and Barroso cases."

Michael Boyer had learned about the death of Mary Beth that morning, the day after it happened, from the circulating nurse as he was preparing a patient for gall bladder surgery. She didn't know any of the details except to say that it didn't appear to be a criminal matter. So all through the surgery, in the back of Michael's mind, he wondered if the transplant virus had anything to do with her death.

Immediately after the surgery, as he began calling around trying to get more details on the Cummings death, he'd learned that Ginny Barroso and her husband were also dead. Now he *really* began to worry. Then, when he was told the

Barrosos died in an auto accident, he didn't know *what* to think. Realizing all three bodies were probably in the medical examiner's possession, he called and verified that. He'd then rounded up Chris and Ash and they'd all headed for the morgue to find out what had happened.

"He's in his office," the secretary said. "It's down the hall to your left, third door on the right."

As they all filed out, Chris was praying that the deaths they were there to inquire about were some monstrous coincidence unrelated to the virus they'd all carried.

Below Hugh Monroe's name on his office door there was a big brass knocker shaped like a whale. Michael rapped the whale three times on the underlying brass plate, sending the sounds echoing down the uncarpeted hallway.

"Come in."

They found Monroe dressed in green scrubs. He was seated at a huge desk with a glass top, several stacks of file folders neatly arranged near his right hand. On a table behind him was a glass case containing a model of a large gray whale. The walls were covered with color photos of whale action shots. Here too the floor was uncarpeted, as though the designers figured that even the offices might occasionally need to be hosed down.

Monroe was a small, tidy man with a big brush mustache. He didn't get up, but made them all reach across his desk to shake his hand as they introduced themselves.

"Please, everyone have a seat."

When they'd arranged themselves in the chrome and leather visitors chairs, Monroe said, "What's your interest in the Cummings and Barroso cases?"

As Michael explained, Monroe became upset. "You mean to tell me that those bodies were infected with some unstudied virus and I wasn't informed?"

"Dr. Monroe, with all due respect," Michael said, "how could we have informed you when we didn't know what had happened?"

"They should have all been wearing ID bracelets with your phone number and instructions to call you if they needed medical attention."

"In retrospect that seems like a good idea," Michael said, "but we had no idea anything like this would occur. We've kept close track of the virus in the blood of the three and have found that it disappeared about a week ago and hasn't reappeared. So we thought the immune system might have destroyed it and they wouldn't now be infectious in any way."

"I'm sure you don't always know if a body is carrying HIV and, because of that, have adopted safety practices in your autopsy attire," Ash added.

Remembering that it wouldn't be wise to antagonize anyone at this sensitive stage in the search for a new chief examiner, Monroe backed off. "Of course. I was just thrown a little by what you told me."

"Even though the virus was no longer in the blood of the three victims and didn't appear dangerous," Ash said, "we were concerned that there might be a long-term problem. Who was driving the Barrosos' car?"

"The wife," Monroe said.

"Did she have the accident because she died at the wheel?"

"Actually, no. The driver of the pickup she hit said she was alive afterwards."

"But could she have been impaired in some way just before the accident?" Michael asked.

Chris was thinking that they should just let Monroe talk, when he said, "Why don't I simply tell you what I've found?

"I have to say that this was a tough one. I examined the Cummings woman first and was completely baffled, because except for acute hair loss, she appeared perfectly healthy. I thought she might have been on some sort of chemotherapy, but I didn't find any evidence of cancer or any surgeries that might have removed a tumor. And she looked well nourished. No reason at all for her to have died so suddenly. Nor did toxicology find anything. So I was stumped. Until I examined Virginia Barroso.

"When I started her autopsy . . ." Monroe's face was now glowing as he recounted his great triumph. "I found no marks on her to suggest she'd suffered more than minor bumps in the accident. Yet she was dead. To my surprise, I soon discovered that she too was suffering from acute hair loss. Later, when I was examining her heart, I found a large thrombus totally blocking a major branch of her left coronary."

"So she died of ventricular arrhythmia induced by a cardiac infarct," Michael said. "A heart attack."

Barely able to conceal his irritation at having his conclusion snatched away from him, Monroe said, "That was the immediate cause, but the question is why did she *make* that thrombus? Answer. Because the wall of the affected vessel was grossly inflamed. But the Cummings woman's coronaries were unobstructed and *not* obviously inflamed. So what killed *her*?

"Of course, before I knew the history of those women, there was no real reason to believe their deaths were related. The hair loss in both could have been totally coincidental. But I had a hunch . . ."

It was obvious to Chris that Monroe was taking every opportunity in his account to make himself look good. Even so she listened with rapt attention, for she'd already heard enough to know for certain that had the two women never cared for her father, both would still be alive.

"The driver of the pickup the Barrosos hit said the wife appeared to be blind after the accident. She was also under the delusion her clothes were on fire and she was being burned alive.

"As I said earlier, I didn't find any external head injuries that might account for blindness. But after examining the tissue sections from her brain this morning, I'm pretty sure I know what happened."

No one had ever held Chris's attention more fully. Michael and Ash were equally riveted.

"Considering what I found in her heart," Monroe said, "you may be thinking there were clots in the vessels serving her visual cortex. But that would be highly unlikely. To make her totally blind, as she appeared to be, clots would have to arise in the vessels on both sides of the brain at the very same moment. Otherwise, she would have had some sight left. Realizing something was wrong, she would have moved onto the shoulder of the highway. No, the facts attending the accident show that she became blind in both eyes simultaneously.

"Have any of you ever heard of scintillating scotoma?" He paused to see if he had any takers. "No?" Happy that his audience was so ill informed, Monroe continued. "It's a condition in which sight suddenly fails, but instead of darkness the afflicted individual sees bright multicolored montages. Interestingly, the condition always lasts almost exactly twenty minutes. It's caused by vascular spasm.

"When I examined the brain sections, I found evidence of inflammation in the branches of the cerebral arteries that serve the visual cortex. So that's what caused the accident: vascular spasm with resulting blindness. I also found evidence of inflammation in some of the cerebral vessels serving the thalamus. It's my belief that the burning pain she felt was caused by spasm in those vessels as well, setting off the well-known phenomenon of central pain. A burning sensation is the most common modality reported by patients suffering from this condition.

"Which brings us to Mary Beth Cummings. Not to draw this out any longer . . . She showed microscopic evidence of inflammation in all the same vessels as Virginia Barroso. So it's my contention that she too died of cardiac arrhythmia.

"Just out of curiosity I also looked at sections of the scalp in all the victims. Both women showed massive inflammation and cell death in the region of the germinal matrix in most of their hair follicles. That's why their hair was falling out: the matrix cells had stopped making hair, so a discontinuity developed in the hair shaft, allowing it to be easily pulled out."

"What about Dominic Barroso?" Chris asked.

"Not as advanced. But I definitely saw signs of inflammation in all the same places as the two women. In my opinion, if he hadn't died from injuries he received in the accident, he soon would have suffered the same fate as the others."

"Well, there's no doubt in my mind that the transplant virus is responsible for this," Michael said sadly. He looked at Chris. "It sounds like when the virus left the blood it set up shop in the vessels Dr. Monroe discussed and hadn't really disappeared at all. Just went into hiding."

"Would it be possible for us to get some blood samples and small pieces of the pertinent vessels as well as vessels from other non-involved sites in all the victims?" Ash asked. "I'll check them for virus."

"That can be arranged," Monroe said. "But it'll take a few hours."

"Would you give me a call when they're ready? I'll come back and pick them up."

"Sure."

Ash gave Monroe his phone number and Monroe jotted it down on a small piece of clean paper from a stack in a little wooden box.

"In return I'd like to know what you find," Monroe said. "For my report."

Ash deferred to Michael.

"That's fair," Michael said.

"And someone needs to tell the health department what's going on."

Michael nodded. "I'll do it."

"Am I going to be seeing any more cases of this?" Monroe asked.

Intending to stay in Atlanta for a few weeks longer, so his status could be monitored at Monteagle, Wayne Collins had moved from Chris's apartment to a small efficiency closer to the hospital. Before departing for the ME's office, Michael had called him at his new place. Relieved to hear his voice, Michael had quizzed him briefly about how he was feeling. Hearing nothing ominous, he had asked Wayne to stay by the phone for the next couple of hours. Now, he was glad he'd done that.

"We've got one more person at risk," Michael said. "But we're going to be watching him closely, so I don't believe you'll be meeting him."

On the way to the car, the phrase "no harm, no foul" flashed on and off in Chris's mind like a defective scoreboard. When there was no evidence the virus had harmed anyone, she had let the phrase ameliorate her feelings of guilt over the backup respirator. Okay, so now there was harm. So a foul *had* to be called. And it was hers to bear.

CHAPTER 12

"LOOKS LIKE YOU were right, Chris," Ash said from the backseat as she pulled out of the ME's parking lot. They'd come in her car because Michael and Ash had driven to her office in Michael's Porsche and it was only a two-seater.

"About what?" Chris said.

"The virus ultimately causing problems."

"Yeah, I think we can definitely classify what happened as a problem."

"I wish I'd never started the pig transplant program," Michael said from beside Chris. "I did it to save lives, not end them. We need to talk to your father right away. Do you know where his new place is?"

"I've never been there, but I know the building. It used to be a motel, but they converted it to apartments."

MICHAEL KNOCKED ON the fading turquoise paint of Wayne's apartment door.

"Anybody want a swim?" Ash said, looking over the railing at the litter- and algae-filled pool in the courtyard below.

Wayne opened the door wearing jeans and a T-shirt with Charles Dickens's face on it. "What's *this* all about?"

"We have to talk," Michael said.

Wayne stepped back and they all trooped into a small living room with rough textured walls and tan shag carpet that looked as though it held many secrets. The parts of a cabinet of some sort were spread all over the floor. Nearby was a yellow legal tablet.

"My latest writing project," Wayne said, gesturing to the clutter. "I think this one really has a chance to make the *USA Today* top fifty. Hello, Chris." His eyes lingered on her for a moment, then he acknowledged the others. "Michael . . . Dr. Ash, is it?"

Ash nodded.

"What's the occasion?"

"We've got some bad news," Michael said. "The two nurses who took care of you after the transplant are dead."

"Oh my God. Not because . . ."

"It looks very much like it was the virus they picked up from . . ." Realizing he was about to make it sound as if it was Wayne's fault, Michael hesitated, then changed his phrasing. "The virus you all shared."

"Dead," Wayne said, "because of me."

"Don't get weird on us," Michael said. "That's an absurd conclusion. But we *are* here to talk about you. I'm concerned that you may be in danger."

"I feel fine. Better than I have in years."

"Have you noticed any unusual hair loss?" Chris asked.

"No. What's that got to do with anything?"

Chris explained, adding, "So you could be in the early stages, before symptoms appear."

"Both nurses dead?"

Michael put his hand on Wayne's shoulder. "I'm afraid so."

"What about the one nurse's husband?"

"Dead from the auto accident the virus caused when it made his wife blind in the middle of the expressway. His autopsy showed early changes that probably would have led to his death in the same manner as the nurses."

Wayne looked at Chris, his eyes asking for help. "And I was just getting used to having a future." He turned to Michael. "Can anything be done?"

"Return to the hospital and let us run some tests. The

virus kills by disrupting the rhythm of the heart. There are drugs to stop that. And other drugs can combat the vascular constriction that leads to the heart problems and the other symptoms."

Wayne lapsed into thought.

"There's no other way," Michael said.

"I don't want to go back."

"You need to be on a cardiac monitor with facilities nearby to treat you if anything develops."

Wayne looked at Chris. "I was the first one to get the virus. Shouldn't I already be dead or showing some symptoms?"

"We don't know enough about how the virus works to predict its course in different circumstances. The two who died were women. Maybe it moves more slowly in men."

"But you said the husband showed signs of it too. He must have got it from his wife—later than the rest of us, but I'm still fine."

"Our belief that the husband was affected was based on microscopic study of his vessels," Michael said. "Most likely he hadn't reached the stage where he had any overt symptoms."

"Doesn't one of the drugs I'm taking kill viruses?"

"But only certain kinds," Ash said. "It's not broad-spectrum. And there's no evidence it's effective against retroviruses, which is what we're talking about."

"But this virus was mutated, right?"

"Yes."

"So it's not like any retrovirus previously known."

"That's correct," Ash said. "But you're making a big assumption to think it's susceptible to the drug you're taking."

"I don't want to go back to the hospital."

"You could die," Michael said.

"I think I'll just risk it."

"Damn it, Wayne," Michael said. "We've got a lot invested in you. You owe it to us to help keep you alive."

"I don't think I'm going to die—at least not from that virus. I don't know why, but I just don't believe I will."

"That's reckless," Michael said.

"I'm a reckless kind of guy."

"Chris, talk to him."

"You should come with us."

"I'm going to be okay."

"You don't know that. It's nothing but a guess and a hope."

"No, it's more. God, or whatever, has given me another chance and I'm sure it's not going to be taken away from me. I've been spared to make up for the life I've lived and so far, I haven't fulfilled my part of the bargain. I've still got work to do." His brow furrowed and his eyes became those of a hurt child. "But those people who died . . . Now I've got to carry that burden too."

"You need to be where we can help you," Chris said. "Will you . . . do it for me?" That wasn't a card she wanted to play but she didn't know what else to say.

Wayne looked into her eyes and the flow of time slowed to a trickle . . . then dried up as they waited for his answer.

"Two days," he said finally. "No more."

Wayne packed a few things in an overnight bag and they all left for the hospital by way of Wal-Mart, where Wayne picked up a couple of paperbacks.

When Wayne was once more installed in his old room at Monteagle, a biopsy sample was taken from his scalp and sent to the pathology lab for frozen sections. Blood was sent to hematology with orders that it be tested for inflammation-related substances. Michael and Chris stayed with him while they waited for the results. Because there was no evidence he was infectious and they'd already had a lot of contact with him, they wore no protective clothing.

Forty minutes after the biopsy was taken, the phone rang.

Michael answered. He listened to a brief message, said, "Okay, thanks," and pressed the disconnect button with his finger. "The biopsy was negative," he said. "No inflammation or cell death in the hair matrix. So maybe there's none in any of his vessels either. I'm going to check on those blood tests."

He called hematology and explained what he wanted. After a brief wait, he once again expressed his thanks and hung up. "No evidence of inflammation there either."

"See, I told you," Wayne said. "Now can I go back to my apartment?"

"You gave us two days. I'm going to hold you to it."

"Nothing's going to happen. It's just a waste of my time and your resources."

"I really hope that's true."

Michael was concerned that the circumstances might make it difficult to find members of the nursing staff who would be willing to care for Wayne. And he was right. But medicine is, after all, a noble profession and someone on each shift agreed to do it. He was also satisfied that should a cardiac crash team be needed they *would* respond.

By the time all this had been accomplished, it was nearly four o'clock. While Michael and Chris were waiting for the elevator in the hall outside the isolation ward, Michael said, "What do you think? Is he in the clear?"

"The biopsy was good news, but I find it hard to believe the ganciclovir he's taking to ward off CMV would be effective against this virus. There are even CMV strains it doesn't work against. So why should we be so lucky that it would knock out this new bug?"

"By God, I think we deserve a break."

"I can't argue with that."

"I'm feeling really crappy over all this. And there's no one who could understand that better than you. Could we get together tonight for dinner?"

Mary Beth Cummings and the Barrosos also sat heavily on Chris's mind, and she now saw how her culpability in those deaths extended far beyond her carelessness with the backup respirator. If she hadn't sent her father to Michael, none of this would have happened. Knowing that when her work was done for the day, the three deaths would loom over her like great black birds, her resolve to keep Michael in check seemed unimportant by comparison. It would not be a good night to be alone.

The elevator arrived and the doors opened. As she got on, Chris looked back at Michael. "What time would you like to go?"

"How about seven o'clock?"

"Let's do that."

"Before I leave here tonight, guess I need to e-mail everybody on the team and bring them up to date."

"You better include Scott."

"I wouldn't be surprised if he already knows."

The trip to the ME's office had materialized before Chris had finished her rounds for the day. So when she got back to her hospital, she knew she'd have to move fast to see everyone and still get home in time to change for dinner. Sensing her stress level getting out of hand, she spent a few minutes in her office centering her emotions before hitting the wards.

She walked out of her last patient's room a little before six and returned to her office to check her e-mail. Finding nothing urgent there, she shut off her computer and sat staring at the dark screen.

With her professional day at an end, remorse for Mary Beth Cummings and the Barrosos once more engulfed her, so that even though she had no time to waste, she lacked the energy to get moving. As she sat reflecting on the ugly turn the transplant program had taken, her quiet surroundings allowed her to confront a concern that had been courting her all afternoon.

From the moment she'd left Monteagle, she'd been carrying around the uneasy feeling that the three deaths the virus had caused were merely a prelude to something more. And she wasn't sure why. Maybe it was the possibility that her father wouldn't remain healthy and he too would succumb to the virus. But she didn't think that was it. But what more was there? All the evidence showed the infection had been contained—limited to just four people. So what else could happen?

She looked past the computer monitor, at the wall where she'd hung the certificate she'd received from the CDC upon completion of her stint there as an EIS officer.

The border of the document was a series of shoeprints indicating all the footwork involved in figuring out the cause of an epidemic. In one corner, a cartoon showed an EIS officer in a rowboat about to be swamped by a towering ocean wave much larger than the one he'd just survived. The point being that about the time you think you've got an epidemic under control and you start to relax, it breaks out again, and this time it's worse.

That was probably the source of her discomfort, she thought—that picture. Realizing it was just a cartoon that had caused her to be so uncomfortable, she felt the worry fade.

It was getting late and she needed to get home. She rose and hung up her white coat. But as she flicked off the lights and shut her office door, she saw that the cartoon wasn't the source of her concern, it was the *message*, forged from the mistakes and experience of generations of bug fighters, many of whom had died by underestimating the enemy. That thought accompanied her all the way to the car.

CHAPTER 13

TR PULLED UP to the old farmhouse on the hill and sat for a moment admiring it. He'd bought it at a foreclosure auction for twenty thousand under its appraised value, figuring he'd rent it out and let someone else pay off the note. At the time, it had seemed like a good idea; a step, albeit a small one, toward the financial status he longed for. But the venture had been nothing but trouble.

He'd specified no pets in the lease, but a few weeks after the first couple had moved in, they bought a prehistoric mutt that had chewed up half the doors and the corner of a kitchen cabinet before he'd seen what was happening and evicted them. The deposit he'd required only covered half the cost of the repairs.

The second family's kid had set his room on fire. The insurance had paid for that, but the place still smelled faintly smoky, making it hard to find anyone else who'd live in it.

Eventually, he'd rented it to a schoolteacher and his wife, with no kids and no pets—landlord Nirvana. But this month's rent was now two weeks overdue. He'd been unable to contact them, so he'd come out here to see what was up. It appeared, though, that they weren't home. Maybe their car was in the barn.

He shut off the engine, got out, and walked across the scrubby lawn to the front steps. Fearing that he'd driven all the way out here for nothing, he went onto the porch and rang the bell.

While waiting for a response, he noticed that the porch needed painting. It was always something with this place.

He rang again.

The windows, too, needed paint. Afraid of what else he might see that needed work, he averted his eyes to the fields across the country road in front of the house. It *was* a fine, peaceful location, though.

Still no one answered his ring.

He went to a window, shaded his eyes, and looked under the partially raised blinds.

Son of a bitch. The place is empty. They've moved out.

He fished his keys from his pocket, unlocked the front door, and went in.

Christ, what a mess. The floor was littered with newspapers and mud. And there were big scratches in the hardwood. He went into the kitchen, where there was more mud, and food of some sort splattered on the wall, spaghetti sauce maybe. And grease all over the cook top. He didn't want to imagine what he'd find in the bathroom, but he had to look.

He went down the hall and pushed the door of the first-floor bathroom open. Jesus. The toilet was nearly overflowing.

That's it, he thought. He was through renting the place. People were animals. He'd let it sit empty.

He hadn't brought his plumbing kit, so he had no way to fix the toilet. Damn it. Now he'd have to make another trip.

He shut the bathroom door and started through the house looking for a coat hanger.

Animals. Nothing but filthy animals.

God, how he hated people.

He didn't have time for this.

All the downstairs closets were bare. At the staircase, he saw that one of the balusters was broken. What did these people *do* in here? At the top of the stairs, he found a large stain on the carpet.

The first two closets he checked upstairs were also empty. But in the third, on a shelf that ran down the side wall where it couldn't be seen from the doorway without leaning in, was a shoebox. He took the box from the shelf and removed the lid. Inside was a pair of women's high-heeled shoes that looked new. He lifted the box to his nose and inhaled deeply, filling his lungs with the aroma inside.

Immediately he was calmed.

He took the box to a spot near the door to the room and sat on the floor. Back against the wall, he put the box to his face and breathed the comforting mixture of glue and leather and solvents. Even when shoes had been long removed from their box, he could detect the minuscule amounts of manufacturing chemicals that had seeped into the cardboard. In this, he was a true savant. For many years he had not understood why he could do this or why it pleased him so. Then one day his mother had given him the explanation.

"IF YOU COULD push a little harder, this'd all be over a lot sooner," Arnetta Selvie said as the sweating woman on the bed screamed again. Laura was good at screaming, but poor at bearing down, Arnetta thought. So the baby inside her wasn't likely to make an appearance any time soon.

"I can't do this anymore," Laura screeched, her voice like fingernails on a blackboard. "It hurts too much."

Arnetta slid her hand inside Laura and checked the baby's position. "Well, it's not moving."

"Can't you give her something for the pain?" Laura's husband, Ben, asked.

"I'd rather not. It'd be better if she'd just do her job and join all the other women in the world who've shown a little character when it was needed." Arnetta spoke a little louder than usual to make sure Laura would hear.

The old midwife's rough manner irritated Ben, making him wish he could have called someone else. But she was three dollars cheaper than the other practitioners in the area. "We're getting nowhere this way," he said. "She's not a strong woman, never has been. You've got to help her. I know you can."

"It'll cost extra."

"How much— Never mind, I don't care," he said, letting

his concern for his wife overrule the knowledge that there was no extra money.

Resigned to the fact that it had to be done, Arnetta dug into her embroidered bag for the ether. She uncorked the bottle, put a little on the clean cloth she carried for this purpose, and put it lightly over Laura's nose and mouth. *"Just breathe it in, honey, and you'll feel like you can fly. Breathe it in, nice and regular."*

Arnetta had to be very careful now. If she left the cloth on too long, Laura would pass out and then they'd be in real trouble.

After a minute or two, she removed the cloth. *"Now, let's give a big push."*

And for the first time that night, Laura generated a decent effort.

Over the next hour, with the intermittent application of ether, Laura made good progress, so that Arnetta could now see the crown of the baby's head at the vaginal opening.

"Okay, girl, now give me another big push."

This time, Laura neither screamed nor pushed.

"Come on. One more."

"Something's wrong," Ben said from the end of the bed where he was making sure he couldn't see the part of his wife he usually found uncommonly interesting. *"She's not moving."*

Oh Lordy, Arnetta thought, wiping her hands on a towel. She pulled her stethoscope out of the pocket of her smock and went to see what was wrong. *"Laura, can you hear me?"* she asked, leaning down into her patient's face. *"Open your eyes for me, honey."*

Arnetta put her stethoscope over the woman's heart and listened hard. *"She's fine,"* she said a moment later. *"Just got a little too much ether. I warned you about that."*

"What about the baby?"

"It's far enough along that I don't need her help now. Where's the nearest electric plug?"

"Over there by that chair, but it doesn't work."

"Then why did you tell me about it?"

Ben floundered for an answer. *"It's the nearest. There's one over here that works."*

Arnetta went to her second bag and fished out a long rubber hose with a suction cup on the end. She put this on the bed and went back to the bag for a small pump with a long extension cord. She threw the plug to Ben. "When I say so, plug it in."

Arnetta put the small end of the hose on a fitting that extended from the pump. Then she applied the suction cup to the baby's head. "Give me some power."

The pump began wheezing and grunting. In a few minutes the vacuum it had created sealed the cup to the baby's head with sufficient suction that Arnetta felt it would hold. She began to pull steadily on the suction cup, and the baby slowly began to move. Its head emerged from the vagina like a turtle coming out of its shell. Accompanied by a soft sloshing sound, the body quickly followed, sliding onto the towels between Laura's legs in a gush of blood and amniotic fluid.

Arnetta was about to crow, "I've got it," when she realized the baby's color wasn't right and he looked limp.

"Pull the plug."

Ben did as she said and the cup fell free. Arnetta turned the baby over. Too concerned about its condition to even announce it was a boy, she clamped and cut the cord and carried the baby to a shallow bureau drawer lined with towels and warmed by a three-bulb floor lamp Laura's mother had given her as a wedding gift.

Arnetta laid the baby in the drawer on its back and suctioned out its nose and mouth with a bulb syringe. She then lifted the baby's feet and slapped them on the soles to stimulate him to breathe.

He didn't.

She slapped him again.

No response.

"Come on, little man, help me," Arnetta urged. She massaged his sternum for a few seconds, then slapped his feet again.

And still he wouldn't breathe.

Her mouth suddenly as dry and dusty as the road she'd taken to get there, Arnetta took the umbilical cord between her fingers and felt for a pulse.

"What's wrong?" Ben asked, crowding her. "Why isn't he crying? Aren't they supposed to cry?"

Arnetta could feel no pulse.

She put her stethoscope over the baby's heart, but her own heart was clanging so hard and fast that was all she could hear. She bent down and covered the baby's nose and mouth with her own mouth and blew a little air into him. With two fingers under his sternum, she pumped his little chest gently five times, then gave him another breath. Behind them, the uterine contractions that continued even with Laura unconscious delivered the placenta, spilling more blood into the towels between her legs.

Still the baby refused to breathe. Unable to watch, Ben turned away and paced, his normally ruddy complexion as pale as the baby's.

Five minutes stretched to ten and then to fifteen and still Arnetta saw no signs of life in the boy. She had once revived a baby after eighteen minutes, but that time, too, passed without success.

Twenty minutes . . .

Twenty-five . . .

After another five, Arnetta finally said it. "I'm sorry. Sometimes it happens this way. Under the circumstances, there's no charge."

As he looked at his lifeless son, Ben couldn't help but wonder if Arnetta had somehow bungled the delivery. If he hadn't used the cheapest midwife in the area, would his boy be alive now?

"Where's my baby?" Laura said, suddenly back from her ether holiday. "I want to see it."

Ben went to her and stroked her hair, his eyes glistening, trying to be strong for her. They had nothing else. The baby was their hope, their only light in a hard life that held little comfort. Now he had to tell her even that had gone wrong.

"I'm sorry, honey. He didn't make it. But we'll try again. It'll be okay. Next time we'll succeed."

The screams Laura had emitted during her labor were nothing compared to the one she now produced.

Then she turned ferocious. "I want to see him. Where is he? Give him to me."

Afraid to resist, Ben went to the body, gently picked it up, and carried it to his wife, who folded it into her arms.

Arnetta quickly gathered up her things, and when she left, she closed the door as quietly as it had ever been shut.

For the next two hours, Laura held the cooling body of her baby, warming it as best she could with her own heat, her quiet sobbing nearly driving Ben crazy with remorse. Finally, weak from crying and all she'd gone through, she let Ben take the body from her.

It was too late to bury the child and the sheriff would probably want to see him first, but it would be hell having the body there in the house reminding them of what could have been. So while Laura drifted off to sleep, Ben went to the closet and got the shoes he'd bought her a few weeks earlier for her eighteenth birthday with money he'd made helping a couple of local farmers repair their machinery after his regular shift at the siding plant.

He removed the shoes from the box and put them back in the closet. He then lined the box with his best undershirt, the one with only a single small hole under the right arm.

He carried the box to their dead baby and gently laid him inside. He put the lid on the box and took it out to the shed, where he set it on an old door resting on two sawhorses. As he closed the shed door, he said quietly, "Good night, son."

It was a languid spring evening and the stars were as bright as he had ever seen them, a night for happiness, not death, not this. As he looked up, he asked God the question he was sure would remain on his heart the rest of this life. Why?

Then he went back inside to face the long hours until dawn.

A little after midnight, the dead baby kicked the lid off the shoebox.

CHAPTER 14

CHRIS CONTEMPLATED THE gray Glen plaid blazer and pleated trousers lying on the bed. Deciding that she wanted to look less businesslike, she chose instead a dark-rose silk matka jacket, a rose jewel-neck sweater, and ivory slacks. She was just putting on her earrings when the buzzer from the lobby called her to the intercom.

"Who is it?"

"Michael."

She let him in, then hurried to the bathroom to brush her hair and make sure it curled just right over her forehead. When Michael rang the bell, she was as ready as she'd ever be. Surprised at how nervous and excited she felt, she opened the door to find him standing there holding a potted miniature orange tree full of fruit. Despite the terrible things that had happened that day, his gift seemed so odd she smiled and shook her head.

"What is it—this?" Michael said, lifting the tree. "I was just trying to be original. I thought it might do well on your balcony."

"Thank you. It was very thoughtful."

"Where do you want it?"

"Out there, I guess."

He followed her to the French doors that opened onto her little woodland.

"It could have been worse," Michael said. "I considered getting you a Saint Bernard puppy."

"Hooray then for the orange tree," Chris said, opening the doors.

As he put the tree down and came back inside, Chris studied his choice of clothes: ecru shirt under a gold-and-black checked sport coat; a gold, black, and ecru tie in a diagonal box pattern; and black pants—Halloween colors that could have been *so* awful, but actually made him look like a fashion ad. Five points for the wardrobe and . . . okay, five for the orange tree.

For dinner, they settled on Terra Firma, an upscale eatery so chic it was in an area that most folks would normally avoid after dark. Entering it was a surreal experience, for the building itself had grungy old planking on the floors, and walls with huge sections of missing plaster that allowed the rough brickwork underneath to show. Yet the place was packed with happy, well-dressed Atlantans at tables with crisp white linens.

Michael had made reservations, so they were shown directly to one of five tables arranged in front of a long pew attached to the wall. Chris chose the pew; Michael, the free-standing chair opposite her.

"I feel like a Nazi in occupied France," Michael said over the din.

So far Michael had been acting as though they'd just lived through a day like any other. Also wanting respite from the truth, Chris joined the pretense.

"Well, you *are* blond and blue-eyed."

They ordered a stuffed mushroom appetizer and two glasses of wine to start. While waiting for those to arrive, they were suddenly surprised to find Sidney Knox, the immunologist member of the transplant team, standing by their table.

"Hello, Chris."

"Sidney . . ."

"Michael, I got your e-mail about those nurses. Terrible, just terrible. And I have to say I'm not proud to have been a part of it. But I take heart in remembering that I voted against accepting Mr. Collins. If we had rejected him, as I recommended, none of this would have occurred."

"You don't know that," Michael said.

"I understand your need to believe otherwise, but I'm correct. He was the wrong choice and now we've got this mess on our consciences."

Noticing that the couple at the next table were showing undisguised interest in this conversation, Michael said, "Sidney, you're forgetting where we are."

"I don't care. And don't lecture me." His face grew red. "I won't be lectured to."

Now the occupants of other tables were beginning to listen.

"I'm sorry. I didn't mean to offend you," Michael said.

"Well, you did. I just hope there isn't more trouble ahead. But if there is, I'm not sharing any of that blame either. Enjoy your dinner—if you can."

And with that, he turned and stalked away, nearly knocking the dishes from a waiter's hand.

"I'd say he was upset," Michael said.

"Nice of him to remind us of what we came here to forget for a little while," Chris said.

Michael could probably have flattened Knox by blowing hard on him. Chris was impressed at the way Michael had kept his temper and hadn't tried to intimidate the man in retaliation.

Knox's comments and the general din of forty conversations inhibited Michael and Chris from saying much to each other during dinner. Afterward, Chris made a suggestion that surprised even her.

"Would you like to see where I go to be alone and think when I'm feeling really out of sorts?"

Pleased that she would take him to a place with such personal significance, Michael said, "If you wouldn't mind sharing it."

Following Chris's instructions, Michael drove to I255 and turned north.

"Where are we going?"

"You'll see."

A few minutes later, as the exit sign for state 410 was illuminated by their headlights, Chris said, "Get off here and go east."

"Stone Mountain?" Michael said, referring to the huge dollop of granite that sat on the Georgia landscape like the top half of a bald head. It was such an odd, unexpected thing that it had been a major tourist attraction even before the three Confederate heroes on horseback had been carved into it.

At the gate, while Michael reached for his wallet to pay the parking fee, Chris said, "That won't be necessary." She got out of the car and waved at the attendant. "Hi, Bill, it's me."

The white-haired guy in the kiosk broke into a grin. He opened the door of the kiosk and waved. "Hello, Dr. Chris. Good to see you. Just a second . . ."

The old man ducked back inside. He reappeared a few seconds later with two small bottles in his hand. Chris went around the back of the car and he gave her the bottles. "One for you and one for your friend."

"You never forget, do you?" Chris said.

"I always try to be ready. You two have a nice night."

"How do you know him?" Michael asked, driving on when Chris was back in her seat.

"I used to work here when I was in college. Got to know everybody, and a lot of the same people are still around."

"What's in the bottles?"

"Apple juice. I used to bring it in my lunch, so Bill keeps some for me in a little fridge."

"Sounds like he's got a crush on you."

"I don't know . . . maybe. Boy, they're cold. Is it okay to put them in the glove compartment till we get there?"

"Sure."

It was now late enough that all the park's attractions were closed. And at this time of year, the laser show at the carving was only given on Saturday night. So despite the presence of folks who were spending the night at the inn and the campground on the property, the wooded roads were deserted.

Michael followed Chris's directions along the winding roads for several minutes, until she pointed at a smaller road that went to the left, into the woods. "Turn here."

About fifty yards down that road, they came to a metal gate.

"Now what?" Michael asked.

"Be right back."

Chris got out, lifted the latch, which wasn't locked, and swung the gate open. She motioned Michael through, then closed the gate and rejoined him.

Their destination soon became obvious to Michael from the way the road quickly rose into a steep grade and left the trees behind, so that on both sides there was only bare granite. Another couple of minutes and they arrived at the mountaintop, a desolate moonscape with a smattering of lights illuminating a snack bar and the skylift landing.

"Park over there by the building," Chris said.

Since this was her world, Michael did as she said.

Chris got the bottles from the glove compartment, then opened her door and got out. "Come on."

A moment later, she handed Michael one of the bottles and led him to a natural wide pocket in the granite where they could sit side by side, their feet comfortably supported by a ridge below.

"Is it clean?" Michael said, eyeing the stone seat suspiciously.

"Don't be so fussy," Chris said, sitting down.

When they were settled, Chris opened her bottle, put the cap in her pocket, and took a sip.

Following her lead, Michael did the same.

"What do you think?" she asked, gesturing to the view.

Eight hundred feet below them and sixteen miles to the west, the lights of Atlanta sparkled and glittered.

"Beautiful," Michael said. "Makes me feel insignificant."

"And, therefore, your problems don't seem as big."

"If they were just *my* problems that might work better. But people are dead because of me."

"And me."

"Why you? I'm the one who started the program. And coerced you into helping me."

"If I hadn't called you about my father, we wouldn't be having this conversation."

"Now you're sounding like Sidney."

"So are you. There's just no way I can be detached about this. Regardless of how I got there, I'm the infectious disease person on the team. That makes what happened primarily my responsibility."

"I don't agree, but it's good of you to be willing to share the blame."

"I'm glad you suggested dinner. If I were alone right now, I'd be feeling far worse."

"Why does it take something like this for us to get together?"

Chris looked out over the trees to the lights of Atlanta. "Because I'm . . ."

Michael waited patiently for her to continue, worried that if he prompted her, she might not finish her thought.

"I'm afraid," she confessed.

"Of me?"

Still looking away from him, she said, "Yes."

"For God's sake, why? I'd never hurt you."

"I don't mean physically."

"Or any other way."

"You say that now, but things change. Time works on our minds so that we lose the taste for some things and acquire new ones."

Suddenly Michael realized what was behind her fears. "This is about your father, isn't it? What he did to you and your mother?"

Chris didn't answer.

"I'm not Wayne. We don't look alike, you could tell us apart on the phone just by our voices, his politics and mine are miles apart, and we don't think the same things are funny. We're separate people. So why would you believe I'd ever do what he did? I should be judged by who I am, not by the actions of someone I didn't even know until three weeks ago."

"What you say makes perfect sense," Chris said, looking at him now.

He reached out and took her hand. "You're cold."

"In more ways than one, I suppose."

"Maybe I can help."

"You think so?"

Michael leaned toward her and she responded. They met halfway in a soft kiss that Chris interrupted before Michael was ready.

"That was a good start," he said.

"It's all I'm capable of right now."

"Sometimes slow is okay."

"Is this one of those times?"

"Actually, I'm not at my best on granite."

Having reached a consensus on where they stood with each other, they were both content to just sit, drink their apple juice, and enjoy the moment. But soon the seriousness of that day's events again commandeered their thoughts, until Michael said, "Remember when Sidney said 'If anything else happens . . .' What do you think about that? I mean, I know there's a chance Wayne may still . . . could die. But that's it, isn't it? You don't think anyone else will get sick, do you?"

Chris remembered the EIS cartoon in her office and the dictum behind it. Seeing no point in telling Michael about that or making him worry any more about what appeared to be a well-contained outbreak, she said, "Sidney was just trying to upset you. You shouldn't be influenced by anything he said."

Micheal nodded. "You're right. I'm putting it out of my mind."

And right then, Chris decided that she would, too.

DAN AND KELLY Gaynor paused in their walk to admire the twenty-foot waterfall that was the centerpiece of their fifty-acre retreat and meeting center in the woods around Dahlonega, an old gold mining town sixty-five miles from Atlanta.

"I'd forgotten how beautiful this was," Dan said, watching the fish in the pool at the base of the falls pluck floating insects from the surface. All around them birds filled the evening air with chatter about their day. "Those two weeks I was gone felt like two months."

"It seemed like forever," Kelly said, putting her arm around his waist.

"Lousy timing, too, with that big church group coming on Friday. But I'm sure we'll be ready, because of you."

"I felt terrible leaving you like that and only visiting you once. I should never have listened to you. This place could have just gotten along without me."

"We couldn't risk not being ready for that group. We need them to be totally satisfied so they'll tell others. We're living too close to the margin to make any errors." He looked down at Kelly. "While I was gone, I missed *you* a lot more than the falls."

"I should hope so. I'm warmer, funnier, and have certain skills that give me a big advantage."

"These skills . . . Would you be interested in giving me a demonstration?"

"Someday . . . when you're up to it."

"Wouldn't your skills take care of that?"

"Lech." Then her brow furrowed. "You feeling okay?" She reached up and put her hand on his forehead. "You're sweating and you feel hot."

"Guess I got a little out of shape while I was gone." Forgetting he shouldn't do that, he ran his fingers through his hair, pulling out another thousand strands that the evening breeze blew from the back of his hand so they rained down in front of him.

"What time do I see that dermatologist tomorrow?"

"Ten-thirty."

"I hope this is just a temporary condition."

"It's probably a reaction to the medicine you've been taking."

"Ow . . ." Dan lifted his right foot.

"What?"

"I just had a stab of hot pain in my foot. Ow. There it is again. Damn, what *is* that?" He dropped to the ground and pulled off his hiking boot and his wool sock.

Kelly knelt beside him and examined his foot. "I don't see anything."

"Jesus, it's moving up my leg."

"Maybe if I massaged it." She grabbed his foot and began to work it with her fingers.

Dan's scream silenced the birds. "That's *worse*."

"Cold water might help. Let's get back to the house. Can you walk?"

"I think so."

She helped him up, but when he put his tormented foot on the ground, he screamed again.

"God that hurts. Oh no. Now it's starting in my other foot."

Suddenly, the forest was obliterated by a shimmering cloud of colors.

"Kelly . . . I can't see. What's happening to me?"

Normally, the worse a situation got, the calmer and more efficient Kelly became. But not this time. This was so bizarre, her mind unspooled. Stay with him and help him to the house or leave him and call for help? She couldn't decide.

Dan screamed again in agony.

She had to leave him and get to the phone.

"Babe, I'm going for help. You just—" Abruptly, Dan became a dead weight in her arms. He slipped from her grasp and fell backward onto the lip of the steep drop to the river. Then he began to slide. Kelly grabbed at him, but it was too late. Helplessly, she watched him roll down the hill until he was stopped short of the water by a small pine tree.

CHAPTER 15

"MICHAEL, IT'S CHRIS."

It was now mid-morning the day after their evening together. Chris had received Michael's page while she was in the ICU and she'd returned it immediately.

"Your father is still upset at being confined again in the hospital," Michael said. "But otherwise, he's fine. Thought you'd want to know."

"I called over there myself first thing this morning and checked on him. Thanks, though, for telling me. I don't understand why he's doing well, but it's good news."

"Could the virus have gained virulence *after* he transmitted it to the others? That would explain why it's not affecting him."

"I don't think so. It would have had to change in the same way in three people. It seems more likely that it already had the potential to cause vascular inflammation when they acquired it."

"Well, so far, it hasn't got Wayne yet. Say, are you busy tonight?"

Between thoughts about her patients, the Barrosos, Mary Beth Cummings, and her father, Chris had replayed the previous night with Michael at least a dozen times in her mind. She shouldn't have kissed him. In a way it was understandable; both of them grappling with their own culpability in the deaths of three people. They'd needed each other. But regardless of what Michael had said about never hurting her, he couldn't possibly know what he'd do five or ten years from now. He drove a Porsche, a rake's car. How would he adjust to having a family? Like any test, it would have to be taken to find out the results. Suppose he failed? She couldn't risk that.

"I'm sorry, but I *do* have plans." It was true, she told herself. Wash her hair, read, watch a movie—those were plans. "But I'll be over there this afternoon to check on a patient. Maybe I'll see you then."

Chris arrived at Monteagle at two-thirty. As she turned into a section of the outside parking lot reserved for the staff, she saw at the end of the row a Channel 5 news van blocking the way and behind it another, from Channel 46. In front of the vans, two guys, each with a big camera on his shoulder, had them pointed at a pretty black woman and a tall gray-haired man who were each holding a mike in the face of someone in a white coat.

Wishing to avoid the congestion, Chris backed up until she could enter the adjacent parking area, where she took the first empty slot. By the time she'd locked her car, a van from Channel 11 had joined the fray. By now, she'd begun to wonder if this had anything to do with the transplant program.

As she neared the action, she saw that the subject of the reporters' attention was Michael, who now had three microphones and another camera pointed at him. She heard the newest reporter, a curly haired guy she often saw on the news at accident or crime scenes, ask, "Dr. Boyer, is it true that you recently transplanted the liver of a pig into a human male patient?"

"I can't discuss this under these conditions," Michael said. "I don't wish to be rude, but I have to go."

He turned and hurried for the hospital entrance, pursued by more questions.

"Dr. Boyer!" The female newshound jostled her male counterparts out of the way so she got a step on them. "There are rumors that two nurses and a man in Dahlonega have all died after contracting a virus from the patient who received the pig liver. Will you comment on that?"

Abruptly Michael stopped walking and spun around to face his inquisitors. All the reporters held their mikes at arm's length to catch his every utterance.

"Who told you a man died in Dahlonega?" he asked.

Chris, too, was shocked at this news. But she saw that by responding as he had, Michael was tacitly admitting that everything else the reporter had said was true. She swooped in to save him, taking him by the arm.

"Dr. Boyer, we're very late for our meeting."

"Chris, they said a man died of the virus in Dahlonega."

"We *must* get to that meeting," Chris insisted.

"Are you Dr. Chris Collins?" the female reporter asked.

"Sorry, no," Chris replied.

Ignoring her denial, the gray-haired newsman said, "Dr. Collins, was the recipient of the pig liver your father?"

Seeing now that the entire situation was out of hand, Michael gave ground and joined Chris in full retreat for the hospital's front entrance.

The reporters and their minions followed, but Chris and Michael were able to put some distance between themselves and their pursuers when the cameramen were slowed getting their equipment through the doors. The extra time allowed the pair to dart onto an elevator whose doors were just closing.

Unable to say anything because of the other passengers, Chris and Michael used the forced silence to catch their breath. When the doors opened on the second floor, they got off and headed down the hall.

"We don't want to stay here," Michael said. He pushed the door to the stairwell open and they went up one floor, popped into the hallway, and slipped into a linen supply room.

"They said somebody else died," Michael said, breathing hard. "Is that possible?"

"I don't see how," Chris replied, her heart hammering on her breastbone. "But they seemed to know everything. Where'd they get their information?"

"There's clearly a big leak in the HMS Monteagle," Michael said. "I certainly don't think it came out of Scott's office. If the transplant was nothing but a big success without the other baggage we've picked up, he'd be the first one on the phone to the press. But he doesn't want this kind of publicity. He's really going to be steamed over this."

"Sidney," Chris said. "My money's on him."

"Sure, he could have provided them with our names and all the other things they seemed to know. But what's with the guy in Dahlonega? What's that all about?"

"We need to call the Dahlonega sheriff. They should know about any recent deaths up there."

Chris got her cell phone from her bag and called information for the number. A few seconds later, she had the Dahlonega sheriff's office on the line.

"This is Dr. Chris Collins in Atlanta. May I speak to someone there who could talk to me about any recent deaths you've had in the community?"

While the call was relayed to the appropriate person, Chris was entertained with the theme from the TV show *COPS*.

"Deputy Govan."

Chris identified herself again. "Deputy, have you had any deaths lately in your jurisdiction that were unusual in any way?"

"Had one last night. Local man went blind, then just keeled over dead. Young fella, too."

"Had he recently started losing lots of hair?"

"I believe somethin' was mentioned about that."

"Where's the body?"

"On its way to the medical examiner's office there in Atlanta."

"When did it leave?"

"I'm not sure. The coroner took care of that."

"What's the deceased's name?"

"Danny Gaynor. Ran a place a few miles out of town where church groups and companies could bring their employees to make plans for the year and not be disturbed by their daily chores. What's your interest in this?"

"There may be some health risks associated with the body."

"Guess that would explain why I got three other calls from Atlanta today about the case."

"From whom?"

"TV stations. I asked them, too, why they were interested,

but they wouldn't go into it. Made me sorry I told 'em anything."

"Did they know the victim's name?"

"No. Say, Gaynor had a wife. Is she or any of the folks who handled the body in danger?"

It certainly sounded as though Gaynor had been a victim of the transplant virus. But without knowing that with certainty and having no idea how it could have traveled so far, Chris was no font of wisdom on the matter. But she had to respond. What should she say? Should everybody up there who'd come in contact with the victim be quarantined?

No. It wasn't her place to be making those decisions. That responsibility rested with the state health department.

"Dr. Collins, you still on the line?"

"There's currently no proof anyone else is at risk," she said. "If that changes, someone will get back to you."

"I'd appreciate knowin' where you could be reached just in case."

Chris gave him all the numbers where she could be contacted, then terminated the call.

"It sounds bad," she said to Michael. "A local man died suddenly with all the earmarks of our virus."

"How can that be? Dahlonega is more than sixty miles from here."

"I don't understand it either, but the guy I talked to said the body was sent to the ME here. And I want to see it. Do you remember the ME's number?"

Michael didn't, so Chris used information again.

"Medical Examiner."

"This is Dr. Chris Collins. It's my understanding that earlier today, the Dahlonega coroner sent your office the body of a man named Dan Gaynor. Has it arrived?"

"Hold on, I'll check."

Appropriately, there was no music when she was put on hold, only dead silence.

Then— "Dr. Collins, the body's here."

"Thanks."

"It's there," she said to Michael. "Did you inform the state health department about the Cummings and Barroso deaths?"

"Pretty much had to."

"They also need to be told about this Dahlonega case. But I want to see the body first."

"Why? There's not much to be learned from a superficial exam. To be sure this new one is related to the others, we'll need the autopsy results and whatever Ash can learn from the blood and tissues."

"I know, but I still want to see it. Have you heard from Ash yet on the others?"

"I called this morning, but he hadn't had enough time to complete his tests."

"Let's check on those reporters."

They left the supply room and went to a bank of windows that looked onto the staff's outdoor parking area. There were now only two vans there. The female reporter and her cameraman were leaning against one of those remaining having a cigarette. A short distance away, the curly haired male reporter was talking on a cell phone while his cameraman was kicking a bean bag into the air and trying to catch it behind his back.

"We can't get to either of our cars without them seeing us," Chris said. "I need a few minutes anyway to check on a patient in the ICU. Maybe they'll be gone after I've finished."

Michael accompanied Chris to the ICU, where she perused the chart of a forty-seven-year-old man with septicemia, examined him briefly, then wrote an order to start him on Cipro.

Looking at the parking lot now from a window four floors higher did nothing for the view, for the reporters were still there.

"We could take a cab," Michael suggested.

"I wonder where Ash is parked."

"Let's ask him."

The virology lab was tucked into a corner of the east wing on the sixth floor. Ash's office was to the left of the counter where specimens to be tested were received. They found him at his bookshelves thumbing through a tome almost too large for one man to hold.

His office was immaculate, no stacks of paper or journals on the floor, all his books side by side on their shelves, none lying on the tops of the others. One wall was covered with black-and-white photographs of hexagon and spiked ball viruses with and without tails, and one that looked like a big

Cheerio with a lumpy rope attached to it. Chris recognized this one as the deadly Ebola. Another wall was decorated with what looked like hand-tinted prints of mushrooms from some old taxonomy book.

"Michael," Ash said. "I was just about to call you. Hello, Chris. I didn't find virus in the blood of any of the three who died, but there was virus in the vessel samples."

"Guess there's no doubt now about what killed them," Michael said.

"And we may have another victim," Chris said. She explained the situation and said, "We're on our way to the morgue, but there are reporters out by our cars looking for us. Somehow, the media know everything."

"My car's in the parking tower," Ash said. "We can use it."

"We hoped you'd say that."

"I SEE YOU'VE heard what we got in this morning," Hugh Monroe said, joining Chris and the others in the ME's reception area for the living. As on their previous visit, Monroe was wearing green scrubs. "How'd you find out?"

"Some reporters showed up at the hospital to question us," Michael said. "We heard it from them."

"They didn't get the information here," Monroe said defensively.

"We know that," Michael said.

"Not that there's anything much I could have told them. We've been swamped today, and since I did the others, I wanted to do these as well. In fact, I was just about to start on the Dahlonega case. So it'll be—"

"I don't understand," Michael interrupted. "You said you 'wanted to do *these* as well.' What do you mean, *these*?"

Monroe gave Michael a puzzled look. "The Dahlonega case and the one that came in an hour ago from North Druid Hills."

CHAPTER 16

"THIS IS THE first we've heard about one from Druid Hills," Michael said.

"Forty-two-year-old female bank teller," Monroe said. "She was just getting ready to open her station when she suddenly went blind. One of her coworkers was taking her to an emergency room, but she died screaming in pain before they could get there. I haven't done anything with her yet either, except take a look at her hair."

"And?" Chris prompted.

"Like all the rest, there's a discontinuity in the shaft of most of the hairs so they no longer connect with the matrix, which makes them easy to pull out."

"I'd like to see both of them," Chris said.

"Is everybody coming?" He looked at the two men.

"Might as well," Michael said.

"I'm not keen on it," Ash said, "but lead on."

They followed Monroe into the hall, where he stopped at the elevator and punched the down button. "Are you finished with your tests on those samples from the other cases?" he asked Ash.

"Just wrapped it up before we came here. There was no

virus in the blood of any of the three, but it *was* present in all the vessel samples."

"That strikes me as odd."

"In what way?" Chris asked.

The elevator arrived and they all got on.

"Seems peculiar that the virus would be in the wall of blood vessels yet not be in the blood," Monroe said. "How does it move around?"

"It was in the blood the first few days after they were infected," Ash said. "It must have gotten into the vessel wall then."

"I see. I believe you told me that on your previous visit."

They rode down to the first floor, where Monroe led them to a supply room with disposable autopsy attire in open boxes on metal shelves.

"Even though we're not going to be doing any cutting, you'll probably want to gear up," Monroe said.

A few minutes later, dressed in white disposable jumpsuits, booties for their shoes, caps for their hair, masks over their noses and mouths, and latex gloves encasing their hands, Monroe took them to a room lined with stainless steel cabinets and a cement floor painted with gray epoxy. The floor sloped gently to a drain in the center of the room.

"Where the hell *is* everybody?" Monroe said. "Must I do *everything* around here myself?"

He went to the door of a big cold room, unlatched it, and swung it open. Inside, on either side of a wide aisle, was a row of stainless gurneys, each bearing a naked body with a tag on the big toe.

"I could use a hand here," Monroe said.

Both Michael and Ash started toward him.

"Just one of you is enough."

Since Michael was the closest, he went into the cold room with Monroe. They emerged a minute later with a gurney bearing the body of a young man, lying on his back, arms at his side, a blue towel modestly covering his genitals.

They positioned this gurney so there'd be room for the other one, then returned to get it. While they did that, Chris went to the first body for a closer look.

His hair was relatively long, but even so, Chris could see patches of scalp. She pinched a small number of hairs between her gloved fingers and pulled. They came out with less effort then it would take to pick an onion. She shifted position so she could get a better look at the man's face, a self-imposed penance to fix in her mind the life that had been cut off through the chain of events she had started.

A phone call to Michael . . .

A conversation that lasted less than ten minutes the day her father reappeared.

Such a small event. And as a result, five people were dead.

Five.

Three was horrible, but five was . . .

Her mind suddenly rebelled against adding this one and the Druid Hills body to her tab. Because if she accepted these, she'd be acknowledging that there might be more.

No.

There *mustn't* be more. These *can't* belong to us.

She reached down and took hold of the cadaver's right arm, intending to fold it across the chest so she could see the hands better. But the body was in rigor and resisted, as though even in death the victim was holding a grudge.

Unable to move the arm, she bent closer.

And found hope.

As Monroe and Michael emerged from the cold room with the second body, she crossed to the other side of the gurney bearing the male victim and examined his other hand.

It was the same.

The second gurney came to a stop and Chris moved quickly toward it. Looking at the first victim's face had been a mistake, so she made a point of not doing that this time. She also ignored this one's hair and looked instead for the hands, but they had somehow become lodged under the cadaver's thighs.

"May I have some help here?" Chris said. "I want to see her hands, but they're under her."

"And shouldn't be," Monroe said, irritation obvious in his voice.

He looked at the two men. "You take her right shoulder," he said to Ash. "And Dr. Boyer, you, her leg. When I say 'lift,' roll her up and I'll move her arm."

This body, being fresher than the other, was not yet in rigor, so the maneuver Monroe had outlined was easily accomplished. He folded the freed arm across the blue towel over the victim's breasts and the three men moved to the other side, where they repeated the procedure.

In less than a minute, Chris had completed her examination, finding that, like the Dahlonega victim, this one's lunulas were normal in color, not gray like those of the others who'd been infected.

"That's all I wanted."

"Should we put them back in the cold room?" Michael asked.

"We've done enough," Monroe said. "I'm going to have a tech prepare him anyway, so he'll be going to an autopsy suite. If you all can find your own way out, I'm going to stay down here for a few minutes. Guess you'll be wanting samples from these cases, too."

"Definitely," Michael said.

"I'd ask if I'll be getting any more, but since you weren't expecting these, there doesn't seem much point."

"Please call me right away if there *are* more," Michael said.

Then they all left Monroe to his work.

"Took us longer to get dressed than it did to look at the bodies," Ash muttered as they stripped off their disposables and dropped them in a big cardboard box in the little room between the hall and where they'd been.

"What were you looking for?" Michael asked Chris.

"Something . . . anything that would show us those deaths weren't caused by our virus. And I did—"

"C'mon, Chris," Ash said. "The hair loss, sudden blindness . . . What are the chances it was something else? Let's keep this in the real world."

Only a few minutes had passed since Chris had seen the new victims' fingernails and been encouraged. But now, separated from those observations by even such a small interval, Ash's remark made the normal color of their lunulas seem insignificant, so that the evidence pinning the new deaths on the transplant virus washed over her little sandcastle of hope.

"You're right," she said. "It has to be the transplant virus. I just didn't want it to be. But that means we've got to figure out how these people were exposed and whether *they* passed it to anyone."

"This is turning into a nightmare," Michael groaned. "What do we do now?"

Chris took a moment to think, then said, "Wayne's transplant took place two weeks ago yesterday. He passed the virus to the two nurses the next night and after that became noninfectious. Assuming we're right about the transmissibility window being only a few hours, these new cases must have come into contact with either the nurses or Dom Barroso while *they* were infectious."

"But Cummings went to bed early the night she was sick and wasn't even aware she had any symptoms," Michael said. "So didn't we conclude that she couldn't have passed it to anyone?"

"Which leaves the other two."

"But according to what Ginny Barroso told us, she never left home the night *she* had symptoms. And neither did her husband."

"Well, there's something wrong somewhere. We need to talk to relatives and friends of the two new victims and try to figure out where they were the week before last and whether they knew Mary Cummings or the Barrosos."

"But they wouldn't have to know them," Ash pointed out. "Suppose Dom Barroso just forgot that the night he had his cough, he ran to an E-Z Serve for a loaf of bread. While waiting to pay, he coughed on the bank teller, who was also in line."

"I didn't say this was going to be easy," Chris said. "But we have to make a start."

"And the bank teller could have coughed on someone and that person could have done the same," Michael moaned.

"The next twenty-four to forty-eight hours are critical," Chris said. "If we get through that period with no more cases, we may be in the clear. But meanwhile, we need to start charting the movements of the new victims. That may teach us something about transmissibility we don't already know. And we certainly don't know much. Let's go upstairs and see what information they've got."

A few minutes later they all trooped into the main office and gathered at the desk of the secretary who'd been handling all their inquiries. She didn't have any information yet on either case, but after she called downstairs and they'd all stood around wasting time, a morgue tech appeared with the available information. This included the full name, address, and phone number of both victims. There was no next of kin known for the bank teller, but they learned that Dan Gaynor's wife was named Kelly.

Back in the car, Chris retrieved her handbag from under the seat, where she'd left it, and got out her cell phone. "I hate to do it this way, but Dahlonega is too far away for a personal visit." She looked over her shoulder. "Michael, do you have your Palm Pilot?"

"Yes."

"Good. We may need to take down some names or phone numbers."

Chris punched Kelly Gaynor's number into her phone. "Hope she's home. If she isn't I don't— Hello, Mrs. Gaynor? This is Dr. Chris Collins. I'm an infectious disease physician in Atlanta. I am so sorry about your husband. I was hoping we could talk briefly about what happened . . . I know . . . It's terrible timing, but there's a chance your husband's death may have been caused by an illness we know very little about. And others may be at risk. I understand that shortly before . . . it happened, your husband began losing his hair. You're not experiencing that, are you?"

Chris looked at Ash and then at Michael, shaking her head so they could follow what Kelly Gaynor was saying.

"We think the incubation period for this illness is around twelve days and that he may have acquired it by coming in contact with one of its earlier victims. Did he know a woman named Mary Beth Cummings?"

Chris shook her head.

"What about Virginia Barroso or her husband Dominic?"

Again, Chris shook her head.

"Had your husband been in Atlanta at all in the last twelve days?"

From the shocked look that appeared on Chris's face, Ash concluded that Kelly Gaynor had just said something important.

"No, at this time I don't think we could say that for sure," Chris said. "But it's a possibility to be considered. Mrs.

Gaynor, I don't want to bother you any more, so I'm going to leave you alone now. Thanks for talking with me."

Chris looked at Ash and then at Michael, who was leaning over the seat, impatient to hear what she'd learned.

"Twelve days ago Dan Gaynor was in Monteagle Hospital with pneumonia."

CHAPTER 17

"HE CAME HOME from the hospital just the day before he died," Chris said.

"So that's where he got it," Ash replied.

"But how? We checked all the staff and none of them got it. How could one patient become infected, but no one else?"

"I'll bet there was at least one more," Ash said.

"Of course . . . the *other* new case," Chris said. "Michael, what's the Monteagle main number?"

Michael gave it to her and she punched it into her phone.

"Medical Records, please . . . This is Dr. Collins. Could you tell me if we've recently had a patient named Lucy Cowles, anytime in the last two weeks? I'll wait."

"I'll bet she was there," Ash said.

They all waited in silence for the verdict.

Finally, it came. Chris repeated it for them.

"She was there from April thirteenth to the twenty-first for evaluation and treatment of kidney stones and a kidney infection." Then, to the clerk on the phone, "I'm away from the hospital just now but should be there in thirty minutes. When I arrive, I'd like to review all the records of that patient and those of Dan Gaynor from Dahlonega. He was an inpatient about the same time. If you'd have that material ready, I'd appreciate it."

"I JUST DON'T get it," Chris said, closing the hospital files on Lucy Cowles. She and Michael were in his office next door to Monteagle in the Medical Arts Building. Ash had returned to the virology lab. "Her entire stay she was on the med-surg floor. Gaynor spent only his two last days there. For most of his confinement he was in the ICU and the step-down ICU. If we're right about the incubation period, they were on different floors from each other when they were infected and in any event were never on the same floor as the transplant iso ward. How did they come into contact with the virus?"

"And why was it so selective?" Michael said. "The ICU and the step-down are open wards. Why didn't it get any of the other patients in there with Gaynor?"

"We can't say yet that it didn't. Who knows what we'll see tomorrow? Someone needs to call every patient who was in any of those wards when Gaynor and Cowles were there and tell them they're at risk. If they start losing their hair, they should come to the hospital immediately."

"We can't set that in motion without clearing it with Norm Stewart."

He was referring to the hospital's medical director.

"Let's find him then."

Michael picked up the phone and called Stewart's office. "This is Dr. Boyer. Is Dr. Stewart available? It's very important . . . Would you please page him then?" Michael gave his direct number and hung up. "He's out of the office, but somewhere in the building."

"Every minute that passes without those calls being made could mean someone else dies," Chris said.

"I did what I could."

"I wasn't criticizing you. I'm just feeling powerless."

They lapsed into a waiting silence where each second moved slower than continental drift. Two minutes slid into three, then four.

"If he doesn't call in the next two minutes," Chris said. "I'm—"

Her threat was interrupted by the phone.

Michael snatched up the receiver. "This is Dr. Boyer . . .

Norman, thanks for getting back to me. There's something urgent Chris Collins and I need to speak with you about . . . Great . . . We'll be right there." He hung up and said, "We're to meet him in his office."

The Monteagle administrative offices occupied most of the hospital's top floor, where the terrazzo underfoot in the rest of the building was replaced with a rose Berber carpet. It was the first time Chris had ever been there and she marveled at how far away the microbe wars on the floors below seemed.

Across from the elevator, a large framed color photograph of the hospital hung over a French console bearing a fresh flower arrangement. To the left of the table, the names and office numbers of the administrators were listed on gold strips in a dark cherry frame. Chris noted that all the strips were removable, but the CEO's name was etched on a gold plate at the top that looked like a permanent part of the directory.

"He's down here," Michael said, striking out to the right.

Stewart was a big enough fish to rate a secretary of his own. He'd chosen an elegant-looking young black woman for the job.

"I'm Dr. Boyer. Dr. Stewart is expecting us."

"Go right in."

They found Stewart standing in front of a framed orange football jersey. There was an orange flag in the corner and on the wall beside it an orange University of Tennessee national championship pennant. Orange caps sat on the bookshelves and orange pillows leaned against the walls. The carpet bore a huge orange UT logo. Stewart straightened the framed jersey and turned to face his visitors.

"So," he said. "The pig transplant program is in trouble."

Because a man of his age should have had at least a little gray in his dark hair, Chris thought he was probably coloring it, which, considering how badly he'd let his weight slip, seemed like trying to hide the county dump with a daffodil.

Thinking that he was likely referring only to the three original deaths, Michael said, "More than you know." He quickly explained the situation and told Stewart what they wanted.

"Michael, do you have any idea what will happen to the reputation of this hospital if we do that?"

"It'll be worse if we don't and more people die," Chris said.

"I can't assume this responsibility myself. We need to take it to Scott." He reached for the phone, entered four numbers, and conveyed the urgency of the matter clearly enough to Scott's secretary that he was put through immediately. A few seconds later, they were all hustling along the rose Berber carpet to Scott's office.

It was now a few minutes after five o'clock and they met Scott's secretary, an older woman with her handbag over her shoulder, an umbrella in one hand, and a silver striped bag from one of Atlanta's better clothing stores in the other, leaving for the day.

"He's waiting for you," she said. "Just knock first."

Scott's outer office was decorated in a southwestern theme; sand-colored walls, Indian carpets, big colorful paintings of cavalry columns and Indians in full regalia. They went to his closed office door, where Stewart tapped a few times to be polite and went in.

The inner office was more of the same, but with a sizable collection of bronze horses—with and without riders—added to the mix. Scott was sitting in a big tan leather chair beside his desk, reading a stapled document on legal-sized paper. He flipped the pages back to the beginning, put the document on the rough-hewn trestle table beside him, and stood.

"Well, this is quite a group. I have to tell you all that I'm damned upset over the deaths of those three people. I'm trying to keep this as quiet as possible, but it's a pot ready to blow."

"I'm afraid it's even worse than we thought," Stewart said. He looked at Michael.

"There have been two more deaths," Michael said. "Almost certainly caused by the transplant virus. And both victims were patients here around the time the two nurses became infected."

Scott's face, already looking as though he'd received a mild sunburn, grew as crimson as the beaded band decorating the Indian headdress on a bronze bust behind him. Jaw set, he raised his hand and wiggled his fingers for more details.

Michael laid it out for him.

"Explain how this can be," Scott said, when Michael finished. "These new cases weren't anywhere near the isolation ward and I can tell you the ventilation system couldn't have been at fault. I went over the specs for them myself with the architect before it was installed."

"Maybe it was the phlebotomist who drew Wayne's blood the night he was infectious," Chris said. "I suppose that person could have become a carrier and passed it to the two new victims if he or she also drew their blood that night."

"But no one on the staff other than the nurses who died tested positive for virus," Scott said.

"Maybe it was carried on a blood kit."

"Is that reasonable?" Scott said, implying by his tone that he didn't think so.

"With this organism, who can say? It's been a strange one from the start."

Scott shook his head. "I don't believe the new victims were infected in the hospital. There must be some other explanation."

"What might that be?" Michael asked.

"I don't think the virus had anything to do with the transplant." He looked at Chris. "Your father probably picked it up somewhere before he came here. Same with the others."

"It's a pig virus," Michael reminded him.

"Coincidence."

"I'm afraid it isn't," Chris said. "When Ash tested the blood taken from my father before the transplant was made, there was no virus in it, so he didn't arrive already infected."

Scott gave Chris a malevolent look.

"They want us to call every patient whose stay in the med-surg ward, the ICU, and the step-down coincided with the time the new victims were here," Stewart said. "And tell them to return to the hospital immediately if they start losing their hair."

"Do you know what's going to happen if we do that?" Scott said. "Everyone who finds one hair on their shoulder will be in the emergency room. And that's what . . . a couple hundred people. How can we keep this quiet if you spread it around like that?"

"We can't," Chris said. "It's just the price for doing what's right."

"I'm not going to expose the hospital to that kind of—"

There was a knock at the door and Carter Dewitt, Monteagle's VP for financial affairs, came in.

"Sorry to bother you all, but John, there's something you need to see on TV."

Dewitt went to a big rugged armoire, opened it, and turned on the TV inside. A second later, the female reporter who'd ambushed Michael that afternoon appeared on the screen standing in front of Monteagle's main entrance.

". . . using a liver from a strain of pigs genetically modified to resemble a human organ. Scientists have long been concerned that transplantation of animal organs into people might allow an animal virus to become established in the transplant recipient and that this could produce a previously unknown disease that would spread throughout the population. Channel five has learned that apparently something like this has happened here at Monteagle Hospital, where two nurses who cared for the pig liver recipient died yesterday of a mysterious illness. The husband of one of the nurses is also dead, reportedly showing early signs of the same disease. Then today, the disease claimed two more victims, a man from Dahlonega and a woman from the North Druid Hills area. Both were patients at Monteagle at the time the pig liver transplant was made."

"Jesus," Scott roared. "They know everything."

"The hospital information office was unavailable for comment," the reporter said.

"Unavailable," Scott shouted. "I pay that son of a bitch Alford to be available twenty-four hours a day. And now I'm blindsided by this." He looked at Chris. "Okay, do whatever it takes to inform all those patients about the danger. Anyone who doesn't cooperate, tell them they resist at their own peril. Find Alford and put him to work, let him spearhead the thing. It may be the last act he does here. Dr. Collins, when you're through contacting those patients, I want you to figure out how those last two victims became infected. Now all of you get out. I've got some thinking to do."

"I need to speak with you for a minute," Dewitt said.

"All right, you stay."

When the others had gone, Dewitt said, "With these five deaths and now that it's all out in the open, I don't see any of the drug houses we've been negotiating with over rights to the virus still being interested, at least not for the kind of money we've been talking about, and maybe not at all. I wanted to prepare you for that."

"The same thought occurred to me while I was listening to that damned reporter. Was that all, because I need to call the TV stations and see if I can smooth any of this over."

"You can tell them we're doing the responsible thing in calling all those patients."

"Why do you think I agreed?"

CHAPTER 18

"FIRST THING WE should do is get Medical Records started drawing up a list of the patients we need to contact," Chris said in the hall outside Scott's office.

"Someone needs to tell the ER director what's going on," Stewart said. "I'd be glad to do it."

"That'd be a big help," Chris said. "If he expresses concern that the ER staff will be exposed to the virus, tell him that all the evidence indicates it'll no longer be in the blood of anyone who comes to the hospital, so they won't be infectious. Stress to him that only people with sudden and significant hair loss are at risk."

"What do you mean by significant?"

"Hair that comes out in patches when it's gently pulled. If he's in doubt about whether a particular person should be considered at risk, he should take a blood sample and have the lab do a sed rate and C-reactive protein determination. Anyone with an abnormal value for either test should be admitted and hooked up to a cardiac monitor with drugs standing by to combat the heart problems that might develop. You'd better get a cardiologist in on this, too. Whenever anyone is admitted to the ER, I want to be informed." She gave him her pager number and they all headed for the elevator.

After visiting Medical Records, Chris and Michael called Chuck Alford, Monteagle's public relations director, at his hospital number, but got no answer. With no better idea on how to find him, they went to Michael's office and looked up his home number in the city directory, which listed three Charles Alfords.

No one answered at the first number.

The next one was not him.

With every second that passed, Chris worried that somewhere in the city, another former Monteagle patient might be about to die.

Michael punched in the third number.

A woman answered.

"Is this the home of the Charles Alford who works at Monteagle Hospital?"

"Yes."

Nodding at Chris, Michael said, "May I speak to Charles, please?"

"One moment."

Michael put the call on speaker phone.

"This is Chuck Alford."

"Chuck, Michael Boyer here." He quickly outlined the situation and said, "John Scott wants you to take charge of the contact process. We've already got Records drawing up a list of the appropriate patients."

"Do you know . . . Did the TV station try to contact the hospital before airing that story?" Alford asked.

"I'm afraid they did, Chuck. But you weren't in."

"Was Scott upset about that? Never mind, I know the answer, but sometimes family has to come first. My little girl— Ahh, forget it. You don't need to hear my problems. Look, I'll be there ASAP, but with the traffic, it could be a while. How many people are we gonna be calling? Doesn't have to be accurate—ballpark."

"Two or three hundred."

"And we need to do it fast," Chris added.

"Who's that?"

"Chris Collins."

"Are you both available to make calls?"

"I am," Chris said.

"Me, too."

"Can you enlist anyone else?" Alford asked. "They don't have to be physically at the hospital. Once we get the patients' names and numbers, we can relay them to those making calls."

"I'll try to get the other members of the transplant team to help," Michael said.

"I'll call my secretary and I'm sure my wife will come on board. Where are you both now?"

"My office."

"How many phone lines there?"

"Four."

"That's one more than I have. How many phones?"

"Also four."

"Let's use your office as a command post. Where is it?"

"Four-o-six Medical Arts Building."

"What's your phone number?" After getting it, Alford said, "We should always keep one line open for incoming calls. For tonight, let's give each patient your number to call if they have questions. And tell them after eight A.M. tomorrow, all calls should go to my office."

"That means someone will have to stay here all night. I don't know how long this is going to take, but I don't think we'll be here till morning."

"I'll stay," Alford said. He made sure Michael had his office number. "Okay, I'll see you soon."

Over the next few minutes, Chris and Michael added Bill Hessman, the team vet, and Robin Victor, the psychiatrist, to those who would be helping. Both were working late, so they'd been in their offices. Ash couldn't be located. That left Sidney Knox.

"I don't look forward to this," Michael said, punching in Knox's Monteagle number.

There was no answer. Michael checked his Palm Pilot for the number and called Knox at home.

No answer there either. Michael then called Medical Records and identified himself. "How are you coming on those patient lists I asked for?"

They had all the names from the first half of the target period but were still working on the others.

"Fax me what you have so far," he said. "And send the rest as soon as they're available."

The first list came in six minutes later. Michael scanned the list into his computer.

"How many names should we give each person?" he asked Chris.

"Let's start with twenty-five."

He copied the master list, chopped off all the names and numbers but the first twenty-five, and was preparing to send that group to Bill Hessman via e-mail when the phone rang.

It was Alford, still en route to the hospital. He outlined what he thought each patient should be told, and let them go back to work.

Michael sent the first list to Hessman, then called to tell him to check his e-mail. He repeated Alford's instructions to Hessman and went back to his computer to make a second list for Victor, which he relayed as he had the first.

Michael assigned Chris the next twenty-five names and he took the following group.

Chris checked her watch. "It's five-thirty," she said. "Lousy timing. A lot of people on our lists probably aren't home from work yet."

"We'll do the best we can, leave messages where there are machines and call back when there aren't. Why don't you use the phone in the main office. That means you'll also be handling any incoming calls on the open line."

"I don't mind. Just show me how to handle the system."

Of the first ten calls Chris made, she spoke directly to a person on her list only twice. Three times she left a message with another member of the household. Twice she got a machine. Three calls went unanswered. When Michael came out to see how she was doing, she learned that his numbers were about like hers.

"Anyone tee off on you about being put at risk?" Michael asked.

"One; a patient's wife. Doesn't the FCC have a law against swearing over the phone?"

"Can't say I blame them. I better go back to work."

Before he could do that, Chuck Alford arrived.

"How we doing?" he asked, slamming the door behind him.

Though he'd been called out without warning, his pants and shirt looked freshly pressed and his tie was well chosen.

While Michael was telling him what had been accomplished, the fax machine began pumping out pages. Chris went over to see what it was.

"More names coming in," she said.

"You two have done well without me," Alford said. "I hope when this is all over I still have a job. My wife is six months pregnant with our second child and we just moved into a new house with more room. It figures that this would be the exact time for something to go wrong. Let me work on the new names. I'll fax some to my wife, some to my secretary, and I'll take some. Where can I set up?"

Michael let him into the office of his practice partner and everybody went back to work.

A few minutes later, Chris took an incoming call.

"Who's this?" a male on the line said with obvious impatience. Chris recognized John Scott's voice.

"Chris Collins."

"Is Alford there?"

"In the next room."

"Put him on."

Chris sent the call to Alford, and though she wanted to listen in, she resumed working her list.

Shortly, Alford came out of the adjacent office. "I'm sorry, but I have to go see Scott. The papers are calling for information about the transplant and the people who died. We need to decide exactly what we're going to tell them. Be back when I can."

"We're not reaching everyone on our list. Some aren't home and have no answering machine. Tell Scott we need for the papers to include the warning we're trying to get out."

"I don't *tell* Scott anything. But I'll suggest it."

Alford was gone about twenty minutes. He returned looking pale and ill used, the notes he'd made during his conversation with Scott clutched in one hand.

"How'd it go?"

"Apparently I've still got a job, at least until we're through this crisis. I've got to call both papers and then I'll get back to my names."

"What did he say about asking them to run our warning?"

"Thought it was a good idea."

Contacting so many people was a tedious business, and after another thirty minutes of it, Chris had to switch the receiver to her other ear because the one she'd been using was aching from the pressure on it. A few minutes later, the calls started coming in from homes where they'd left messages. Chris handled the first few herself, then began sharing them with Michael and Alford. Victor and Hessman also called wanting more names. All told, the team they'd assembled had to contact three hundred and twenty-nine people. By eight o'clock, the entire number had been called at least once. At the homes of thirty-three of the patients on their lists there had been no one home and no answering machine. With the number yet uncontacted so small, they let Victor and Hessman go home.

They'd now spoken directly to a considerable number of the patients at risk or to their immediate family members, and had picked up no signs of trouble.

"It's been a couple hours since we started," Chris said. "And I haven't been paged from the ER. So I guess they haven't admitted anyone."

"Or they just forgot to tell you," Michael said.

"I better check." She picked up the phone and had the operator ring the ER. "This is Dr. Collins. May I speak to the doctor in charge, please?"

The seconds slid by with no one picking up. "They must be busy."

Finally a voice. "This is Dr. Allen."

Chris identified herself and said, "I haven't been paged so I guess we've had no one admitted . . ." She shook her head to show Michael and Alford that was correct.

"Any candidates down there waiting for lab results? Okay, thanks." She hung up. "The ER is clear."

"There's no need for you two to stay any longer," Alford said. "I'll keep after those remaining names and field incoming calls."

"I think I will go home," Michael said. "I've got surgery in the morning."

"I'll see you both sometime tomorrow," Chris said. "Hopefully, things won't be any worse then."

On their way out, Michael said to Chris, "I should be

through with my case by eleven. How about meeting me for lunch in the Monteagle cafeteria at eleven-thirty?"

"Okay."

"If I get delayed, I'll let you know."

Instead of going home herself, Chris went up to the isolation ward, where she found her father watching TV, his cardiac monitor showing nothing but a normal heart rhythm.

"Looks like you're doing okay," she said.

"As I predicted," Wayne said. "I'll stay the night, but in the morning, I'm leaving."

"Did you know that the virus killed two more people?"

His expression showed he didn't. "Who?"

She explained the latest developments, then asked, "How do you feel about that?"

"Responsible," he said. "And shitty. What were you expecting, euphoria? I'm sorry I ever came here." He whipped aside the sheet covering him, pulled off the leads to his cardiac monitor, and slid from the bed. He went to the closet and gathered up his clothes.

Chris had come there to hurt him with the news of the latest deaths, but she hadn't expected this.

"You shouldn't go. You could still be at risk."

"I don't really care."

"What are you going to do?"

"That's my business."

Following the first deaths, he'd agreed to return to the hospital only when Chris had asked him to do it for her. She thought that might work again, but she was in no mood to prostrate herself before him like that.

"Okay, do what you want. Your impulses have always been impeccably correct. Why should they be wrong now?" She turned and steamed from the room.

Wayne got dressed in his small bathroom, grabbed his overnight bag, and headed out.

"Mr. Collins," the nurse on duty protested. "No one notified me that you were to be discharged."

"It's criminal, isn't it, how people fail to communicate these days."

Wayne made his way to the hospital's main entrance and called a cab on a pay phone in the lobby.

•   •   •

TR PARKED HIS car in Monteagle's outside lot and sat watching two nurses walk by. Man . . . there was something about those white stockings. In his mind, he could see them up under the girls' dresses, flaring out as they covered their thighs. He knew they were probably panty hose, but preferred imagining that they were held up by garters.

The women passed behind a car and their legs were lost to sight. Having no further reason to sit there, TR reached for the bag of items he'd just picked up to make his role in everything that was happening appear legit, and got out.

As he approached the hospital's main entrance, he was surprised to see Wayne Collins standing at the curb with a small suitcase beside him. TR almost turned around and went back to his car because he didn't want to talk to the man. But Wayne was looking the other way, toward the entrance to the parking lot, so it might be possible to get past him without being seen.

TR picked up the pace and moved as far to the left of the sidewalk as he could. Just a few more steps . . . Keep looking that way, Wayne.

Suddenly, Wayne turned and looked right at him.

"Mr. Collins, I see you're leaving," TR said brightly.

"There's no need for me to be here. As you can see . . . as everybody can see, I'm fine. I probably should be dead by now, but I'm not. And I'm sick of this place."

"Sometimes I feel the same way."

"Two more people died from the virus," Wayne said.

"That's what I heard. Very confusing."

"Do you think it's my fault? The virus mutated in *me*. If someone else had received the liver I got, it might not have changed and become lethal."

"No court in the world would buy that. You had no control over the virus. It was purely a matter of biology. We can only be responsible for events whose outcome we can influence and whose consequences are fully known to us. This situation in no way meets those conditions."

With his attention on TR, Wayne didn't see the cab approaching.

"That's a generous view," Wayne said.

The cab pulled to a stop in front of him and the driver got out. "Either of you Wayne Collins?"

Wayne signaled the cabbie with his hand, then extended it to TR. "Thanks for the pep talk."

They shook hands and Wayne threw his suitcase in the cab's backseat. He climbed in after it and the cab pulled away.

Watching it leave, TR thought back to what Wayne had said about being fine but thinking he probably should be dead. That was the truth. No way he should still be walking around. That was as disturbing to TR as being forced to articulate all that crap about blame.

CHAPTER 19

"WHERE WE GOIN?" the cabbie asked.

Wayne recited his address and lapsed into thought. More deaths. From the virus that had mutated in his body. Why? What was there about him that brought misfortune and misery to everyone he had anything to do with? And the last two, he'd never met them, never even seen them, and they were dead. He'd been wrong. His life hadn't been spared so he could put his balance sheet in order. Whatever had led him to all those mistakes in the past had saved the biggest screw-up for last.

Ahead on the left, Wayne saw a sign that suddenly made his palms sweat and his mouth go as dry as a Dead Sea Scroll.

"Cabbie, pull in at that liquor store."

A few seconds later, with Wayne almost ready to jump out with the cab still moving, they pulled into the parking lot.

"I'll just be a minute."

Wayne got out and went inside, where death and pleasure were displayed in thousands of colors and shapes. He looked for the old familiar: Bombay Sapphire gin in that beautiful topaz-blue bottle. He found it among the clamor with the precision of a bloodhound and hurried to its shelf, where he took a liter bottle in each hand and carried them to the cashier.

Back in the cab, as they set out once more for his apartment, Wayne sat with the bagged bottles in his lap, holding them against him, the contact warming him. Gin was Wayne's escape hatch. Plan A was to stay sober. Bombay gin had always been plan B. He'd been warned at AA to avoid the big four that might kick off plan B. He should never let himself be hungry, angry, lonely, or tired. Well, at least he wasn't hungry.

When he reached his apartment, he went inside, threw his little suitcase down, and took both bottles out of their paper sleeves. He put the bottles on the TV and sat down in front of them, a follower paying homage to his deity.

ALL THE WAY home, Chris regretted that she hadn't done whatever was necessary to keep her father in the hospital. It appeared that when the virus killed, the interval between noticeable hair loss and the onset of blindness and fatal heart arrhythmia was only a matter of hours. So even though Wayne presently had no symptoms, it could all happen fast. But not so quickly that he couldn't get to the hospital in time. *If* he was thinking clearly. He seemed so upset over the latest deaths. And that could mean . . .

Damn it.

She hurried down the hall, unlocked her apartment, and went directly to the phone, where, fearing that he might be about to go on a drinking binge, she punched in Wayne's number.

THE PHONE BEGAN to ring, but Wayne had no interest in anything but the blue bottles and the contents that would take all the pain away. He got out of his chair and went into the apartment's kitchenette, where he filled a glass with ice from the freezer of his little refrigerator. He carried the glass back to the other room and set it on the TV. With trembling hands, he broke the seal on one of the gin bottles, spun off the cap, and slowly poured the gin onto the ice, mesmerized by its sensuous beauty as it snaked over the cubes.

•   •   •

CHRIS HAD LOST count of how many times Wayne's phone had rung, but she stayed on the line hoping that if he was home and just didn't want to be bothered, he might answer anyway just to stop the noise.

Finally, believing that he probably *wasn't* home, she gave up.

She'd been running on adrenaline since she'd rescued Michael from those reporters, and it was time now to get off it. A few minutes of meditation put her feet back on the ground, but it didn't keep her from thinking about the backup respirator.

Then a darker consideration that no one had yet voiced rolled into view. The drugs they could use to combat vascular spasm, cardiac arrhythmia, and inflammation simply treated the symptoms of viral infection, not the cause. If there were any new cases, could they really be cured? Or would they be as intractable as some of those tropical viruses like Ebola? It was a possibility too horrible to contemplate.

Maybe getting drunk wasn't such a bad idea.

She went to the kitchen and located the gin she and Wayne had argued about and that he'd left there when he moved out. She didn't know why she'd kept it, but was glad now she had. She opened the bottle and poured a little in a glass. After pausing to smell the contents, she tried it.

It felt like Drano going down and when it hit her stomach it set off an inferno that made her face flush. And her mouth and tongue were now numb. *Oh yeah, this is great,* she thought. She poured the rest of the bottle into the sink.

If only she'd noticed that the backup had no filters in it.

Now a part of her tried to lay the blame off on Wayne. If he hadn't come to her for help, she wouldn't be in this mess. But instead of helping, that train of thought just reminded her to also feel guilty about letting him leave the hospital.

How bad was it going to get? Would a hundred people die? Two hundred?

How did that damned virus get into the two new cases? Maybe those weren't her fault. If it wasn't a respirator problem, maybe she could get them off her conscience. *If* she could also forget that she'd set the whole thing in motion by the first call to Michael.

With the twin rats of guilt and worry chewing on her, she

decided that if she couldn't thwart them by getting drunk, sleep might do it. Because she suffered from occasional bouts of insomnia, she kept a bottle of melatonin on hand. She didn't like taking it, but tonight, knowing that she'd need help, she took one before slipping under the covers and, within the hour, found temporary relief from the mess her life had become.

WAYNE'S GIN ON the rocks sat on the TV as yet unsampled. He was back in his chair staring at it, sliding his two AA poker chips around in his right hand, rasping them against each other. He'd been given the traditional white chip at his first meeting. His sponsor, Asa Gray, had handed him the red one for ninety days' sobriety just before Wayne had left Kansas City to come to Atlanta. Fifteen minutes earlier, when he'd been about to take that first drink after returning to his apartment, he'd heard Asa's gravelly voice.

"Okay, bud, you been clean for ninety days. So that entitles you to this red chip. But you ain't accomplished shit. Ninety days is nothing. It's a long burp. You're still just one drink away from disaster." He had held the chip in front of Wayne's face and wiggled it. "It's red because it's a danger chip. You're feeling smug and satisfied, like you got this thing whipped. But you ain't. It's still got you by the short hairs, and if you don't watch yourself every minute of every day, you'll be flat on your ass, drunk in some alley. Then you get another white chip. And I'm gonna give it to you."

Asa reached in his pocket. "It's already got your name on it. See, here it is." He showed Wayne a white chip with Wayne Collins scrawled on it with a black marker. "White means you're back where you started—no progress, no pride, no guts."

Asa Gray . . . God, how Wayne hated that SOB. The way he squinted at you when he was ragging on you, that voice, like transmission gears being stripped. Where was the hug for ninety days of denial, the compliments, the encouragement?

Asa Gray . . . It was the thought of having to take a white chip from him that a few minutes ago had stopped the gin bottle a few degrees short of starting Wayne down that old road.

But now the gin was reasoning with him. *You don't ever have to see Asa Gray again,* it said. *He can only give you the chip if you let him. Or if you admit to what you did. You can always lie. You've had plenty of practice.*

But then Wayne thought of Chris. By entering the transplant program, he'd promised her he'd stay sober, gave her his word. *So what?* the gin said. *She isn't around. You can get drunk tonight, alone here in your apartment, and no one would ever know.*

But he'd know.

Chris.

He did love her. But she wouldn't believe him. Still didn't trust him. This was his last chance with her.

But people had died because of him. It had all gone wrong. Why? He'd been so sure the transplant was meant as a reprieve. Could there be something about all this he didn't see, something positive?

He looked at the beautiful blue bottles, and the gin assured him he saw it all clearly.

CHRIS WOKE FEELING even lower than the night before, and her first thoughts went to the Monteagle ER and the medical examiner's office, so that even before she got dressed, she had the ER on the phone.

Because there had been a shift change during the night, it took a while for the new crew to understand what she was talking about, but eventually, they coughed up the information that no one had been admitted in the last eight hours for possible viral-induced inflammatory disease.

Harboring some doubt about the accuracy of their report, Chris then called the ME's office, where, of course, Hugh Monroe wasn't in yet and the skeleton crew couldn't tell her anything about new arrivals. Needing to get out in the world and confront whatever was waiting for her, she dressed quickly, started some coffee, and picked up the morning paper from the hall.

And there it was, front-page headline, above the fold: "KILLER DISEASE GRIPS ATLANTA."

The story was fairly accurate but was written in a sensationalizing manner that made her feel even worse, especially when she was mentioned by name as the transplant recipient's daughter. A boxed sidebar carried the warning she'd wanted publicized, but in the context of the accompanying story, it just made the situation sound even more dangerous for the city's general population. Now, absolutely dreading this day, she gulped down half a cup of coffee and headed for her car.

When the elevator reached the floor below hers, the doors opened for an older couple that had lived in the building longer than she had and whom she often encountered in the mornings. Seeing her, they stepped back and waved her on, apparently afraid she was infectious.

Subsequently, as she left the apartment building, a blue van came speeding down the circular drive that ran past the front door. It came to an abrupt stop and people started piling out as though it was about to explode.

A well-dressed man with a big mustache came toward her as though the mike in his hand was some kind of radiation detector and she was fresh in from Chernobyl.

"Dr. Collins, may I speak to you for a moment?"

Jesus, it was Jeffrey Latoria, from CBS. Close behind him were two cameramen, who deployed themselves on each side of him.

"Sorry, but I'm very busy today," she said, taking off at a quick pace.

Undeterred, Latoria pursued her. "Doctor, please . . . We'd like your view on the danger this city faces from the transplant virus in the liver given to your father."

Chris kept walking.

"Give us some idea of how bad you expect this epidemic to be."

Chris realized that if she didn't talk to him it would appear that she knew the situation was terrible. It would have been a good opportunity to calm people if she had anything optimistic to say. But she still didn't know the extent of the problem. So all she could do was leap into her car like a fugitive embezzler and take off, which she did.

Not in the mood now to see anyone associated with her practice, Chris headed in the opposite direction. Without making a conscious decision to go there, she soon found herself in the parking lot of the Cabana Grove, her father's apartment building, where she saw by the presence of his red pickup that he was probably there.

She'd seen the truck many times since he'd reappeared in her life, but for some reason, today, it brought back memories of that day when she'd spotted an earlier version through the hole in Mrs. Lipinski's closet. Thinking about it, she began to feel silverfish crawling over her and she remembered how she'd cried out for him to save her.

A Richter level ten shudder ran through her and she brushed a ghostly silverfish from her neck.

"Save *me*," she muttered. "Why, he couldn't even save *himself*."

Now that she was here, she believed she'd come to find out if he'd gotten drunk last night. So as she got out of her car and made her way to the metal stairs leading to the second-floor units, she was afraid of what she was about to see.

At his door, she paused, wondering if this was really something she needed to know. Then, not at all sure she was doing the right thing, she knocked.

Prepared to see a red-eyed rumpled derelict, she was rocked by the neatly dressed normal Wayne that opened the door.

"This is a surprise," he said.

"May I come in?"

He stepped back and she went inside, where she immediately saw the two bottles of gin on the TV.

He closed the door. "I'm not going back to the hospital, if that's why you're here."

"I want to apologize for last night. When I told you about the two newest deaths, I wanted to hurt you."

"Mission accomplished."

"I called last night afraid that I might have caused you to . . ." She gestured at the gin.

"I thought about it and nearly did. But in the end, I couldn't. I still have things to do and I can't do them drunk."

"Have you seen the paper?"

"Not yet."

"The whole story was on TV last night and it's in the paper this morning. When I came out to get my car a half hour ago, Jeffrey Latoria from CBS jumped out of a van and wanted an interview."

"What did you do?"

"I ran. I didn't know what to say. I feel so bad and so responsible for what's happened."

"Why?"

"Mind if I sit down?"

He pulled the armchair where he'd fought the gin wars last night around so it faced the bed. When they were both sitting facing each other, Chris told him about the filter mix-up.

"I don't see how that makes you responsible," he said when she was finished. "You can't do everything yourself. You spoke to that first nurse about the problem and she told you it was being taken care of. You did what you were supposed to. Others didn't. Why should *they* be exonerated? This is a heavy load that just can't be carried by one person. If you want to point fingers, stick one in *my* chest. I'm the one who nourished and brought that little bastard into existence."

"Sorry, but you don't get any points for that. The mutation and growth of the virus was nothing but a set of biochemical reactions over which you had no control. No ability to intervene, no blame."

"I don't agree with you, but I appreciate you saying it. I'm glad you came. It's not the kind of happy family chat I imagined we might have, but I'll take what I can get. Where do we go from here?"

"Maybe if we're real lucky, the disease will have run its course. If not . . ."

"I mean about us."

"I have no idea." There was an awkward pause in the conversation, then Chris said, "If you hadn't needed a liver, would you have *ever* come to find me?"

"I don't know. I may have been too afraid of facing you."

"And yet you say you care for me?"

"My lack of courage is no argument against that."

"You didn't even come to Mom's funeral."

"I wasn't aware she died until months later. Otherwise, I would have been there."

"Unless you were too drunk to find your way."

He nodded. "That would have delayed me. But a moment ago when you were arguing that I shouldn't feel responsible for the deaths of those five people, you were willing to absolve me because I lacked the intent to harm them. Can't I get the same consideration for my actions toward you and your mother?"

"You're twisting my words. I didn't say you lacked intent to hurt those people, though I'm sure that's true. Control was the issue. You had no ability to stop the virus from mutating. You weren't forced to leave us. It was a choice, freely made. So you have to accept the consequences and the blame for how we struggled."

"She could have remarried."

"You're forgetting the little detail that you were never divorced. Till the day she died, she believed you might come back. She loved you, you dope."

"If I could go back to that day I left, I wouldn't make the same decision."

"Regret is a cheap commodity. Believe me, I know, because I'm loaded with it. I regret that I didn't make sure those new filters were on hand when they were needed. But my regrets change nothing. I think I better get to work."

"Will you let me know if there's more trouble?"

"Sure."

After she left, Wayne reflected on what Chris had expressed about him not being at fault for the five deaths. And he began to feel less culpable because what she'd said couldn't have been motivated by a daughter's love for her father. She didn't even like him, so maybe there was some truth in her view of what happened.

Out on the highway, Chris, too, was thinking about their conversation. It was true that if the supply clerk had promptly brought the new filters instead of letting an entire day pass, things would have been different. And when the new ones didn't arrive, the nurse on the day shift should have followed up before going home. And if Mary Beth had taken more responsibility for understanding the operation of her respirator, or had called someone and asked about the yellow filters, everyone might still be alive. Ginny Barroso, too, could have been more careful about the kind of filters she put in her mask.

But then Chris remembered whose views she was drawing on to defend herself.

Yes, I'm really not at fault here. The blame actually resides in everyone else involved. I'm sure that's true because my advisor in these matters, the eminent runaway husband and father, Wayne Collins, has told me so.

Seeing now just how self-serving and despicable it was to even consider that Mary Beth and Ginny Barroso might be responsible for their own deaths, Chris once more assumed the entire burden.

CHAPTER 20

"WELL, IT'S JUST like I predicted," Carter Dewitt said as he came into John Scott's office. "Every one of the drug companies we were negotiating with for rights to the transplant virus has withdrawn their offer."

Scott threw his pen down. "How'd they find out so soon that it turned lethal?"

"The Atlanta paper put it on their wire service. Apparently it's front-page news in every city in the country."

"Any of them make a revised offer?"

"They all wanted out completely."

"This has turned so ugly I can't believe it. In just a few days we go from the likelihood of a hundred-million-dollar payday to being smeared in the media as a dangerous, sloppy operation. I'm sorry we ever got involved in xenotransplantation. Is there any way we can shift all the heat to Michael Boyer or Chris Collins? Set them up in the media, then take away their hospital privileges?"

"Not a good idea. Right now, we need to be the model of decency and a caring institution. I called the ME's office this morning and there haven't been any new cases. Nor has the ER turned up anyone who appears to be in danger. The worst could be over. If that's the case, this will soon all go away. In a few weeks or a month, the public won't remember much about it. I do have *some* good news . . . sort of.

"This morning, after taking the fifth call from drug companies pulling out of negotiations, I got a call from Iliad Pharmaceuticals, a small firm in New Jersey that we hadn't heard from. They made us an offer, nothing like what we were considering, but at least it's money on the table."

"How much?"

"A hundred thousand for all rights."

"A hundred thou . . . That insults my intelligence."

"I know it's poor, but I think we should accept. At least we'll get something for all the trouble this situation has caused us. And I don't think we'll be getting any other offers. Let's just wash our hands of this thing."

"What's the hurry? If we wait, maybe someone else will come in."

"Or there'll be more deaths and Iliad will reconsider. When there was no downside to the viral therapeutic effects, the projected R and D costs for getting a product on the market were reasonable. Now whoever takes it on has to figure out how to separate the therapeutic effects from the lethal ones. That could prove to be impossible. At the least it'll require a huge financial commitment."

"Where's Iliad going to get that if they're small?"

"Not our problem. I say take their money and run."

Scott thought a moment, then batted the air with his hand. "All right. Tell them they've got a deal."

CHRIS TOUCHED THE hand of the last patient on her morning rounds, a fifty-seven-year-old woman who had developed peritonitis after her appendix burst.

"I'm sorry you're still feeling so badly," Chris said. "You have a very stubborn bug in you that just doesn't want to give up. But we're going to take care of that and get you out of here."

She gave the woman's hand a final pat and left the room to write orders for increasing the dose of the antibiotic she was using to treat her. She found Jerry Kennedy, the senior partner in her practice, waiting for her at the nurses station. He was wearing a solemn expression.

"There's something I'd like to discuss with you," he said.

"Go ahead."

He glanced at the nurses behind the counter. "Not here."

"Give me a minute."

Chris wrote her orders in the woman's chart, set the order flag on the spine to red, and put the chart back in the carousel where they were kept. Then she walked over to where Jerry was waiting. "What's up?"

He guided her to a corner away from the bustle. "That article in the paper this morning . . . It's stirred people up."

"What people?"

"The physicians who hire us. They're afraid of you, worried that you'll pass that transplant virus to their patients."

"There's no basis for their concern. I'm not carrying the virus. It didn't get into me."

"Right now, in the heat of this epidemic, telling them that isn't going to make them relax. You need to take some time off. Just until this situation plays out."

"What does Dale think?"

"He agrees. We've already lined up someone to fill in for you. It's just temporary."

"I don't like this. There's no reason for it."

"The success of our practice depends on our clients having faith in us. If that goes, *we* go."

"And do I get paid while I'm on this forced leave?"

"We couldn't do that. We have to use the funds generated by your replacement to pay her. We need you to do this for the team. And believe me, we appreciate it."

"How long?"

"Let's say, three weeks. Then we'll see where we are."

"You're all heart, Jerry."

"I don't feel good about this. It's just sound practice management. Now I've got to get going. Thanks again for being so understanding."

CHRIS ARRIVED AT the Monteagle cafeteria for her lunch date with Michael thirty-five minutes after talking with Jerry, still brooding about how easily people you think are your friends will sacrifice you to the mob. She got in the salad bar line behind a woman who chose each item from the bowl of mixed greens as carefully as if she were picking a justice for the supreme court. With each decision, the chosen item was carefully arranged in her Styrofoam take-out container, re-arranged, and patted in place while Chris's patience grew ever shorter and the line behind them grew longer.

When the woman had finally finished her masterwork and moved on, a voice behind Chris whispered, "Obviously a case of obsessive-compulsive disorder."

Chris turned to see Robin Victor, the psychiatrist member of the transplant team, also in line.

"Hi, Robin. Didn't know you were there." Chris plunged the salad tongs into the bowl and grabbed at the contents even more indiscriminately than usual, showing Victor she had no trace of salad-related OCD. She quickly finished with that and moved down, letting Victor take her place.

"How are you doing?" he said. "I spoke to Michael a few minutes ago and he said you were taking the problems we're having with the transplant virus very personally."

"I am," Chris replied, adding two carrot sticks to her salad. As she moved down, she was thinking that this was no place to get into that. She added a dollop of ranch dressing to her salad and crossed to the other side of the bar for a couple of cheddar cubes, hoping to get away before Victor could move close enough to reopen what should be a private conversation.

But he caught her as she turned to go. "If you'd like to discuss all this, I'm at your disposal. I'll rearrange my calendar to fit you in right away."

"Thanks. I'll think about it."

Chris went to the drink dispenser, put some ice in a cup, and filled the cup with unsweetened tea, absolutely sure that she wouldn't be calling Victor. She didn't need psychiatric help. And even if she did want to talk to someone, which she didn't, it wouldn't be a man she worked with.

She took her tray to the nearest cashier's line and queued up behind four other folks.

"I know how these things are," Victor whispered again to her back. "The same thoughts just keep looping through your head. And you can't get rid of them. If you don't feel like talking about it, and I certainly understand that, I'll give you some advice right now."

Chris turned. "That's really not necessary."

"Do something to blow out the cobwebs, something you

wouldn't ordinarily do. Just one evening. Get out of the rut. I promise it'll help."

Thankfully, he stood quietly for the rest of the time it took for her to reach the cashier. She paid and carried her tray into the seating area, hoping Michael was already there and that Victor wouldn't sit with them.

She spotted Michael at a table near the far wall, under a row of big circular openings that allowed people on the floor above to look down on the unusually light crowd.

"Is Victor right behind me?" she asked, arriving at the table.

"He's heading a different way."

"Good." She put her tray down and sat to Michael's right. "The whole time we were getting our food, he tried to coax me into coming to see him professionally because I'm upset over this virus debacle. And I don't want to talk to him about that. How'd your case go this morning?"

"About as expected. But since that article in the paper appeared, I've had three surgical cases cancel. They all cited some schedule conflicts, but I'm sure they're afraid to come here, worried that I'll infect them with the transplant virus." He gestured to the small crowd. "Some of the staff are even so afraid of the hospital *they're* staying home. Oh, and the FDA has suspended permission to do any more pig transplants pending an investigation. Big surprise there."

"I'm sorry about your cancellations. I'm having the same problem. I've been forced to take a temporary unpaid leave from my practice until our clients are convinced I'm not Typhoid Mary."

"What about your infection control duties? Do you still have those?"

"So far, but that doesn't take much effort."

"I've got a couple of research papers I never seem to have the time to write. Guess I can get to them now."

Apparently seeing someone he knew, Michael's head turned forward and he lifted his chin to acknowledge them. Chris looked, too, and saw Carter Dewitt coming their way with a tray.

"I don't want to interrupt," he said when he reached them, "but I wanted to give you some information." He put his tray on the table, leaned close, and lowered his voice. "I was with

John Scott less than an hour ago and he was very upset at the beating the hospital's reputation is taking over these deaths. It's also caused a huge reversal in some business negotiations we've been in. You didn't hear it from me, but Scott is thinking about publicly blaming you two and then suspending your privileges here. I think I convinced him not to do that, but you can never tell about him once he gets an idea."

"We appreciate you speaking up for us," Michael said.

"I'm not telling you this to be a hero. I just thought a little heads-up might be useful. You know, forewarned is . . . something, I forget. But you get the idea."

"We do. Thanks."

He winked and nodded and picked up his tray, then headed for a table that had just cleared.

"What are we going to do about all this?" Chris said.

"I don't see that it's in our power to do anything. This is one we just have wait out."

"At least there aren't any new cases at the ME's office, and no one has been admitted through the ER. A couple people with minor hair loss showed up in the ER, but they were inflammation negative."

"I hope things stay that way. Did you know that Wayne left the hospital last night?"

"My fault, I'm afraid. I went up to see him after we finished making our calls and I said some things that made him leave. He's okay, though. I just came from his apartment. Which reminds me, you should be careful when you leave the hospital. Jeffrey Latoria is in town looking for interviews."

"Whose that?"

"A reporter from CBS."

"You saw him?"

"Spoke to him very briefly outside my apartment this morning."

"What did you say?"

"That I couldn't talk."

"I'll bet we'll be on the national news tonight."

"I can hardly wait."

"Made any progress in figuring out how that virus got into those other people?"

"Haven't had time to work on it yet today. But after we finish here, I'm going to check on the phlebotomist angle . . . see if one of them could have carried it to the other wards. And I'm not doing it for Scott. I'm doing it for myself."

They finished lunch without much additional conversation. While taking their trays to the collection area, they ran into Eric Ash coming from the food line.

"You're eating a little late today," Michael said.

"I wanted to finish up with the samples from those two cases yesterday. Didn't find virus in the blood of either one, but the vessel samples were loaded. Of course, considering how they died, none of that is surprising. How we doing so far today?"

"No new cases," Chris said.

"I feel like a held breath over this. And my appetite isn't what it used to be."

Michael looked at the food on Ash's tray. "At least you're trying."

They left Ash to his lunch and went into the hall, where Michael said, "I'd be glad to help you work on that viral transmission problem."

"Thanks. If I get into a situation where I need assistance, I'll let you know."

"Do you want to get together tonight . . . dinner, a movie maybe?"

"It's tempting, but I've got too much on my mind to be good company."

"I understand. Another time. Give me a call later today or tomorrow and we'll compare notes and see where we are."

From the cafeteria, Chris took the elevator to the fourth floor and followed the tiled corridor to the hematology lab. At the counter where outpatients who needed blood work initiated it, a young man with a goatee and mustache and his hair a storm-tossed oil slick offered assistance.

"I'm Dr. Collins."

"Well, I'm pleased to meet you, Dr. Collins," he said, buttering his words with sexual innuendo.

"I'd like some information."

"For you, anything."

"Good. First, you can cut the crap. I'm not amused, excited, or interested by it, so put your libido back in your pants. Do we understand each other?"

His slouching posture improved dramatically. "Yes, ma'am. What did you want to know?"

"Do you keep a record of the patients each of your phlebotomists sees?"

"It's in the computer."

When Chris first realized the two nurses had become infected with the transplant virus, she'd been particularly concerned that Karen Casoli, the phlebotomist who'd drawn Wayne's blood the night he developed the cough, might have also been colonized. But as with every other living member of the staff who had contact with him, her blood had tested negative, so Chris had stopped thinking about her. But with the new cases, she had to be investigated as a possible link.

"Are the records kept by phlebotomist or patient names?"

"I can do it either way."

"Did Karen Casoli ever draw blood from a patient named Dan Gaynor?"

The young man moved down the counter to the computer on his left and worked the keyboard. In a couple of minutes he said, "Once."

"When?"

"The night of April tenth."

That was the night *before* her father received his transplant. "Any other time?"

"No. That was her only visit."

"How about a patient named Lucy Cowles?"

It took another couple of minutes to get that data. "She didn't see her at all."

"Did anyone other than Karen Casoli draw blood from Wayne Collins while he was here?"

"Why do I know that name? Oh yeah, he's the guy who got the pig liver." His eyes widened. "And you're . . ."

"Never mind. Just check the records."

"Without looking I can tell you that he probably did have someone other than Casoli. Whenever possible, we always assign the same person to draw a patient's blood the whole time they're here. So they see a familiar face. But most draws are done during the day and Casoli works at night. So . . ."

"Could you just look, please."

He soon had another name. "His usual vamp was Pearl Ritchie."

Vamp meant vampire. "Did she do draws on either of those other patients?"

"She was Gaynor's vamp, but not that other woman."

"She never saw Lucy Cowles?"

"Don't think so."

"Look again to be sure."

He returned to Lucy Cowles's records, perused them, and shook his head. "Never."

"Could the records be wrong? Could the person who was assigned to Cowles have one day sent Pearl Ritchie in her place?"

"What do you think, I'm gonna stand here and tell you we keep incorrect records?"

"That's not an answer."

"You don't believe me, ask Pearl. There she is."

Chris looked behind her and saw an overweight young woman with a blood kit in one hand come in and head for the swinging door to the lab.

"Pearl, Dr. Collins would like to talk to you."

The woman walked over to where Chris stood.

"Pearl, in the last two weeks, do you remember doing a draw on a patient named Lucy Cowles?"

Pearl's gray eyes rolled upward as she mulled the name over. "No."

"She wouldn't have been one of your regular patients. You would have seen her as a favor to . . ." Chris looked at the fellow helping her.

"Dawn," he said.

"No, I haven't covered for Dawn or anybody in months. And I might not ever do it again, considering how they're always too busy to help me."

"You're sure?"

"Did I sound uncertain? I'm sure."

When Chris stepped from the hospital a few minutes after talking with Pearl Ritchie, she emerged slowly, making sure there were no TV crews hanging around. She made a clean escape to her car, then sat thinking about her visit to the heme lab. If Casoli had seen the two patients who'd died, it would have suggested that she had somehow become a carrier even though she showed no evidence of having been infected herself. But her one visit to Gaynor was *before* the transplant, and she'd *never* seen Cowles. Pearl Ritchie wasn't there the night Wayne was coughing, but she was his usual vamp. So maybe *she* became a carrier from handling his blood. And she *did* see Dan Gaynor after the transplant. But not Lucy Cowles. And if Ritchie *was* a carrier, why hadn't any of her other patients become infected and died?

With discordant possibilities tossing around in her head like junk in a Venetian canal, she started her car and drove to the parking lot exit, where she had to decide on a destination.

Her practice office?

Definitely not.

Home?

To do what? The laundry?

Noting for the first time that it was a fine spring day, she realized she'd been so involved with her work and the transplant situation she hadn't bought any seasonal plants for her little high-rise woodland.

An hour later, she was on the elevator of her apartment building hitting the up button with her elbow because both hands were occupied with a flat of mixed bedding plants. She couldn't open her apartment door with her elbow, so at that point she had to set the flat down. When the plants were safely out on her balcony, she returned to her car for the other things she'd bought.

She loved almost everything about her apartment, but trying to garden ten floors from street level was not one of them. Someday, she'd buy a house, with some land, where she could wash her own car and not have to lug potting soil up in an elevator with people staring at her.

She spent the next ninety minutes planting impatiens, petunias, celosia, and begonias in the big decorative pots she used for annuals. When everything was fertilized and the pots arranged so they'd get the correct amount of sun, she changed out of her gardening clothes, then returned to the balcony to admire her work. Coming back inside, she was suddenly aware of how cold and empty her apartment felt. For as long as she'd lived there, she'd had almost more professional work than she could handle, so she was always too tired and preoccupied to reflect on much else. Now, with no patients to think about, she realized how barren her personal life was.

She thought about the week when Wayne had stayed with

her. At first it had been awkward, but then, when she'd become more used to him, it wasn't so bad . . . to have him there when she'd come home, busy making dinner . . . like a family.

She shivered and went to find a sweater.

Sorting through the French armoire she'd bought at an estate sale for a fraction of its value, her thoughts went back to lunch that afternoon. She should have agreed to meet Michael tonight.

She remembered their kiss on Stone Mountain, how good it felt.

"Do something you've never done before," Victor had said. She imagined herself and Michael in her bed, naked, pressed against each other . . . Stone Mountain times ten, times a hundred. Her face flushed and she could hear her heart in her ears.

Thump thump. Thump thump. *Call him. Call him.*

She pulled on a sweater and looked at the phone.

Thump thump. Thump thump. *Call him. Call him.*

She moved slowly to the phone and stood beside it, her hands folded together in front of her, lest one betray her and reach for the receiver.

Call him. Call him.

She picked up the receiver and punched in the first three digits of Michael's pager. Then her finger hit the disconnect.

She stood there a moment, immobile.

Her finger returned to the keypad and traveled over it.

One ring . . . two . . . An answer . . .

"Dr. Monroe, please."

After a short wait, the ME came on the line.

"This is Chris Collins again."

"Nothing new," he said, knowing why she'd called. "I still have your pager number. I'll call you if there's another one."

"Thanks. Sorry for not waiting."

She followed that call with one to the Monteagle ER and received the same news.

She hung up and went back to the kitchen. There, she poured herself a cup of coffee and carried it to where she'd put the copy of *Billy Runyan* Wayne had given her.

She took the book to a comfortable chair, opened it, and

read the inscription Wayne had ostensibly written there years ago.

Whatever else you might think of me, please believe that I do love you.

As though she might now find the insights into Wayne's mind that had eluded her all the other times she'd read the story, she started on it again.

At five o'clock, with eighty pages to go, she put the book aside and turned on the national news. It led off with the transplant story, Jeffrey Latoria as the on-site correspondent. After he had laid out the bones of what had taken place, including her dual involvement, he said, "An hour ago I spoke with the recipient of the pig liver, Mr. Wayne Collins."

Chris stiffened in her chair as the live feed faded to tape.

And there was her father, beside his red truck.

"Mr. Collins, how does it feel to be the world's first recipient of a pig liver?"

"Of course I'm grateful. It saved my life. I just wish it hadn't come at the price it did."

"Are you referring to the people who died?"

"Right now, I can't see how those lives for mine is a fair trade. And I want their families to know that I'm so sorry."

"In your opinion, could those deaths have been avoided?"

Recognizing this as a loaded question, Chris tensed, hoping Wayne could handle it.

He thought about it a moment and said, "Mistakes were made."

"Wrong answer," Chris muttered.

"Could you expand on that?"

"Say no," Chris muttered again. "Don't play his game."

"I'd rather not," Wayne said.

"No," Chris muttered, banging the arm of her chair in irritation. He'd made the right decision refusing to say any more, but the way he'd phrased it sounded so clandestine it was bound to stimulate interest in the details of how this terrible thing had happened. And when that became known, the spotlight would swing her way.

"I'm sorry, I have to go now," Wayne said, turning and opening the door of his truck.

"Mr. Collins, how does your daughter feel about the situation?"

Wayne turned to the camera and Chris clutched the arms of her chair, hoping he wouldn't say anything stupid.

"You'll have to ask her about that."

Her fingers uncurled in relief.

The camera switched to Latoria. "And that's the situation here in Atlanta."

The network anchor returned. "Fearing for the safety of their members, the Southeastern Association of Independent Realtors has canceled their annual convention, which was to be held next week in Atlanta. With the death toll at five, Atlantans are sleeping uneasily tonight." The anchor turned to face a different camera. "In the Middle East today . . ."

Chris got up and switched off the set.

She considered calling her father and telling him how dumb it had been to let himself be interviewed, and how he'd compromised her privacy by telling the world mistakes had been made.

But in his defense, it wasn't easy to be rude and just walk away from someone trying to speak to you. With the cameras on him, he had to have been nervous and talking without any time to think. Who knows what *she* might have said under those circumstances? No, it wouldn't be fair to criticize him.

MILES AWAY, ON the administrative floor of Monteagle Hospital, John Scott was on the phone.

"Governor, as I explained to the state health department, there's no need to bring in the CDC."

Scott was trying hard to control his temper. The hospital's reputation was already muddied and there was no way he was going to let the CDC troop through the halls snooping in every corner, making his operation look totally inept.

"We've got one of the best virologists in the world as well as a former EIS officer from the CDC working on the problem. We don't need any help. In fact it's been over twenty-four hours and we've had no new cases. So it looks like the thing may have burnt itself out . . . Yes, of course, it's too early to know that for sure. I *do* realize the pressure you're under, but give us seventy-two hours to work on it. If there are any more new cases, we can talk again.

"Governor, this is a situation that calls for mature judgment. And I've always believed that was your great strength. It's why I contributed so generously to your last campaign . . . I'm sorry, I shouldn't have said that. Please just erase it from your memory . . .

"Right, seventy-two hours . . . Yes, Governor . . . Well, I certainly appreciate that. Thank you. Feel free to call me anytime. Yes, sir . . . Have a nice night and don't worry. We're on it."

As Scott hung up, he was very glad he hadn't followed through with his earlier inclination to pillory Chris Collins.

DESPITE TAKING A melatonin, no Atlantan slept more poorly that night than Chris. Everything kept running through her head in a disturbing collage that made her grind her teeth. Prominently featured in this cerebral extravaganza were the puzzles associated with the five deaths. Her father alive, all the others carrying the virus dead. The two patients . . . infected like the nurses, but how? Fingertips whirled through her brain, some with white lunulas, some gray. Pearl Ritchie, Karen Casoli . . . Karen Ritchie, Pearl Kasoli . . .

Finally it was morning. She sat up and brushed at her hair with her fingers, feeling like an intern just finishing a thirty-six-hour shift. She couldn't go through another night like that. But how could she avoid it?

It was that damned virus, moving around in unknown ways, affecting people differently. Until she understood all of that better, she'd never be able to sleep.

She sat on the edge of the bed, at a loss for what to do. Then the answer came to her.

Sam Fairborn.

CHAPTER 21

CHRIS PULLED INTO the Fairborns' dirt driveway and got out of her car.

Sam Fairborn had retired from the CDC even before she had arrived there for her training as an EIS officer. But she'd heard about him regularly because he was a legend among the staff. He'd earned a lot of that reputation during the outbreak of Sudan encephalitis in Seattle that killed twenty-eight people during the late fifties. Prior to that, the disease was unknown in the U.S., so no one believed him at first when he identified it. Through that kind of insight and open-minded thinking, he'd played a major role for decades in every significant investigation the CDC had undertaken. When everyone else was stumped, Fairborn, it seemed, had the answer.

Chris had learned where he lived from one of his friends at the CDC. But her contact didn't know his phone number; nor could Chris get it from information. So she had just come out here in hopes he was home.

She'd driven twenty miles from Atlanta on the interstate and gone another three on a narrow country lane, until she'd seen his name on a mailbox. She now discovered that he lived in a small white stucco cottage covered in yellow roses that were blooming so prolifically she paused at the foot of the brick walkway to the house to admire them. Then, thinking that she'd better announce herself, she walked to the front door and rang the bell.

It was answered by a lovely older woman with high cheekbones and her pure white hair swept up into a stylish coiffure. She was wearing an elegant black knit duster over a sheer gray knit dress, pearls at her ears and throat. Looking like that, Chris thought she was apparently expecting someone or about to go out.

"I'm sorry to have come without calling first, but I couldn't find your number. I'm Dr. Chris Collins. I once worked at the CDC. I've never met your husband, but I'd like to talk to him about some puzzling features of a new virus."

"Was that your father on the news two nights ago?"

"I'm afraid so."

Chris half expected the door to be slammed shut, but instead the woman said, "Come in."

Chris stepped into a room with exposed rough-hewn beams that would have made the place oppressive were it not for the décor, which was bright and cheery, with many layers of interest, and had that crowded eclectic look that was difficult to clean but pleases the eye.

"I'm Ann Fairborn." She offered her hand and Chris shook it.

"Sam's working in the backyard. I'll show you the way."

Chris followed her to a study with the same beams and professional décor and through a pair of French doors into a modest-sized garden enclosed by walls of old brick. Along the wall on each side, a deep border of summer-flowering perennials was coming on strong behind the deep green of peonies heavy with buds. In front of the peonies, tulips were just fading, their petals falling away, so there were gaps in the blooms.

"He's back here," Mrs. Fairborn said, leading the way to a stucco outbuilding in the rear of the garden.

They found Sam Fairborn standing at a potting table behind the outbuilding, a row of clay pots to his right on the table, several bags of caladium bulbs to his left, their identifying labels still on them.

"Sam, this is Dr. Collins. That man who got the pig liver is her father. She'd like to talk to you."

Chris was shocked at Sam Fairborn's appearance. With his lovely wife and charming home, she was expecting Mr. Fezziwig from *A Christmas Carol*. But Fairborn looked like someone who stepped out of one of those old torn paintings you see in antique shops. What was left of his thin hair was pure gray like his wife's. But his eyebrows and his mustache and goatee were coarse and black. Both eyebrows extended well above the upper rim of his glasses, but the left one in particular seemed to be trying to reforest his scalp. His eyes were hooded with suspicion, the right distinctly more than the left. She waited for him to speak, but his mouth remained frozen in a drooping arc of displeasure.

"I'm sorry I didn't call ahead, but I couldn't find your number."

"That's why it's unlisted," Fairborn growled. "Who told you where I live?"

Not wanting to get that person in trouble, Chris said, "A mutual friend."

"I don't have any friends."

"Acquaintance, then."

"Imprecision in speech leads to fuzzy thinking." His big hand reached for a bag of caladium bulbs and he ripped it open.

"Dr. Collins, would you like something to drink?" Mrs. Fairborn asked. "We have tea, coffee, and diet cola . . . not a common brand, but one Sam likes."

"No need for that," Sam said. "She's not staying."

"No, thanks," Chris said.

Ann Fairborn put her hand on Chris's arm. "I'll just leave you two to talk then." Her smile encouraged Chris to remain there. She waited for Sam to ask her what she wanted, but he just kept working.

"I'd like to talk to you about the pig liver transplant initiative at Monteagle Hospital."

"Damned irresponsible program if you ask me." He looked at Chris and shook a caladium bulb at her. "To proceed with a transplant even when you know ahead of time that all pig cells contain a retrovirus is a recipe for disaster." He turned back to

his work, pulled a clay pot toward him, and plunged the bulb
into the waiting soil.

"It's certainly *been* a disaster, there's no debating that. But
there are some features of what's been happening that don't
make sense. As the infectious disease member of the team, I
feel very responsible for what's occurred."

Fairborn looked at her. "Was it your idea to start the program?"

"No."

"Not your fault then." He dug in the bag for more bulbs.

"Certain events took place that make me feel I could have
prevented the spread of the virus."

"I'm not a psychiatrist."

"I don't need a psychiatrist."

"If you need absolution, see a priest."

"And I didn't come for absolution. I want to talk to you
about facts in this epidemic that don't fit into a coherent pattern. As I understand it, that's your specialty."

"*Was,* past tense." He plunged another bulb into the soil.

"I know you're retired. I was hoping you'd just talk to me
about these facts and give me your opinion."

"Not interested."

"Why not?"

"I don't owe you an explanation. I don't even know you.
Isn't it time for you to go?"

Irritated at his rudeness, Chris said, "Fine. Thanks for
being such a public-spirited citizen. I don't see how your wife
puts up with you. Enjoy your garden. And by the way, all
those bulbs you've planted while we've been talking—
they're upside down."

Appearing shocked, Fairborn glanced at the bulb in his
hand and looked back at Chris. "What do you mean?"

She took the bulb from him and pointed at the end he was
about to push into the soil. "That isn't the root. This is."

His eyes grew even more hooded. "How do you know?"

"When I was in high school I worked part-time for a landscape company. I've planted thousands of those things."

He stood there sizing her up for several seconds, then said,
"Let's go inside and you can tell me your story."

Standing aside so he could lead the way, she was surprised
to see that he walked with a considerable limp. She followed

him into his study, where he motioned her to an oxblood-colored leather sofa while he lowered himself into a similar armchair whose cushion whooshed under his bulk.

"Now," he said, folding his hands over his belly. "What doesn't make sense?"

For the next fifteen minutes, he listened intently to what she had to say, barely blinking, hardly moving. She told him how the virus at first seemed to be therapeutic, but then became a Judas, turning lethal and killing its victims by causing coronary artery spasms that led to cardiac arrhythmia. She related how it moved through the hospital by mysterious routes, striking two patients in different wards but, so far, harming no one else. She talked about how her father was still alive even though the virus had surely mutated into its lethal form inside him. She finished by telling him how the virus had caused her father's lunulas and those of Mary Beth Cummings and the Barrosos to turn gray, but had not affected those of the two patients who'd died.

"So what do you make of all this?"

Fairborn reached for the tobacco pouch on the table next to his chair, unzipped it, and nestled it in his lap. He picked up the pipe from the ashtray on the same table and dipped it into the pouch. "Well, there are two possibilities," he said, bringing his pipe out of the pouch. "Most of these observations that are troubling you could just be individual differences in the way people respond to an infectious organism. Or . . . and I think this is the more likely explanation . . ."

Chris waited eagerly for him to finish his thought.

Instead, he concentrated on his pipe, tamping the tobacco into the bowl, then putting the tobacco pouch back on the table. He picked up a lighter and struck a flame that he applied to the bowl, puffing on the pipe until his little campfire was well stoked.

"Or?" Chris prompted.

He took a long puff on the pipe, blew a plume of smoke at the ceiling, then looked back at her. "Or, there are two viruses."

CHAPTER 22

.

"TWO VIRUSES," CHRIS echoed. "Why do you say that?"

"If the virus that causes the lethal effects is different from the one producing the therapeutic events, that would explain why the two patients who died didn't have gray lunulas."

"Because they weren't infected with the transplant virus, only the lethal one."

"It also explains why you can't figure out how the transplant virus got into them. It didn't."

"And my father . . . *He's* still alive because he was infected only with the transplant virus?"

"Perhaps."

"That just leaves us with a *different* question. How did the lethal virus get into the five who died?"

"A different question, true, but now it's the right question. The transplant virus appeared to be moving around in puzzling ways only because it didn't fit with everything you knew about it. We know nothing about the second virus, so its movements may be perfectly reasonable."

"But where did it come from? Why did it appear first in the two nurses who were taking care of my father? If you look at the history of everything that's happened, the flow of infection seems so obviously from my father to the nurses, to the one nurse's husband."

"I can't explain that, but I seem to remember reading a long time ago about a disease that produces symptoms very similar to those in the people who died. I first thought about it when I saw the symptomatology in the paper last night. But I can't recall *where* I read it."

"Maybe I should hit the library and see what I can dig up."

"Good idea. Meanwhile, I'll try to remember where I saw it. Sometimes if I just sit quietly and think about a problem for a while the answer will come to me in a day or two. The wait used to be only a few hours, but I'm not the man I was."

"Well, the man you are is certainly man enough."

It was just the barest hint, but Chris thought she saw a little upward tug at the corners of Fairborn's mouth. "I've taken too much of your time," Chris said, getting up.

Fairborn, too, rose.

Chris got a card and a pen from her bag and jotted her home phone and pager number on it. She crossed the space between them and handed it to Fairborn. "Call me anytime."

"You should have my number, too."

He recited his phone number and Chris wrote it on another of her own cards.

On the way to the door, Ann joined them.

"Did you have a productive talk?"

"I think so," Chris replied.

"I'm happy you came. Sam spends too much time just working in the garden. He needs more intellectual stimulation."

"Don't let her fool you," Sam said. "It's all I can do to keep up with *her*."

When Chris was gone, Sam told his wife what he and Chris had discussed, then he went back to the study to smoke his pipe and let his brain know how much he wanted to remember where he'd read about those symptoms.

After finishing his smoke, he returned to the potting table and resumed work on the caladiums, starting by digging up all those he'd planted upside down and replanting them correctly.

A little before noon, while Ann was preparing lunch, she saw Sam through the kitchen window, coming toward the house as fast as his bad leg allowed. Worried about him, she wiped her hands on her apron and met him as he came through the door to his study.

"Are you all right? Did you cut yourself again?"

"I think I know where I read about those symptoms." He went to the phone and entered a number from memory.

From the doorway, Ann watched him with affection, happy to see him so excited. She returned to the kitchen, humming, forgetting in her insulated little world that this was not a problem affecting some primitive tribe in a God-forsaken part of the world, but was in Atlanta, barely thirty minutes from her door.

In the study, Sam's call to the CDC had been answered.

"Marcy . . . Sam Fairborn."

Marcy Sandoval had been Sam's secretary when he was a virology section chief at the CDC. She was still there, serving his successor.

They exchanged the usual banter appropriate to the situation, then Sam said, "I'm trying to track down something I read years ago and I think it was in an epi one report."

He was referring to the field report written by epidemiology teams the CDC sends to places experiencing an outbreak of a new disease. This report was usually followed by the epi two, a full account of the disease, written after blood and tissue samples were completely analyzed and the causal organism identified. The epi two was often published, or at the very least presented at the CDC's annual conference. While Sam's memory of the investigation in question was very dim, he seemed to remember that there had never been a full account published or presented at conference. Which meant that the only record of this investigation, if indeed he was on the right track, was in the CDC's files.

"Are those old epi one reports computerized?"

"How far back do you need them?"

"Let's say fifteen years, but forget the five I've been gone."

"They've been trying to get all that old material on CDs, but I don't know if they've made it back that far yet."

"Could you make copies for me of what there is?"

"How soon do you need them?"

"You mean you haven't started yet?"

Marcy laughed. "I see you haven't changed. When I get

them, should I mail them to you or do you want to pick them up?"

"I'll come and get them. Do visitors still have to be ferried by security van up to the lobby?"

"Yes."

"Leave them at Security for me then. And thanks. I'll speak to your new boss and tell him you need a raise."

After hanging up, Sam considered calling Chris and telling her what he'd remembered, but since there was a chance he was wrong, he decided to keep it to himself until he'd gone through the old reports.

AFTER HER VISIT with Fairborn, Chris spent the rest of the day in the library at Emory University trying to find a previously described disease that caused hair loss, bilateral blindness, central pain, and vascular inflammation. Finally, unable to read another word, she gave up, having found nothing. When she'd first heard Fairborn propose that there were two viruses, it had sounded plausible, even likely. But now, walking back to her car, she had serious doubts about his theory.

TR PICKED UP the ringing phone and identified himself.

"It's all set," a familiar voice from New Jersey said. "I just hope there's plenty of sand over your tracks."

"You worry too much," TR replied.

"I don't think *you* worry enough."

"What phone are you using?"

"A safe one, but your question makes me feel better. Just be careful."

SAM FAIRBORN TURNED right and proceeded slowly down Michael Street, looking through the black chain-link fence at the complex of buildings that comprised the CDC, where he'd spent thirty-five years of his life. It was the first time since he'd retired that he'd come back, and he was surprised at how detached he felt looking at it. It was as if it had all happened to someone else. He'd once been the best epidemiologist in the world, and now he was just an old man who used to be somebody. And the funny thing was, that was okay. But he had to admit this was fun—the puzzles, tracking down a vague memory of something that could have enormous significance.

One more time, he thought. Just to prove he still could.

It was now Monday afternoon. Considering that he'd asked Marcy for those old epi ones on Friday, and she'd already rounded them up, it was obvious she was just as reliable and effective as ever.

The road ran along the eastern end of the Emory campus and Sam was amazed at the amount of construction going on there. But then, Emory always did have a lot of money. At the end of the street, he turned right and pulled into a slot in front of the so-called visitor's center, which was actually a security operation designed to keep someone from getting into the complex with a bomb.

He went inside and stepped up to the visitor sign-in counter.

"Yes, sir, what can I do for you?" a burly black man in a uniform and carrying a big sidearm asked.

"I'm Sam Fairborn. I think you have a package for me."

"I believe I do." He went to a desk behind him and picked up a manila envelope. He checked the name on the front and brought it back to the counter.

"Now, sir, if you'll just show me some identification."

Amused that he had so quickly gone from being the most universally recognized figure at the CDC to someone who needed to *prove* who he was, Sam gave the guard his driver's license. After the guard perused it and checked the real Sam against the photo on the license, he handed over the envelope. Going back to his car, Sam felt apprehensive and excited in a way that gardening never produced.

SAM FOUND TWO CDs in the envelope he'd picked up. The inclusive dates of the reports they contained were written in magic marker on each one. He loaded the disk with the oldest reports into his computer and waited for the icon to appear on his monitor. When it did, he clicked it open and read the title of the first report: *Outbreak of Dengue Fever in Sao Paulo.* Well acquainted with the symptoms of Dengue fever, he nevertheless skimmed the report to see if it contained any surprises. Finding none, he moved on to *Human Herpes Virus Infection in Malaysian Blood Donors.*

And so it went for the next hour.

Growing stiff from sitting so long, he got up, filled his pipe, and went outside, where he watched two young squirrels chasing each other through the trees on the other side of the garden wall. He didn't like squirrels because they were rodents and rodents were the vectors for so many diseases . . . rodents and mosquitoes. So he didn't belong to the army of ecologists who believed that every species was valuable. If it had been in his power, he'd have destroyed every rodent and mosquito on the planet. Still, those damn squirrels *were* cute. He continued to watch them until they dropped out of sight, then he resumed his stroll around the garden, always vigilant for fungus or marauding insects.

He finished his stroll and his pipe at the same time, and returned to his study. There, he settled once more into the chair in front of his computer and replaced the CD he'd been working on with the next one.

He clicked the disk open and read the title of the first report on it: *Outbreak of a New, Lethal Disease in Northern Kazakhstan*.

Kazakhstan . . .

The location created a flutter of recognition in his memory circuits. As he read further, the salient facts came at him in a rush: rodent-borne, universally fatal, onset signaled by hair loss, followed by bilateral blindness . . .

This was it.

CHAPTER 23

THE DISCOVERER OF the Star of India sapphire couldn't have been more excited than Sam was. He ripped through the rest of the report, neglected parts of his brain stirring again, lighting up, buzzing.

Preliminary studies done on blood samples of both the rodents and the human victims showed that they cross-reacted with antibodies against a genus of organisms known as hantaviruses.

This struck Sam as quite surprising, for no known hantavirus acted as this one did. But of course, prior to the outbreak in the four corners regions of the U.S., everyone thought hantaviruses only caused kidney problems. But the four corners strain killed by causing acute respiratory distress. So why couldn't this be a new hanta strain? And why had there never been a full report published? It was long enough ago that it should have been written up while he was still active.

He looked at the author's name. Bill Lansden. Yeah, he remembered Lansden; a tall lanky guy with a permanent chapped look to his face. Worked in the Special Pathogens section.

Sam pulled the phone toward him and entered the general number for the CDC. When they answered, he asked for Lansden.

The phone in Lansden's office rang four times, then Sam heard it roll over to a different number.

"Special Pathogens," a female voice said.

"I'm trying to find Bill Lansden."

"I'm sorry, but Dr. Lansden is on medical leave."

Stretching a point, Sam said, "We're old friends. What happened?"

"He's had a stroke."

"Is he at home?"

"I believe he's still in the hospital."

"Where?"

"Emory University."

Though Sam was really warming to the chase now, he'd become such a penny pincher in retirement he didn't even consider calling Information, but lugged out the phone book and looked up the hospital's number.

A few minutes later, having verified that Lansden was indeed still hospitalized and having gained possession of his room number, Sam got Chris's card out of his desk drawer and called her pager.

CHRIS HAD AWAKENED that morning ready for another stint in the library. But as on Friday and during the few hours she'd spent searching on Saturday, she had still found nothing useful. As she scrolled down another list of titles, she felt her pager vibrate. She retrieved it from her pocket and looked at the displayed number. Failing to recognize it, but grateful for an excuse to take a break, she got her cell phone from her handbag and punched in the number.

Whoever had placed the call picked up before the first ring was finished.

"This is Chris Collins."

"It's Sam Fairborn. I found the report. It was an old epi one in the CDC files."

"All the symptoms were the same?"

"Identical."

"What caused them, or didn't the investigator know?"

"Couldn't say for sure, but the blood of the victims and the rodent vector cross-reacted to antibodies against the hanta genus."

That jogged Chris's memory. "My father's medical records showed that about ten years ago he had some kind of respiratory disease, but he got better. And he was living in New Mexico at the time . . ."

"If that was four corners hanta he had, he's probably loaded with hanta antibodies, which would explain why he's still alive," Fairborn said.

"Surely you're right. It all fits so well. But I'm going to have his blood tested to be sure. Where was the outbreak the epi one was describing?"

"Kazakhstan."

Chris's first reaction to this was to wonder how a lethal Kazak virus that had apparently never come to the medical world's attention in any other place got to Atlanta. Then she saw the obvious answer. "But the investigators of that outbreak likely brought blood samples back here to the CDC for further study . . ."

"That'd be the usual procedure, but there's never been a full report of the study published. I guess you didn't find anything."

"No."

"If they had samples, why wasn't it published?"

"Who wrote the report?"

"Guy named Bill Lansden. He still works at the CDC, or at least he did until recently. When I called over there to talk to him, I found out he's had a stroke."

"How bad?"

"Don't know. But he's still in the hospital."

"Suppose he *did* bring viral samples back to the CDC. How did the organism get into my father and everybody else? We need to talk to Lansden."

"I had the same thought. Are you available now to meet me at Emory Hospital? That's where he is."

"I'm at the Emory library now."

"If I don't get involved in some traffic snafu, it'll take me about thirty minutes to get there. I'll meet you at the hospital's front entrance."

With plenty of time to spare, Chris then called Monteagle. "Dr. Ash, please."

While waiting for the call to be transferred, she had to listen to a recorded message touting Monteagle as one of the world's leading medical institutions. The recording did not mention the two patients who had died from what now appeared to be a rogue Kazak virus.

"Ash."

"Eric, this is Chris. Can you test my father's pre-transplant blood samples for antibodies to hantavirus?"

"I'm not sure I have the reagents on hand, but I can get them. Why?"

She related what she'd learned from Fairborn. "Lansden is still hospitalized, but we're going to meet there in a few minutes in hopes he's well enough to answer some questions."

"Ask him one for me. If we really are dealing with two viruses, why does this Kazak organism flow along the same infectivity pathway as the transplant virus?"

"I doubt he'll be able to answer that one."

"Ask Fairborn then."

"Sounds like you don't believe his theory."

"Just because the virus in Kazakhstan produced the same symptoms as those we've seen in the people who died here, it doesn't have to mean that the Kazak virus is here. Whatever mutation made our virus lethal could have also occurred independently in the one from Kazakhstan."

"I seem to remember you telling Scott in our big meeting when the infections first occurred that such a thing was unlikely."

"Unlikely, but possible."

"Sorry, but I think Fairborn is on to something."

"Maybe . . . maybe not. Get us a sample of the Kazak virus or antibodies against it and we'll have something to work with to figure this out."

"We'll ask Lansden what he has."

"Where'd you say he was hospitalized?"

"Emory."

"And you're going over there right now?"

"I'm supposed to be at the front entrance in thirty minutes."

"Let me know what you learn. Meanwhile, I'll get right to work on those hanta tests."

CHAPTER 24

WHILE CHRIS AND Sam Fairborn waited at the stroke unit's nursing station for Dr. McKee, Bill Lansden's neurologist, Fairborn picked at a white thread on his tweed jacket.

"What's that on your ear?" Chris asked.

"Can you be more specific?"

"That brown smudge."

"I painted my potting bench today before I picked up those reports from the CDC. Guess I scratched my ear while I had paint on my fingers. How's it look?"

"Very distinguished."

Their conversation was interrupted by the arrival of a fair-skinned woman wearing a white lab coat. She came directly toward them and stood in front of Fairborn.

"Dr. Fairborn?"

"Yes."

She offered her hand. "I'm Evelyn McKee."

Fairborn shook her hand and introduced Chris. Then they got down to business.

"As I told you on the phone," McKee said, "this isn't going to be easy. Dr. Lansden's stroke has damaged his speech centers so that he can't express a coherent thought. His sentences are rhythmic and complex, but the important words are usually inappropriate."

With her neurology rotation in medical school long behind her, Chris couldn't remember the details of the kinds of strokes that affect language, so she simply asked the question that occurred to her. "Can he write coherently?"

"His right arm is paralyzed, but even if he was left-handed, he doesn't know what to do with a pen. Typically, a patient with these deficits can't understand what's said to them. But he seems to have some comprehension."

"Can you boil all this down into a set of guidelines for talking to him?" Fairborn asked.

"Do you mind if I tape this session? I'd like a record of how he responds to new people. There's a TV camera in his room and a tape machine in the room behind me."

Fairborn looked at Chris, who shrugged.

"Sure, go ahead."

"Then let's start by seeing how he responds to questions that require more complicated answers than yes or no. If he has trouble with a question, rephrase it. If he still has trouble, shift to yes or no questions. Now, here's an additional complication. Sometimes he says no when he means yes. So we've been having him answer yes by blinking his eyes once, twice for no. This works because the centers that control his blinking movements aren't damaged and therefore won't betray his intent. We tried asking him to just nod or shake his head, but his meds are keeping him on the edge of vertigo so that head movements make him nauseous. He hasn't been an easy patient to manage."

IN THE SUPPLY closet of the stroke unit taping room, TR could hear everything that was being said. He was well aware of the terrible risk he was taking by being here, but what choice did he have? When he'd learned what Chris and that old peacock from the CDC were up to, he absolutely *had* to know what they were going to get from Lansden. Before ducking into the closet, he'd turned on the intercom that allowed conversations in Lansden's room to be heard in the taping room.

• • • •

"LET ME TURN on the recorder, and we'll begin," McKee said.

She went into the taping room, put a fresh VHS-C tape in the machine, and pressed the record button.

In the supply closet, TR tried not to breathe so loud.

When McKee came back into the hall, Chris said, "What's his prognosis?"

"Hard to say. Ordinarily, with time, there's some recovery of function. I'm hoping to see evidence of that today. The clots that did the damage came from a heart condition that causes episodic atrial fibrillation. We're trying now to find the right drug and the right dose to control that without side effects, but as I indicated earlier, so far we haven't had great success. He seems to have a low tolerance for the best drugs."

When they entered, Lansden was sitting up in bed watching cartoons on TV with the sound off.

"Bill, you have some visitors," McKee said. "This is Dr. Collins." She gestured to Chris. "And Dr. Fairborn."

Sam had told Chris that he knew Lansden from his years at the CDC, but Lansden showed no sign that he remembered.

"They'd like to ask you some questions," McKee said. She stepped back so Chris and Fairborn could move in closer.

IN THE CLOSET next door, TR could hear every word.

"DR. LANSDEN, I'VE read your very interesting report on the disease you investigated in Kazakhstan years ago," Fairborn said. "And I . . . we've been wondering why was a full account of that outbreak never published?"

Lansden sat silently for a few seconds during which Chris believed his damaged brain was probably trying to make some sense out of the question. Then he spoke.

"I couldn't gender anything because all the frame and tissue horses were misbegotten." His face twisted into a mask of irritation.

Fairborn looked at McKee for a translation, but the neurologist just said, "Try again."

"I don't understand," Fairborn said to Lansden.

"I couldn't gender anything because all the frame and tissue horses were misbegotten." It was obvious from his tortured expression that Lansden knew he wasn't making any sense.

Seeing that Lansden was just going to keep making the same mistakes, Fairborn decided to try a different question.

"What happened to all the blood and tissue samples you brought back with you?"

"I didn't smoke any here."

"I'm sorry . . ."

"I didn't smoke any here."

Fairborn looked at McKee. "I think we're going to have to use just yes and no questions," McKee said. "Bill, answer these next questions by blinking in the usual way."

IN THE CLOSET, TR realized he was now going to have to reconstruct Lansden's answers from Fairborn's responses.

"ARE THE SAMPLES you brought back from Kazakhstan stored at the CDC?" Fairborn asked.

Knowing they had to be there, Fairborn was so surprised when Lansden blinked NO that he forgot the questioning format. "Then where *are* they? I'm sorry . . . Are you saying they were lost?"

YES.

"*After* they arrived in this country?"

NO.

"They were lost en route?"

YES.

"Before they left Kazakhstan?"

YES.

"Dr. Lansden," Chris said. "were you alone in Kazakhstan?"

TR LISTENED HARDER now, as though he could hear Lansden blink.

NO.

"Someone was with you in an official capacity?"

YES.

"Someone from the CDC?"

YES.

"A man?"

YES.
"Can you tell us his name?"

TR'S HANDS HAD turned so cold they felt as if they belonged on a corpse.

"EMBER," LANSDEN SAID.
"His name was Ember?" Chris asked.
NO.
"Try again."
"Ember."
Lansden's eyelids began blinking erratically.
"What's wrong, Doctor?" Chris asked McKee. "Why is he suddenly blinking so much?"
"He does that from time to time, and I haven't yet figured out why."
"Course mode," Lansden said.
"I don't understand," Chris said.
Lansden slapped his sheet with his left hand. "Course mode."
No one in the room could figure out what was going on, but in the closet, TR thought he did and it made his scrotum shrivel.
If the Kazak viral samples really were lost before arriving in the U.S., Chris was unable to see how they could be at the heart of the deaths in Atlanta. But considering Lansden's condition, it seemed possible that he might have misunderstood Fairborn's questions. It therefore appeared that if they were to ever get the straight story on where those samples were, they'd have to talk to the other person who was with Lansden in Kazakhstan. So they had to get his name.
"I've got an idea," Chris said. "Let's just go through the alphabet and get the name one letter at a time with the yes and no technique."
"That should work," Fairborn said.

THERE WAS NO doubt now in TR's mind that in about two minutes, his life would be over. Back when he'd first heard about Lansden's stroke, he'd gone to the university hospital to check on him, hoping to learn that he might die. But he had found him irritatingly healthy. Sure, he couldn't communicate, but brains can recover.

Still concerned that Lansden might one day link him to the murders of the two Frenchmen, he'd thought then about killing Lansden. But with each room in the stroke unit flanked by these recording and viewing rooms with their one-way mirrors, you could never be sure you weren't being watched. So he hadn't felt comfortable enough to do anything. Nor was there any real need to take the risk.

But now . . . Damn it. He should have fixed this problem when he'd had the chance.

FAIRBORN TURNED TO Lansden to resume questioning him, but Lansden suddenly looked very pale and his breathing was labored. He threw the covers off with his good arm and started to get up on the other side of the bed. Then he vomited.

"It's his meds," McKee said as she went around to the other side of the bed. Watching where she stepped, she went to Lansden and helped him to his feet. As she guided him to the bathroom, she glanced over her shoulder. "Would one of you please press that call button for some help?"

Fairborn pressed the button, then looked at Chris. "I think we should leave him alone for now."

IN THE CLOSET, TR was elated. He'd been yanked from the lip of the abyss. But he now had a lot to do. First, he had to get his hands on the tape that had recorded the session with Lansden. He'd heard Fairborn say they were leaving, so he'd wait about two minutes to allow them to get off the floor, then he'd grab the tape and try to get out of there without being seen.

But before he could even start his mental countdown, he saw, through the louvers of the closet door, Fairborn come into the recording room, turn off the tape machine, and remove the tape. To TR's horror, Fairborn put the tape in the plastic box it came in and slipped it into his pocket.

"ARE WE LEAVING?" Chris asked, hurrying to keep up with Fairborn as he moved quickly toward the elevators.

"I want to see that part just before he became ill."

"But you stole the tape."

"No, I borrowed it."

"Why didn't you ask for a copy?"

"Didn't want to wait around."

"Is this how you behaved when you worked at the CDC?"

"Pretty much. They called me unconventional and some other things you're probably thinking of right now. They never understood that the investigation always takes first priority."

"We shouldn't need more than a few minutes tomorrow to get that name from Lansden using the alphabet approach. Why bother with the tape?"

"You never know what might happen between now and then. In some countries I've worked in, the government could change twice between dinner and breakfast. So I always observe the Fairborn uncertainty principle: If a situation can harm you by deteriorating, it will, usually so quickly nothing can be salvaged."

"What a pessimist."

"It's the safest way to view the world."

Outside the hospital, Chris said, "I'm going to let you study that tape alone."

"I'll call you if I find anything."

CHAPTER 25

WHEN CHRIS GOT home from Emory Hospital, she thought about Wayne and how he believed he was responsible for the five deaths that had occurred. She looked at the phone.

Should she call and tell him about the Kazak virus? Then she remembered his TV interview. "Mistakes were made . . ."

She shuddered at the inept way he'd handled himself. Suppose he did that again and told a reporter about the second virus? It was too soon for that to become public.

Better he be left uninformed.

THE FAIRBORNS HAD been invited to dinner at the home of Myra and Bob Quinn. Ann had met Myra when they'd both served on a committee to raise money for the local volunteer fire department. Sam thought Myra was okay, but Bob, a retired soybean farmer, was a bore. Obviously intimidated by Sam's education and accomplishments, Bob would always monopolize the conversation talking about his coin collection, describing in excruciating detail how each one was acquired. The first time Sam heard those stories they were interesting. Now he faced an evening at the Quinns with all the enthusiasm of someone about to step into a p4 lab without a space suit. But he went nevertheless, for Ann's sake.

They arrived home from the Quinns a little after ten.

"Well, I thought that was nice," Ann said, taking off the light jacket she'd worn.

Sam muttered something that he hoped sounded like he agreed, then said, "I've got some work to do."

Ever solicitous when it came to Sam, Ann said, "I'll bring you a cup of tea."

Sam headed for his study and turned on the TV. Somewhere in the house there was an adapter that would allow VHS-C tapes to be played on a VCR. But even if he could find it, his VCR had lately been unable to play a tape without making the image flutter. No matter. When legends find one path blocked, they use another. He went to the shelf under the bookcases and got the camcorder he'd bought to film the grandkids when they came to visit. Carrying the camera back to the TV, he connected the two by the camera's video and audio output cables. Then he reached into the pocket of his sport coat for the tape he'd taken from the hospital.

NO WONDER I couldn't find it, TR thought, watching Fairborn through a window on the right side of the cottage. *It wasn't in the house.* He could strike now and take the tape, but then he'd have to kill both of them. Better to wait and get it while they slept. But that would only work if Fairborn didn't figure it out first.

FAIRBORN STARTED THE tape rolling. There was Lansden and his own voice: "Dr. Lansden, I've read your very interesting . . ."

He watched and listened to the replay carefully, but everything that sounded like gibberish earlier remained that way. The tape reached the part where Lansden kept saying the man with him in Kazakhstan was named Ember. Then Lansden's eyelids began flickering.

No. Not flickering, because sometimes they remained closed for a beat or two.

On the tape Lansden said, "Course mode."

"I don't understand," Chris said.

Lansden slapped the sheet and said it again: "Course mode."

What was he trying to say?

Ann came in with his tea.

"What are you doing, dear?"

"Trying to make sense of this tape."

Ann leaned down to look, but the tape had gone beyond the recorded images.

Sam briefly explained the situation and rewound the tape. As he played it again, Ann stood by his side, her hand on his shoulder.

When the tape reached the end, Sam hit stop, then started rewind.

"What do you think?" Sam asked.

"I think course mode means Morse code."

Sam's mouth gaped in amazement at how stupid he'd been. That's exactly what it meant. "You've done it," Sam said. "He's telling us the name we wanted by blinking in Morse code. Thank you."

"Happy to help, dear," Ann said. "Don't stay up too late."

OUTSIDE, WHERE HE'D heard everything that had been said, TR dropped to the ground. Believing that he knew what Fairborn would do next, he got out his knife.

MORSE CODE. LORD. Pretty soon I'll need a walker for my brain, Sam thought, hurrying to his computer and turning it on. This was not the kind of performance he would ever let himself forget, but for now, he was so interested in deciphering the name, he didn't have time to dwell on it. He didn't know anything about Morse code, but it should be easy enough to find what he wanted on the internet.

In just a few seconds he was looking at the first page of results the Go To search engine had given him for Morse code. He chose the fourth entry, "A Morse Code Primer," and waited for the page to appear.

And waited.

And waited.

A small box appeared on his screen advising that he had been disconnected.

Muttering and threatening to change to another internet

provider, he went through the log-on sequence again, but still couldn't get access.

He picked up the phone.

Dead.

Damn. The one time when he really needed a phone line, it was down. And it was too late tonight to do anything about it. He considered trying to at least convert Lansden's eyelid movements to dots and dashes on paper, but then, thinking he'd be better able to do that after reading a little about Morse code, he shut everything off and went to bed.

SITTING ON THE cool ground with his back against the house after cutting the phone line, TR was pleased to see the light that had been spilling from Fairborn's study window suddenly go out. While he waited for the couple to fall asleep, his thoughts took him back to the day he'd first been called TR, the hated nickname that even his own mind wouldn't free him from.

HE HADN'T CRIED during the taunting, but now that he was alone, the tears flowed. Embarrassed at the way he looked, he left the roadside and followed the path into the woods that would take him home the long way.

His route soon took him past the place where the high school kids brought their dates and did bad things in their cars. Friday and Saturday nights after ten o'clock were the best times to be there, and if you were careful and there was only one car, you could sneak up and watch them through the window. On those nights, back in his bed, thinking about what he'd seen, he found it impossible to sleep or keep his hands from his private place.

Today, walking past the spot, he saw, through his tears, a book of matches that looked clean and fresh enough to still be good. He picked up the matches, pulled one free, and scraped it across the igniter strip. He watched the resulting flame until it crept so close to his fingers he had to drop it. Then he took off his pants and threw them on the ground.

It took a few seconds for the second match to ignite his pants, but he was soon standing in front of a smoking little poplin fire. After watching the pants burn until they were al- most completely consumed, he took off his shirt and tied it around his waist so his tattered shorts were partially covered. Then he headed for home, ready at an instant to leave the path and take cover should anyone come along.

The woods ended about thirty yards from his house, which meant he'd be exposed for only the time it took him to bolt across the yard. He took a deep breath and started running.

Thirty yards . . . twenty . . . ten . . .

He reached the house and dropped to his knees. With practiced skill, he skittered under the house and crabwalked to the boards he'd loosened in the floor of his closet one day when his mother's arthritis had improved enough so she could drive his father to the doctor. Those boards were how he got out at night to watch the high school kids.

His plan today was to sneak inside, change into his other pants, then go back to the woods and arrive home the regular way. Should his mother say anything about his pants being different than those he'd left in that morning, he'd convince her she was mistaken. If he could manage that, the burned ones would have just disappeared.

He pushed the loose boards up and out of the way and hiked himself inside. Suddenly, the closet door flew open and there was his mother, his only other shirt on a hanger in her hand.

They looked at each other for a moment in disbelief, then she pulled him out of the closet and inspected the floor. Turning, she skewered him with a fierce stare. "Where are your pants?"

Though he was already an accomplished sneak, he was a fledgling liar and had no answer.

She hung up the shirt in her hand, then grabbed him by the arm. "I think your father needs to hear what you've got to say about all this."

His father was on the sofa watching the tiny fluttering TV the church had given them. Unable to work or even walk very much because his lungs had been hurt at the asbestos siding plant, that was how he spent most of his time.

"Ben, your son has something to tell you."

His father struggled to a sitting position and went off on a coughing jag, covering his mouth with the handkerchief he always carried.

When he could speak, he said, "I'm listening."

Genuine tears welling up in his eyes, his son said, "I burned up my new pants."

"Why?"

"Because they came from the church rag bag. They weren't new, they were used, *like everything that comes into this house. They belonged to Jimmy Demarco, but his mother got that bleach stain on them and so she gave them away. But Jimmy recognized them today and he told everybody where I get my clothes and he said . . ." Now he was sobbing.*

"He told everybody that when I was born you put me in a shoebox and threw me away like garbage and he started calling me TR, saying it with my last name so it came out, 'TRash.' Then everybody was doing it. Why are we trash? Why can't I have clothes that nobody else has had first? Why do we have to live in this ugly house? Why does our car have to be so rusty? I hate my life."

His father reached out for him. Fearing that his father would start coughing again, Eric reluctantly moved closer.

His father put his hand on his son's shoulder. "Eric, I know what you're going through. But there's no shame in being poor. It's what's inside a man that counts."

No shame? *Eric thought. It was nothing* but *shame. And that's when he lost what little respect he still had for his father.*

SUDDENLY, ASH WAS yanked back to the present by light once again coming from Fairborn's study window.

Was that old fart still up?

Lights began blooming all through the garden. Two feet away, one came on at the base of a spruce, illuminating its branches and him, too. He heard the sound of the sliding door to the study rasping along its track. Panicking, he rolled onto one knee and lurched for the spotlight giving him away. Ignoring the heat, he unscrewed the bulb. Once again hidden by darkness, he pulled his automatic from his jacket pocket and focused on the corner of the house. He didn't want to kill the old man, but if he had to, he would. And his wife.

FINDING SLEEP AN elusive commodity, Sam Fairborn stepped outside wearing a robe over his pajamas, his pipe in

his hand. He stood for a while on the porch smoking and surveying the garden, enjoying the damp smells of the night.

Then he began to think of his hostas in that shady spot
under the cherry tree and how if he was to preserve that beautiful unspoiled spring foliage, he needed to be vigilant, which
meant he'd have to come out at night and pick the cutworms
off them.

Did he want to do that tonight? No.

But this very minute those little wrecking machines were
probably crawling up the stems to begin feeding. And once
the damage was done, there was nothing you could do about
it. The plant would look lousy until the next spring.

He took a few more puffs on his pipe, all the while imagining cutworm jaws chewing and slicing. Finally unable to
take it any longer, he returned to the study, where he put his
pipe in an ashtray and picked up a flashlight, then went back
outside to do battle.

Before engaging the enemy, he stopped by the storage shed
and put on a pair of disposable rubber gloves from a jar he
kept there.

CROUCHED AMONG THE foundation plantings on the side
of the house, Ash could see Fairborn pissing around in the
garden. What was he doing? Looked like he was picking
something off the plants. Then he'd put whatever it was on the
brick walkway and jab at it with a stick. But it was the flashlight that worried Ash. If Fairborn got it into his head to replace the bulb Ash had unscrewed, the old man was going to
die.

IT TOOK FAIRBORN a little less than ten minutes to rescue
his hostas, and when he was finished, his lower back was
aching from all the bending. Still, it was a reasonable price for
putting an end to the cutworm threat. Playing his flashlight
once more over the verdant green leaves, in a final salute, he
thought about how dramatically his world had shrunk. Where
entire countries had once looked to him for help, his influence
now was limited to a quarter acre of land around his house. Or
at least it had been until Chris Collins came to him.

How did that Kazak virus get into those folks who died at
Monteagle? As he began to stroll back toward the house,

along the perimeter walkway, he idly played his flashlight into the foliage around him, looking for more nocturnal pests.

TURN THE FLASHLIGHT off and go inside, old man, Ash silently urged. But Fairborn kept coming, his flashlight swinging from side to side. Ash began to think ahead. He'd kill the old man and immediately go inside and find his wife, which shouldn't be hard because she'd likely come running to meet him. When he'd searched the house earlier for the tape, he hadn't seen a cell phone. So with the phone line cut, there was probably no danger she'd be able to call for help . . .

Unless she carried one in her bag. Damn. This wasn't good.

Fairborn was now about ten feet from the corner of the house and he was still working the flowers and bushes with his light.

Then he was eight feet away . . .

Now six . . .

He was back-lit by a couple of spotlights and he was a big target, so even if Ash hadn't been a skilled shot, there was no chance he'd miss.

Four feet . . .

Fairborn swung his light from his left, bringing it across his body. There was no doubt now, the beam was going to rake Ash's hiding place.

Ash pointed the muzzle of his automatic at Fairborn's heart and his finger tightened on the trigger.

CHAPTER 26

JUST BEFORE ASH'S gun fired, Fairborn switched off his flashlight and disappeared around the corner.

Ash rolled back into a sitting position, the tension of the last few minutes leaving him in a rush. In just a few minutes, his mind took him back to the events that occurred after he'd told his parents how everybody was now calling him TR.

THE NEXT DAY they did it again, led as before by Jimmy Demarco, the asshole who'd thought it up. But this time Ash didn't cry, because he had plans for Demarco.

After school, with a piece of broken glass in his pocket, Ash headed directly for the woods. There, he took a path that led to the field behind the home of the widow Massy, who made ends meet by doing other folks' laundry, so she always had a lot of sheets and stuff hanging outside, all of which would make good cover for what he needed to do.

Sure enough, when he got there, her yard was rippling with white panels fluttering in the breeze like the sails of great ships carrying spices and slaves. Dropping into a crouch, Ash made his way through the weeds to the edge of the widow's grass and began yanking clothespins off a sheet

*in the middle of the yard, well hidden by all the unmolested
laundry.*

*He worked quickly, throwing the pins to the ground and
letting the damp sheets lie where they fell. In under a minute,
the rope clothesline he coveted was bare. Careful to keep from
slicing himself, he began sawing at the rope with the broken
glass he'd brought.*

Hurry . . . Hurry . . .

The first strand popped free.

One by one, others joined the first.

Then that end was done.

*Making sure he didn't leave any footprints on the sheets
he'd let fall, he raced to the other end of the line and sawed it
free as well. And ran away into the woods.*

*He hid the rope under some leaves near the place where
he'd burned his pants, then set off through the woods along a
route that couldn't even be called a path, but which he could
follow with ease.*

*This course led him to the Ledbetter place, a family that
never threw anything away, so that his advance on their shed
was hidden by stacks of old tires, piles of lumber, and every
kitchen appliance the family had ever owned. That his family
was considered more lowly than even the Ledbetters was a
hard apple to swallow.*

*Reaching the shed, he worked a loose board free and
slipped inside. Amid the gloom and spiderwebs, he began
pulling out drawers and looking in rusty cans for what he
needed.*

*Outside, the handlebar shadow of the rusting motorcycle
behind the shed crept steadily across the ground. Just before
it started up the back of the shed, he came out with a handful
of #16 spikes, an old hatchet, and an oily rag. On his way
back to the woods, he picked up a gray board with about a
hundred slugs stuck to the underside in a slime fest. But it was
just the right length.*

God bless the Ledbetters.

SUDDENLY, ASH HEARD the sound of a car pulling into
Fairborn's driveway.

Who the hell was that?

He remained where he was, trying not to let his mind run

wild with unfounded speculation on how much this might
screw things up. Fairborn was in bed. He *couldn't* be expecting someone. Every nerve sizzling, Ash listened hard to the
engine out front, which didn't seem to be getting any closer.
Then, it revved up, slowed again, and . . .

Yes, the car was leaving . . . probably just someone using
the driveway to turn around.

With this latest threat extinguished, Ash's thoughts soon
returned to the Jimmy Demarco saga.

*ASH HID THE spikes and the board he'd taken from the Led-
betters under the leaves with the rope. Hatchet in hand, he
went in search of the final item. He found it eighty yards from
where he'd hidden everything—a tree about ten inches in di-
ameter that had been snapped off in a windstorm, so he only
had to cut it at one end.*

*But even that wasn't easy, for the hatchet was rusty and the
blade badly nicked. He was so hindered by his poor equipment that when it was time to go home, the tree was only cut
halfway through.*

*That night, before falling asleep, he went over his plans for
tomorrow again and again, until he believed he had thought
of everything.*

*The next afternoon, he went immediately from school to his
hidden cache of supplies and picked up the hatchet. Soon, he
was whacking away at the fallen tree, wood chips flying into
his hair and sticking to the sweat on his brow. This was the
bad part, making so much noise. Because if anybody saw him
doing this, they might remember it later. So he'd chop awhile,
then stop and listen and look around. Finally, one last blow
ended the job.*

*He had lopped off a section about three feet long, and
when he tried to pick it up, he found it almost too heavy to
carry. But it had to be heavy to work properly, so he just made
the best of it, staggering under its weight a few yards at a
time, then putting it down to rest.*

*It took nearly an hour to move the log to the big catalpa
tree beside the path Jimmy Demarco took to school each
morning. Then he had to go back and get the rest of his stuff.*

*When he returned, he didn't have much time left. Even in
rural Alabama, kids knew about fingerprints, so he wiped his*

from all the spikes with the oily rag he'd taken. Holding each spike with the rag, he used the blunt end of the hatchet to drive a dozen of them through the board in two rows several inches apart. With the last two spikes, he nailed the board to the log so the sharp end of the other spikes faced outward.

He notched the log a few inches from each end, then cut some pieces off the rope he'd stolen and fashioned a sling for the log. In about twenty minutes he had the log properly suspended from a big limb in the old catalpa. Now it was time to test it.

Positioning himself high in the tree so he could lean back against a limb big enough to support his weight, he began pulling the fetching rope on the log hand over hand until the log swung up almost to where he stood.

His location among the leaves did not allow him an unrestricted view of the path, but he could see well enough to know when someone on a bicycle was coming, and judge their progress. He imagined now that he saw Jimmy Demarco come into view.

Coming . . . closer . . . closer . . .

Now.

He let go of the rope and the log swung down in a perfect arc, not even twisting. He'd remembered to tie the end of the fetching rope to a little branch so he wouldn't lose it when he let the log go. This made it easy to pull it back into position for another trial.

He practiced for a few more minutes, until he had a good feel for the timing he'd need, then he pulled the log up and tied the fetching rope to a branch so the whole thing would be hidden from view.

Back on the ground, he approached the catalpa from both directions on the path to make sure the log couldn't be seen. Of course he could see it through the leaves because he knew it was up there. But he didn't think anyone else would. Before leaving, he cut down a small tree a good distance from the catalpa and used it like a big brush to freshen the trampled weeds around the old tree. He wiped his prints from the hatchet and wrapped it in the rag. On the way home, he threw the hatchet in a deep pool in Aker's creek.

There was never much food in the house, so he was always hungry. Seven days a week, dinner consisted of white beans and cornbread, and in the summer, whatever vegetables his mother's little garden produced. On Sunday, sometimes his mother would add a little chicken or pork to the beans if they could afford it. Breakfast was a piece of cornbread and a glass of water. Lunch was nonexistent. It was monotonous fare, but because he was perpetually hungry, he always looked forward to dinner. And with all the work he'd just done, he now felt as though there was a hole drilled completely through him where his stomach should be.

That night, in his dreams, he was in the tree practicing. But his mind never put Jimmy Demarco in the picture, so the big log always swung down and hit nothing.

Needing to be in the tree well before Demarco passed, he left the house the next morning a half hour early, telling his mother he'd promised his teacher he'd clean all her erasers before school.

Fifteen minutes later, he was in the old catalpa tree, poised and ready, the rope coiled in his hand so it wouldn't catch on anything when he let it go. He heard the clatter of Demarco's bike before he saw him. Then he came into view, standing up as he pedaled to get over the little hill leading to the old tree.

Having bested the hill, Demarco settled into his seat and pedaled on. It was all happening so fast there was no time to think or anticipate. Ash let the rope go and the big log swung down.

When it hit Jimmy, his bicycle skittered off into the weeds. But Jimmy wasn't with it, because he was stuck on the spikes bristling from the log. The Jimmy-log swung up and then reversed direction, retracing its original arc until Jimmy's feet dragging on the ground brought it to a stop.

Ash watched from above for a few seconds to see what would happen next, but Jimmy just hung there, not moving.

Ash climbed down and looked at what he'd done. One spike had gone into Jimmy's head just above his ear. The one below was in his neck. The upper wound wasn't bleeding at all, but blood from his neck wound had already soaked his shirt all the way to the cuff on his sleeve. And it was still dribbling from around the spike.

Looking at him, Ash found the whole scene extremely interesting, like a white garter snake or a toad so flattened and dry on the road you could sail it like a Frisbee. It was already

too late to stop the TR taunting. That would continue no mat-
ter what he did. But Jimmy Demarco wouldn't ever do it
again, or hit a baseball or ride his bicycle or drink lemonade.
He had stopped Jimmy from doing all those things. He recog-
nized the severity of the punishment he had inflicted on
Jimmy, but felt no sorrow for the boy, because it had all been
Jimmy's fault.

LOOKING BACK ON it, sitting there against the Fairborns' house, Ash was amazed at how inept the county sheriff had been in his investigation of Jimmy's death. He had asked him a few questions along with all the other kids who knew Jimmy, but that was it. No one had even picked up on his lie about the erasers.

There'd been some kids knocking mailboxes over around that time, and everyone had come to believe that's who killed Jimmy. But the sheriff never figured out who *they* were either.

But that was all in the past. And now there was work to do. Ash got to his feet, pulled on a pair of rubber gloves from his pants pocket, and crept around to the back of the house.

CHAPTER 27

WHEN HE'D SEARCHED the house earlier in the evening, Ash had opened the door into the laundry room with a credit card . . . a credit card, for Christ's sake. So he couldn't help but think that Fairborn wasn't as smart as everybody said.

Gun in hand, he entered again through the same door. Guided by nightlights, he moved quietly through the kitchen and stepped into the carpeted hall that led to the study.

From his previous excursion through the house, he knew that the Fairborns' bedroom was to his right at the end of the hall. Before proceeding, he looked at their closed door to make sure it wasn't opening. Satisfied, he moved down the hall and went into the study, also dimly lit by a nightlight.

He went directly to the TV, which was still connected to the camcorder. Needing more illumination, he got out his penlight and played the beam over the area, looking for the tape.

Not there.

So it must still be in the camera. This was perfect. He'd been aware on his earlier visit that when the tape came up missing, it was likely Fairborn and Collins would realize why it had been stolen. And when they learned about the other job he had to do tonight, everybody would start digging harder. But he'd had no choice. He had to take the tape. But now, if he also took the camera, they might think it was just a simple burglary. He needed to be sure, though, that the tape really was in the camera.

Leaning closer, he examined the camera looking for . . .

There it was.

He put the penlight in his mouth and pressed the camera's eject button. With a gentle whirr and a tiny click, the tape compartment popped open. And there was the tape. Leaving it in place, he closed the compartment and unplugged the audio and video cables from the TV.

SAM FAIRBORN HAD always possessed a remarkably acute sense of hearing. And while certain of his other faculties had eroded with age, that had not. The very slight sound of the laundry room door opening had not awakened him, but it had brought him from a deep sleep to a shallow slumber. When the tape compartment on the camera opened, so did his eyes, and he sat up.

WITH THE CAMERA cradled in one hand, his gun in the other, and his penlight still in his mouth, Ash looked around for more to take, something small and visible so he wouldn't have to open a drawer or a cabinet.

IN THE BEDROOM, Fairborn listened for another noise, but he heard nothing. Nevertheless, he got out of bed, went to the closet, and got his shotgun. A shotgun was a great weapon for shooting rodents outside, but a clumsy one for defending yourself in the house. But it was all he had.

Always slow to wake, his wife slept on.

Sam went to the bedroom door, which was not latched, and slowly pulled it open, lifting the doorknob to lessen the chances of any hinge squeak. His finger on the shotgun's trigger, he looked into the hallway. Seeing no one, he moved into the hall and started toward the study.

WHEN HE'D BEEN in the house earlier, Ash had been thinking only of the tape and hadn't paid much attention to any-thing else. So he didn't have any memory of what he might steal in addition to the camera. Certainly nothing on the mantel looked valuable enough to promote the fiction that the camera had been taken in a routine burglary.

FAIRBORN GLANCED INTO the kitchen.

Nothing there.

He crept forward along the hallway and looked into the study.

Oh my God. His legs grew weak. There . . . over by the mantel. Someone *was* in the house.

Sam suddenly began to tremble. Conflicting thoughts barked for his attention.

If he shot into the study, the damage to the house from the blast would be horrendous. Better to warn the guy and hold him for the cops.

But he was probably armed. Warning him would give him an opportunity to shoot first. Sam remembered reading an article that said crooks always have the advantage in a showdown because law-abiding people hesitate to shoot. Crooks don't.

So he should just fire the damn gun.

But he might kill the guy. At the very least, he'd maim him. Could he do that?

Absolutely.

He raised the gun to aim it, but his elbow hit the wall behind him and the gun fired before he was ready, filling the house with a deafening blast.

CHAPTER 28

"DR. MCKEE, THIS is Chris Collins. I was there yesterday with Sam Fairborn, talking to Bill Lansden. Is Dr. Lansden feeling well enough today for us to came back?"

"I'm sorry, Dr. Collins, but Bill Lansden passed away last night."

Though Chris hadn't really known Lansden, having seen him alive just the day before, she was rocked by the news. "That's terrible. What happened?"

"His heart stopped and we couldn't get it going again. I'm sorry."

"I didn't think atrial fibrillation ever led to cardiac arrest."

"That wasn't the only heart problem he'd had in recent years."

"Was he married?"

"A widower, I believe."

"At least that keeps his death from destroying another life."

"It's sad, though, to die alone."

"He didn't have any relatives?"

"We found an aunt who's handling the funeral arrangements, but they apparently weren't close. If you'll excuse me, I'm being paged."

After hanging up, Chris sat for a moment reflecting on what McKee had said. Dying alone . . . It was more than sad, it was horrible to contemplate. To have your life mean so little that when you leave it, there's no one to hold your hand or stroke your brow. It was her worst fear, and the way she was going, far too likely a prospect.

Shaking off those thoughts, she dialed Sam Fairborn's number to tell him the news, but the line was busy.

Lansden dead. How were they going to get that name now? The CDC had more than eight thousand employees scattered all over the world. And Lansden was in Kazakhstan over a decade ago. Who else would know that name? If Lansden had been married, his wife might have known. Maybe Fairborn could come up with an idea.

She dialed his number again, but it was still busy.

Though it was hard to concentrate, she reviewed the hospital's infection reports for the last week, then tried Fairborn again.

Still busy. Probably on his computer surfing the net.

Wanting badly to discuss their next move with him, she decided to just drive out to his home. Perhaps it was the conversation with McKee about Lansden dying alone, or maybe it was simply that she hadn't spoken to Michael at all about Sam Fairborn and what he'd found. Whatever the reason, she paged Michael now, leaving the number of her cell phone.

Without waiting for him to respond, she headed for her car. He called back just as she slid behind the wheel.

"Hi, Chris. It's funny you should call. I was just thinking that we hadn't spoken for a couple days and needed to make contact."

"Some things have happened you should know about. Are you free to take a ride?"

"Sure."

"Where are you?"

"Monteagle, checking on one of my few remaining patients."

"I'll pick you up in twenty minutes out front."

On the way to Monteagle, Chris tried Fairborn's number again, but it was still busy.

Michael was waiting for her when she arrived. Despite the stress she was under, the sight of him lifted her spirits.

When he got in, he banged his knee on the dash.

"Sorry."

"I'm okay. Where are we going?" he asked, sliding his seat back.

"Ever heard of Sam Fairborn?"

"From the CDC? Sure."

For the next few miles Chris related what Fairborn had discovered, and their visit with Lansden.

"But when I called the hospital this morning, I learned that Lansden died last night."

"That is one weird story. And you think the Kazak virus is what killed our nurses and the others?"

"How could it not be involved? But Lansden said none of the blood and tissue samples he took in the field ever got to the States."

"What happened to them?"

"It was so hard to communicate with him we didn't even try to pursue that, but he indicated there was another man from the CDC in Kazakhstan with him. So we went after that name, thinking he'd be a lot easier to talk to. Lansden kept calling him Ember, but when we asked him if that was what he really meant, he said no. Or rather, he blinked no. When he spoke, he often used the wrong words."

"Was he married?"

"No. I thought of that, too."

"Maybe someone at the CDC who was there when Lansden was in Kazakhstan would remember who was with him. Or there could be some old records that would tell us."

"That's why we're going to see Fairborn. It's his territory. And he's someone you should meet anyway."

For the next couple of miles Michael quietly mulled over everything Chris had told him. Then he said, "Suppose we do find this guy. What could he possibly say that would explain what happened? If the samples never got to the States, they couldn't be the source of the virus that killed those people. Why does the lethal virus appear to be tied to the transplant virus? And why is your father still alive?"

"Can't answer your first two questions, but as for my father, we think the respiratory illness he had in New Mexico was a hanta infection. Antibodies to that organism probably protected him from the Kazak hanta."

"Ash could tell us if that's true."

"He's already working on it."

"Boy, I *have* been out of the loop."

"It wasn't intentional. There was just so much happening."

"It's okay."

"We better make sure Fairborn doesn't leave before we arrive. Get my cell phone out of my bag will you and call him. Just hit redial."

"He doesn't know we're coming?"

"His phone's been busy all morning."

And it was again.

"At least he's still there," Chris said.

Just before they reached the Fairborns' cottage, Chris realized it might be *Ann* on the phone or their computer and that Sam *could* be away. But no, their car was in the drive.

"Pretty place," Michael said as Chris pulled to a stop.

"He's a gardener."

They got out and Chris led the way to the porch, where she rang the bell. While they waited, a mockingbird in a flowering cherry showed them what he could do, his song setting his whole body in motion like a little bellows.

Chris rang the bell again.

"Hope he doesn't come to the door in his pajamas," Michael said.

"He doesn't strike me as a man who sleeps late."

They stood there for another minute, then Michael said, "Maybe the bell isn't working."

This time Chris knocked.

Still no answer.

"They could be out back," Chris said.

Michael followed her to the wrought iron gate that led to the rear of the house.

"Dr. Fairborn . . . it's Chris Collins. Are you there?"

But they heard only the buzz of a nearby bee.

"Dr. Fairborn?"

Chris opened the gate, went inside, and followed the brick walkway to the rear patio and garden. Seeing no one, she continued through the garden to the potting bench which, as Fairborn mentioned earlier, had recently been given a fresh coat of brown paint. But *he* wasn't there.

Michael walked back to the house and tried to look inside

through the drape over the sliding glass doors to the study. Unable to see anything, he knocked on the glass.

No answer.

He looked at Chris. "Let's try the phone again."

They went back out front and Chris gave that another try. "Still busy."

Michael scowled. "This is weird." He walked back onto the porch and tried the door.

It wasn't locked. He pushed the door open and put his head inside. "Dr. Fairborn . . . is anyone home?"

He went into the little foyer and started to call out again, but all he got out was "Doc—" for on the floor, where a hallway led to the left, he saw a slippered foot and part of a leg.

Thinking that Fairborn might have had a heart attack and was still alive, Michael rushed forward. When he saw the entire situation, he froze. Fairborn was lying on his left side, facing away from him. His scalp was torn into twin starbursts from two gunshots delivered with the muzzle of the gun so close to his head the gases had exploded the skin. There wasn't much blood associated with those wounds, but the front of his pajamas looked to be soaked with it. Behind Michael, from where she saw the body as clearly as he, Chris's legs grew weak.

Michael knelt and put a finger on Fairborn's neck to feel for a pulse, then quickly pulled back. "He's already cold. We need to call the police."

Chris looked into the study. Seeing a lot of damage over by the fireplace, she went inside to inspect it more closely.

"I don't think we should be doing that," Michael said.

Ignoring him, Chris surveyed the wreckage of a TV and a splintered magazine rack. "This looks like shotgun damage," she said. "He must have fired on whoever did that to him. But where's the gun?" Then she got an ugly premonition that things were even worse than they looked. "Oh God . . . his wife, Ann."

Chris backtracked to the hallway, tears glistening in her eyes. She looked at Fairborn's body, then stepped past it and went down the hall.

"Chris, don't go back there."

But again she paid no attention.

Seeing that the door at the end of the hall was standing

open, she went past the kitchen and entered the Fairborns' bedroom, where she saw with relief that there was no body on the bed. But the room had been ransacked—drawers pulled out, socks and underwear scattered over the carpet. On the floor was a small jewelry box, its contents apparently plundered except for an earring that lay nearby.

Where was Ann?

Chris moved toward the open closet door, afraid of what she might find inside, but unable to keep from looking. She stood for a second at the edge of the open door, then slowly leaned around it. And found what she feared she might: Ann Fairborn, sitting on the floor, back against the wall, blood trailing down her face from two obscene entry wounds in her forehead.

"Chris . . ." Michael touched her arm. "Really, we shouldn't be in here."

In shock over the brutality the Fairborns had suffered, Chris let him guide her from the room and out onto the porch.

"Why them?" she said.

"A chance occurrence," Michael replied. "Just shitty luck that the creep responsible chose this house."

"She was the *sweetest* woman. And he was unique, and so brilliant. This is monstrous."

"Let's go to the car, where you can sit down."

In the car, while Chris sat pitched forward, her head on the steering wheel, Michael dialed 911 on her cell phone.

"This is Dr. Michael Boyer. There's been a double murder at . . ." He glanced at the house number above the front door. "Sixteen twenty-three Parham Road."

"DID YOU KNOW that when a phone line is cut, outside callers get a busy signal?" Chris said, driving back to Atlanta after being detained at the Fairborn crime scene for over an hour by the county sheriff.

"First I heard of that was when the sheriff mentioned it."

"The line being busy . . . and their car in the drive . . . I thought it was just a normal day for them. I never expected . . . I don't ever want to go through anything like that again."

"It's not the best morning I ever spent either," Michael

agreed. "We seem to be surrounded by death . . . the five at Monteagle, that guy Lansden, and now this."

"What are you saying?"

"That it's a lot to bear. What did you think I meant?"

Chris didn't give him an answer and Michael didn't press her for one.

They drove for a while without talking, but Michael could tell Chris was thinking hard about something.

Then she said, "Do you have time for us to run by Emory Hospital?"

"I'm available. What are we doing?"

"I want to talk to Lansden's neurologist again about his death."

"Why?"

"I know this is probably off the wall, but think with me . . . The key to figuring out what happened to the Kazak virus samples is learning the name of the man who was there with Lansden. And I believe we could have done that today by getting Lansden to spell it a letter at a time, either by pointing to them on something or blinking yes or no as we recited the alphabet. But before we can get there, he dies."

"Okay, so?"

"While we were there the first time, they filmed the session. Before we left, Fairborn stole the tape, or at least borrowed it without asking."

"Did he tell you why?"

"No. But he must have believed he could learn something by reviewing it. And now *he's* dead. Suppose someone doesn't want the man who was with Lansden identified."

"I don't know what to say."

"I wonder what happened to that tape."

"You're suggesting Fairborn was killed just so someone could get their hands on it?"

"Isn't that possible?"

"I agree the odds are long on all this simply being the result of random events, but highly unlikely things happen all the time. And there's every indication the Fairborns were killed by a burglar—the missing shotgun, for example. That was certainly taken by the killer. And when we were in the study, I saw some floppy disks on his desk, but no computer. So that was probably taken, too."

"In the bedroom I did notice an emptied jewelry box with one earring the robber missed."

"There you go."

Chris lapsed back into thought. A few minutes later, as she changed lanes to avoid a slab of rubber from a shredded retread, she said, "Suppose the killer just took all those things to hide his real intent?"

"If that's true, someone could also be watching you."

CHAPTER 29

"HERE SHE IS," Chris said, seeing McKee get off the elevator in the Emory stroke unit shortly after they'd paged her.

"Dr. Collins, it's good to see you again."

She introduced Michael and the two shook hands.

"You know, a very peculiar thing happened yesterday," McKee said to Chris. "After you spoke with Dr. Lansden, I went to get the tape from the session, but it was gone."

"I'm sorry about that. Dr. Fairborn took it. He wanted to review it at home."

McKee was obviously irritated. "He should have requested a copy. I'd have been happy to provide it."

"It's all moot now. He and his wife were murdered last night."

McKee grew pale. "That's awful."

"I can't give you all the details, but his death following so closely on Dr. Lansden's makes me think the Fairborns were killed during an attempt to steal that tape. So my question to you is was Lansden's death suspicious in any way?"

"What do you mean?"

"Could it have been caused by someone?"

"There was nothing to suggest that."

"Have you arranged for an autopsy?"

"There was no need. And no one to pay for it."

"Where's the body?"

"I don't know. Maybe it's still here, maybe it's been transferred to a funeral home. That's not my area."

"I understand. Thanks for talking to us."

As McKee walked away, Michael said, "Boy, you really laid it on her."

"I didn't know how else to make her really think about the circumstances of Lansden's death."

She dug in her bag for her cell phone.

"Let me guess, you're calling the medical examiner."

"I want *his* opinion on what killed Lansden."

Hugh Monroe was appropriately skeptical of what Chris told him, but more importantly, he agreed to locate the body and have it transported to the morgue so he could perform the autopsy she wanted.

"Okay," Chris said, putting her phone away. "Let's go see if Ash has the hanta antibody results on my father's blood."

WHEN THEY REACHED the Monteagle virology lab, one of Ash's lab techs said he'd already gone to lunch. After what they'd seen at the Fairborns', neither Chris nor Michael felt like eating, so they bypassed the serving lines in the cafeteria and went directly to the seating area, where they saw Ash sitting with Carter Dewitt and Henry Bechtel, VP for legal affairs.

"I don't want to talk in front of those other men," Chris said.

"I'll go over and arrange for us to meet Ash in his office when he's finished here."

"No, wait, Bechtel's leaving . . . So's Dewitt."

They headed for Ash on a route that would put a couple of tables between them and the two VPs when they passed, a distance that required only a nod of acknowledgment.

Watching them heading his way, Ash wondered if Chris had heard about Fairborn yet. She was wearing a serious expression and her eyes looked a little red. He needed to be careful now. She was probably going to ask him about the hanta antibody test on her father.

He'd been thinking about how to handle that and it seemed best to just admit the truth. If he lied and she became suspicious, she could draw a fresh sample from Wayne and take it elsewhere for testing. What a screw-up that had been. Boyer had told everybody at that first meeting Wayne had some kind of respiratory illness when he'd lived in New Mexico. He should have paid more attention.

"You're not eating?" he said, when Chris and Michael reached him.

"We saw some things this morning that dulled our appetites," Michael said, pulling out a chair and sitting down.

Chris did the same.

"What do you mean?"

Chris told him about the murders, Lansden's death, and the tape Fairborn took. "Michael thinks the Fairborns were killed by a burglar who had nothing to do with Lansden. But I'm not so sure. I'm wondering if the killer was after that tape."

"What did the police think?" Ash asked.

"I haven't told them any of this. I didn't think about it until they let us go and we were on the road home."

"And you haven't called them?"

"It could just be my imagination. I'm at least going to wait until I hear what the ME finds when he does the autopsy on Lansden."

An autopsy.

This was something Ash hadn't expected. While Lansden was sleeping, he'd plunged a syringe into the injection port of his IV and slipped him a bolus of potassium chloride, a common substance that would stop his heart. And untraceable in an autopsy. So there was nothing to worry about there. But this whole enterprise was getting very treacherous.

"I don't mean to sound like I'm pushing you," Chris said. "But have you finished those hanta antibody tests on my father's blood?"

"Got the results about an hour ago." Then, even though it was just going to add to his problems, he said, "That infection he had in New Mexico clearly must have been hanta."

"So Fairborn was right," Chris said.

"And I've got some other news. Michael, you particularly are probably not going to be happy about this, but you saw Bechtel and Dewitt just leave . . . Before lunch they came to my lab and picked up all the blood and tissue samples from everybody associated with Wayne's transplant. Said they'd sold the rights to the therapeutic virus to some pharmaceutical company. Under the terms of the sale, I'm to have nothing more to do with the virus."

"Did you get it sequenced?" Michael asked.

"Unfortunately, I've encountered significant problems with that, so it's still undone."

Michael scowled. "Who bought the rights?"

"They didn't tell me."

"How can they take all that material out of the public domain?" Michael said. "What happened here has stopped xeno-transplantation plans all over the country. We have to know exactly what occurred."

Ash threw up his hands. "Hey, don't kill the messenger."

When he lifted his hands, Chris saw something that shocked her. On the side of his right wrist, where he obviously hadn't noticed it, was a smear of brown paint, the same color as the paint that was on Sam Fairborn's ear the day before he was murdered.

Wanting to get out of there, Chris reached for her pager and looked at the display as though a call had come in.

"I've got to go. Eric, thanks for the news. Michael, would you drive me back to Good Samaritan?" Without giving him a chance to remind her that they'd come to Monteagle in her car, she walked off.

Puzzled, Michael came after her.

"Chris, what were you talking about back there? You drove us—"

"Not here."

Michael followed her into the hall, where she took him to a corner that would allow them to talk privately.

"Ash has paint on his wrist the same color as the potting table Sam Fairborn painted yesterday before he was killed. With the cool temperatures we've been having, that painted table might not have been completely dry last night."

"You think Ash—"

"I don't know what to think except I'm running into too many coincidences to believe they're all unrelated."

"But I've known Ash for years."

"What does he do in his spare time?"

Michael thought a moment. "I don't know."

"Where did he grow up?"

"You've made your point."

"I wonder if he ever worked at the CDC . . . say about twelve years ago."

"Let's go up to Human Resources and see if we can get a copy of his CV. They must have one on file."

IN THE CAFETERIA, Ash was concerned about the way Chris had abruptly cut off their conversation. She'd said she was paged, but there was something about the way she glanced at the display; looking toward it, but not *at* it. If he could roll back the weeks, he would, and this time he'd ignore the opportunity that had been dangled in front of him. But that wasn't possible. He'd made his decision and now he'd just have to play it through. But Chris Collins had better watch her step.

DEANNA HUNT, THE director of Human Resources, made no attempt to hide her interest in Michael. It was in her eyes, her posture, and the way she touched him when she spoke. It irritated Chris. And the fact that it irritated her, irritated her even more. She had no claim on Michael, so why did she care if this woman was acting like a whore?

"You just wait right here," Deanna said, "and I'll get you a copy of that CV." As she left her office, her eyes raked Chris with a cold look.

Unschooled in the rules of feminine warfare, Michael had no idea Deanna had just thrown the gauntlet at Chris's feet.

"Nice office," Michael said. "Wonder where she got that." He gestured at the wall behind Deanna's desk where she'd hung a long fabric tube that appeared to have been woven from old burlap bags and had colored knitting needles sticking out all over it.

"I hear the Georgia psychiatric hospital has an arts program," Chris said.

Michael was still trying to figure out if she was serious about that when Deanna returned.

She gave him a stapled set of papers and a big smile. "Did you notice I didn't even ask why you wanted this?"

"Chris and I have a little bet about how many publications he has."

Deanna turned to Chris. "Doctors at play. How interesting."

"I guess we better go and take a look at this," Michael said. "Thanks for the help."

"If you ever need me, you know where I am."

In the hall, Chris muttered, "If you ever need me, you know where I am."

"What?"

"Nothing. Let's go to your office and take a look at that CV."

"BORN IN CLAYTON, Alabama," Chris said.

"Sounds small and remote," Michael said.

"Undergraduate degree from the University of Alabama, Ph.D. in molecular biology and virology from Cal Tech. One post-doc at the University of Chicago, another in Germany. Four years on the faculty at Florida State, another three at Iliad Pharmaceuticals, then he came here. No mention of any stint at the CDC." She flipped the page and scanned the contents. "And a really impressive list of publications in the best journals, including three in *Science* and two in *Nature*. You just can't *get* in those journals."

"I knew he was good. If he wasn't at the CDC, then I guess he wasn't the one in Kazakhstan with Lansden."

"I don't know . . ."

"What's the big picture here? Let's say Ash *was* with Lansden and that he has the samples of the Kazak virus . . ."

"Keep going."

"Did he accidentally infect the people who died with it and now he's trying to cover up his involvement?"

"How could this accident have occurred?"

Michael shrugged. "I've gone as far as I can."

"I can't take it any further either, but it could be something like that. In any event, we should tell the police about that paint."

"What if we're wrong? We don't know it's the *same* paint."

"If it's not, there's no damage done."

"It could embarrass one of our colleagues. And you have

to admit we're just groping in the dark here. And think about this. If he's responsible for infecting the dead with Kazak hanta, wouldn't he have lied about the anti-hanta tests on your father? By telling you that Wayne has those antibodies in his blood, he provided support for Fairborn's theory."

Chris thought about that a moment, then said, "He didn't have much choice. If we ever decided to get a second opinion with a fresh sample, we'd not only learn the truth then, but would know he lied."

"On the other hand, if we got different results on a second test, he could just say he made a mistake due to deteriorated reagents, something like that."

"As good a virologist as he is, he'd always run positive controls to prove the reagents were working. We have to tell the police about that paint."

Michael raised his hands in resignation. "Make the call."

CHAPTER 30

DETECTIVE LENIHAN FROM the Fayette County sheriff's office was a big man with a square head and an equally rectilinear body, so that he reminded Chris of a refrigerator with a TV sitting on it. She and Michael were meeting him at a restaurant about a mile from Monteagle to make sure no one saw them together. Because it was too late for lunch and too early for dinner, they had the place practically to themselves.

Chris had thought that detectives were supposed to have poker faces, but Lenihan's skepticism at her story had been plainly visible in *his* from the moment they'd met, so she wasn't surprised when he said, "To be frank with you, Dr. Collins, this isn't what I'd call a hot lead. This guy Ash . . . how could he even know that Fairborn had a tape of the interview with the man who had the stroke? Did you tell him?"

"No, but he knew we were going over there. Maybe he went to Fairborn's home that night to talk to him about it and learned then of its existence. The tape's missing, isn't it?"

"We haven't finished our inventory of the home's contents yet. But I'll tell you what, that paint on Ash's wrist isn't going to stay there long, so I'll just drive over to Monteagle and see it for myself, maybe take a sample for comparison with what's on the potting table. Where would I find this guy?"

Chris gave him directions to the virology lab, then said, "Will you let us know what you think after you talk to him?"

"I don't know. We'll see."

LENIHAN STEPPED ONTO the elevator in the Monteagle lobby and pressed the button for the sixth floor with the knuckle of his right hand so he wouldn't be touching hospital germs with his finger. Damn bugs should be visible, he thought as the doors closed and the elevator started to move.

Sneaky little shits . . . He inspected the floor and walls of the elevator, wondering if he was riding with whatever killed those people here. And wouldn't you know Ash would be the director of the virology lab . . . That's gotta be one of the *worst* places in the whole hospital.

The elevator stopped on the second floor and Lenihan was joined by a nurse and her patient, a comatose-looking old man on a gurney. The only thing that kept Lenihan from bolting into the hall and taking another elevator was the belief that real men don't do such things.

IN HIS OFFICE, Ash still couldn't concentrate. What had made Chris Collins leave the lunch table so abruptly? He thought back to their conversation.

They'd been talking about Scott selling the rights to the transplant virus and Boyer had complained about it. In response, he'd said, "Don't kill the messenger," and he'd thrown up his hands.

That's when Collins left.

Ash looked at the palms of his hands, then turned them and . . . *What the hell was that?*

Paint.

Where did that come from? Is that what Collins reacted to? Was there a chance he'd bumped into something freshly painted last night at the Fairborns'?

Damn.

He got up and went into the lab through the rear door of his office. He crossed the lab, without speaking to either of the techs he passed, and stepped up to a chemical cabinet, where he took down a bottle of acetone. Grabbing a box of Kimwipes, he carried everything to a nearby sink.

LENIHAN STEPPED OFF the elevator on the sixth floor, looked briefly at the sign on the wall pointing to the virology lab, and walked that way.

ASH SCRUBBED AT the brown paint on his wrist with a wad of Kimwipes soaked in acetone. Slowly, the stain gave ground. He turned the wipes to a fresh area and went after a particularly stubborn spot, rubbing until his skin reddened.

There . . . finished. He washed the used wipes under some running water so the acetone wouldn't dissolve the plastic wastebasket liner, then he tossed them away.

On his way back to his office after washing the acetone from his hands, he saw a heavyset man in street clothes come into the lab and approach the clerk at the counter. They spoke briefly, then the clerk turned and said, "Dr. Ash, there's someone here to see you."

Ash walked to the counter.

"Doctor, I'm Tony Lenihan. May we speak privately?"

"About what?"

"Privately?" Lenihan repeated.

Ash pointed to Lenihan's left. "That's my office. Just go on in and I'll be there shortly."

Ash had chosen to enter his office by the back door to give himself a few seconds to think about who this guy might be. With all that had been happening recently, he had to wonder if Lenihan was a cop.

Was he here to arrest him . . . take him away in cuffs in front of the staff . . . through the hospital like some freak on display? Ash's mind went back to the day Jimmy Demarco had first taunted him. "T R-ash, T R-ash . . . If you want him, he'll be there in a flash, cause he's T R-ash." Then the others had joined in: "T R-ash . . . T R-ash."

The voices raged in his brain.

He would never allow himself to be humiliated like that again, *never*.

But he could see no alternative to going into his office. If he ran, it would be an admission of guilt. And they'd surely catch him.

But maybe he's not a cop. He could be anybody. Just calm down and talk to him.

Ash entered his office by the rear door and found Lenihan studying his picture of Ebola, the office door shut to ensure the privacy he'd requested.

"What's that?" Lenihan asked, referring to the picture.

"One of the most dangerous viruses on earth."

Lenihan shivered. "Don't know how you work around these things."

"Carefully," Ash said, forcing himself to grin amiably.

Lenihan returned the smile. "I'm a detective with the Fayette County sheriff's office . . ."

Ash's heart quickened, but he made sure his face remained calm.

"Do you know a man named Sam Fairborn?" Lenihan asked.

"By reputation, certainly, but we've never met. I heard he and his wife were killed last night. Terrible. What happened?"

"I can't discuss it."

"I understand. What brings you here?"

"I wonder if you'd do me a favor? It's going to sound kind of strange, but I'd appreciate it."

"What?"

"Do this with your right hand." Lenihan put his hand out and rotated it slowly back and forth.

Worried that this might be a ploy so Lenihan could snap the cuffs on him, Ash hesitated.

"Please," Lenihan prodded.

Seeing no cuffs in Lenihan's possession, Ash did what he asked.

"Great. Thank you. And now the left."

Having survived it once, Ash now willingly repeated the maneuver.

"Excellent. The things we detectives need to ask . . . I just have one more question for you. And please don't read anything into this. It's just a question I have to ask everybody I talk to for my records. It's like department policy. Whether it's appropriate or not, I gotta ask. Where were you last night between seven P.M. and two A.M.?"

"At home. I read until about ten, then went to bed."

"I didn't see a wedding ring, so I guess you were alone?"

"Yes."

"I love a good book. What were you reading?"

"*Gerald's Game*, by Stephen King."

"Oh yeah, that one where the wolf eats the guy's body while the wife is handcuffed to the bed. I read that, too."

"It wasn't a wolf. It was a stray dog."

"That's right, a dog. Grisly book, but good. Okay, that's it. I won't take any more of your time. Have a good rest of the day. And . . ." He pointed at the Ebola picture. "Watch out for the little things."

What a fiasco, Lenihan thought, heading for the elevators. *I got a double homicide to solve and I'm over here chasing my ass.*

WITH THE DETECTIVE gone, Ash's legs grew rubbery and he dropped into his chair. There was no doubt in his mind that Lenihan had been looking for paint on his hands. And him saying the dog in *Gerald's Game* was a wolf—it was a test to see if he'd lied about being home last night reading.

A detective right in his office.

And there could only be one person responsible for that.

CHRIS AND MICHAEL would never forget the Fairborn murder scene, but by the time they'd spoken to Lenihan, a translucent membrane was already growing over its memory, obscuring the brittle clarity of the moment, so that they'd remained behind in the restaurant to at least try to eat something. They were just finishing when Chris saw Lenihan come through the front door and head their way.

"Did you see him?" Chris asked when he reached the table.

"Ordinarily I wouldn't do this, but as I was driving back this way I saw the white Porsche was out front, so I figured you were still here."

"How'd you know the car was mine?" Michael asked.

Lenihan lowered his chin and looked at Michael through the tops of his eyes.

"Right," Michael said. "You're a detective."

Lenihan sat down. "I saw no paint on his wrist or his hands."

"But there *was*," Chris said.

"That doesn't help me."

"Did you ask him where he was last night?"

"He was home alone, reading."

"So he has no alibi."

"For someone who lives alone, having no alibi for a given period of time is the default position. It's what you'd expect."

"So why'd you ask?"

"Habit, I guess. My point here is that there's no reason for me to think about this guy anymore."

"You're not serious."

"I don't joke about murder. There's no proof he was at the scene and he has no motive."

"I gave you a motive."

"What you told me was a hypothesis you'd strung together from a lot of guesswork. That's not a motive."

"You aren't even going to try to find out if he was in Kazakhstan with Lansden?"

"It's effort and time I can't afford. But thanks for the call."

When Lenihan was out of earshot, Chris said, "Where were you in that conversation? I could have used a little help."

"That wasn't a mind looking to be changed."

"I suppose you're right."

"And maybe the paint on Ash *wasn't* from Fairborn's table."

"Ever heard of epidemiologist's itch?"

"Sounds like something you'd get in the jungle."

"It's the intuitive ability all good epidemiologists have to assemble apparently disparate facts into a cohesive hypothesis that will lead to the truth."

"And you've got that itch about Ash."

"I definitely do. You've got an internet hookup in your office, haven't you?"

"Yes."

"Let's go back there. I want to look up some people on the CDC website, see if they're still on staff and if one of them can help us learn who was with Lansden in Kazakhstan."

FIFTEEN MINUTES LATER, with Chris working at his computer, Michael said, "I'll be right back. I'm going to make a pit stop."

He left and walked down the hall toward the men's room.

Three doors ahead, Robin Victor, the transplant team's psychiatrist, came out of his office.

"Michael, how goes it?"

"My practice is still suffering fallout from that transplant virus mess."

"Mine, too. People don't even want to come to *this* building. I may have to move. But I'm going to give it a few more weeks and see what happens. Did you hear that Scott sold the marketing rights to the transplant virus?"

"I know. And he took all the blood and tissue samples away from Ash so we can't do any more work on the organism. Under the circumstances, I'm surprised any company would want to get involved. The development costs to bring this thing to market will be prohibitive . . . *if* it's even possible. I wonder who it was."

"I heard it was a small firm in New Jersey, Iliad Pharmaceuticals, I think."

Iliad . . .

That name . . .

Forgetting for the moment the reason he'd come into the hall, Michael left Victor and returned to his office, where Chris was just finishing the call she'd planned to make.

"Thanks, Larry, I'll be waiting to hear from you." She hung up and looked at Michael. "I found someone at the CDC who'll help us, but he can't promise results."

"What was the name of that pharmaceutical house Ash worked for just before coming to Monteagle?"

Chris picked up Ash's CV and looked for the pertinent entry.

"Iliad," she said.

"You know all those coincidences you mentioned a few minutes ago? Here's another one. Robin Victor just said the development rights to the transplant virus were sold to Iliad."

"That *can't* be a random event."

"But what does it mean?"

"I don't know. Let's see what we can find out about Iliad on the net."

"I ran into Victor before I made it to where I was headed, so I'm going to try again."

As Michael left, Chris typed Lycos.com into the URL address box on the internet browser and hit the return key. When the site was loaded, she typed in Iliad Pharmaceuticals and initiated the search.

The first hit was the Iliad home page.

Over the next few minutes she got a quick profile of the company, which was located in Newark, New Jersey. In existence for only twenty-three years, its primary income appeared to be from two cholesterol-lowering drugs whose names she didn't recognize and an antibiotic she rarely used because of its potential side effects. The company also sold surgical dressings impregnated with an agent that promoted wound healing.

Having a feel for the company now, she returned to the first page of the site and studied the picture of the CEO. Paul Danner was blond and not bad looking. But, appearing to be in his mid-forties, he was pushing the age limit on his chosen hair style—casual and loose with a faint part down the middle. He was wearing a smug expression that made him look like a guy who enjoyed firing people. From Danner's stated tenure as CEO, he'd been in that position when Ash worked there.

Feeling that she'd learned all she could from the corporate site, Chris went back to the list of hits the search engine had produced.

The fifth entry caught her attention: "Drug Industry Rogues." She clicked on the link.

The page loaded quickly. Under the same title that had drawn her there, an additional line explained the site's content: "Certain drug companies in the U.S. have a history of unethical and sometimes illegal behavior. Below are the worst offenders."

The second company on the list was Iliad. Among the six cited offenses they'd committed was manipulating clinical trial data to downgrade reported side effects of one of their cholesterol drugs. In another instance, they'd paid a large fine for submitting falsified efficacy data to the FDA to get approval for a hepatitis C vaccine. The accounts of the company's various offenses were written in the style of tabloid exposés, in which Paul Danner's name often appeared. But there was no mention of Ash. The fraudulent nature of the hep C data had been brought to the FDA's attention by Frieda Sepanski, a company employee involved in drafting their FDA reports.

The door opened and Michael returned.

"Look at this," Chris said. "Iliad is on a list of drug companies with a history of unethical conduct. During the time Ash was there, they were slapped with a big fine for falsifying data on a hep C vaccine."

"Scott better hope their check clears."

"There's no mention of Ash in the article about the vaccine, but I wonder if he was involved."

"Maybe that's why he left: *He* was the one who cooked the results."

"If that's what happened, I'd think his references from Iliad would be lousy. And Monteagle wouldn't have touched him. Actually, Iliad had similar troubles even before Ash joined them."

"Even so, I'd sure like to know more about that hep C situation."

"Me, too. I wonder . . ."

"What?"

"The name of the woman who blew the whistle on the hep C data is mentioned in the article. I wonder if she'd talk to us."

Chris went to the AT&T web site and clicked on the white page directory. She entered Sepanski and Newark in the appropriate blanks, chose New Jersey in the state list, and waited for the search.

It found only two Sepanskis, a Joseph N. and a Delano S.

Chris looked at Michael. "Do you mind if I call from here?"

"I think I can afford it."

The call to Joseph N. was answered on the third ring by a man.

"May I speak to Frieda, please?"

"You've got the wrong number," the man said. "That's my daughter-in-law."

"Is she at . . ." Chris recited the other number.

"That's her."

"Sorry to bother you." Chris hung up and looked at Michael. "Fifty-fifty chance of getting the right one and I lose—typical."

Her second call rang four times and raised only a machine. She hung up without leaving a message.

"I'll try again later."

ASH PACED IN front of the convenience store's outdoor pay phone, hoping he'd get his call before someone else wanted to use it. As he walked, he replayed once more his movements at the Fairborn house.

He'd worn gloves, so he couldn't have left any prints. With the Fairborns both dead, he'd been free to take a lot of stuff to make it look like a bungled burglary, all of which was now at the bottom of Lake Lanier. The gun he'd used was under three feet of dirt. He'd brushed away the tire tracks he'd made when he'd brought his car to the house to load the things he'd taken, and he'd thrown away all the clothes he'd worn, including the shoes. So there was no possibility they could prove he was there.

Still, there shouldn't have been any way for that paint to get on his wrist either, but it had.

Thinking about all this made him so edgy that when the phone rang, it startled him. He hurried to the phone and picked up the receiver. "Ash."

Hearing the voice he'd expected, he said, "I've got a situation here I can't handle myself."

He went on to explain the nature of his problem. "So this needs to be addressed as soon as possible." He listened to the voice on the other end for a moment and said, "You *know* what I mean . . . Look, you could have opted out when I first brought the idea to you, but you didn't. Now get on the truck or it'll run over you as well as me, never doubt that . . . Ask around for a name. It's New Jersey, for Christ's sake, how hard could it be to find someone? Just be careful who you talk to. I'll take a digital photo of her and send it to you. Of *course* I won't send it by computer. I'll overnight it by FedEx. Then you have to move fast."

CHAPTER 31

"FRIEDA SEPANSKI, PLEASE."

"This is she."

Finally . . . Chris had called twice the night after her first attempt in Michael's office and had tried again three times today. "Mrs. Sepanski, my name is Chris Collins. I'm a physician in Atlanta and I'd like to talk to you about Eric Ash, who I believe was employed by Iliad Pharmaceuticals when you were there."

"Why are you calling *me*?"

"Because you were the one who reported the company to the FDA for falsifying their hepatitis vaccine data. And I was hoping you might know if Ash was involved."

There was silence at the other end.

"Mrs. Sepanski . . ."

"That was a long time ago."

"I know, but surely you remember the details."

"That's not what I meant. Why do you want to dredge all that up again?"

"Believe me, I wouldn't be interested if it wasn't very important."

"That part of my life is over. I don't want to relive it."

"Could you just tell me if Ash was involved?"

"Take my advice and stay away from him."

"Why?"

"I've said too much already. I'm sorry, I can't help you."

The line went dead.

Chris hung up and reflected on what Frieda Sepanski had said. There was clearly a lot she could tell about Ash, but for some reason, she was afraid. Something must have happened to her after she'd blown the whistle on Iliad. All this convinced Chris even more that Ash was involved in the Fairborn murders. But as Michael would say, "What's the big picture here?" And what to make of Lansden's death? The autopsy had found nothing suspicious. Maybe it *was* simply a coincidence of timing. It would have helped a lot if her CDC contact had been able to find out who had been in Kazakhstan with Lansden, but he hadn't. Needing to clear her head, she left her apartment and went to her car.

FORTY MINUTES LATER, Chris pulled to a stop at the entrance to Stone Mountain Park and rolled down her window. As usual, on weeknights, Bill Spain was on duty.

"Hello, Dr. Chris," Spain said, coming out of his kiosk. "How are you?"

"I've been better, Bill."

"Heard about all the trouble you been havin' at that hospital. How's that goin'?"

"No new cases for several days, so I think it's over, but keep your fingers crossed for us."

He showed her one gnarled hand, his long index and middle fingers overlapped. "I'll do that." His other hand held the customary bottle of apple juice, which he gave her without comment. "It's been on the cool side here the last few nights, but I see you're wearin' a jacket, so you should be fine."

"I'm sure I will. Have a good one."

Chris had not noticed that a black Chrysler had been following her since she'd left her apartment building's parking lot. When she was about fifty yards into the park, that car stopped at the entrance kiosk, where the driver paid Bill the admission fee and told him to keep the change.

It was still early in the year and the park roads were as deserted as usual. Then a pair of headlights appeared behind

Chris. She much preferred making the short drive to the mountaintop service road without the intrusion of any other vehicles. But at least she was in the lead, so if there was any wildlife by the roads, she'd be the one to see it. And a few seconds later, she did spot a rabbit that darted off into the woods.

When her lights picked up the old familiar oak tree she used for a landmark, she slowed the car. Just beyond the tree, she turned onto the unmarked service road. When she reached the gate and got out to open it, she saw the black car pass the service road and keep going.

IN THE BLACK car, Earl Garland, freshly in from New Jersey, was assessing the situation. He'd come to Atlanta to kill Chris, but after seeing her picture, he'd decided that a long-range shot to the head with his sniper's rifle would be wasting a valuable resource. Exploit the resource, then kill her, was the way he looked at it.

Of course, this meant a considerable increase in risk, but it was the old cost-benefit ratio. And to Earl, the benefits in this case clearly outweighed the cost, especially if, as he suspected, she was a natural redhead.

Figuring he'd gone far enough, he pulled off the road onto a service path and put the car in neutral. He didn't know where that side road she'd taken went, but as deserted as this place was, if he followed her onto it, she'd probably become suspicious.

He waited a couple of minutes, then backed onto the pavement and returned to the road the pigeon had taken. When he reached the gate, he stopped to think.

Where did this thing lead? He could see in his headlights that beyond the gate, the road rose steeply. Was this the service road to the top of the mountain? If so, what was up there?

He always liked to have a second escape route, but this looked like it could be the only way up. All his experience told him to leave it alone, pick another time and place. But that red hair . . .

ON THE MOUNTAINTOP, sitting in her favorite niche in the granite, Chris sat looking over the lights of Atlanta, wondering what to do about Frieda Sepanski. Maybe she should call her again. Probably wouldn't do any good, though. The woman would likely just hang up.

Then her mind turned to the Fairborns, and a thought like fingernails against a blackboard clamored for her attention. If Ash did kill the Fairborns to get that tape, those deaths, too, were on her head, because if she had never contacted Fairborn, he and his wife would still be—

Her thoughts were interrupted by the sound of a car. Turning and looking up, she saw the mountaintop bathed in light. She heard the car stop. A door opened and closed. Someone stepped into view.

"Excuse me, miss," a man's voice said. "This part of the park is closed."

Chris stood up. Though it was difficult to see much about the man because he was standing in the glow of his car headlights, he appeared to be dressed in jeans and a leather jacket.

"It's all right," she said. "I'm Chris Collins. I used to work at the park and I have permission to be up here."

"If you're accustomed to visiting places like this at night, I hope you're carrying something to protect yourself."

"I have a little mace canister on my key ring. But I've been coming up here for years and have never had a problem."

"Would you mind showing me some identification please?"

Chris left the ledge where she was sitting and made her way up to where he was waiting.

"My bag is in my car." She gestured to her car and started toward it. Suddenly, the man grabbed her from behind and she felt something cold against her neck just below her chin.

"Stay calm or I'll bleed you out," he hissed into her ear. "Where are your car keys?"

This can't be happening, Chris thought. This wasn't Metropolitan Boulevard. It was *safe* up here. And always had been.

But it *was* happening and she was so scared she couldn't remember where her keys were.

The arm across her chest tightened. "Keys."

Where *were* they?

She remembered. "My jacket," she croaked, her voice unrecognizable.

"Remove them slowly and throw them on the ground."

Chris reached into her right pocket and found the keys.

"Slowly," he reminded her. "If I feel your muscles tense, I'll slit your throat."

She removed the keys and held them up so he could see them. "I'm going to throw them now."

"Just with your wrist."

She flicked her wrist, sending her keys and her mace canister jangling to the pavement.

"Now drop your pants."

No, not that, her brain howled. She'd once lost control of her car on an icy patch and had believed she was about to hit another car head-on. Until now, that was the most frightened she'd ever been.

But this was worse.

Far worse.

And knowing that, her heart, her breathing, her brain, every system in her body, deserted her, unwilling to be a witness to this.

"I'm not a patient man," he said, sliding the knife slightly against her skin. The resulting flow of warm blood forced her senses back to work. She undid her belt and her zipper and let her pants drop to her ankles, allowing the cool night air to assault her skin.

"All the way off."

Holding the heels down with the opposite foot, she slid out of her cross trainers and stepped out of her pants.

"Now your panties."

Unable to do otherwise, she followed his order . . . and stood there on the top of Stone Mountain half-naked.

He began pulling her toward her car, dragging her so fast her feet scraped the asphalt. Reaching her car, he pushed her facedown onto the hood. Most of her mind tried once more to board a ship for distant ports, but a tiny part of it resisted. And that opposition spread, so she was soon able to think.

"Now I want you to turn over," Garland said. "I'm going to remove the knife from your throat so you can do that. But if you make any sudden moves, I *will* cut you."

She felt the knife withdraw.

"Slowly now . . . *very* slowly," he said.

She turned onto her back and finally saw his face—an ordinary face, not that of a monster. And she knew then, because he'd made no attempt to hide his identity, that after he raped her, he planned to kill her. Eyes glittering in the penumbra of his car's headlights, he stared at her coppery triangle.

"I knew it," he said. He unzipped his pants, freed himself, and leaned onto her, the knife again at her throat.

In the instant before the act began, she knew what she had to do. Her hand slid into her jacket pocket and her fingers curled around the small bottle of juice she hadn't yet opened. She'd only have one chance, so she had to make it count.

He was so occupied he didn't sense the movement of her arm as she pulled the bottle from her pocket and raised it as far as she could. Pouring all her fear into the stroke, she brought the bottle down, bottom first, in a powerful arc onto the back of his head. A breaking egg sensation ran up her arm, and without making a sound, Garland went limp on top of her.

Wanting to howl and beat her chest like an alpha gorilla, she shoved his knife hand away from her, disarmed him, and pushed him aside so he rolled off her and cascaded to the asphalt.

She got off the hood and put her foot heavily on the front of Garland's neck. "Now who's got the upper hand, asshole."

Having taking the edge off her need to gloat, she grabbed her clothes and pulled them on. She scooped up her keys, hurried around to the driver's side of her car, and with a shaking hand, jammed the key in the lock. She wrenched the door open, tossed the knife onto the passenger seat, and threw herself behind the wheel. Quickly, she locked herself in.

From the moment she'd taken her foot off Garland's neck, her goal had been to just get dressed and get out of there. Now, as her car's engine roared to life and she pulled on the lights, she hesitated.

How easy it would be to put it in drive "by mistake" and run over this bastard as a parting gift. Resting on the transmission lever, her hand quivered with the desire to do that.

But she couldn't, for she'd spent too many years saving lives to so easily take one—if he was even still alive.

She yanked the transmission into reverse, made a tight turn, and headed for the service road, her right hand digging in her bag for her cell phone. Finding the phone by touch, she slowed under a light pole so she could locate the button for the preset number of the park police.

"This is Chris Collins, I've been assaulted on the mountaintop and you need to send someone up here. No . . . he's unconscious, but I'm not staying here. I'm coming down to the station house." She hit the disconnect button and headed for the service road.

A few seconds later, as she entered the mouth of the road, she looked in the mirror and the joy of survival she'd felt a moment earlier was tainted by the sight of Garland barreling toward her in his car.

The slope of the road was steep and could not be traversed safely at high speed. Nevertheless, she poured on the gas.

For a couple of swift heartbeats, the road's sharp descent hid the pursuing car from view, then it popped into sight, still coming fast. The only illumination of the pavement was her headlights, which, even on high, didn't let Chris see far enough ahead to feel comfortable. And the thin metal rails lining the road were flashing by at a disturbing rate. One mistake at this speed and she'd be into those rails and probably through them into the abyss beyond.

She was going far too fast, but she didn't want her assailant to catch her. She had no idea what he intended and didn't want to find out.

Too fast. Damn it, this wasn't good.

But the car behind was slowly getting closer.

The gate below . . . It was closed. What would she do when she reached it? She couldn't get out and open it. Her eyes strained to see beyond the limits of her lights. Where the hell were the park police?

As worried as she was about the car behind, she couldn't make herself go any faster. She began to reason with herself. He just wants to escape, that's all. If he catches up, he'll simply pass on by and it'll be over.

Behind her, the pursuing vehicle was only a few car lengths back. It swung into the adjacent lane.

And still Chris didn't see any sign of the cops.

The headlights of the other car pulled even with her rear bumper.

THE SEEPAGE FROM Garland's head wound had now stopped and the blood in his hair was beginning to clot. But it still felt like someone was using his brain as a polo ball. His eyesight was fine, though, and his hands were steady. He pressed the button that controlled the passenger window and it disappeared into the door, letting in a hurricane. He picked up the automatic in his lap and got ready, aware that he'd have only one shot.

He knew he should be concentrating only on escape, but the bitch had hurt him, and now she had to pay.

CHRIS GLANCED QUICKLY to the left and saw that the black car was nearly even with her, but it was dark inside it, so she didn't see the gun.

JUST A SECOND or two more, Garland thought.

CHAPTER 32

SEE, HE JUST wants to pass and get away safely, Chris thought. *So just ease up on the gas and let him by,* that same voice urged. Then another, more suspicious quarter was heard from. *You nearly killed him. He has to be upset about that. What if he's got a gun and when your window is lined up with his . . .?*

Her foot came off the gas and hit the brakes.

THERE WAS NO doubt in Garland's mind the instant before he fired that the upholstery in Chris's car was about to be decorated with little pieces of her brain. But as the gun bucked in his hand, her car was suddenly yanked backward.

THE GLASS BESIDE Chris shattered and she felt a burning sensation across the bridge of her nose. At almost the same instant, the window on the passenger side crystallized around a hole blasted through it. Stunned by all this, she flinched. The resulting tug on the steering wheel accentuated the rear-end slide her panic stop had induced, and her right rear wheel left the pavement.

Before she could react, the back half of her car collided

with the metal rail, taking out one support after another, each second bringing her closer to the beckoning abyss. So disoriented she had no idea how to stop this deadly progression, she fought the steering wheel, spinning it one way then the other in mad confusion, out of control, out of luck.

HE'D MISSED, GARLAND was sure of it. He stomped on his brakes and slid to a stop, his car blocking the road. She'd destroyed a big section of the guard rail, and the ass end of her car was now hanging out in space, but it didn't look like it was going over. He glanced down the road, toward the gate. If she had a phone in her car, she could have called for help by now.

A part of him urged that he accept the call as a fact and save himself. But she'd hurt him and he still hurt. You just can't let something like that pass. He pulled forward as much as he could, then put the car in reverse and backed up, bringing his headlights around to where they illuminated Chris's car. Automatic in hand, he got out and ran toward her.

NO, CHRIS THOUGHT. *Here he comes.* She gunned her engine, but there was nothing for her tires to bite into.

Where were those cops?

Running was a lousy idea. Sitting there waiting for him was worse. She looked for the knife, but it had fallen off the seat and was hidden from her. With no time to look for it, she threw her door open and attempted to get out, the steep angle of the road making what should have been a simple act a fight.

She struggled onto the pavement and tried to get moving up the road, but the incline made her feel as though there were heavy rubber straps on her legs holding her back. At least that was also slowing the guy coming for her. She heard a sound like a willow switch being whisked through the air and something ticked the sleeve of her jacket.

This was no good. She was making it too easy for him. She tried to run harder, but the fronts of her thighs were already burning. There was no way to escape. The mountaintop was too far away, and there was nothing there to save her even if she could reach it.

A few yards ahead she saw the tops of some pine trees poking above the guard rail. Knowing there had to be a flat outcropping not far below, she urged her body forward. She heard the willow switch again, but the slug must have missed her. At least she didn't feel as though she'd been hit.

GARLAND CURSED AT his poor performance. Normally, he was a better marksman than this, but he didn't usually have to contend with a raging pain in his head. In addition, the steep slope had thrown his balance off and his headlights were casting weird shadows over the fleeing target. But there was nowhere for her to go and he had another full magazine in his pocket, so there was no doubt how this would end.

CHRIS REACHED THE rail and looked down into a void that was so dark she couldn't tell how far the ledge below was. At least the shoulder of the road seemed to angle down to it rather than fall off precipitously. As sanctuaries go, it didn't have much to recommend it, for the entire stand of trees was no more than twenty feet long and obviously narrow. In addition, if she went down there, she'd be trapped. But then so would he, which meant he wouldn't follow her.

A slug ricocheting off the rail beside her right hand made the decision for her. She dropped to the ground and threw her legs onto the sloping granite below. Praying it wasn't a thirty-foot drop, she shoved herself forward.

The granite wasn't as smooth as it looked in daylight, and her butt found every ridge and pothole in it. Teeth clenched in fear, she rode the mountain, which lifted her then slammed her down onto the tail end of her spine over and over. Her descent seemed endless, as though the ledge below were racing her, trying to stay out of reach. Suddenly, she felt the cold stone fall away and she was airborne. BAM. She was slammed once more onto the granite, so hard her clenched jaw popped open. At the same instant, her face was raked by pine boughs. Then, with a jolt, it was over.

As she spit out the pine needles that had somehow found their way into her mouth, she came to realize she was straddling the trunk of a pine tree whose bark was less than a finger's breadth from her crotch. And with a granite wall against her spine, she couldn't lie back enough so she could free herself.

Expecting at any second to be shot from above, she rolled to the right until she was nearly upside down and her shoulder was grinding into the thin soil beneath her. Squirming onto her back, she swung her trapped leg into the air and brought it around the tree. With a flurry of kicking and pushing against whatever purchase she could find, her lower body moved across the granite wall in an arc until she was lying on her side. In the darkness, she scrabbled to her feet.

Before she had time to think, she sensed the arrival of her pursuer. Looking up, she saw him dimly outlined by the light from his car. He raised his gun, pointed it directly at her, and fired.

The slug hit the ground an inch from her foot and ricocheted into a tree behind her.

He can see me, her brain howled.

It seemed impossible. When she'd looked down here herself, she'd been able to see nothing. How could *he* do it?

But then he moved his gun a little to the left and fired again. Then back to the right.

He can't see, Chris thought. He was firing blindly, concentrating on the place where she'd disappeared. Another shot hit a granite outcropping to her left and ricocheted past her, so close it whispered in her ear. Another hit the tree beside her, spraying her with sap. With slugs flying in all directions like that, there was simply no place to hide.

Carefully, she began backing up to at least get some tree trunks between her and the gun. But the trees, having struggled to grow at all in such a place, afforded her almost no protection. The willow switch sounds were now coming too close together to be timed, producing a deadly hail that at any moment could end her life.

With no other option, she continued to edge her way deeper into the trees, well aware that she was approaching a precipice. A slug grazed her hand and she cried out in pain. Hearing the sound, the gunman focused his efforts on the source.

She could go no farther, for she had reached the edge of the granite shelf. Trying to become a smaller target, she dropped to one knee. As she did, her right hand strayed over the edge of the cliff and found that the granite below did not form a sheer drop-off, but slanted away into darkness.

She tried to move forward and get out of that spot, but a tree growing right on the edge of the shelf blocked her. Then she got an idea. She looked over the edge of the shelf. There was no telling how distant the ground was, probably far enough to turn her into a bag of broken bones if she fell.

Her assessment was accurate, for the slope she'd felt with her hand extended for only fourteen feet before it ended in a sheer drop to a rocky jumble two hundred feet below.

With no time to debate the wisdom in what she was about to do, she flattened herself on the ground and wrapped both hands around the trunk of the tree in front of her. Scooting sideways with her legs, she worked her body off the ledge and onto the slope. With a little more scuttling, she lay in a line directly below the tree, all of her body except her hands under the trajectory of any slug fired from above.

But this refuge came at a high price, for the hand that had been shot ached, and the granite was punishing her knees. Moreover, the strength it took to hold on was pushing her physical limits. And now that she was down there, she knew she'd never have the strength to pull herself back up.

BELOW, IN THE park police station, the dispatcher who had taken Chris's call was so angry at the malfunctioning radio transmitter that had so far not allowed her to contact anybody, she began pounding on it with her fist.

CHAPTER 33

SLUGS WERE STILL flying above and there was a chance Chris might be hit again in the hands. If that happened, she'd never be able to hold on. But even if it didn't, the hand that was already throbbing from her earlier injury was threatening to pack it in. And she was certain that under the strain of her weight, her shoulder joints were slowly separating.

She'd long believed and taken comfort in the evidence that as one dies, the brain releases chemicals that produce a kind of euphoria, so there is no fear at the end, only a quiet pleasure. Now, though she was not mortally wounded, the pain and her flagging strength started tripping those switches and she began to accept the thought of death.

Just let go and the pain will be over. It'll be fine, it really will. Don't be afraid, it'll be lovely.

Eyes closed, she felt as though she were floating and if she released her hold, she would flutter harmlessly to the earth like a piece of confetti.

Just let go . . .

But then, the coarser, knuckle-dragging parts of her brain that were not deceived by soft voices and false promises, the ones that had seen the species through famine and flood and pestilence, joined the fray. And they urged her to hold on. *Save yourself. Death is not the answer. Hold on. Hold on.*

The willow switch suddenly grew silent. Had he given up? Was he out of ammunition? A voice cut the night.

"Drop your weapon."

There was someone else up there.

She heard the gunman begin firing again, but obviously not at her. Other, unsilenced shots rang out.

Hold on, she told herself. *Help is coming.* Somehow, she found a tiny reserve of untapped adrenaline. With it she bought the strength to maintain her grip for a few more seconds.

The shooting stopped and she heard running footsteps. There was a sliding sound followed by a grunt and a thump nearby. Then the rustle of pine boughs.

"Over here. Hurry." She was so weak now her voice was hardly above a whisper.

The rustling grew closer. At practically the same instant that she wondered why the park police didn't have any flashlights, the cop they'd sent to save her reached her on hands and knees and put his hand on her arm.

"Thank God you're here," she said.

Then she felt hard cold pressure against her head and she knew . . . It wasn't a cop, it was *him*.

The beam of two flashlights from above cut twin swaths through the darkness.

"Good-bye, Red," the gunman said.

Her resources drained and in no position to stop him even if she weren't exhausted, there was nothing she could do to prevent him from shooting her in the head, except release her hold and slide into oblivion. That at least would be *her* choice on how she would die, not his.

But help was *so* close.

An instant before he fired, she jerked her head to the right. The silencer slid down her skull and off it, so the round hit the granite beside her and caromed off into the darkness.

ON THE ROAD above, both cops saw the gunman crouching by the shelf's edge. Having already been fired upon, they were both so scared neither bothered to give him another warning before they began blasting away at him.

Although a moment earlier they'd managed to wound the gunman severely enough that he fell onto the shelf with Chris, they were poor marksmen, and seven of the eight rounds they fired this time missed. But one tore through his skull, tunneled through thirty-eight years of experience and memories, and blew a picture window in the other side of his head as it exited.

The gunman toppled, hit the granite slope with a dull thud, then began to slide. Greased by his own blood, he created a new ride for the park and went on its inaugural run.

Too depleted to feel any emotion over her close escape, Chris concentrated on letting the cops know she was there.

"Help . . . I can't . . . I'm down here . . ."

The two cops searched the shelf with their flashlights, then the younger of the two spotted Chris's hands. Without hesitating, he swung under the rail and slid down to the ledge on his rump.

Because he'd suffered from undiagnosed dyslexia, he'd twice failed the exam for the Atlanta police department. But physically, he was more than adequate, so he had little trouble pulling Chris to safety. At the sloping wall that led to the road, he dropped to his knees so Chris could step onto his back and then onto his shoulders as she stood up. This raised her high enough that the other cop could pull her onto the road.

"What took you so long?" Chris croaked.

"Our radio transmitter is on the blink," the cop said. "Sometimes it works, sometimes not. So we didn't get the call right away."

"I need to sit down."

The cop turned and looked below at his colleague. "I'm gonna take her to my car, then we'll get you up."

Sitting in the police cruiser's front seat while the older cop helped the younger one climb back to the road using a set of jumper cables as a rope, it almost seemed to Chris that what had just happened wasn't real . . . that a few minutes ago she *couldn't* have been about to die. But the throbbing pain in her hand and another across the bridge of her nose reminded her that it had all been horribly real. She reached up and carefully touched the side of her nose. The skin there felt oddly corrugated, making her want to look at it in the rearview mirror. But she didn't have the strength to fight the steep angle on which the car was parked. So she just lay back and closed her eyes.

After the young cop had successfully climbed the jumper cables, he and his colleague spent a few minutes discussing the situation. Then the older cop drove Chris to the park police station, where she went directly to the rest room and looked in the mirror.

What she saw shocked her, for the wound on her nose had bled incredibly, leaving a veil of dried gore across her right cheek. She carefully cleaned it off with moist paper towels, then did the same with the blood around the small knife cut on her neck. When she reached the wound on the back of her hand, that one began bleeding again. Holding some paper towels against the flow, she went back into the ready room, where the dispatcher, a heavyset woman with a prison guard look about her, sat her down and applied some gauze and tape to the bleeding wound and put a bandage on her nose.

"I've called an ambulance," she said. "When they get here, I'll have them look at you."

"I'm okay," Chris said. "I don't need that." Though she knew it wasn't a likely possibility, she so desperately wanted to be away from these people and be surrounded by her own things, she said, "Could we just get my car down and let me go home?"

An incredulous expression crossed the woman's face. "A crime was committed and a man was shot. There are reports to fill out, questions to be answered. No, of course you can't go home. Not for a while."

That while turned out to be three hours, during which she did two performances, one for the park police and another for the county sheriff. The flow of information in those interviews wasn't entirely one way, for in the process she learned that the man who had attacked her was dead. By the time she'd been told this, the caffeine in two cups of hot coffee had a couple of her generators back on line.

The side of her car was scraped and crushed, but it was still as functional as she was, so when she'd answered the last question and was allowed to leave, she drove away at the wheel of her own car. As desperate as she was to get home, she stopped at Bill Spain's kiosk and surprised him with a big hug and a kiss on the cheek for giving her the juice bottle she'd used to get out from under Garland's knife.

HOME . . . STANDING IN her living room, she thought what a fine word that was . . . to have a place away from the dangers of the world, where you could be safe and warm and your arms weren't being pulled out of their sockets and there wasn't a gun to your head. She walked through her apartment with new eyes, appreciating the old, thrilled by the familiar.

Then she showered.

Hot water piped right into your bathroom.

What an invention.

After she showered, she put on her favorite pair of flannel pajamas and a robe and curled up in one of the big upholstered chairs in the living room. There, her mind began replaying the horrors of the evening, reformatted, of course, for home viewing. In minute detail she relived the attack, felt once more the knife against her throat, heard again the crack of the bottle against her assailant's skull, and saw the lights of his car coming toward her. She cringed at the sickening sound of her own car ripping out metal posts, and felt the pain in her arms, the cold metal silencer against her head.

And after the last frame slid from view, there was, for a few seconds, only a white screen in her head. She began to wonder why this had happened. Why, after so many years of going up on the mountain in utter safety, a man driving a rental car, for that's what the sheriff had said he was driving, attacked her. And why was he carrying a silenced automatic as though . . .

For hours there had been a distant voice in her head, trying to get her attention. But there had been too much else going on for her to hear. Now that it was quiet she finally got the message.

CHAPTER 34

THE MORNING AFTER the attempt on her life, Chris met with Michael in his office and told him what had happened. When she finished, he pulled her out of her chair and wrapped his arms around her.

"What a horrible night you had. I feel awful that I wasn't there to help."

Needing the comfort his arms provided, Chris let herself enjoy the moment. But then, fearing that she was cooperating too much, she gently pulled free.

"There's no reason for you to feel bad," she said. "You couldn't have known what was going to happen."

"What was that guy doing up there anyway?"

"He wasn't there by accident. Just in from out of town . . . carrying a gun with a silencer . . . The guy was a pro."

"What do you mean a pro—a hit man?" Michael's skepticism was obvious in his voice.

"And I think Ash hired him."

"Why would he do such a thing?"

"He must have figured out I was behind the visit he got from Lenihan."

"Nothing came of that. Why risk drawing more attention to himself?"

"If that goon had succeeded, the connection probably would have gone unnoticed."

"Have you told Lenihan all this?"

"He was very sympathetic about what happened, but was even more skeptical than you are."

"Chris, that's not fair. I'm just trying to look at this objectively."

"Which is exactly what I'm doing."

"I didn't mean—"

"I know you didn't. But I need some support here. I'm out on this limb all by myself."

Michael put his arms around her waist. "I'm with you wherever it takes us."

"You mean that?"

"Yes."

"Than we better get packed, because we're going to Newark, New Jersey, and talk to Frieda Sepanski."

WITH MICHAEL BEHIND the wheel of their rental car and Chris checking house numbers, they slowly cruised Bingham Street looking for the Sepanski house. As they drove, Chris couldn't help thinking that the area looked like a Stepford community: neat little brick bungalows, varying only subtly from each other, the yards greening up from winter in synchrony, not a speck of litter anywhere, all the sidewalks in perfect repair.

They'd moved fast after Chris had voiced her intent to make the trip, and three hours later, they were airborne, having paid a surprisingly modest amount for their tickets considering the lack of advance planning.

"*There* are some people I'll bet the neighbors talk about," Michael said, pointing a few doors ahead on the right, where the yard showed some bald patches, and a half dozen different species of weeds had a good head start on the grass. The wooden trim on the house was faded and the paint was flaking off in long strips. From the way the roofing shingles were curled up, Chris suspected that the next cold front blowing through would take a bunch of them with it.

Then she saw the house number. "That's the Sepanski home."

They pulled into the empty driveway, stopped short of a big oil stain on the pavement, and got out. Beyond a chain-link gate, the driveway continued into the backyard, to a small garage also in poor repair. There was no car back there either.

"Doesn't look like anyone's home," Michael said. "Hope they still live here."

"The AT and T internet directory showed this address for their phone number."

"They should know."

Chris stepped up on the dust-covered porch and pressed the doorbell, which she could hear ring inside.

No one responded.

She tried again.

"It's only four o'clock," Michael said, looking at his watch. "They're probably still at work."

"Maybe I should have called ahead," Chris said. "But I thought she'd be more likely to talk to us if we just showed up in person."

"There's no reason yet to doubt that. Let's go take a look at Iliad, get something to eat, and come back. That'll give them time to have dinner, too. Be better not to interrupt them in the middle of a meal."

Chris agreed and they returned to the car.

Using the Newark map they'd bought at a gas station and the map Chris had printed from the internet showing the location of the Iliad plant, they arrived there less than twenty minutes after leaving the Sepanski home.

The plant was in a light industrial area not far from Newark Bay, where concertina wire and loading docks meant more than aesthetics. Remaining in the car, they studied the place.

Housed in a neat three-story brick building with a row of Bradford pears growing from iron-grated holes in the sidewalk, the Iliad building was an oasis. Though the structure was no architectural gem, the front entrance was flanked by a pair of obelisks carved into the stone trim work. Each obelisk was capped by a Horus eye and there were three rows of hieroglyphs cut into the lintel stone.

"I don't get it," Michael said. "What's Iliad got to do with Egypt?"

"Look up there," Chris said, pointing through the windshield at some more carved work up near the roof, well above the big white letters that spelled Iliad.

"Nile Fishing Nets," he read. "It's a retrofit. I guess it was cheaper to set up here than in some exclusive industrial park."

A small white truck that resembled the kind used by wholesale meat distributors to make restaurant deliveries passed by, temporarily blocking their view of the plant. On the side, green lettering identified it as an Iliad truck. It turned and went through the gate in the chain-link fence on the far side of the plant.

"The place looks pretty normal," Michael said.

"Yeah, where's their sign that says, 'Rogue Business. Faked FDA Reports Our Specialty'?"

Michael grinned. "It must be inside."

Suddenly, Chris's door was yanked open and a man looked in.

"Can you folks spare a couple of dollars? I need somethin' to eat."

Red-eyed, sallow-skinned, and festooned with a stringy gray beard, he looked as though he'd been on the street a long time. Somewhere in his travels he'd found an aviator hat, which he was wearing with the flaps down. An acrid odor of urine, tobacco, and wine filled the car, making Chris's eyes water.

"I know I shouldn't have opened your door like that, but my experience has been that if I'd merely tapped on the window, you'd have ignored me. It's got somethin' to do with havin' glass between us."

"I'll make you a deal," Chris said. She pointed at his grocery cart, which was loaded with clothes and cardboard. "I'll give you the money if you'll stand over there while I get it."

"Where would we be without the art of negotiation?" He pulled his head back and retreated to the cart.

Chris dug in her bag, but could only find one single in her wallet. Instead of just giving him that, she pulled out a five, left the car, and handed it to him.

Seeing that it was more than he asked for, the old man

grinned, and it was not a pretty sight. "You're a good person," he said. "Anybody asks me, I'll tell 'em so."

"Then we're even."

"You be sure and keep your car door locked. Never can tell when somebody on the outside will try to open it."

Chris got back in the car and locked the door.

"We should have thought of that by ourselves," Michael said. "Why'd you give him money? He'll probably just drink it up."

"When someone says they need money for food, it's hard to say no. It's up to him how he chooses to spend it."

"Speaking of food, I could use some myself." He pointed at the Iliad building. "Did you want to go inside?"

"I'd like to spend a few hours going through their files, but I suppose they have a policy against that sort of thing. So I don't see any point in going in. I was just curious to see what it looked like and where it was."

Having no idea where they should eat, Michael headed for an area of strip malls and other high-density commercial activity they'd passed on the way to the Sepanski home. But before he reached it, he saw a little neighborhood restaurant called the Newark House, which had a Cape Cod look about it—gray cedar shingles, a white picket fence along the sidewalk, yellow and purple tulips in the flower beds.

He looked at Chris. "How about here?"

"Looks good."

And it was. Michael had the best salmon he'd ever tasted. The small steak Chris ordered was cooked to perfection and came with garlicky new potatoes that were so good she thought about the old vagrant they'd met at Iliad.

"I feel guilty eating like this when that old man has nothing. I should have given him more."

"I was thinking about him, too. I should have kicked in something instead of just sitting there."

"He could be someone's father."

It wasn't hard for Michael to see the connection between that comment and Chris's family situation. Unsure of what to say, he sorted through the available responses. "He'd certainly be better off with his family, if he has any."

"Then why isn't he there?" Chris said, her eyes sparking.

Despite knowing it was somewhere in the area, Michael

had stepped into the trap. Trying to climb out, he said, "Maybe he's mentally ill."

"He didn't sound that way to me. His comment about the glass between us making it easier to ignore him was pretty perceptive."

"Chris, the man is a total stranger. We can spin all the stories we want about how he became what he is, but only *he* knows what happened."

The sparks in Chris's eyes died. "Of course you're right. And he's not Wayne, either, is he? Let's not talk about that anymore."

Trying to kill as much time as possible, they lingered over coffee and dessert, which meant they didn't leave the restaurant until a little after six.

"Maybe we should wait a bit longer before we go back to the Sepanskis'," Chris suggested. "I'd like to swing by our motel first anyway."

Because they'd made no arrangements ahead of time with Frieda Sepanski, there was no way to know when they'd get to talk to her. So they'd only bought one-way plane tickets to Newark, figuring they'd just scramble for a flight home when they were ready. Aware that they'd have to spend at least tonight in Newark, they'd taken rooms at a Hampton Inn.

By the time they reached the motel and spent a few minutes in their respective bathrooms, it was late enough for another visit to Bingham Street. They arrived there shortly after dark and were encouraged to see a car in the driveway and the lights on in the house.

Once again Michael let Chris take the lead. She rang the doorbell as before, and they waited expectantly for a response. After a brief interval, the inner door was opened by a heavyset woman with long black hair and wearing a gray print dress cut loosely to hide her shape. She made no effort to also open the storm door.

Believing this was the woman they sought, Chris said, "Mrs. Sepanski, I'm Chris Collins and this is Dr. Boyer. I spoke to you a few days earlier about Eric Ash."

The slightly puzzled expression on the woman's face changed to irritation.

"I told you I didn't want to talk about him."

"Please, it's very important, and we've come all the way from Atlanta to see you."

"Well, you shouldn't have. I didn't tell you to do that."

"We think he may have been involved in the deaths of several people and that he's a dangerous man who needs to be stopped. Please talk to us. Help us stop him."

"I don't know all that much."

"Whatever you can tell us so we can understand him better will help."

She'd been responding quickly. Now she hesitated. Chris hoped it was a sign her resistance was weakening.

"Please," Chris prompted.

"Show me some identification," Frieda said.

Chris got her wallet from her bag and produced her driver's license and Good Samaritan employee ID, which she held against the storm door.

Michael did the same with his IDs.

Frieda reached out, unlocked the storm door, and pushed it open.

It was a house without a foyer, and when they entered, it was directly into a sitting room containing cheap furniture arranged with no understanding of decorating principles or no money to carry them out. But it was clean. Whatever they'd had for dinner smelled good.

"Please have a seat."

Chris went to the gold sofa and Michael took the green upholstered chair beside it.

Without the storm door between them and in better light now, Chris saw that Frieda's pale complexion was not as flawless as it first appeared, but had the texture of finely ground corn meal. Fidgeting like a squirrel, she offered them some coffee. Both declined. With her hostess obligations out of the way, Frieda sat in the upholstered chair on the other side of the coffee table. "What did you want to know?"

Before Chris could answer, a man with a cane shuffled into view and stood in the doorway that led to the back of the house.

"I dropped my medicine in the bathroom," he said to Frieda.

Frieda got up and went to him. "This is my husband, Ruben."

Ruben's eyes were heavy-lidded and his complexion was the color of nonfat milk. Frieda didn't introduce Chris and Michael, but Ruben seemed too sick to care.

"I'll get his medicine and be right back."

She quickly reappeared and returned to her chair.

"Did Ash have anything to do with the fraudulent hep C vaccine data?" Chris asked.

"It was *his* project."

"Does that mean yes?"

"You can't ever tell anyone we spoke. Promise me that."

"I promise."

She looked at Michael.

"You have my word."

"If anyone asks me, I'll deny we ever met. I'm not going to be dragged into anything beyond this conversation."

She sat there fidgeting, her eyes darting back and forth between her two visitors. "Of course Ash knew the data were faked. He and Paul Danner, Iliad's CEO, were close friends, so I should have realized that telling Danner wouldn't lead to anything. And it didn't. He told me to keep quiet about it, threatened to fire me. But I couldn't look the other way. So I contacted the FDA and I was let go."

"Isn't there a whistle-blower law to shield people in those situations?"

"It's not that kind of law. It just allows whistle-blowers to sue the defendant company on behalf of the government and share in the proceeds of the suit when the fraud cost the government money. This one didn't cost the government anything. So I wasn't protected in any way.

"About a week after I was fired, things began to happen. The windshield on our car was smashed one night, then a few days later, we came home and found white paint thrown all over the back of the house. Two days after that, when I got off work from my new job and went to get my car, I found that someone . . ." Her face twisted in disgust. "Even thinking about it again nauseates me. Someone had smeared feces all over the dashboard and the seats. And the car was only three years old. You can't clean that stuff off of fabric. We had to have the seats replaced. The parking lot attendant remembered seeing someone hanging around the car a few hours earlier. From his description, it had to be Ash. We told the police who was responsible, but they couldn't do anything because we had no real proof it was him.

"For the next week everything was okay. Then one night a siren woke us up. It died right in front of the house and we heard shouts and the gate opening. Ruben looked out to see what was going on and the garage was on fire. They said it was obviously arson, but once again, there was no proof who did it.

"Do you know what that's like . . . never knowing what's going to happen next . . . to be afraid to go to sleep at night or leave your home, wondering if it'll be there when you come back? It was destroying my mind and my marriage. So Ruben decided to take care of things himself. That was before he got sick. He was big and strong then.

"He took a baseball bat over to Ash's home and confronted him, told him that if one more thing happened, he was going to break Ash's legs. And that stopped it. A few months later, Ash left town. That's why you can't tell anyone we spoke about this. I can't have that happen again. Ruben is too sick now to protect us. We're not even able to keep the house up like we should."

"I'm sorry for what happened to you and that Ruben is not well," Chris said. "Please don't think badly of me for asking more questions, but why do you think Ash left Iliad?"

"After the hepatitis C problem, I heard the company lost a lot of business. People just didn't trust their products. There were a lot of layoffs. I guess they just couldn't afford to keep Ash on, or he left for a better-paying job."

"Sounds like that would have been a good time for a company name change. I wonder why they didn't do it?"

Frieda shrugged. "I wouldn't know."

"Have you heard any gossip about how the company's been doing lately?"

"It's been a long time since anyone I know has worked there. But if it's gossip you want, you should talk to the Red Baron."

"Who's he?"

"A vagrant who's been in the area for years. People call him that because he always wears an aviator hat, you know, the kind with flaps."

"That must be the man we met today," Chris said.

"Where?"

"In front of the Iliad plant."

"He lives in the alley around the corner. There's an old broken cement culvert there he uses for a home. I always felt sorry for him, so when I could, I'd give him a little money. And sometimes he'd say things about the company only an insider would know. I once asked him how he did that and he said you'd be surprised what you can learn if you take the time to notice what's going on around you. I'm sure that included going through the company's trash bin. Some people think he's crazy, but he isn't."

With nothing more to ask, Chris stood up and Michael did the same. "We've taken too much of your time." Chris moved to Frieda and offered her hand, which Frieda took in her own. "Thanks so much for talking to us and being so candid."

"I don't see how I've helped you any," Frieda said as they all moved toward the door.

"You've given us a better understanding of the relationship between Paul Danner and Ash."

"Is that significant?"

"It could be. And we now know how vindictive Ash can be."

"That's why you're not ever going to say we spoke. You promised . . ."

"You can count on us."

"I hope he gets what he deserves."

A few seconds later, as Chris and Michael were leaving the porch, Frieda reopened the storm door and leaned out. "Be careful."

In the car, Chris spoke first. "What do you think now about the guy who attacked me?"

"Hiring an assassin is a major step up compared to what Ash did to her, but I think he's capable of it. Now what?"

"Let's find the Red Baron."

"I was afraid you'd say that."

CHAPTER 35

THE STREETLIGHTS IN the Newark warehouse district stood as silent sentinels, illuminating a shunned world.

"She said he lived in a culvert in an alley near here," Chris said, as Michael edged the car past the deserted Iliad plant. "But I haven't see any alleys along this street. Take a right at the corner."

Michael did as she asked and they found pot hole heaven, lined with low buildings of corrugated metal alternating with two- and three-story brick structures that looked as old as the Roman coliseum and in only slightly better repair.

"It looks like there's an opening between buildings down there on the right," Chris said, pointing. "It could be an alley."

Driving slowly so he could maneuver the car around the craters that pocked the street, Michael proceeded toward the dark void Chris had indicated.

And she was right. It *was* an alley. He pulled the car into its mouth and they both leaned forward to see what the headlights would show them.

"There," Chris said, pointing at a cement oval Michael had already seen for himself at the end of the short alley. The culvert was turned so they couldn't look into it and its left end was snugged against the building beside it.

Michael moved the car deeper into the alley, and a head popped out of the culvert. He wasn't wearing his hat, but it was obviously the Red Baron. Letting the car run and leaving the lights on, Chris and Michael got out and walked to the culvert.

Before they reached it, the Red Baron came out with an old sword in one hand.

"Who are you? What do you want?" he said, squinting in the lights from the car.

"I'm Chris and this is Michael. We met earlier today around the corner in front of the Iliad plant. I gave you five dollars."

"What's the matter, you want it back?"

"We want to talk to you."

"About what?"

"Iliad Pharmaceuticals and anything you might be able to tell us about them."

"What made you think of me?"

"You seem like someone who would have an observant eye."

"Did Frieda send you?"

Remembering her promise to Frieda, Chris lied. "I don't know what you mean."

"No, I guess that's right," the old man said more to himself than to Chris. "I embarrass her, so she probably wouldn't admit knowin' me." Then, back in the moment, he said, "Why are you askin' about Iliad?"

"It's a long story. One I'd rather not discuss."

"Well, I don't know anything. You wasted your time by comin'."

Believing he might be afraid he was talking to someone with ties to Iliad, Chris said, "We don't work for them. We're doctors in Atlanta."

"You could be from the Mayo Clinic and it wouldn't make any difference. I have nothin' to tell."

Chris produced her Good Samaritan ID and held it out so he could read it in the lights from the car. He leaned forward and took a good look.

Following Chris's lead, Michael showed the old man his Monteagle ID.

"Atlanta, huh?" the old man said. "I lived there once. Had pneumonia and spent a week in the hospital. Wasn't either one of those you work for. Can't remember the name. I think it started with a G."

"Grady?" Chris asked.

For the first time, the old man relaxed. "Suppose I did know somethin'. My time is valuable."

"We'll pay you, of course."

"Then turn off those damn car lights and come here and sit."

Beside his culvert the old man had constructed a second room that consisted primarily of a roof of corrugated metal supported on one end by the top of the culvert, and on the other by two side-by-side fifty-five-gallon drums. Three strategically placed cement blocks held the roof in place. In this room, Chris saw his grocery cart.

Far back in the culvert, some short boards on more cement blocks served as a makeshift table. On the table a little lamp with a heat-stained shade emitted a warm yellow glow. The floor of the culvert was lined by a rumpled sleeping bag on which there were a couple of paperbacks.

While Michael went back to the car to shut off the lights, the old man ducked into his storage room, where he got another cement block, which he brought out and stood on end in front of the culvert. By the time Michael had returned, the old man had brought out a second block and placed it a few feet from the first.

"It's those or the ground," he said, gesturing to the cement blocks.

While Chris and Michael squatted on their blocks, the old man took one off the roof and set it down for his own use.

"Where do you get the electricity for your lamp?" Chris asked.

"I tapped into a circuit on the outside of the buildin' behind us. It wasn't hard."

"How long have you lived here?"

"I thought you wanted to talk about Iliad."

"I do, but I'm curious about you as well."

"Because I'm a freak?"

"No. I just find you interesting."

"I don't want to be interestin'. I just want to be left alone."

"Okay, I'm sorry."

"Apology accepted. What happened to your nose and hand?" he asked, referring to the bandages over the grazing bullet wounds she'd received.

"A little accident."

"Another story you'd rather not discuss, I guess. You said you'd pay for information. How much?"

"Twenty dollars."

The old man stood and picked up his cement block. "Good-bye."

"Wait a minute . . . I thought you appreciated the art of negotiation."

He put the block down. "I do. What's the new offer?"

"It's hard to put a price on something when you don't know what you're going to get."

"Not my problem."

"So you *do* know something interesting about Iliad?"

"You like the word *interestin'*, don't you?"

"I find it interesting."

The old man smiled. He looked at Michael. "You don't talk much."

"Depends on the circumstances."

The old man gestured at Chris with his head. "You two sleepin' together?"

"That's none of your business," Michael said.

"I suppose not." He turned to Chris. "How much did you say?"

"Fifty dollars."

"Sixty."

"All right."

"Seventy."

"No. You said sixty and I agreed. At that point we had a deal. Unless you're a man whose word doesn't mean anything."

"Okay, sixty. In cash. I don't take checks or credit cards."

Chris got three twenties from her wallet and handed them over.

The old man folded them into a tight rectangle and shoved

them into his right shoe. "I'll see you right here tomorrow night at eight forty-five. Don't be late."

"What do you mean?" Chris said. "Why can't we talk now?"

"I want to show you somethin' and I can't do it now."

"Why not?" Michael said.

"I liked you better when you didn't talk," the old man said. "Could it be because there's nothin' to see now?"

"How do we know you'll be here?" Michael asked.

"Yeah, I might take your friend's sixty dollars and start a new life in another state." He looked at Chris. "You have my word."

"That's good enough for me," Chris said, standing. "We'll see you tomorrow."

IN THE CAR, on their way to a more inhabited part of the world, Michael said, "I don't like the idea of going back there at night. He could be arranging an ambush with some of his friends."

There was merit in Michael's concern, so Chris took it seriously. "Remember him asking me if Frieda sent us? Right after that he said he embarrassed her. That sounds like he's more to her than just some bum she met. Let's go see her again."

CHRIS WAS AFRAID that when Frieda saw them on the porch she wouldn't open the door. But she did.

"Mrs. Sepanski, I'm sorry to bother you again, but we spoke to the Red Baron and made an appointment to meet him tomorrow night where he lives." Considering the Red Baron's place on the social ladder, the word appointment seemed odd even to Chris. "And we're wondering if that's a safe thing to do. I didn't tell him you sent us, but he guessed it and then he said he embarrasses you. Why did he say that?"

A look of resignation crept over Frieda's face. "Because he's my father's brother, Gene. And he does embarrass me, even though I can understand what happened to him."

"Which was?"

"Years and years ago, his wife and daughter were killed in a plane crash and he's never recovered. He's an intelligent, educated man who could have done so much with his life, but he's never found his way out of the grief of their deaths. I can appreciate that to a point, but it's been *so* long."

Frieda's story went straight to Chris's heart. Where Frieda saw Gene as a tragic figure, Chris saw him as a hero. To have loved his family so much that he'd lost all incentive in life after their deaths made such a statement. And surely when they were alive, he'd shown them how he felt. What must that have been like for them to know they were loved so much?

"Frankly, Mrs. Sepanski," Michael said, stepping into the void Chris's reflections left in the conversation. "We're worried about meeting him at night down there with no one else around."

"You can't believe he'd harm you."

"We didn't know what to think."

"Despite the way he lives, he's a good man. You have nothing to fear from him."

"WELL, SHE CONVINCED me," Chris said, as Michael backed out of the Sepanski driveway.

"I still wish we were meeting him during the day. But I guess he sounds okay. We should stay alert, though, when we see him, and keep your cell phone within easy reach."

CHRIS HAD NOT slept at all the previous night, and by the time her head hit the Hampton Inn pillow, her brain was already closing up shop. But sleep would not come that easily, for she suddenly heard the muffled ring of her cell phone.

Forcing herself onto her feet, she turned on a light. She padded over to her handbag, opened it, and retrieved the phone.

"Chris Collins."

"This is Wayne. I just saw on the news what happened to you last night on Stone Mountain. Are you okay?"

"I'm a little bruised, but otherwise fine."

"You shouldn't have been up there all alone."

It was a comment from a worried parent, but Chris was still so wary of him she didn't hear it that way. And she didn't entertain for a second any thought of telling him what was behind the attack on her. Instead, she just said, "I've been doing it for years with no problem."

"That doesn't mean it's a good idea. But I guess you know that now. I'm glad you're not hurt."

"Thanks."

"I haven't seen you in a while. Could we get together tomorrow for lunch?"

"I can't. I'm out of town and won't be back by then."

"Where are you?"

"On a business trip. I'll call you when I get home. We'll arrange something."

"That sounds great. Have a good trip. I'll talk to you later."

Under other circumstances Chris would have spent at least a few minutes thinking about Wayne's call and their situation. But tonight, she just returned to bed, flicked off the light, and fell asleep.

THE NEXT MORNING, Chris and Michael drove over to Manhattan and spent the day as tourists at the Museum of Natural History. Despite seeing many marvelous things there, they often found themselves standing in front of a display and wondering what Gene was going to show them. That afternoon, at the woolly mammoth exhibit, Chris had a flashback to Stone Mountain, when Earl Garland's gun was pressed against her head. For a moment, it seemed so real she was sure that if she reached up, she'd be able to wrap her fingers around the gun's muzzle. But she didn't dare reach up or she'd fall. Suddenly, the pain in her shoulders returned, aching from the weight of her body pulling on them. As it had that night, the hand of death stroked her hair and she heard the black courier whisper her name with a sibilant s: *Chrisss . . . Chrisss . . .*

This time the sound of Michael's voice rescued her.

"Chris, are you in there?"

"Sorry. My mind wandered for a minute. Michael . . . Thank you for coming with me to Newark and for not taking advantage of us being on this trip together."

"What do you mean?"

"Not trying to talk your way into my bed last night."

"Chris, I won't deny that the thought occurred to me, but I don't want it to happen that way. I want all of you. I want to share your hopes and your fears. I want to help celebrate your successes and be there for your disappointments. Sure, I want the physical part, but only with everything else."

"I don't know what to say."

"That says it." He turned and looked at the mammoth.

She put her hand over his, where it rested on the exhibit railing. "I thought you understood. We spoke about this on Stone Mountain . . ."

He turned to look at her. "I remember. I'm sorry. Sometimes my ego talks before I can censor it."

His apology made Chris feel only marginally better. She knew she couldn't hold him in storage forever. There would come a time when he would give up on her. His reaction a moment ago was proof that even now he was fighting that decision. Damn it. She *wanted* to trust him. How she longed to just be normal.

Not even the museum could compete with all that was galloping around in Chris's head, so by the time they reached their car at the end of the day, she couldn't remember much that they'd seen. But at least they were now only a few hours away from learning what Gene had for them.

THEIR HEADLIGHTS ONCE again brought Gene out of his culvert, except it wasn't him.

But then Chris realized that he simply *looked* different, for he was now clean-shaven, his hair was combed, and he was dressed in clean clothes—a pair of dark-blue pants and a fashionable patterned sport shirt. But he was still wearing black sneakers.

Michael switched off the headlights and cut the engine. As they got out, Gene said, "Thought you might not come."

"Had to," Chris said. "I've got money invested here."

"Let me lock up and I'll be ready to go."

"Go where?" Chris asked.

"You'll see."

What he meant by "lock up" wasn't clear, but he went into his grocery cart garage and pushed the cart more deeply into the shadows. For a few seconds they heard the sound of clanking chains, then Gene reappeared.

"Let's hit the road," he said, heading for the car.

With Gene in the backseat issuing directions, they drove

through the empty streets, both Michael and Chris grateful that he'd bathed.

After they'd gone about ten blocks, he pointed to a side street. "Park there."

When Michael had done that, Gene opened his door. "Now we walk."

They followed him farther down the side street and then into an alley, where broken glass glittered in the glare from an occasional bare lightbulb over a loading dock, and little clusters of spring weeds were gathering strength for a summer offensive against the deteriorating asphalt. Gene moved surprisingly fast and they had to hustle to keep up. They followed the alley to its end, where it opened onto a street that, on its far side, ran along a set of railroad tracks. Beyond the tracks there was an almost unbroken line of corrugated metal buildings with loading docks every fifteen yards or so.

Gene put out his arms to keep Chris and Michael back, then he checked in both directions. Satisfied that no one was around, he said, "Now we go fast."

He took off across the street and over the railroad tracks, with Chris and Michael following single file, so that they resembled a small family of urban raccoons. Blending into the shadows of the raised concrete foundation for the metal buildings, Gene turned left and headed for a spot about forty yards away, where, presumably, the same street they'd been on before they'd parked the car passed over the tracks and disappeared between the buildings.

When they reached the street, it became obvious that there was a tall chain-link gate across it. Unlike the gate at the service road on Stone Mountain, this one was padlocked. Without hesitating, Gene crossed the street and squeezed through the narrow opening between the left gate support and the adjacent building. He looked back and motioned for Chris and Michael to follow.

Despite her admiration for the sacrifices Gene had made in the name of love, Chris was growing uncomfortable with all this. "What are we doing here?"

"You want to learn somethin' about Iliad or not?" Gene said. "If you don't, we'll leave. Makes no difference to me."

Chris looked at Michael.

"Just explain what we're here for," Michael said.

"I'd rather show you."

"And I'd rather you *tell* us," Michael said.

"We're wastin' time," Gene said. "We stand here arguin', we'll see nothin'."

"We've come this far," Chris said to Michael. "Let's just go with him."

After the big speech he'd made at the museum about wanting to share Chris's life, Michael felt that this was no time to be pulling back. "I'm right behind you."

There was plenty of room for even Michael to slip through the opening, and soon they were both inside. As Gene led them forward in the shadows along the side of the adjacent building, the air freshened into a light breeze that carried the odor of brine and creosote. Chris could hear the faint sound of lapping water. For some reason, he'd brought them to the waterfront.

They emerged onto a long wooden dock that stretched along the bay in both directions for as far as they could see in the dim illumination cast by the occasional light fixtures on the dock warehouses. Across an expanse of black water, pinpoints of light marked the opposite shore. In the sky to the right, planes were making their approach to Newark Airport, taking people home or to their hotels before their business meeting in the morning. None of them, Chris thought, were here to skulk through the city's deserted streets at night with a vagrant for a leader.

"This way," Gene said, heading left, toward a tall stack of black ribbed drainage culverts strapped together to keep them from rolling. Farther out on the dock there was a cluster of big wooden crates, each with a plastic shroud stapled to the upper half.

As they followed Gene between the black culverts and the adjacent building, Chris said, "Don't they have a night watchman here to protect all this stuff on the dock?"

"Most of the time," Gene said. "But he's been paid to be somewhere else tonight."

Chris had no idea what he meant by that, but decided not to pursue it.

Past the culverts, Gene kept on a course that was taking them to a big yellow crane permanently fixed to the cement apron in front of the warehouses.

When they reached it, he said, "This is where we want to be."

The crane was well beyond the feeble light cast by the last fixture they'd passed, and it was so dark there Chris could barely see Gene's face.

"What we came to see will be on the other side of this crane in a few minutes, so you need to find a good place where you can watch but still be concealed. One of you can stand up there on the platform by the cab and watch through the cab windows. The other can stand on the steps and look through the lower part of the windows. I'll stay down here."

"Are you telling us people are coming? We'll be watching someone?"

"Not comin' . . . already here," Gene said, glancing through the gap between the crane mechanism and the cab. "Get down."

They each dropped to one knee so they couldn't be seen. Chris heard the sound of a car engine growing closer. Then it stopped. A door opened. "Are these people dangerous?" she whispered, suddenly feeling breathless and light-headed.

"Mostly just careless," Gene answered. "Don't worry, I'll take care of you."

"I think we should go."

"Too late. If we move now, they'll see us. You might as well take a look."

Upset at Gene and herself for letting him get her and Michael into this position, Chris nevertheless was curious about what was going to happen. She turned to Michael. "He's right. I'm going up there."

"Wait a minute," Gene said. "He always stands by his car and takes a quick look around before he becomes comfortable." Staying low, he moved to the rear of the crane and slowly rose into a crouch, which allowed him to look out through the angle formed by the crane mechanism and the flatbed on which it was mounted.

The seconds crawled by, then he whispered, "It's okay now."

With Michael close behind, Chris climbed the stairs to the cab and went to the spot Gene had suggested. Michael, too, followed his advice and remained on the steps just high enough so he could see through the cab's widows.

CHAPTER 36

CHRIS CAREFULLY LEANED forward and took a look.

Twenty yards away, a blond man was standing at the edge of the dock facing the bay with a flashlight. He flicked it on and off a couple of times, then turned and walked back to the silver Lexus that had brought him. Able now to see his face, Chris recognized him as Paul Danner, Iliad's CEO.

Danner opened the car and tossed the flashlight inside. Leaving the door open, he produced a cell phone from somewhere on his person. Seeing *his* phone reminded Chris that hers was on. Fearing that if it rang, it would give them away, she switched it to mute.

Danner's call lasted only a few seconds. He put the phone away, then reached into the car's front seat and grabbed a laptop computer that he put on top of the car. He flipped the computer open and began tapping away on the keyboard.

He was still typing a few minutes later when a white truck pulled onto the dock and the driver jockeyed it around so the rear end was facing the bay. Danner closed his computer and put it back in the car. He walked over and began motioning the truck to back up.

There was no lettering on the truck, but it had the same

general appearance as the Iliad truck Chris and Michael had seen yesterday. Looking as closely as she could under the circumstances, Chris thought she could see that a white rectangle of some material had been applied to the truck where the Iliad lettering was on the other one they'd seen.

Danner guided the truck backward until it was just a few feet from the dock's edge. He stopped it with a raised palm and a shout.

"Whoa. That's good."

The driver, a big guy with curly dark hair and wearing jeans and a gray sweatshirt that covered his beer belly like the cover on a bowling ball, stepped onto the dock. They exchanged a few words that Chris couldn't hear, then the big guy went around to the back of the truck and opened the doors.

An interval ensued in which the driver lit up a cigarette and Danner paced. Soon, the steady throb of an engine drifted in from the bay. The sound steadily grew louder. Chris saw two tiny lights appear a short distance out in the water. A launch slipped into view and cut its engines back to a burble. The craft slowly advanced toward the dock; then, because the water was so far below the dock, Chris lost sight of it.

Danner and the truck driver moved to the edge of the dock and looked down. After a minute or so, a head appeared at their feet; someone from the boat, coming up a ladder. Danner extended his hand to help the climber up and a man dressed in dark clothing and wearing a knit seaman's cap stepped onto the dock. He and Danner shook hands and spoke to each other, but once again, Chris couldn't hear what was said.

The seaman gave Danner the briefcase he was carrying. Danner took it to his car and put it on the roof, as he had the laptop, and popped it open. He inspected the contents, then shut it and put it in the trunk. He gave the truck driver a thumbs-up and the driver reached into the truck for a small cardboard box. He relayed the box to the seaman, who looked over the edge of the dock and dropped it, presumably to someone on the boat.

"What are they loading, drugs?" Chris whispered to Gene.

"Crystal meth," Gene said. "They make it at the plant and sell it here at the same time every week."

The transfer went quickly and the driver closed up the truck. There was another verbal exchange between Danner and the seaman, then the seaman patted Danner on the shoulder. They spoke some more and Danner laughed. Danner said something to the truck driver and headed for the ladder that led to the boat. The seaman followed, leaving the truck driver to watch the vehicles.

The driver lit another cigarette and wandered down the dock, where he stood for a moment looking out over the bay. Then he sat down, legs dangling from the edge of the dock.

Seeing him on the other side of the truck, his view of Danner's car totally blocked, a surge of adrenaline rolled through Chris like a tsunami. Even before arriving in Newark, she'd wished there was some way she could get access to Iliad's files. As much as she wanted that, she knew it was never going to happen. But the next best thing, Danner's laptop, was sitting unattended, barely ten yards away. And she was sure he hadn't locked his car.

Had she not been through that terrible experience on Stone Mountain, there was no way she'd have considered doing what she was thinking about. But having been so close to death that night, this seemed, by comparison, only minimally hazardous, especially since she had her cell phone.

Just a few seconds was all it would take.

As she teetered on the brink of go or no go, her body went on red alert, internal buzzers sounding, lights flashing.

The moment wouldn't last forever.

If she was going, it had to be now.

She moved quickly to the steps. "I'm coming down."

Michael descended and remained by the steps in case she needed a hand. Reaching the cement apron, she pulled her cell phone from her pocket and pressed it into Michael's hand. "I want that laptop's hard disk. You two head back the way we came in. I'll get the disk and follow you. If anything goes wrong, call nine-one-one."

Before either of the men could say anything, she darted across the dock to a cluster of blue-painted machinery with tarps lashed over the tops.

Michael couldn't believe what she was doing. But there she was, running along the machinery, toward Danner's car.

"Chris . . . don't do this," he whispered. "Come back."

But she either didn't hear or chose to ignore him. She cleared the machinery and was now out in the open.

Michael certainly wasn't going to leave her and go with Gene to some safer place. And he wasn't going to hide behind the crane while she was at risk. As for calling 911, now seemed like a good time, and if that somehow screwed up the chances of getting that hard disk, it was worth it because what Chris was doing was *nuts*.

Needing to get out there with her and not even knowing how to tell the cops exactly where they were, he turned to Gene, who was now standing beside him. "Take this phone and call nine-one-one." He gave Gene a quick lesson on the phone's operation, then ran for Danner's car, where Chris was yanking on the passenger door.

LOCKED, WOULDN'T YOU *know it*, Chris thought. She'd hoped this side of the car was open, so she wouldn't have to go in through the driver's side, where she'd be more easily seen. There was no way of knowing how long Danner would be on the boat. He could come up on the dock at any moment. Or that other bozo could decide to stroll back down here.

MICHAEL HAD EXPLAINED the phone so quickly Gene wasn't sure which button he was supposed to push to send his call. He thought he knew, but in the poor light behind the crane, he couldn't read the lettering on that button even though the keypad was illuminated. Not wanting to make a mistake, he moved forward where the light was better. As he did, he stumbled over one of the brackets that held the crane to the cement. The phone flew from his hand, skittered onto the dock, and slipped through a gap in the planking. A second later, he heard a faint splash when it hit the water.

"CHRIS, FORGET THAT disk, and let's get out of here," Michael whispered, arriving at her side. "This is a drug deal. These people are dangerous."

"I *want* that disk," she replied. "And I'm not leaving without it."

"The car's locked."

"The other door isn't."

Michael was tempted to grab her and drag her away, but he

couldn't bring himself to lay his hands on her like that. "Then stay here. I'll get it."

He ran around to the other side of the car and jerked the driver's door open. Ignoring the overhead light that flicked on, he ducked inside and grabbed the computer. Before he could leave, Chris tapped on the passenger window and motioned for him to unlock that door. Puzzled, he did what she asked.

Chris pulled the door open. "Give it to me, then get out and close that side."

Michael handed her the computer and crawled out of the car. He shut his door as quietly as possible.

Chris closed hers with the same care, then knelt to remove the laptop's hard disk. She'd decided to take just the disk, hoping that if Danner returned to his car before they were well gone, he wouldn't notice anything was wrong.

On the other side of the Lexus, Michael heard footsteps coming closer; the truck driver returning. What was Chris *doing* over there? She had the computer, but hadn't left. The footsteps were too close to risk telling her to get moving. Making a quick decision, he darted to the truck and stood with his back against it.

The footsteps were slow, so the guy must not have realized anything was wrong. Aware that what was about to transpire was high on the list of things surgeons shouldn't do with their bare hands, Michael kept his eyes trained on the spot where he guessed the guy's head would be when he rounded the truck.

As the driver stepped into view, Michael pivoted so he could use the full force of his upper body and he brought his right fist around in a looping arc. The blow struck the guy full on his nose, breaking it and producing a geyser of blood. Michael had known even before he'd struck that this had to be a one-punch fight. And it was, for the driver's legs gave way, and he went down.

If he'd fallen forward or backward, everything would have been fine, but he fell sideways. Seeing what was coming, Michael tried to catch him, but the guy was too heavy and he went over the edge of the dock like a sandbag.

•   •   •

ON THE BOAT below, Danner and the two men he'd been dealing with for over a year were just shaking hands to seal an agreement to increase future shipments by thirty percent when the truck driver hit the water. The cold brine instantly brought him back from punch land and he came up thrashing and spitting.

Enrique, the seaman who'd been on the dock with Danner, grabbed the driver's hand and with the help of his partner, Luis, they hauled him aboard.

"What the hell happened?" Danner asked the driver, whose nose was still bleeding.

"Somebody sucker punched me," he replied, wiping brine and blood away from his nose with the back of his hand.

"Everybody up on the dock," Danner yelled.

AS THE DRIVER toppled into the bay, Michael ran for the Lexus, where Chris hadn't yet figured out how to remove the laptop's hard disk.

"Come on, we have to go . . . *now*," he said.

With hard disk removal suddenly a moot issue, Chris got to her feet. Still holding the computer, she followed Michael at a dead run.

When they reached the crane, Gene, who'd seen what had happened and heard Danner yell, came out of its shadows. "Not this way . . . over here . . ."

Instead of leading them back the way they'd come, he ran toward the tarp-covered machinery. Not seeing the point of this, Chris and Michael hesitated.

"Come on," Gene hissed, waving them his way. "I know what I'm doin'."

It was clear to both of them that they didn't have any better options. Fervently hoping that Gene wasn't overestimating himself, Chris ran to join him. Her actions pulled Michael along.

BACK AT THE truck, Danner and his three accomplices were now on the dock, all of them armed with automatics. Danner checked the truck and then his car. "Damn it . . . somebody's stolen my laptop. I want these people. Enrique and I'll go this way," he said, pointing in the direction of the crane. "You two, that way. Whoever's here *has got* to be found." Before giving chase, he opened the trunk, made sure the money was there, and grabbed a flashlight.

Chris and Michael followed Gene through the maze formed by the blue machinery to another ladder leading to the water.

"Our best bet is to go *under* the dock," Gene whispered. He swung onto the ladder and started down.

As much as she'd risked to get her hands on it, Chris was afraid she might drop the computer if she tried to navigate the ladder with it. Reluctantly, she tucked it under a nearby tarp and followed Gene.

At the waterline, Gene stepped onto a narrow plank that ran perpendicular to the length of the dock, leaving room for Chris to move down the ladder and Michael to get on it. Bracing a hand against one of the planks that made up the cross ties of the decking above, Gene helped Chris off the ladder. At high tide the plank on which Gene stood was submerged, which meant it was coated with marine algae.

"Watch yourself," Gene said. "It's slippery."

Chris gingerly stepped onto the plank and slowly shifted her weight to that foot. Suddenly, she was sliding.

An umbrella opened in her chest as she fought to keep her balance.

She couldn't . . .

She was going down . . .

But Gene's grip tightened and he became a rock. With his help, she found her footing.

ENRIQUE GUTIERREZ, THIRTY-EIGHT years of age, still owned the Texas state high school pole vault record. This had not kept him from twice serving time for drug trafficking, and he had no intention of becoming a three-time loser. So he was highly motivated to find the *hijos de putas* who were screwing around up here. This would have been a hell of a lot easier had he thought to bring a flashlight from the boat, because the machine maze was a dark and dangerous place. And as he explored it, his nerves felt like they were running on the outside of his skin, making him ready to shoot anything that moved.

Although Enrique tried to make no sound, the water under the dock reflected and magnified his every step, so Chris and

Gene were well aware of his presence. And Michael was still out on the ladder. Afraid even to breathe, Chris tensed for the worst.

Michael didn't have the advantage of an echo effect where he stood, so the slight sounds of Enrique's movements were masked by the gentle slap of waves against the dock pilings. But he didn't have to hear Enrique to know he was somewhere in the maze. How could he not check out such a likely hiding place? The question was, would he notice the ladder?

Michael needed to get out of sight, but was afraid that if he moved, he'd make a noise that would give him away. So he remained still, hugged the ladder, and tried to make himself as thin as possible.

On the dock, as Enrique edged into position to look on the bay side of the last machine in the group, he tried to stay as far from the blind corner as possible. This caused him to brush against the tarp covering the machine behind him.

The rasping sound of Enrique's back against the tarp was so close it sent Michael's senses to Def Con four. The conclusion of this scenario was surely now only seconds away. If whoever was up there discovered the ladder and stepped near enough, Michael decided he'd try to grab the guy's feet and dump him in the bay. But assuming he could even accomplish that, if the guy screamed or got off a shot, the rest of them would come running.

Of course it was important that the people he was searching for be found, but Enrique was, in a way, pleased that he hadn't encountered anyone among the machines and had not been ambushed himself. He was now standing less than three feet from the ladder, and even in the poor light, all he had to do to see it was look down.

CHAPTER 37

ENRIQUE WAS SEARCHING for people, not ants, so when he rounded the last machine and found no one hiding behind it, he had no reason to look down. Though they were still in great peril, Michael, Chris, and Gene all felt relieved as Enrique hurried from the machine maze to search elsewhere.

Michael was more surefooted than Chris, and when he stepped onto the slippery plank after being warned by her of its condition, there were no problems.

"There's another ladder down the dock, near where we came in," Gene whispered. "We can get to it on a line of planks that connects with this one, farther back."

"We should call for help before we do anything else," Chris said. "Michael, I hope you've still got the phone."

"Help is already on the way," Michael said. "Gene called before we had to run for it." Hearing no affirmation from the old man, Michael said, "You did make the call . . ."

"The phone fell in the bay before I could do it. I'm sorry . . ."

His admission was so stunning, neither Chris nor Michael could speak.

"All right, I know, I'm clumsy and stupid," Gene said. "But we'll be okay. We'll get to the other ladder, and when the time is right, we'll climb up and get out of here."

Michael thought about throwing a little criticism at Gene, too, but remembering that he'd set off the alarm by knocking that goon in the bay, he said nothing. Nor did Chris, the primary culprit in their troubles, feel that she had any right to complain.

"The planks are all slippery," Gene said. "So be careful. Let's move."

The timbers in the decking overhead were several inches apart. This allowed a tiny amount of light from above to filter through. It wasn't enough to actually see Gene in front of them, but only to sense him. Without even listening hard, they could still hear Danner and his men running around the dock, looking for them.

The plank on which they were standing was sixteen inches vertically, but presented them with an edge only three and a half inches wide, room for a relatively easy stroll, except that it was treacherously slimy and they couldn't even see it. Holding on to the decking overhead and moving as carefully as possible, Chris and Michael followed Gene deeper into the underdock.

"Here's where we turn left," Gene said. "It's another plank, just like the one we're on."

They all made the turn without mishap and began to move slowly in the new direction. From far off, they heard a shout.

"Here's a ladder. They could be under the dock. Bring that flashlight."

More running footsteps.

"They're coming down here," Chris said. "Gene, what should we do?"

"We have to get in the water—to the land side of this plank we're on."

"Let's hear idea number two," Chris said.

"There's no alternative," Gene said. "The tide is low enough that when we're in the water, the plank will hide us. And we have to go now."

There was a slight splash as Gene entered the water.

Down where the shouting had come from, Paul Danner descended the ladder with his flashlight.

Out of time for discussion, Chris let go of her hold on the overhead decking and carefully squatted until she had one knee on the plank under her. She bent down, got a two-handed grip on the plank, and did an awkward dismount.

As she hit the water, the word that filled her mind was "Cold." And it wasn't like being cold when you were dry. This cold crept into every crevice and secret part of her body. Feeling only water under her feet, she started them in a rhythmic paddling motion.

"No hands showin'," Gene cautioned. "Hold on to the bottom of the plank."

On the ladder, Paul Danner swept the underdock with the beam of his flashlight. Powerful as it was, its beam didn't carry far enough. Dissatisfied with his inspection, Danner climbed back onto the dock. "I didn't see anybody," he said to Enrique. "But we need to look more thoroughly. Go back to the boat and cruise along the dock with your spotlight."

With the immediate danger passed, the trio in the water all moved their hands back to the top of the plank.

"They're going to use the boat to check this area with a spotlight," Michael whispered, telling the others what they'd already heard for themselves.

"Won't matter," Gene said. "Light can't penetrate wood. We stay here; they'll never see us."

"Unless they send someone *in* here with a flashlight," Chris said.

"Then they might," Gene agreed.

Chris didn't know about the others, but her body wasn't getting used to the cold water, and the smell of creosote, gasoline, and rotting fish was making her queasy.

Soon they heard the boat starter being cranked. The engine sprang to life, and whoever was behind the wheel pushed the gas to it, swinging the boat into position so it could parallel the dock, Chris guessed.

The engine dropped back to a lower speed and settled into a steady throb. But instead of getting progressively louder, it grew fainter.

"Went the other way first," Michael said. "You all right, Chris?"

It was exactly that moment when Chris realized this bay was part of the Atlantic. And oceans have sharks. Long ago, she'd loved the shore and had often swum in the sea during holidays in Destin, Florida. One day she'd taken a helicopter ride over the shore, and the pilot had pointed out the many sharks patrolling the surf, some of them less than a hundred yards from swimmers. This was the first time she'd been in the ocean since that day, and here she was, feet dangling like human sushi. The wound on her hand from last night's attack was no longer bleeding, but she worried that sharks could smell it anyway.

"Chris, are you okay?" Michael asked again.

"I can think of a few other places I'd rather be," she replied, not wanting to burden the others with her shark fears.

Far down the dock, the boat's engine began to sing.

"They'll be coming this way now," Michael said.

"Watch your hands," Gene warned.

Very reluctantly, Chris put her hands back in the water.

The engine dropped to search speed and the boat came in their direction. About fifty yards away, a bright circle of light invaded the darkness and methodically explored.

As the boat grew inexorably closer, Chris felt even more nauseated.

The spotlight traveled along the seawall behind them, stopped a few feet short of their position, and crawled downward, across the plank hiding them. Chris's stomach gave a final warning.

No . . . she couldn't . . . not now. Even with the boat engine to mask the sound, she might be heard.

She issued her stomach orders to calm down. And it seemed to be helping, when suddenly, the spotlight returned, raked the wall behind them, then dropped and traveled along their protective plank.

For the first time Chris wondered if the light would penetrate the water and reveal them *below* the plank. As if answering that question, three shots echoed through the underdock. One tore through the plank, shredding it. A second hit the seawall, ricocheted, and zipped into the water. There was a squeal as the third hit its intended target, a big wharf rat that either jumped or was blown off the plank into the water near Chris's right shoulder, where it squealed and struggled and shed blood into the water.

The gunfire brought hurried footsteps into the machine maze above.

"Do you see them?" Danner asked from the edge of the dock.

"Nah, it was just a rat," Enrique said. "And there's nothin' I hate worse."

"Forget the rats and stay focused," Danner barked.

The light and the boat slowly moved on. When it seemed safe to make a little noise, Chris began creating waves with her hands to push the dying rat toward the seawall. Addition of the rat to the stew should have made her even sicker. But the fear she'd felt when the shooting began, and her worry now about any sharks in the area being drawn to the rat's blood, took over her queasy stomach circuitry, so at least on that score, she felt better.

"I was sure he'd seen us," Michael said.

"I told you, light can't penetrate wood," Gene said.

"It was those slugs I was worried about."

"Are we in the clear now, do you think?" Chris asked.

"I don't believe they'll look in here again," Michael said.

"We better stay in the water, though," Gene warned.

"Let's move down and get away from that rat," Chris said.

They worked their way along the plank for about thirty feet and stopped. They heard the boat continue along the dock at low speed for another few minutes. Then its engine began to roar. It came back at high speed, passed by, and returned to the ladder where it had originally tied up.

"There's nobody down here," they heard Enrique shout to Danner.

"Damn it," Danner said. "I don't know where they could be. But I'm not going to stay here all night. We can't meet here anymore. In fact, everything is now on hold. I'll let you know what the new plans are in a few days. If you don't hear from me, just sit tight."

A few seconds of silence elapsed, then the boat engine revved up a notch. It maintained that speed for a few more seconds before its pilot opened the throttle. As the roar of the boat slowly faded and the waves from its wake slapped against the plank that had kept Enrique from seeing more than a rat, the engines of the car and the truck on the dock joined the mix. These sounds, too, quickly faded.

Under the dock, no one spoke right away, but all listened hard, afraid to believe that Danner and his men were truly gone. But they heard only the sound of water lapping against wood and cement. Seconds slid by and it remained quiet.

"Are they really gone?" Chris said. "Or is it a trap?"

"I'll check," Gene said. "If it is a trick and I'm caught, I'll just pretend to be drunk. They're more likely to believe I'm here alone than if they catch either of you."

"Be careful," Chris said.

"I'll go, too," Michael said.

"Weren't you listenin'?" Gene said. "Dr. Collins will be safer if it's just me. You stay with her."

Gene hoisted himself over the plank and back into the water on the other side, where he set out in a breaststroke for the ladder. When he reached it, he climbed up and stepped onto the dock.

Still worried about sharks, Chris said, "I'm getting out of the water." She hauled herself onto the plank and managed to get to her feet. Michael did the same.

Balanced on the thin plank, with water draining from their clothes, they quickly became even colder than they had been, but neither of them complained.

They stood there long enough that Chris began to shiver, and Michael had a thought. "I wonder if he's left us."

"He had a chance to do that when we were both at Danner's car, so I don't think—"

She was interrupted by the sound of someone on the ladder. It immediately occurred to both of them that if it wasn't Gene, they'd be easy targets for someone with a flashlight and a gun.

"It's okay," Gene said. "Come on."

Reluctant to get back in the water, Michael and Chris made their way to the ladder using Plank Avenue. Michael was in front, so he went up first and helped Chris onto the dock. As soon as she was off the ladder, Chris went to the tarp where she'd hidden Danner's laptop.

It seemed unlikely that Danner and his men could have found it, but as her hand slid behind the tarp, that small possibility loomed large.

But the computer was still there.

With it once again in her possession, Chris's spirits lifted.

"I don't know about you two, but I think I've gotten about all this experience has to offer."

Leaving wet footprints on the dock, they headed back the way they'd come in.

When they reached the alley leading to the car and were no longer out in the open, Michael muttered, "That guy Danner is a real lowlife. Considering what we already knew about him, I guess we shouldn't be surprised at what we just saw. He'll obviously do anything for a buck."

Feeling cold and miserable, they plodded up the alley. As they approached the street where they'd parked, Michael suddenly stopped walking and whispered. "Wait a minute . . . Wasn't there a light over that loading dock when we arrived?"

"I don't remember," Chris said.

"I'm sure there was," Gene said.

"Let's get into some cover." Michael guided Gene and Chris into the deep shadows of the adjacent building on their left. "You two stay here."

While the others did as he instructed, Michael crept along the side of the warehouse and took a discreet look around the corner, in the opposite direction from where they'd parked. He lingered there a moment, then came back to the others. "There's a white truck sitting in the dark around the corner. And someone's in it smoking."

"The truck from the dock," Chris said.

"And probably the same guy inside," Michael said. "They must have seen our car and left him here to watch for us."

"Is he alone?" Chris asked.

"I think so, but reinforcements may be on the way."

"What are we going to do?"

"I'm going to let him catch me."

"What do you mean?"

"Don't worry, I can handle him. Once I get him under control, we're not going to have much time, so when I give the word, Gene, you check the truck for his keys, that's probably where they'll be."

"Why not let *me* bait him to the car," Gene said. "Then you could jump him from behind."

"I let you take the lead back there on the dock because it made sense for the situation. But this is different. I can do this alone, and unless you're planning on leaving town, I don't think you want to be seen with us."

"Agreed, that could be a problem."

"Or *I* could bait him," Chris said.

"He's not going to want to believe a woman punched him into the bay, so if he sees you, he'll immediately think you must be with someone."

"Maybe we should just leave the car," Chris said.

"I'd rather ride out of here than walk. I can handle him. I promise."

"I believe you."

Truthfully, Chris wasn't so sure. Without a gun in the equation, she'd have had complete confidence in him, but the guy in the truck was surely armed.

"Okay, here I go." Michael turned and nonchalantly walked down the middle of the alley and into plain view of the truck. He turned right and took no more than half a dozen steps before Chris heard the truck's door open.

"Hey, cowboy," a voice called out. "Hold on there."

The truck driver came into view holding an automatic in his right hand.

"How come you're all wet?" he said.

"Freak rainstorm," Michael replied.

"You're the one who sucker punched me on the dock, ain't you?" the guy said, moving closer. "Where's the computer you stole?"

He was now standing just a few feet from Michael. Seeing no reason she couldn't give Michael a little help, Chris shouted, "Drop the gun, creep."

As the goon reflexively turned his head slightly in her direction, Michael stepped forward, grabbed the guy's gun hand, and drove it upward. A shot rang out and the two men scuffled. In seconds, the gun was on the ground and Michael was behind the guy, his left arm around the goon's neck, his right pinning the guy's gun hand to his back. In another few seconds, the guy quit struggling and Michael let him slump to the ground.

"Time to get those keys," Michael shouted.

While Gene bolted for the truck, Michael picked up the gun and motioned for Chris. "Let's move."

"I got the keys," Gene said, hurrying toward the others.

In moments, they were in their car speeding from the scene.

"Drop the gun, creep?" Michael said, grinning from behind the wheel.

"It was all I could think to say," Chris replied, sitting beside him, Danner's computer safe in her lap.

"Gene, where do you want to go?" Michael asked.

"Home."

Following Gene's instructions and with the heater on to warm them up, they took a route that kept them off the street where the Iliad plant was located. When they reached Gene's alley, Michael pulled up in front of the old man's culvert and they all got out.

"We make a good team," Gene said.

"Thank you for helping us when we were in trouble," Chris said. "You could have saved yourself, but you didn't."

"I wasn't expectin' you to run out and take that computer, but I still felt responsible for you. Even if you hadn't done that, us just bein' on the dock was risky. I could have simply told you what goes on there instead of takin' you. But it wears on you to be a bum, with everybody lookin' down on you. I guess I just wanted a few minutes where I could be with folks like you sort of as an equal . . . Not that I ever could be that."

"I understand," Chris said. "And I also know you're a good and brave man. And I'm proud to know you." She leaned over and kissed him on the cheek.

"That goes for me, too," Michael said. "Except for the kiss." He dug in his wet pants for his wallet. "I want to give you something to help you out."

Gene raised his hand. "You already have. Now you better get out of here before somebody sees us and you ruin my reputation."

"Will you be okay?" Chris said. "With those men, I mean."

"I'm not somebody they'll spend any time thinkin' about. So, sure. I'll be fine. You two have good lives, and I hope whatever you need from that computer is there. I'll make sure it's safe for you to leave."

While Michael and Chris got back in their car, Gene walked to the mouth of the alley and checked the street. He motioned for them to proceed.

Michael backed up quickly and made a tight turn in the

street. He dropped the car into Drive and off they went. Chris turned to wave good-bye, but Gene had already disappeared into the alley.

As the bleak warehouse district sped by, Chris wondered what her life would have been like if she'd had Gene for a father. He certainly would never have left her and her mother. Nothing about their two lives seemed fair. She'd been denied love, and Gene had lost the family he loved. Why did life have to be so perverse?

"Did you bring any clothing on this trip you can't bear to lose?" Michael said.

"I'm sorry. What did you say?"

"Danner obviously believed he'd found our car. If I were him, I wouldn't just post someone to intercept us when we came back to it, I'd try to get inside and go through the glove compartment to see if I could find the name of the owner."

Chris opened the glove compartment. "The rental agreement is in here," she said.

"The car was still locked, but that doesn't prove they weren't in it. And even if they didn't break in, they could run a check on the plates."

"Then contact the rental agency and get your name," Chris said.

"If they had my name, they could find out where we're staying."

"By calling all the motels in Newark? Come on, now you're losing me. That would be *so* much work."

"Considering what we saw at the dock, he's got a lot at stake. Do you want to take the chance he wouldn't do that?"

"No."

"Let's get out of here tonight—right to the airport and out on whatever flight is available to Atlanta."

"Looking like this?"

"We'll find a Wal-Mart and get some dry clothes. We can change at a Burger King or something."

"I guess we have no choice."

"How much do you figure that laptop is worth?"

"A couple thousand."

"That makes its theft a felony. I hope there's something useful on it."

"Let's find out." Chris eagerly flipped the laptop open and

turned it on. The screen quickly powered up and Chris scanned the folders displayed on it.

"Uh-oh." She clicked on a folder, then on a file inside.

"What have we got?" Michael asked.

"Dates and amounts of meth delivered every week for the last six months and the names of the recipients."

"Very incriminating stuff. Anything else?"

She closed that file and looked further. About halfway down the screen, in the middle of a row of folders that didn't seem of any interest, she saw one that definitely caught her attention.

"Here's a folder titled 'Ash contract.'"

She opened the folder. Inside were two files. The title of the first repeated the folder title, but the second made her eyes widen even further.

"Michael . . . there are two files in here. One with Ash's name on it and the other with the name Dewitt."

"Carter Dewitt, the Monteagle VP for financial affairs?"

"His first name isn't there, but it *has* to be him."

Chris opened the file with Ash's name on it and began to read.

Michael waited impatiently for less than a minute, then said, "Well?"

"I need a little more time."

As Chris read, her mind went on a tear, arranging everything that had happened in the last few weeks into a logical construct that was as sickening as it was horrible.

CHAPTER 38

"THEY'RE MURDERERS," CHRIS said. "The Fairborns, Mary Beth Cummings, the Barrosos, Dan Gaynor, Lucy Cowles—they killed all of them."

"What the devil are you reading?" Michael asked.

"It's a contract between Ash and Iliad giving Ash one third ownership of the patent for a therapeutic virus they're calling T-1, but which I'm sure is *our* virus. It's all so obvious. When our virus was purely therapeutic, I'm sure there was a bidding war going on for it, but when it turned lethal, its value must have plummeted. So Iliad got the rights from Monteagle very cheaply."

"But it *isn't* really lethal," Michael said, taking up the story. "Ash somehow infected the nurses and the others with the Kazak hantavirus."

"That has to be what happened. Ash was the one with Lansden in Kazakhstan. He brought hanta samples back with him and for some reason just kept them in his freezer. The epi one Sam Fairborn found said that shortly after an infected person or animal died, the medical team could no longer find any virus in the body, that the virus must have been very sensitive to degradation by all the enzymes the victim's cells release after death."

"Making it untraceable," Michael said. "The perfect murder weapon."

"They could have infected those who died by contaminating the needles used at Monteagle for drawing blood samples from all the victims."

"But why did they kill Gaynor and Cowles?"

"Those were either mistakes—infected needles ending up in the wrong place—or they did it intentionally to draw more attention to the lethal nature of the virus. The bigger the stink, the less competition Iliad would have buying the rights from Monteagle."

"That's where Dewitt came in. He must have helped steer the sale to Iliad."

"Let me check just to be sure . . ." Chris opened the Dewitt file and scanned the first few lines of that contract. "There it is—Carter Allen Dewitt."

"How was the virus in the contract described?" Michael asked.

"It was identified by its RNA sequence."

"But we don't know the sequence of our virus because Ash said he hadn't determined it, which must have been a lie. Without knowing that our virus and the one in the contracts are the same, the rest is just conjecture. And from what I've seen of Detective Lenihan, the cops are going to want proof they're identical."

"How can we get proof? All the blood samples that had our virus in them were turned over to Iliad. Wait a minute . . . There *is* one place where we might be able to get a sample. My father."

"How can we do that? There's no transplant virus *in* his blood anymore. Like all the others who got infected, he was virus positive for only a few days."

"I read a report a few years ago that HIV gets sequestered in lymph nodes. And both HIV and our virus are retroviruses. So maybe we can find our virus by biopsying one of my father's nodes. We could take it over to a virologist at the CDC for sequencing. I know it's a long shot to think we'll find it, especially since our virus doesn't behave like a typical retrovirus, but I can't think of any other way to get a sample."

"Let's do it . . . if Wayne will agree."

By the time they'd found a Wal-Mart, changed into their new clothes, and reached the airport, it was so late the first flight they could get to Atlanta was at five-thirty the next morning. Apart from the dismal prospect of spending the night at the airport, both were concerned that the goon Michael had put to sleep in the alley might cruise the place with some friends looking for Michael. And since the airport was already practically deserted, he'd be easy to spot.

At Chris's suggestion, they'd kept the rental car until they'd checked on available flights, so they at least still had transportation. Deciding that it was being overly cautious to worry about Danner's men cruising every motel parking lot in Newark looking for the car, they bought a few toiletries at an all-night drugstore, then found a cheap place to stay, where they registered under false names and paid for their rooms in moist cash.

The next morning, with Chris's eyes a little bloodshot and Michael's hand aching from punching the goon on the dock, they returned the rental car, caught their flight, and were back in Atlanta a little before 8 A.M., carrying their salt-encrusted clothing and Danner's laptop in a couple of plastic Wal-Mart bags.

"Let's call Wayne," Chris said as they passed a bank of pay phones in the terminal.

"Do you know his number?"

"I remember it."

Wayne answered, sounding a little groggy.

"This is Chris. Michael and I want to talk to you about something. Is it okay if we come over now? . . . Good. We'll be there in about half an hour."

WAYNE CAME TO the door of his apartment looking alert, well groomed, and in good health. This caused Chris to conclude that his lethargy on the phone earlier had been because she'd awakened him, not the effects of a hangover.

"You two are certainly out early this morning," Wayne said, letting them in. Seeing the bandage across the bridge of Chris's nose and the one on her hand, he said, "Boy, you did get banged up the other night."

"It wasn't something I'd want to do again."

"The news said the guy is dead. I was glad to hear it. I'm just sorry you had to go through that."

"Me, too."

"I got some news myself yesterday. I thought about calling you, but I wanted to tell you in person. I almost can't believe it. I've had a novel making the rounds in New York for so long I'd given up hope on it. But my agent called yesterday. She's sold it . . . not to one of the major houses, but another real publisher. They've offered me a two-book deal. The advance isn't six figures or anything, but I'm going to be back in print."

"Congratulations," Chris said.

Michael extended his hand. "Wayne, that's great. I'm happy for you."

As Wayne and Michael shook hands, Chris was surprised to realize that she felt proud of Wayne. To keep writing after what he'd been through—all the rejections—it was a fine accomplishment. A part of her wanted to hug him and tell him she was proud and share his triumph. Instead, she heard herself say, "I met an interesting person while I was gone, a homeless man who once had a wife and daughter. But they were killed in a plane crash. He was so devastated by the loss that he's wandered the streets ever since, unable to forget them, too grief stricken to care about anything else. What do you think of that?"

The joy went out of Wayne's eyes as her dagger found its mark. "I think what happened to him was a terrible thing. But it was his family that died. He didn't. He should never forget them, but he's carried the pain with him far too long. And as a result it's damaged him. I'm sure his wife and daughter wouldn't have wanted that kind of life for him. He needs to let the wound heal."

Seeing that Chris had gone off the tracks, Michael interceded. "Wayne, we're here to ask a favor. We'd like to take a biopsy of one of your lymph nodes to see if it contains any copies of the transplant virus. It's a quick procedure. We'll have you in and out in no time."

Even Chris was aware that her attack on Wayne was counterproductive to securing his cooperation for a biopsy, so she willingly let the focus of the conversation shift in that direction. From the moment she'd suggested that they try to get a virus sample from Wayne, both she and Michael had had doubts he'd agree. Now that he was smarting from having Gene thrown in his face, they both waited for his answer even more apprehensively than they might have if she hadn't done that.

Speaking to Michael, Wayne said, "You've given me back my life. How can I refuse you a favor?"

Michael called the hospital, checked on the availability of an OR, and set up the procedure for one o'clock that afternoon. Then he and Chris left.

"I shouldn't have mentioned Gene to him," Chris said on the way to Michael's car. "I didn't plan to do it; it simply slipped out. My anger toward what he did is like a kitchen fire I think I've got under control, then it suddenly springs back to life."

"With the rocky relationship you two have had, it's going to take a while for you both to find common ground. What do you want to do about the incriminating meth file on Danner's laptop?"

"For now, nothing. Until we get the results of the biopsy, I don't want to alert Ash or Dewitt in any way."

"That seems wise to me, too. What are we going to do with the computer?"

"I'll lock it up in my home file cabinet. As soon as I get cleaned up, I'll call the CDC and line up someone to analyze that node."

"How long will the analysis take?"

"I'll ask."

When they reached the parking lot of Chris's apartment, she put her hand on Michael's arm. "Thanks for going to Newark with me. I don't know what I would have done without you."

"That's what I've been trying to tell you."

WHEN MICHAEL AND Chris left, Wayne slumped into his chair in front of the TV, his book deal tarnished by his daughter's refusal to forgive him for what he'd done as a foolish young man who'd had storms raging inside him he didn't understand or know how to control. If there was some way he could confront that man now, he'd beat him senseless.

Wasn't love supposed to conquer all? Apparently that

didn't extend to strong-willed women wronged by their old man.

He sat there for a long time, until he began to wonder if he even knew the meaning of love. Maybe Chris was right. He *shouldn't* be forgiven. Maybe there was something fundamental missing in him and his wish for forgiveness was just another selfish act to make *him* feel better.

The realization that he was quite possibly a man without a soul blew across him like a cold wind.

CHAPTER 39

THE PAGE IN front of Detective Lenihan was filled with row after row of the letters A, U, G, and C in different combinations. Under each row of black letters there was a row of red letters.

"The black lettering is the nucleotide sequence of the virus in the contract on Paul Danner's computer," Chris explained. "The red lettering is the sequence the CDC obtained from virus found in one of my father's lymph nodes."

Chris paused while Lenihan bent to examine the two sequences. When he'd had enough time to get the picture, she said, "They're identical."

"Obviously, Ash lied when he told us he hadn't sequenced the transplant virus," Michael said. "He did sequence it, but didn't want anyone to know that much about it until Iliad had secured the rights."

"But in order for the contract between him and Iliad to mean anything, the virus had to be specifically identified," Chris said.

"This story you've outlined for me goes far beyond the authority of the Fayette County sheriff's office," Lenihan said.

"We're aware of that," Chris replied. "But we were sure you'd know what to do next."

"I'll have to bring the Atlanta and Newark police in on it."

"Good," Chris said. "The sooner the better."

"I'll need to take that laptop as evidence."

"It's all yours."

"I have to tell you, this alone isn't going to be enough to hang these guys. But I'm pretty sure it'll give us probable cause to get a search warrant."

"Looking for what?"

"I'm not at liberty to say. Was there anything else you wanted to tell me?"

Chris shrugged. "We thought what we already said would be more than enough."

"I'll get to work on it and we'll see what happens."

"I'M NOT ENCOURAGED," Chris said to Michael in the hall after leaving Lenihan's office.

"I admit, I kind of expected them to run right over to Monteagle and arrest both Ash and Dewitt."

"A search warrant . . . What do they expect that to produce? Ash isn't so stupid as to keep any incriminating evidence around. I'll bet he's even destroyed his remaining stocks of Kazak hanta. After all we went through to get that computer, I can't believe it doesn't mean anything."

"It got Lenihan moving."

"Ash has to pay for what he did. He just *has* to."

AS ERIC ASH pulled into the Monteagle parking garage, he was still troubled over the events of the past few days. First, that idiot, Garland, botched the hit on the Collins woman, then there was the conversation he'd had with Paul Danner yesterday. His laptop stolen, with Danner just a few feet away. And with the virus contracts on it.

Damn his carelessness.

But the real worrisome part of that story was the description of the thief: curly blond hair, heavyset. That sounded a hell of a lot like Michael Boyer. There was a woman present as well. And no one seemed to know where Boyer or Collins was yesterday. All that made him feel as though a storm were building that he was powerless to stop. He'd considered marshaling what resources he could and clearing out, but then what? A life where he'd have to live as a fugitive under a phony name, waiting tables for a living? He couldn't do that. It was this life or a better one, nothing less. So he'd have to be optimistic and hope that *wasn't* Boyer and Collins in Newark. Even if it was and they thought they had it figured out, they'd need the transplant virus sequence to prove anything. And they didn't have it. So he'd stay strong, behave normally, and hold on.

Ash pulled into his parking space, got out of the car, and locked it. Suddenly, men in ill-fitting suits were coming toward him from all directions. Behind him, he heard a familiar voice.

"Dr. Ash, I have a search warrant for your car, your office, and your home."

Ash turned to face Detective Lenihan. Though the blood was pounding in Ash's ears, he struggled to appear calm as the men closed in. Lenihan gave Ash a document.

"We'd like to begin with your car. May I have the keys?"

Wordlessly, Ash detached his car key from his other keys and gave it to Lenihan.

"Step back, please," Lenihan said.

As Ash moved out of the way, he noticed that a small crowd of Monteagle employees was gathering to see what was taking place. Embarrassed, his face began to flush and his mind took him back to a spring morning in Clayton, Alabama, a long time ago.

"His parents threw him out with the trash. That makes him trash too. It's even part of his name. Ash . . . T R-ash . . . T R-ash . . ."

The taunting rang in his ears, making his face even redder and suffusing it with heat.

He snapped back to the present, where three of the men with Lenihan were now in Ash's car, rooting through it, violating his privacy. He looked at the small knot of people watching and whispering to each other, whispering about *him*.

Lenihan moved to the trunk, slipped on a pair of rubber gloves, and inserted the key in the lock.

Go ahead and look, you bastard, Ash thought. *You won't find anything.* In addition to getting rid of all the stuff associated with his visit to the Fairborns, he'd also disposed, albeit extremely reluctantly, of all the remaining samples of Kazak hanta. So there was nothing to incriminate him. But being humiliated like this in front of people he knew was intolerable.

The trunk opened and Ash moved around to where he could make an appropriately sarcastic comment when Lenihan realized there was nothing in there. But as Ash moved closer, he saw something inexplicable on the floor of the trunk and he nearly screamed out loud.

As part of his plan to make the Fairborn murders appear to be nothing more than a burglary gone wrong, he'd taken, in addition to a lot of other things in the house, Ann Fairborn's jewelry. Lenihan now reached into the trunk and picked up a diamond earring that had somehow fallen out of the pillowcase Ash had dumped that jewelry into.

Lenihan examined the earring, then laid it back on the trunk carpeting. From an inside pocket of his suit coat, he produced a small clasp-top envelope that he opened and tapped into his gloved hand until the matching earring he'd found on the floor of the Fairborns' bedroom slid into his palm. He slipped the empty envelope into a different pocket, then picked up the earring in the trunk and compared them. Finding them an exact match, he turned to tell Ash he was under arrest for the murders of Ann and Sam Fairborn, but Ash was gone.

Lenihan looked at the small crowd of gawkers. "Did any of you see where Dr. Ash went?"

A couple of them pointed to the garage stairwell.

Lenihan hurried to the front of the car. "He's on the run, boys. Kenny, stay with the car. Doug, you and Blaine come with me."

The three detectives sprinted for the stairwell, where Lenihan sent one of his men up while he and the other one headed down.

AWARE THAT HE was drawing attention to himself, Ash ran along the hallway connecting the second level of the garage with the hospital. He'd taken off when he'd seen Lenihan reach into his pocket for that envelope. He hadn't been there to see what was in the envelope, but he knew it was the matching earring he'd purposely left on the floor of the Fairborns' bedroom to show the cops that the Fairborns had been killed by a robber, and now that very earring had come back to haunt him. Of all the things to leave in the trunk. He should have checked the trunk the next day when there was more light. The improbability that this could have happened made him want to smash something.

But through his anger he realized that even if they hadn't found the second earring, there was a good chance the cops could have used Dewitt against him—promised him immunity in return for the truth. He felt sure now that if they squeezed Dewitt, he'd squeal like one of Hessman's pigs.

Ash pushed the door open to the south wing stairwell and clattered down the steps, brushing past two nurses coming up. He darted onto the first floor and set out in a brisk walk for the far end of the hall, fearing that at any moment he'd hear his name shouted from behind him—or in front.

Lenihan could have had other men with him parked around the building. One could even be coming down that intersecting hallway this minute. Ash slowed to a walk and glanced behind him, then looked back the other way. Anxiously, he set out once more for the far stairwell, his eyes riveted on the corner where the other hallway might at any moment disgorge another detective.

When he reached the dangerous intersection, he moved over to hug the wall and edged one eye around the corner for a cautious look. But all he saw was a member of the maintenance staff reglueing a flap of loose wallpaper. No detectives.

Then he was again on the move.

At the destination stairwell, he yanked the door open and headed for the basement. Sweat running down his spine and pearling on his forehead, he emerged a few seconds later, turned to the right, and froze.

Shit.

Ten yards ahead, an employee from Central Supply was standing by a flatbed cart loaded with boxes, waiting for the elevator. Not wanting anyone to see where he was going, Ash stepped back into the stairwell and shut the door.

After an appropriate wait, he checked the hall. Good. The guy was gone.

Before anyone else could appear and get in his way, Ash hurried down the hall and disappeared into the stairwell that led to the subbasement. At the bottom of those stairs he opened a heavy metal door and confronted hell on earth: the mechanical heart of the hospital—huge generators, submarine-shaped boilers, and great air handlers groaning and hissing, pumping out heat that rolled from the open door in suffocating waves that seemed to crush Ash's chest like a python, everything packed in so tightly there was barely room for the narrow metal grated walkway that led into the depths of the monster. Ash loosened his tie and took a couple of seconds to get his mind right, then he went inside.

He followed the walkway deep into the room, looking for a nook where he could secrete himself and not be seen by anyone else who might come down here, yet would allow him to see them. He soon found such a spot—a flat metal surface up high where he could sit with his back against a big insulated duct firm enough to support him and that wasn't hot to the touch. In front of him, six large pipes formed a vertical wall that made it impossible for anyone on the walkway to see him. But he could look out through the tiny gaps between the pipes. Not that he could do anything about it should they find him. But it was the best he could manage.

He stripped off his tie and briefly reflected on how much he'd paid for it. Then he looked up, wondering if there were any pipes that would support his weight if he used his tie to hang himself, because there was no way he could tolerate the shame of being led to a car in handcuffs and pushed inside.

He knew that after you were arrested there was an arraignment in open court where the participants practically shouted out the sordid details of the case so everyone in the place could hear. And when the media found out about *his* arrest, they'd be there in droves, writing about him—how he acted, how he looked. And there would be TV cameras, their operators falling over themselves so they could broadcast his picture around the country, and they'd recite the charges against him on the five o'clock news, and again at ten and probably again the next morning.

No, by God. He wouldn't be humiliated like that ever again. His act of looking for an appropriate pipe from which he could hang himself was largely a symbolic gesture arising from self-pity. Because this was not the time for that. There was still work to do.

He carefully folded his tie and put it beside him, thinking

of Jimmy Demarco, his chief tormentor when he was a schoolboy. Why couldn't Jimmy have left him alone? Instead, Jimmy chose to ridicule him, to insert himself into matters that didn't concern him. And he'd paid for it. That was important work worth doing, making Jimmy pay. But there were still too many Jimmy Demarcos in the world.

Lord, but it was hot in here.

He unbuttoned his shirt to his waist, pulled it open, and began what would be a long ordeal if he wasn't discovered.

For the first hour, he was nervous and extremely uncomfortable, but gradually the repetitious sounds of the machinery and the unceasing heat lulled and baked him, until, senses dulled, he lapsed into sleep.

He woke thirty minutes later and for a brief instant didn't know where he was. But then it all came back in a sickening rush. He'd perspired so much his shirt was soaked. And despite having lost all that water, he still had to pee.

To fit into his hidey hole he had to sit with his knees bent and his feet drawn up. Now, as he tried to shift his position, he found his legs stiff. Moving like an old man, he climbed down and relieved himself into the grated floor of the walkway, aware now that his shorts, too, were wet with sweat.

Bladder emptied, he climbed back onto his perch, the incessant noise around him dimming his memory of what silence was like. What a horrible place this was. But that was its attraction, for no one would expect him to be hiding in such an inhospitable place. Terrible as it was, he would have to remain until after dark, which meant . . . He looked at his watch; 9:30 A.M. Another ten hours. How could he manage to stay here *ten* more hours?

Suddenly, he heard a new sound over the old—the door to the room opening. His view of the doorway was blocked, so he couldn't see Lenihan surveying the room.

Appalled at the noise and the heat, Lenihan hesitated. Then he came inside.

CHAPTER 40

TWO STEPS INTO the machine room the heat was far worse than it had been standing in the doorway, so bad, in fact, Lenihan didn't think that even a man on the run for murder would choose this as a place to hide. With a final quick glance around, he turned and left.

For Ash, time became another enemy, making him increasingly uncomfortable and draining his patience as it tried to drive him from his nest. But he remained resolute and stayed put, determined that he, not Lenihan, would decide how the final events of his life played out.

A little after two in the afternoon he woke from one of the fitful little snatches of sleep he'd been able to manage a couple of times each hour. He'd now lost so much fluid from sweating he had none to spare for salivation and his mouth was as dry as a dead man's.

In the basement hallway there was a water fountain beside the elevator. He was sure of it. He could run up there, satisfy his raging thirst, and be back in a minute or two.

But suppose someone saw him. Surely by now the news that he was being pursued by the police would be all over the hospital. If he was seen at the water fountain . . .

He couldn't risk it.

Instead, he began to explore, looking for a water pipe with a faulty connection. And in a few minutes, he found one. But it was so close to the floor he had to lie on his back to get his mouth under the drip, which delivered only one drop of tepid water every minute or so.

It was a precarious situation because he was lying with his feet in the walkway and anyone who came in would see him. This drove him back to his hiding place before his thirst was slaked, but the little water he'd been able to consume made him feel better.

WAYNE WAS WAITING for Chris when she pulled up at the gate leading to the apartments overlooking the Cabana Grove's pool.

"What happened to the side of your car?" he said, getting in.

"It got banged up when I was being chased by that guy on Stone Mountain. I'm taking it over to the insurance claims agent tomorrow."

"You never told me exactly what happened up there."

"I don't want to think about that again."

"Fair enough. I was surprised to get your call."

"Didn't you say you wanted to have lunch?"

"I thought you forgot."

"Before we go, I need to talk to you about some things."

"Okay."

She pulled into a nearby parking slot and turned to face Wayne. "The transplant virus didn't kill those five people."

"What do you mean? I don't—"

"They were actually killed by a hantavirus Eric Ash brought back from Kazakhstan years ago. He and Carter Dewitt, the Monteagle VP for financial affairs, conspired to infect the five who died, and you, with the Kazak virus to make it appear that the transplant virus had turned lethal."

"Why?"

"To decrease value of the transplant virus in the pharmaceutical marketplace so Dewitt could steer its sale at a cut-rate price to a drug company he and Ash were in partnership with."

"How long have you known this?"

"I've suspected there were two viruses for a couple of weeks. Actually, it was Sam Fairborn, a friend of mine from the CDC, who figured it out."

"Fairborn . . . Weren't he and his wife murdered?"

"By Ash, to cover his tracks. And that guy who assaulted me on Stone Mountain—he was hired by Ash and his friends to stop me from investigating."

"So Ash and Dewitt have been arrested?"

"Ash is on the run. Detectives found evidence this morning that he killed the Fairborns, but during the search of his car, he slipped away. I'm sure it's only a matter of time before they get him."

"Why didn't Ash's virus kill *me*?"

"You're immune. The respiratory illness you had in New Mexico was caused by a hantavirus. Your blood is full of antibodies against the whole hanta group."

"You've known about this other virus for two weeks and you didn't tell me? You let me continue to think I was responsible for those five deaths when you knew better?"

"We've discussed that. Even if the transplant virus *had* been the cause, you couldn't be blamed."

"But I *felt* like I was. And you *knew* that."

"When Sam Fairborn first came up with the idea that there might be two viruses involved, it was merely a guess. We had to do a lot of work to prove that was the case. And we didn't want our efforts publicized."

"I'd hardly call telling me publicizing them."

"Do you remember saying 'mistakes were made' when you were interviewed on TV?"

"So?"

"That comment could have caused me a lot of trouble. I'm lucky none of the relatives of those who died have come after me with a malpractice suit."

"I agree, I shouldn't have said that. But I was miserable thinking I'd caused those deaths. Didn't that mean anything to you?"

"Of course it did. At one point I almost did call you, but then I remembered that interview. I'm sorry, maybe I should have told you. I don't know . . . I just . . ." Chris turned and looked out the window. An awkward silence settled over the car.

"Life can be confusing, can't it?" Wayne said eventually. "It certainly has been for me. I wish you'd told me about Ash's virus, but I understand. In your eyes I'm still a disreputable sort that's not to be trusted. But I'm going to keep working on that and maybe, someday, we can at least be friends."

He got out and gently closed the door. Chris watched him as he walked to the apartment gate and disappeared through it.

DURING THE LONG day, Ash returned to the leaking pipe many times, telling himself each trip would be the last. Finally, his long wait was over and it was time to go. Leaving his tie behind, he went to the door and threw it open.

The air in the stairwell was stagnant and warm, but it was so much more tolerable than the machine room, Ash found it invigorating, and the lethargy that had dogged him for hours lifted. He went up the stairs, pushed the door at the top open, and looked down the hall.

No one in sight.

In addition to Central Supply, which was now closed, this part of the basement housed only Radiation Oncology, which was also closed. So the chances of him being seen by anyone if he should stop at the water fountain were remote. He thought about the cold unending stream of water that could be had there by the mere press of a button and his dehydrated body urged him to go get it.

But he was afraid, for the water fountain was right out in the open.

His body and mind engaged in a brief skirmish, then, ignoring the water fountain, he darted across the hall and into another stairwell. Keeping to those parts of the hospital that were the most uninhabited at night, he made his way to the virology lab without being seen. Grateful he hadn't given Lenihan his entire key ring in the garage that morning, he unlocked the lab door and slipped inside.

There was no glass in the door to the hall, but Ash still left the lights off, afraid someone might see the illumination under the door and know he was there. Moving by instinct and memory, he went through the swinging door of the receiving counter and carefully moved along the central work island in the main lab until he found the computer they used to post lab results. He switched it on.

In a few seconds the glowing monitor gave him enough light to navigate by. He looked for the liquid nitrogen container where, until he'd destroyed them, he'd stored the Kazak hanta samples.

It was gone, apparently taken by Lenihan. No matter, he'd never need the thing again. Safe for the moment, he hurried to the nearest sink, turned on the tap, and drank water from his hand until his stomach pushed against his belt.

In the machine room, heat had been the problem. Now that he was in temperate surroundings his sweat-soaked clothing lay cold against his skin. So he went to his office and changed into a set of green scrubs he'd kept on hand for the lab work he'd been doing that he didn't want any of his techs to know about. Then he went into the lab and got a small screw-top bottle of chloroform from one of the reagent cabinets. He took the bottle back to his office and shoved it into a pocket of the pants he'd worn all day. Carefully, he folded and rolled all his wet clothing into a tidy bundle he secured with a couple of strips of cellophane tape.

There was no way he could return to his car. The cops were probably waiting for him in the garage. He looked at the phone on his desk. Dare he use that? Was there a cop sitting somewhere picking his teeth and listening to any calls made from it?

Deciding it was too risky, he tried to think of an alternative. The hospital pay phones were too public, and it was a long walk to the nearest gas station, all of it along well-traveled roads where somebody in scrubs might attract the attention of any cops in the area. So it came down to relative risk. Make a choice and hope it was the right one. Door number one or number two. Where was the tiger?

He lifted the receiver of his phone and quickly pressed the disconnect button with the index finger of his left hand. Gripping the receiver against that same hand with his thumb, he unscrewed the mouthpiece with his other hand and looked at the mechanism inside. He didn't see anything that looked like a bug, but of course, he didn't know what a bug looked like.

Resigned to this option, he reassembled the mouthpiece,

then lugged out the phone book, looked up the number, and made the call.

"I'd like a cab sent to Monteagle Hospital." His voice didn't echo or sound unusual in any other way. Did that mean the phone was okay?

"Pick me up at . . ." He hesitated, wondering where the safest location would be. In a bold move, he said, "The Emergency entrance. This is Dr. . . . Demarco. How long? Ten minutes? That'll be fine."

He hung up, grabbed his clothes, and left the office. Returning to the lab, he got a simple nose-and-mouth mask from a box near the fume hood and pulled it on. It was going to look a little odd for someone to be wearing a mask in the hallway, but it was better than being recognized if he should pass anyone.

Once again taking the most obscure route possible, he made his way to a maintenance door about twenty yards from the Emergency entrance, where he could wait for the cab behind a big tank of liquid oxygen hidden by a dense cotoneaster hedge. His idea in coming there was that a guy in scrubs walking to a cab wouldn't look out of place. But now the mask had to go. He pulled it off and tossed it on the ground.

While waiting for the cab, he wondered once more if his phone had been bugged. If so, Lenihan and his men could be posted out of sight waiting for him to show.

There were three ambulances sitting near the ER entrance. Any of them could have detectives inside ready to jump out and grab him. He looked at the vehicles in the ER parking lot, where he saw two vans, more potential hiding places for cops.

By the time the cab arrived, Ash had become so convinced he'd put himself into a trap, he couldn't leave the safety of the hedge.

The cab sat there, waiting.

But if he didn't go now, when would he have another chance?

It was back to the old risk/benefit ratio.

Finally, tired of the indecision, he stepped into the open. His eyes went to each of the ambulances, then to the vans in the parking lot.

No movement in any of them.

He started walking at a brisk pace, his eyes darting over the landscape, the tension in the moment making it harder to breathe than when he'd been in the machine room.

He was halfway there now, and nothing had changed.

Two thirds of the way . . .

The emergency room doors flew open . . . a uniform . . . *cops* . . .

But then he saw a gurney and another uniformed figure pushing it—two paramedics, that's all.

He reached the cab, pulled the door open, and lunged inside. "I'm Dr. Demarco. Let's go."

He gave the cabbie the location of the convenience store where he always made his sensitive calls on the phone out front, then looked back at the rapidly disappearing ER, incredulous that he'd made it.

At the pay phone he let that cab go and called another, using a different name, wanting to create a rift in the continuity between the hospital and his ultimate destination should Lenihan start questioning cabbies.

While waiting for the second cab, he quieted the rumblings in his stomach with a packaged ham and cheese sandwich, a bag of chips, and a Coke. When the second cab arrived, he had the driver take him to an ATM, where he withdrew the maximum amount he could get. With the next address he gave the cabbie, he made the guy's night.

CHAPTER 41

THE CAB PULLED to a stop beside the darkened farm-house. While they were coming up the drive, Ash had been looking for cops. He'd never spoken to anyone at Monteagle about owning this place, so it seemed unlikely that Lenihan would know about it. But the possibility still bothered him.

"This the right address?" the cabbie said, prompting him to make a decision.

"It's correct."

"Don't look like anyone's expecting you."

"But of course that's not your concern, is it?"

Ash paid the considerable fare and, even though his net worth would soon be an irrelevancy, added a measly tip. He picked up his bundle of clothing and got out.

Before the unhappy cabbie had even reached the road out front, the crickets on the property went back to work, creating a din that made Ash feel he'd be safe here for the short time it mattered.

It was a cloudy night and the moon was obscured, so it was too dark for him to read his watch. But he'd checked it at the convenience store and judged that it was now around nine o'clock, too late to get started. But that was fine with him, for he was worn out.

He went up on the porch and let himself inside. With all that had been going on, he'd never gotten around to having the utilities cut off and there were lights if he wanted them, which he didn't. No use showing passersby there was someone here. Again moving by memory, he went up the stairs, surprised at how much creakier they seemed in the dark, and entered the largest bedroom, where he cast around with his foot until he found the empty shoebox he remembered leaving there. He then lay down on the floor, put his clothing under his head, and drew the shoebox close to his face. Lulled and comforted by sweetly aromatic residues that took him back to his first home on this earth, he soon fell into the deep dreamless sleep of the innocent.

ASH WOKE AT first light, made a pit stop in the upstairs bathroom, then went downstairs and out the back door to the barn, where he unlocked the big main door and threw it open. Most of the barn he made available to whoever was renting the farmhouse. But there was a section in the back he kept locked. He went there now and opened that door.

Inside were some tools and an old blue pickup truck he used to carry supplies for maintenance and repairs of the place. He grabbed a shovel and went back outside. Hustling around to the rear of the barn, he scraped aside some strategically placed dead leaves and began digging.

Ten minutes later, he reached down into the hole he'd made and pulled out a zip-top plastic bag containing the gun he'd used to kill Sam and Ann Fairborn. He took the shovel and the gun back into the barn and stowed the gun under the driver's seat of the truck. He then slipped the key into the truck's ignition and turned it. The old vehicle hadn't been used in months, but it had always been reliable. And today, it was again, for after cranking a couple of times, the engine started and ran smoothly.

He drove the truck into the yard, got out, and closed the main barn door, reviewing in his mind what he needed. There was a well-equipped tool box in the back of the truck, but he'd have to pick up welding equipment, rebars, duct tape, some hose and a clamp, and a canary. If nothing went wrong, he should have everything ready by tonight. Then came the hard part.

"HOW DID YOUR case go?" Chris said into the phone to Michael, trying to be polite before she poured out her news. She'd called him an hour ago, but he couldn't come to the phone because he was involved in an unscheduled surgery.

"It was a tough one," Michael said.

"Then they were lucky to have you as the surgeon." Unable to hold back any longer, she blurted out what she'd learned. "They caught Ash."

"How'd they find him?"

"Tracked him from a couple of cabs he took yesterday to get away from Monteagle."

"How do you know that?"

"Lenihan's office called. They also said the Atlanta police are grilling Dewitt hoping he'll turn on Ash to save himself."

"Sounds like something that could be very productive."

"As they say on TV—wait, there's more. The cops in Newark have thrown a blanket over the entire Iliad operation and have arrested Paul Danner."

"Looks like we did some good."

Chris's reply was interrupted by the sound of the buzzer from the lobby. "Hold on. Someone's calling me from downstairs."

She put the receiver down and walked to the intercom. She pressed the button so she could respond. "Yes, who's there?"

"One of your neighbors from the third floor," a male voice said. "I'm afraid I've backed into your car. I'm dreadfully sorry but I've created quite a bit of damage and I wanted to let you know. I'll pay for it of course, but you should probably take a look. I don't think your car is driveable."

Not again, Chris thought. "How could you hit it that hard in the *parking* lot?" she said, making no attempt to conceal her irritation.

"I'm a fool, I know. My foot slipped off the brake and hit the gas."

"All right. I'll be right down."

She went back to the phone and picked up the receiver. "Michael, I've got a minor crisis here I need to deal with, so I have to go."

"What happened?"

"Someone backed into my car."

"That's incredible. Same side as the other damage?"

"I don't know, but the person who did it thinks I won't be able to drive it now."

"If I can help in any way, let me know."

"I will. Thanks."

Chris hung up, grabbed her handbag, and hurried to the elevators.

She thought she'd find the guy who'd called waiting for her in the lobby, but it was empty. Believing he'd returned to the accident, she went outside.

The parking lot was nicely landscaped with lots of trees and shrubs dividing it into sections. It was one of the features that had made her choose to live in this development. There were no assigned spaces in the lot, but each tenant was expected to park in a specific area. Hers was section D, off to the right, behind section C.

Arriving there after a short walk, she saw a blue pickup with its back end hard against the rear fender of her car on the previously undamaged side. Even before she got close, she could see collision ripples in her fender and pieces of taillight on the asphalt . . . and something that looked like a sheet of paper stuck to her car in front of the damage. But she didn't see the truck's owner anywhere.

When she reached the two vehicles, she took a quick look at the damage, which certainly didn't appear as though it would make her car undrivable, then reached down for the note.

She'd just begun to read it when she was grabbed from behind and a cloth impregnated with a pungent odor was pressed to her face. She tried to struggle free, but her assailant had one arm wrapped around her, pinning both her arms and crushing her back against his chest. The chemical in the cloth went up her nose and infiltrated her brain, making her feel as though her feet weren't touching the ground. Then she was falling—into a deep black pit.

CHAPTER 42

CHRIS OPENED HER eyes, disoriented and slightly sick to her stomach. Gradually she became aware that she was sitting on the floor, her back against a hard surface. In front of her, slightly to her left, was a chrome kitchen chair and beyond that she saw vertical stripes.

Where *was* she?

Then the accident in the parking lot came back to her: the cloth against her face, the smell . . . But now she could place the odor. Chloroform. She vaguely recalled regaining consciousness earlier in some kind of closed container with her hands and feet bound. And she'd felt the sensation of movement. Then, after a long interval, the motion had stopped and the container was opened. That's all she could remember.

She struggled to her feet, her palms picking up dirt and grit as she used them to help herself. Standing, she became even more nauseated, and it felt like someone was stroking a huge brass gong in her head.

The light in her immediate surroundings was poor, but seemed brighter in the direction of the vertical stripes. She shuffled in that direction and found herself confronting a series of metal bars of the type used to reinforce concrete. Beyond the bars was a larger room, obviously a basement, illuminated by a single bare lightbulb.

She heard a door open and someone came down the stairs, which were on the other side of the basement, angled so they hugged the far wall. Legs clothed in green scrubs came into view, then a torso, then . . .

Ash.

It was Ash.

How could that be? He was . . . Then, even though her mind was still recovering from the chloroform, she realized it hadn't been Lenihan's office that called her. It had been Ash, to make her relax and not be suspicious of his scheme to get her outside.

He left the steps and came over to stand by another chrome chair that matched the one in her cell. He was unshaven and his hair was uncombed.

"I see you're awake," he said.

"What are you doing? Why am I here?"

"Do you know what you've done to me by your meddling?"

"Whatever happens to you now is your own fault. You can't blame me."

"Oh, but I can. And I do. I'll tell you this, I'm not going to be taken. I won't go through that . . . be humiliated in front of the world. I won't."

"What are you going to do?"

"Kill myself. It's the only way."

Dreading the answer, Chris asked the next obvious question. "What about me?"

"We're going to die together. You wanted to be part of this. Now you are."

The trials Chris had been through in the last few days had taken more out of her than she'd thought was in her. Now she was faced with another. And she didn't think she could bear it.

"How will you . . . ?"

"Carbon monoxide." He turned and pointed at the upper part of the wall behind him. "There's a hose already in that hole up there. All I have to do is hook the hose to the tailpipe of my truck. It's a slow way to die, but I want you to have time to think about it as it happens and to feel it coming."

"When are you going to do it?"

"I don't want to be found looking like this. So in the morning, I'm going to get some decent clothes and get cleaned up. I'd guess we'll be dead before lunch."

"And in the meantime, I stay here, with no toilet and nothing but that chair to sit on?"

"There's a bucket and a roll of toilet paper back there in the corner. And that's more than you deserve."

Ash's mind was obviously so monstrously warped Chris felt there was no way she could reason with him. But she had to try.

"Eric . . . look at it from my perspective. I had the responsibility to protect everyone in the hospital from any infectious organism that might arise from my father's transplant. When those people died, I *had* to investigate. It was my job and I felt I had let everyone down. How *could* I have done nothing?"

Ash looked at her for a few seconds, his jaw muscles flexing. His face began to twist like a child about to cry. "At the little school I attended when I was a kid, if anyone misbehaved, the teacher would banish them to the room where we put our coats and where those who could afford to bring one kept their lunch until it was time to eat. In my home, some days there was no food at all in the house and I'd go to school so hungry I'd kick another kid or act up in some other way just so I'd get sent to the coat room. While I was there, I'd steal little bits of food from the other kids' lunches . . . a cookie, a couple of raisins, some meat from a sandwich . . . Not enough from any one lunch to be noticed." Tears sprang to his eyes and he wiped at them with his fingers. "So I've paid my dues in this world. I've earned the right to enjoy life, and that virus was my ticket."

"Eric, I can sympathize with what it was like for you as a kid, but my God, that didn't give you the right to destroy people."

His expression suddenly hardened. "Yet I'm expected to accept what you did."

"It's not the same."

"*You* destroyed *me*." A vein rose in the center of his forehead. "I am so sick of people getting in my way. It's happened my whole life. People just will *not* mind their own business. They've got to pick and pry and ridicule, and talk behind your

back, interfere with *everything* you want to do. We're a per-
nicious species and you're right there among the worst. So
don't try to justify yourself to me, because I know *exactly*
what you are." He raised a dismissive hand. "I don't want to
talk about this anymore." He turned and walked away. At the
steps, he paused and looked back at her. "This didn't have to
happen. You've only yourself to blame."

He went up the stairs and closed the door. Then the light
went out, plunging Chris into utter darkness.

She'd been through so much in the last few days she wasn't
ready to give up hope that she'd find a way out of this. At the
same time, she was acutely aware that on Stone Mountain and
at the Newark waterfront, she'd had help. Here, she was
alone.

During the short time the light had been on she'd realized
Ash had fashioned her cell by constructing a barred door over
the open end of a small alcove that had probably once served
as a coal bin. While talking to him, she'd seen that the brick
wall to her right continued past the bars as one of the basement's perimeter walls. Considering how narrow her cell was,
it was reasonable to suppose that the brick wall to her left was
not backed by dirt, but merely divided the basement, which
meant if she could get through that wall, she'd be free, at least
free of her cell. Then . . . She cut off any thought about what
she'd do next so she could concentrate on the problem at
hand.

She moved along the bars to her left, reached through
them with her right hand, and felt around the corner. Her fingers encountered only the other side of her cell wall. So she
was right about it being freestanding. Running her fingers
carefully along the front edge of the wall, she could count
the joints.

Three of them.

So the wall was four bricks thick.

Next she went along the wall pounding on it with her fists
and leaning on it with her shoulder and the side of her
leg, testing its stability. Of course, it felt very solid. She returned to the bars and shook them. The door rattled a little,
but with a heavy sound that indicated it was strong and well
made.

She went back to the divider wall and got down on the

floor. Bracing herself with her hands behind her, she kicked at the wall with both feet. But it was like kicking herself in the head, because each time her feet hit the bricks, a mushroom-shaped cloud exploded in her skull. Despite the pain of her headache, she tested the entire length of the wall for as high as her feet could reach and still have some force behind them. Finally, realizing that even a horse probably couldn't kick this wall down, she got up, brushed herself off, and sat down in the chair to think.

A chrome kitchen chair . . .

Sitting in the dark . . .

Her mind took her back to Mrs. Lipinski's closet, and her life suddenly seemed like it had all been a sham in which the chair and the darkness had seemed to grow more distant, but were actually approaching from a different direction, a journey in a circle. But at least Mrs. Lipinski always returned to release her. Now there was no one to open the door.

If Lenihan had known about this place, wherever it was, he'd probably have staked it out and grabbed Ash when he'd first showed up. And even if Michael figured out that Lenihan's office hadn't called her and that she was missing, what could he do? It all seemed preordained and utterly hopeless.

Then she got an idea.

She got out of the chair and carried it to the bars, where she tried to find a way she could use one of its legs to pry on the door. But there was no arrangement where she could get any leverage. She put the chair back on the floor and once again sat in it. Upstairs, she could hear the floor creaking as Ash moved around.

She sat there in the dark for nearly twenty minutes, her mind turning her situation over and over, examining every side of it, looking for a weakness she could exploit. But there was nothing. She'd been right the first time. It was hopeless.

It hurt to think, so she stopped doing it, closed her eyes, and once again let her mind drift.

A minute or so after she'd let her sails take her where they would, a single word popped into her head.

Mortar.

Eight months ago, Good Samaritan had had to have the entire brick facade of the main building repointed because the mortar was failing. Everything looked and felt solid, but the mortar had lost its integrity.

She got up, stripped off her belt, and folded the buckle back so she could get the tongue between her fingers like a pen. Then she went to the wall about a foot back from the bars, felt for a joint between the bricks at chest level, and scraped at it hard with her makeshift gouge. But the gouge simply stuttered along the joint.

Did that mean the mortar was solid everywhere? Probably. But this was no time to make a mistake based on an untested assumption, especially since she had no other ideas. She moved to her left a couple of bricks and tried again . . . with the same result.

Damn it. With so much shoddy workmanship in the world, why did the person who built this wall have to be so *competent*? She scraped another joint and found it as impenetrable as the others. She let her arms fall to her side. She was just going to have to face the truth. There was no way out of this. In the morning, she was going to die. She went back to her chair and dropped into it.

Dead before lunch.

Dead . . . lunch . . . Had those two words ever been used before in the same sentence? She doubted it. Probably the most momentous word in the English language juxtaposed to one of the most trivial.

Dead.

But she wasn't that way yet. And until she was, she wasn't going to accept it as inevitable.

She shot to her feet and returned to the wall, where she once more set to work.

She'd been at it for perhaps another two minutes when she raked her gouge along a joint and felt the mortar crumble. Afraid to believe it was more than simply an air pocket, she pushed harder against the gouge and made a long sweep with it.

It was rotten.

The whole joint was weak.

And so was the one below it.

And the one to the left.

Invigorated, she began scraping at the wall with a feverish

intensity. But the sound of the gouge against the mortar was quite loud in the otherwise silent basement, and as she worked, she feared Ash would be able to hear it.

No, he couldn't. It wouldn't be fair. Her only chance, thwarted by the sound. There was a door at the top of the stairs and it was closed. She'd heard it shut. He couldn't hear the noise through that.

Then the basement light came on.

CHAPTER 43

THE BASEMENT DOOR opened and Chris heard Ash on the stairs. She looked down and saw with horror a pile of gray mortar on the darker floor at her feet, a clear indicator of what she'd been doing. She knelt and scattered the mortar with her hand, then stuffed her belt in her pocket and made for the chair.

Because of the way the stairs were constructed, Ash had to descend facing away from Chris's cell. For him to get a clear look at her, he had to turn to his right when he reached the bottom and take a few steps in that same direction. By the time he did that, Chris was in the chrome chair trying not to look as though she'd been up to anything.

Ash's manner as he walked toward the cell, and the sandwich and Coke can in his hands, suggested that he hadn't come down because of the sound.

"Oh, I see you're still here," he said. His face changed from a mocking expression to one of concern. "Why is your face so red?"

Chris's heart lurched at the question and she prayed he wouldn't notice the scattered mortar on the floor behind her.

"I've been out jogging," she said. "How do I know why it's red? Maybe it's some aftereffect of being chloroformed."

"Maybe . . ." He stared at her for what seemed like a long time, during which she stared back, trying to hold his eyes and not let them wander.

But his eyes *did* rove—to her feet, then across the floor to her left, then back along the wall where she'd been working. She could barely breathe now and her face grew redder. Wedged tightly between her fear of death and the anticipation that Ash was about to discover her secret, time ceased to move and the moment hung in the air like an insect trapped in amber.

Ash's eyes returned to hers. "I thought you might be hungry or thirsty." He held up the items he'd brought. "I'll just leave these things here on this chair and you can get them when you like." He smiled mockingly, then he turned, walked to the stairs, and left without looking back.

He didn't see the mortar, Chris thought in letters two stories high. *He doesn't know.*

Eagerly, she returned to work.

In about forty minutes, she had the mortar in all the joints of the first brick excavated to where she couldn't reach any deeper with her gouge. But the brick wouldn't come loose. And there wasn't any way to get a good grip on it.

How could this happen? She'd found the answer and now it wasn't going to work?

She thought about using the entire buckle, but it would only reach a tiny bit deeper into the joints than the tongue did.

Wait . . .

She went to the far rear corner of her cell and picked up the galvanized bucket Ash had given her to use as a toilet. Returning to the wall, she wedged the handle of the bucket into the joint she'd excavated below the first brick. When she exerted pressure on the handle, it rolled in the joint until it hit the bricks below. Using them for leverage, she pried up on the loosened brick.

Nothing gave.

She rolled the handle upward an eighth of an inch and slammed it down into the lower bricks. It made too much noise and it hurt her hands, but she did it again . . . and again . . . and then miraculously, she felt the brick move. A

couple more thrusts of the handle and the brick came free. She
put the bucket down and pulled the brick from the wall.

No Oscar, no Nobel Prize, no Pulitzer ever produced in its
recipient more joy than Chris felt holding that lowly brick.

With the first brick removed, she had better access to the
joints of the adjacent bricks, but it was hard to grip the buckle
tongue hard enough to use it effectively, and occasionally
she'd scrape her knuckles against a brick, making them raw
and sore. Despite that, the progress she was making spurred
her on. As she worked, however, she constantly worried that
Ash might return before she could get out. If he did, there was
no way she could hide the loose bricks on the floor and the
hole in the wall.

By now, her fingers were aching from holding the gouge.
Being right-handed, she wasn't as efficient holding it in her
left hand. And that was the hand the bullet had injured on
Stone Mountain. So whenever she grasped anything in those
fingers, it hurt. But in order to keep going, she had to switch
hands.

She settled into a routine in which she alternated hands
every ten or fifteen minutes. Even with this approach, by the
time she'd removed seven bricks, the fingers on both hands
hurt so badly she had to take a break.

What time was it? In the dark it was impossible to read her
watch. Was she proceeding at a reasonable rate? Was there
time to finish? Afraid that it had taken far longer to remove
those seven bricks than she thought, she forced herself back
to work.

Stopping only when the pain in her fingers became unbearable, she labored into the night and slowly the pile of
bricks at her feet grew. To produce a hole large enough for her
to crawl through required the removal of fifteen bricks. When
she reached that number in the first layer of the wall, she
stopped and tried kicking her way through the remaining layers. But they held firm.

Deeply disappointed and aware that she was once again
faced with a first-brick-in-the-layer situation, she wrapped her
sore and protesting fingers around the gouge and attacked.

The constant friction against the gouge was slowly wearing it away and it was steadily growing shorter. By the time
she'd removed the fifth brick in the second layer of the wall it

was no longer usable. So she switched to the buckle itself. Though not shaped as appropriately, it did work, but progress was slower.

Mind numbed by the repetitious labor, arms and fingers tortured by the unusual demands she was placing on them, she pushed herself on through the night.

She'd heard no squeaking of the floor above for a long time and she assumed it was because Ash was asleep. But suddenly, it started again. Did that mean it was morning? Without any windows in the basement, she had no way to tell.

Surely it couldn't be dawn. She was still just working on the second opening. There was too much yet to do. It *couldn't* be morning.

Afraid that it was, she kicked at the remaining parts of the wall through the holes she'd made in the first two layers. But the opening in the second layer was still so small she kept hitting protruding bricks, blunting the force she could exert and nearly destroying her foot.

She was so tired and frustrated she felt like screaming. But instead, she redirected that energy into her hands, and returned to work.

A few minutes later, she heard an engine start outside. The sound grew louder as the vehicle got underway, then it faded—Ash off on an errand, presumably in the truck he'd used to damage her car. So it *was* morning.

Knowing she had very little time left, she somehow found the reserves to work faster.

All too soon, she heard the truck return. A door slam . . . an interval with no sound, then the floor above began to squeak. She sawed furiously at the brick that was interfering with her ability to deliver a good solid kick to the outer shell of the wall.

Come on . . . come on . . .

She grabbed the free edge of the brick that projected into the opening, and pulled on it.

Let *loose*.

But it wouldn't.

She rocked back on her left leg and gave the brick a kick. No effect.

She kicked it again.

Still it wouldn't come loose.

She bent forward and raked the buckle into the joint with the most remaining mortar, her heart hammering, her hair soggy from perspiring into it all night. The mortar of this brick was not as rotten as the others, so it resisted, consuming time she couldn't afford.

Totally focused on the defiant brick, she sawed and pulled and kicked it. What was holding it in there?

Too much time was passing.

She heard Ash start the truck. The sound grew louder as he gave it gas, then even louder—and closer.

He was backing it up to the hose he'd put through the foundation.

She kicked at the brick again and felt it move. Another kick distinctly loosened it. She could hear scraping sounds outside; Ash connecting the hose to the truck's exhaust.

She grabbed the brick and wiggled it back and forth, yanking so hard the brick tore the skin of her hands. And then it came free and tumbled to the floor.

Outside, the truck's engine rose above the idling sound it had been making and began a steady hum, which was surely the result of Ash rigging the gas so the engine wouldn't stall. For the first time Chris smelled the sickly sweet odor of exhaust fumes.

How long did it take for carbon monoxide to work? She didn't know.

She shifted into a sideways kicking stance and delivered a trial blow in slow motion to get a feel for exactly where the target was. Then she lashed out with all the force she could generate.

Her foot struck the wall solidly in the right spot, but didn't accomplish anything. She kicked it again, another solid well-placed blow—with all the effect of a cigarette butt hitting the sidewalk.

She wasn't big enough . . . couldn't get enough . . .

A thought flashed into her head. She grabbed the chrome chair and hauled it in front of the hole in the wall. Overhead, the floor was squeaking again.

She dropped into the chair, grabbed the seat with both hands, and drew her legs up and back. A trial run for aiming, then she kicked out with both feet, exploding with all the energy she had left in her body.

Both feet hit the wall solidly and the chair went over backward, tossing her onto the rubble around her, which bruised her in so many places she was reincarnated in pain. But as she'd tumbled from the chair, she'd heard a new sound, a sliding, rumbling mixed with the clink of bricks striking each other.

Picking herself up, she went to the divider wall and pushed her hands forward . . . farther and farther . . .

She'd done it.

She was through.

She plunged into the opening she'd made, barely aware of the perimeter bricks that clawed at her legs, and the loose ones that shifted and rolled when she put her hands on them, scraping her palms and pinching her fingers. On the other side, she scrambled to her feet.

Before she had time to think, the light came on and she heard the door at the top of the stairs open. On the floor she saw a small pile of iron reinforcing bars apparently left over from Ash's work on her cell. She picked one up that was about four feet long and moved quickly to the stairs, taking up a position just under the point where they began their descent.

Ash's feet came into view . . . then his legs.

Her timing needed to be perfect.

His waist appeared.

He came down another step and she could now see that he was carrying a bird cage.

His head cleared the floor above, but he was still a few steps too high for her to reach him. To see her or the damage to the wall, he'd have to stoop and turn to his right, which he didn't.

When he reached the next to last step, Chris rushed forward, the rebar cocked in a batter's stance. Before he could react, she swung the bar, aiming it high. It hit him in the throat and he collapsed. With feathers flying and the canary in the cage squawking, Ash and the cage tumbled to the basement floor, where the bird continued to squawk and flap, but Ash lay still.

Chris dropped the metal bar and darted to the foot of the stairs. She skirted Ash's body and ran up the steps, the joy of knowing she was going to live overwhelming every other sensation. At the top of the stairs, she grabbed the doorknob and turned it.

Locked.

The blasted door was locked.

The discovery that she was *not* free settled on her like a shroud. She looked down at Ash's body, which was still in the same position. Reluctantly, she went halfway down the steps and paused.

The keys were probably in his pocket.

She watched him for a couple of seconds, looking for any sign of movement. Seeing none and realizing that with every breath she took more of her hemoglobin was combining with the carbon monoxide pouring into the basement, rendering her blood incapable of carrying oxygen, she went down the remaining steps and knelt by Ash's body.

He was lying on his left side, which made his right pocket the most accessible. She reached inside . . . and found it empty.

Surely, he had the keys. They couldn't be upstairs. So they had to be in his other pocket.

She pushed on his right shoulder to roll him over, but he went much too easily. Having expected resistance, she fell across him. For an instant she didn't know what was happening. Then she felt his arms close around her and tighten.

CHAPTER 44

IT WAS CLEAR that whatever injuries Ash had sustained from the rebar and the fall hadn't affected his strength, because Chris couldn't break his hold. And her arms were pinned at her sides, rendering them useless. She was lying slightly askew on top of him, so she couldn't even try to head-butt him.

She *had* to get away from him and somehow get out of there. She squirmed in his grip, but he doggedly held on.

"The more you fight me, the quicker you'll die," Ash said, his voice now hoarse from the damage the rebar had done to his larynx.

The bird cage was lying nearby and Chris saw that the canary had stopped squawking and was now sitting quietly. Ash had obviously brought the bird down here as an indicator that the carbon monoxide was working. Because of its high metabolic rate it would succumb before either of them.

Chris should have seen the answer to her situation in Ash's comment about fighting him. But it was the bird that showed her the way.

Drawing on the lessons she'd learned from Gloria Ting, her Chinese classmate in med school, she turned inward and focused on the shining orb that lay at the center of her consciousness. Even as the journey began, her heart slowed by three beats a minute and she started to breathe more slowly and less deeply.

Like a time-lapse film of a blooming flower running backward, her outward manifestation collapsed and folded, homing in on her spiritual core. And her heart slowed even more.

Soon she was breathing only five times a minute and taking in less than twenty percent of the air normally needed to sustain her. But she went deeper still, spiraling downward to a place most people never know is within them.

Down and deeper she went, each second bringing her closer to her final destination.

Deeper . . .

Calmer . . .

Quieter . . .

Touchdown.

And there she remained, her skin cool to the touch, her pulse barely detectable, seeming not to breathe at all.

Beneath her, Ash was puzzled. Had the carbon monoxide affected her already? Thinking she might be faking, he held on. In the upended cage, the canary toppled onto its side.

One of the tricks in meditating so deeply is to leave a line open to complete consciousness as a protective measure. If your house catches on fire, it would be best to cease meditating and call for help. Gloria had likened this to tying a rope onto your belt before entering an undersea wreck wearing scuba gear. If anything goes wrong on the surface, a signal can be sent by way of the rope.

Twenty-two minutes after Ash had grabbed Chris, she felt a tug on her rope.

Returning to real time and space she found that Ash was now well under the influence of carbon monoxide and she was easily able to disentangle herself from him. Still clearheaded herself, she jammed her hand in Ash's left pocket and got his keys. When she drew her hand out, Ash made a feeble attempt to grab her wrist, but she pulled free with little effort.

With nothing now holding her back, Chris flew up the stairs. Below her, Ash rolled onto his side and tried to get up.

It took Chris a few seconds to find the right key, some of that time spent keeping one eye on Ash. Then the door was open and she was free. Though Ash seemed incapable of climbing the stairs, she shut the door and locked it.

She'd emerged into the kitchen, so she had no trouble finding her way outside. When she went onto the porch, she saw Ash's truck backed up to the foundation.

She ran down the porch steps and headed for the truck, where she threw the driver's door open and climbed in.

Standard transmission—no problem. She reached down, picked up the brick lying on the gas pedal, and tossed it aside. She slammed the clutch to the floorboard, threw it into first, and took off, figuring that the hose conveying carbon monoxide into the basement would either come off the truck or pull · out of the foundation. Either way was fine with her.

The hose was firmly attached to the truck's exhaust pipe with a hose clamp, but Ash had merely pushed the other end into the hole he'd made in the foundation, and packed the gap around it with toilet paper. So as Chris sped down the dirt driveway, the hose trailed after her.

At the road out front she hesitated. She had no idea which way to go because she had no idea where she was. Across the road was a farmer's field with young corn plants stretching along the road for as far as she could see. But on her side of the road, beyond a smaller field of some other kind of crop, she saw a small house. Needing a phone and a geography lesson, she headed for the house.

THE DOOR OPENED and an old man in overalls gave her a puzzled look.

"May I use your phone, please? It's an emergency. There's someone who needs help in that house down the road."

The old man hesitated, looking at her with rheumy eyes from behind wire-rimmed trifocals.

"I know I'm a mess, but there's no time to explain. Please . . ."

The old man stepped aside and let her in.

"It's over there," he said, pointing to a small end table by a well-worn sofa.

Chris went to the phone and picked up the receiver. "What's this address?" she asked the old man.

"Fifty-five sixteen."

"And the name of that road out front?"

"Robertson Pike."

Chris dialed 911.

When the dispatcher answered, Chris identified herself and recited her home address and phone number. "There's a man in the basement of the two-story farmhouse just down the road from fifty-five sixteen Robertson Pike. He's suffering from carbon monoxide poisoning. So you'll need an ambulance. That man is Dr. Eric Ash and he's being sought for the murders of half a dozen people including Dr. Sam Fairborn and his wife. Fairborn . . ." She spelled the name. "For details of this case, contact Detective Lenihan at the Fayette County sheriff's office . . . Lenihan . . ." She spelled *that* name.

"No, I'm not at the scene. I'm calling from the Robertson address I mentioned. But I'm not staying here, I'm going home. If anyone wants to talk to me, that's where I'll be."

The dispatcher started to tell her she needed to stay where she was, but Chris hung up. She got directions to the expressway from the old man, thanked him, and left. It wasn't until a few minutes later that she realized she still had the keys to the farmhouse basement. But there was no way she was going back there. The cops and medics would just have to improvise like she had.

ACTUALLY, WHEN THE county sheriff's car arrived at the farmhouse a few minutes before the ambulance, the officer driving didn't have to improvise at all, for the basement door was standing open and there was no one in the house. From the burn marks on the door where the lock had been and the welding torch on the steps inside, it sure looked as though somebody who'd been locked in had cut their way out.

CHAPTER 45

THE EMERGENCY CASE Michael had worked on the day before was a car accident victim with so much abdominal damage it had pushed his skills to their limits and beyond. As a result, he was very apprehensive about the girl's chances and had been hovering around Intensive Care ever since. But there was something else that also worried him, and this sent him once again to the phone.

"Wayne, this is Michael Boyer. Is Chris there?"

"In case you hadn't noticed, we don't spend much time together."

"I know. It's just that I can't locate her. I've called her home, her office, her cell phone, and I've paged her. It's not like her to be out of reach like that. After some of the things she's been through, I'm worried."

"Now so am I. When's the last time you saw her?"

"I talked to her on the phone last night around eight o'clock. She had to hang up because someone called from the lobby of her apartment building and said they'd backed into her car."

"I think we should go over to her apartment and look

around. I've still got the key she gave me when I stayed with her."

"I'll meet you there."

"HER CAR'S IN the parking lot," Wayne said, coming up to Michael in the lobby of the Ethridge.

"I know, I saw it, too. It's got some new damage, but could still be driven. So where is she?"

"Let's go up."

Both of them deeply concerned, they went through the card reader, using the key card Chris had obtained for Wayne, and headed for the elevators.

At Chris's apartment door, Wayne knocked, waited a few seconds for a response, then slipped his key in the lock and let them in.

"The lights are on," Wayne said. "Chris, are you home? Chris?"

Michael headed for the hall bedrooms.

Wayne went to the French doors leading to the balcony, opened them, and walked outside. Unable to see the entire balcony for all the trees and shrubs, he called out again. "Chris, are you out here?"

Less than a minute later, the two men met in the front room.

"Where could she be?" Wayne said.

Then Michael had a horrible thought. "Have you heard anything on the news about Ash being caught?"

"No. Has he?"

"That's why Chris called me last night, to say that Lenihan's office told her he had, but there was nothing about it on the news last night or in the papers this morning."

"You think it was a setup and that it was Ash who called from the lobby about her car?"

"God, I hope not." He went to the phone on the English secretary and dialed Information. "Would you connect me with the Fayette County sheriff's office, please?"

A pause . . . one ring, and a woman answered.

"Detective Lenihan, please."

Another pause, then an automated woman's voice said, "Detective Lenihan is on the phone. If you would like his voice mail, press one." Michael didn't want the guy's voice mail, he wanted Lenihan. He thought about calling again and telling the woman who answered the last time just to interrupt Lenihan, but then, hoping the detective would be available in a minute or two, he pressed 1.

"This is Michael Boyer. It's urgent that I talk to you. Please call me at . . ." He gave the number of Chris's phone. "As soon as possible."

He hung up and looked at Wayne. "He's got another call."

"So we just stand around here and wait?"

"Not for long. If he doesn't call back in the next few minutes, I'll try again, and next time I won't be so cooperative."

DOWNSTAIRS, A MATRONLY woman carrying a cat in a cardboard travel box slid her entry card through the reader by the glass security door, changing the red light over the door to green. Across the lobby, Eric Ash pretended to be looking for a name on the mailboxes. Cupped in his left hand he carried a folded copy of the *Wall Street Journal*. Nestled inside the paper was the automatic he'd used to kill Sam and Ann Fairborn. After he'd cut his way out of the basement with the welding equipment that was still down there, he'd grabbed the gun and set out across the field of soybeans behind the barn. Emerging onto a county road about a quarter mile away, he'd waved down the first car he'd seen and hijacked it, caring not at all that he'd had to kill the driver, who was now in the car's trunk.

The carbon monoxide he'd inhaled had made him weak and disoriented and he shouldn't have been able to accomplish all that he'd done already, but he was being driven by hatred.

Chris Collins . . .

How he detested that name . . . that nosy, meddling, double x chromosome *cunt*. She was harder to kill than a cockroach.

He wasn't so confused that he believed his final attempt to end her life was without flaws. He didn't even know where she was. She'd taken his truck, but it wasn't in the parking lot. Would the cops she'd have called let her drive it home? Probably not. And they'd surely keep her busy for a while telling them what had happened.

So it seemed likely she wasn't home, which was good. He

could get in and wait for her. And if she showed up with someone, Michael Boyer for instance, there were enough rounds in the gun for everybody.

Believing that sufficient time had passed for the woman with the cat to have caught an elevator, Ash produced the key card he'd found in Chris's handbag and walked to the security door.

UPSTAIRS, MICHAEL FELT his pager vibrate. He took it from his pocket and checked the number displayed.

Intensive Care.

"No, not now," he moaned.

He looked at Chris's phone. He didn't want to tie up the line and block the call from Lenihan, but his cell phone was in his car. He looked at Wayne. "I have to do this, but I'll make it quick."

He picked up the receiver and dialed Intensive Care.

"This is Dr. Boyer."

His face darkened as the caller informed him that his patient from yesterday was bleeding internally. "Okay, I'll be right there. Wayne, I have to go to the hospital. If Lenihan doesn't call back in the next few minutes, you call him. If Ash hasn't been caught, tell him about Chris."

Because he was so worried about Chris, Wayne let Michael get away with talking to him like he couldn't have figured all that out for himself.

Michael pulled out his wallet, got one of his business cards, and began writing on it with one of the two pens he always carried. "This is my cell phone number. When you talk to Lenihan, call me and let me know what he says."

AS MICHAEL WAITED for an elevator less than a minute later, Ash was four floors away, riding up.

The indicator light over the middle elevator of the trio facing Michael blinked on and the doors swooshed open. He stepped on and punched L. Barely after the doors on his elevator closed, they opened on elevator number 1 and Ash stepped into the hallway.

CHAPTER 46

ASH WENT DOWN the carpeted hallway to Chris's apartment, checked in both directions to make sure no one else was around, then drew the gun from the folded paper. Gripping the weapon tightly in his right hand and holding it in front of him where it couldn't be seen by anyone who might come along, he dropped the paper and slid that hand into his pants pocket for Chris's key ring.

He tried one of the three keys that looked like an apartment key . . .

No good.

The next one slid neatly into the lock.

INSIDE THE APARTMENT, Wayne was about to draw himself a glass of water from the kitchen tap when he heard someone at the door. From where he was standing he didn't have a direct sight line to the entrance, but he could see its reflection in a mirrored screen to the right of the TV cabinet. In that reflection he saw Ash and what was in his hand. Thinking that if he could see Ash, Ash could also see him, Wayne dropped to the kitchen floor.

Then the phone rang.

Ash closed the door and stood motionless, waiting to see if Chris would come into the room and answer the phone. It rang a second time and then a third, and a fourth.

The answering machine came on. "This is Chris. I can't come to the phone right now. Please leave a message."

"This is Detective Lenihan returning your call. It's now eleven-twenty. I'll be here for another thirty minutes."

Ash didn't understand the content of that call, but he took it as proof Chris wasn't there. He went over to a chair in front of the TV and sat down, grateful for the chance to rest.

BEHIND THE KITCHEN cabinets, Wayne was scared. If Ash decided to check out the apartment, he'd see him right away, for there was just no place to hide. Wayne looked across the kitchen at the hall leading to the other rooms. If he could get back there, he could use the phone in Chris's study to call for help. But he couldn't risk moving.

With his body tingling like a high-tension wire, he listened hard for any sound that would tell him what Ash was doing or where he was. But he heard nothing.

WHEN MICHAEL REACHED the exit of the apartment parking lot, he turned right. Three minutes later, Chris appeared from the other direction still driving Ash's truck. Even before she was halfway home, she'd realized she left the farmhouse without looking for the handbag she'd been carrying when Ash abducted her. She'd then stopped and looked in the tarp-covered truck bed, hoping it might be there, but it wasn't. So in addition to losing her wallet, she had no key to her apartment.

She pulled into the parking lot and dumped the truck into the first space she found near the Ethridge's main entrance. Looking forward to being safe again in her own home and getting the grime washed off her, she hurried inside and pushed the intercom button over the manager's mailbox.

"Yes, may I help you?"

"This is Chris Collins. I've lost my key and my security card."

"Come on down. I'll give you replacements."

The security door buzzed and the light over it changed from red to green.

•   •   •

BEHIND THE KITCHEN cabinets, Wayne felt as though he was breathing so hard Ash had to hear him. But so far, nothing had happened. What was the guy up to?

There was no doubt in Wayne's mind that if Ash saw him, he was a dead man. Surely his life had not been saved just so he could be killed by this lunatic. When he'd learned from Chris that he wasn't responsible for any of the deaths they'd all thought had been caused by the transplant virus, he'd felt reborn for the second time in a month. He'd even started working on a new novel. And it was going to be terrific.

Suddenly, he heard a sound that sent another thousand watts coursing through him.

A key in the lock . . .

Silently he prayed, *Please don't let it be Chris.*

CHRIS STEPPED INSIDE and closed the door behind her. Inexplicably, she began to cry. All the horrors she'd experienced cascaded from her eyes. It was over. She was home.

Then, through the tears, she saw the impossible: Ash rising from her favorite chair, turning toward her. He stepped around the chair and Chris saw the gun dangling at his side.

"The way I had it planned at the farmhouse, our bodies would have looked good," he said, his voice rattling like an apparition from the grave. "Now they're going to be a mess. And once again it's *all your fault.*" He clenched his teeth. "I wish I'd never met you. I wish you'd never been born. I wish your father had never been born. Now die."

The hand with the gun began to move, lifting toward her. And this time she had no answer. When the gun was a few degrees shy of horizontal, she saw a blur from her right—her father, charging toward Ash, growling like an animal.

Ash spun toward Wayne and began firing—

Once . . . Twice . . .

Both rounds thudded into Wayne's body, but he kept coming. Wayne's head and shoulder hit Ash in the midsection and drove him backward. Ash's gun hand flew upward and a third round hit the ceiling. Though he was hit twice, Wayne's legs kept churning like a linebacker pushing a training sled. Ash backpedaled, but didn't go down. Wayne's momentum carried them into the French doors leading to the balcony and they splintered open.

Seeing what was coming, Chris had time to scream, "No," before they hit the balcony railing and it gave way. Then they were gone.

CHAPTER 47

CHRIS LOOKED AWAY from her father's newly installed headstone to the huge oak tree nearby and the little artificial waterfall beyond.

"It's a pretty site, don't you think?"

"Very," Michael said.

"Was I wrong to bury him next to my mother?"

"I'm sure he would have approved."

"I know it's what she would have wanted. She always hoped that one day he'd come back and they'd be together again."

"There can't be any doubt in your mind now that he really loved you. He could have remained hidden in the kitchen and Ash would probably never have known he was there. But he put his life on the line to save you."

Chris looked at the rolling green hills dotted with markers. "And I made it so hard on him; throwing Gene up to him, refusing to accept him, holding on to my anger. And ultimately being responsible for his death."

"You weren't responsible. He just did what any good father would have done under the circumstances."

"He wanted so badly for his life to have meant something."

"And so it did. With every patient you save from now on, he gets some of the credit. Then there's that other little thing."

She looked up at him. "What?"

"The transplant virus. There's something very important there, and now that the entire viral sequence is known, someone will eventually figure out the secret behind its ability to stimulate tissue regeneration. And the mutation that caused it all, that once-in-a-million chance event, occurred in your father. So when we've learned how to harness that potential . . . Well, it couldn't have happened without Wayne."

Chris's lips arced in a thin smile and she nodded. "It's going to take me a while to sort all this out. And I'm going to need some help. Are you available?"

"I'll have to check my schedule, but I think I can find some time for you."

EPILOGUE

WITH WAYNE GONE, there was some discussion at the publisher that had bought Wayne's novel about canceling the
book because Wayne couldn't help with the editing and there
wouldn't be a second one. Despite these problems, they ultimately decided to proceed with the single book. As sole heir
to Wayne's estate, Chris signed the contract. Following its
publication, Wayne's novel was nominated for the National
Book Critics Circle Award, but lost to a book that in Chris's
opinion wasn't nearly as good. After a lot of thought, Chris
accepted John Scott's offer and became the medical director
of infection control at Monteagle. There, she started her own
infectious disease practice, which quickly had to add two
more physicians to handle all the work. When the stress
mounts, Chris still goes to Stone Mountain to relax, but only
when Michael is free to accompany her. Research on the therapeutic effects of the transplant virus continues.

AUTHOR'S NOTE

Over the last decade a variety of biotech and pharmaceutical companies in the real world have collectively spent more than a billion dollars on research aimed at the use of pigs as organ donors for humans. Much of that money was spent trying to eliminate the severe rejection reaction that occurs when a pig organ is placed in a primate. While that problem has not been fully overcome, considerable progress has been made. Should it become possible for pig transplants to function normally in humans, no one needing an organ would die for the lack of one. But there really *is* a functional retrovirus in the DNA of all pig cells, and there's considerable concern that it could pose a transplantation health hazard. Best estimates are that the first pig organ transplants are still a few years away. What will happen when that becomes a reality? Will the pig retrovirus as it currently exists cause human disease? Will it mutate into something far more dangerous? When can we relax—after ten transplants with no problems? A hundred? No one can answer these questions. But one thing seems certain: We're about to embark on a great adventure.

**When an elite prosecutor faces the most lethal
predator she's ever encountered, it all comes down to
a choice between justice and ...**

RETRIBUTION

Turn the page for a taste of one of the most exciting
debuts in years! Jilliane Hoffman's first novel,
Retribution,
is guaranteed to have you holding your breath until you
turn the very last page.

**On January 5, 2004,
retribution will be claimed!**

Available January 5, 2004,
wherever Putnam books are sold.

PROLOGUE

CHLOE LARSON WAS, as usual, in a mad and blinding rush. She had all of ten minutes to change into something suitable to wear to *The Phantom of the Opera*—currently sold out a year in advance and the hottest show on Broadway—put on a face, and catch the 6:52 P.M. train out of Bayside into the city, which was, in itself, a three-minute car ride from her apartment to the station. That left her with only seven minutes. She whipped through the overstuffed closet that she had meant to clean out last winter, and quickly settled on a black crepe skirt and matching jacket with a pink camisole. Clutching one shoe in her hand, she muttered Michael's name under her breath, while she frantically tossed aside shoe after shoe from the pile on the closet floor, at last finally finding the black patent-leather pump's mate.

She hurried down the hall to the bathroom, pulling on her heels as she walked. *It was not supposed to happen like this,* she thought as she flipped her long blond hair upside down, combing it with one hand, while brushing her teeth with the other. She was supposed to be relaxed and carefree, giddy with anticipation, her mind free of distractions when the question to end all questions was finally asked of her. Not rushing to and fro, on almost no sleep, from intense classes and study groups with other really anxious people, the New York State Bar Exam oppressively intruding upon her every thought. She spit out the toothpaste, spritzed on Chanel No. 5, and practically ran to the front door. Four minutes. She had four minutes, or else she would have to catch the 7:22 and then she would probably miss the curtain. An image of a dapper and annoyed Michael, waiting outside the Majestic Theater, rose in hand, box in pocket, checking his watch, flashed into her mind.

It was not supposed to happen like this. She was supposed to be more prepared.

She hurried through the courtyard to her car, rushing to put on the earrings she had grabbed off the nightstand in her room. From the second story above, she felt the eyes of her strange and reclusive neighbor upon her, peering down from behind his living room window, as he did every day. Just watching as she made her way through the courtyard into the busy world and on with her life. She shook off the cold, uncomfortable feeling as quickly as it had come and climbed into her car. This was no time to think about Marvin. This was no time to think of the bar exam or bar review classes or study groups. It was time to think only of her answer to the question that Michael was surely going to ask her tonight.

Three minutes. She had only three minutes, she thought, as she cheated the corner stop sign, barely making the light up on Northern Boulevard.

The deafening sound of the train whistle was upon her now as she ran up the platform stairs two at a time. The doors closed on her just as she waved a thank-you to the conductor for waiting and made her way into the car. She sat back against the ripped red vinyl seat and caught her breath from that last run through the parking lot and up the stairs. The train pulled out of the station, headed for Manhattan. She had barely made it.

Just relax and calm down now, Chloe, she told herself, looking at Queens as it passed her by in the fading light of day. Because tonight, after all, was going to be a very special night. Of that she was certain.

PART ONE

CHAPTER ONE

JUNE 1988
NEW YORK CITY

THE WIND HAD picked up and the thick evergreen bushes that hid his motionless body from sight began to rustle and sway. Just to the west, lightning lit the sky, and jagged streaks of white and purple flashed behind the brilliant Manhattan skyline. There was little doubt that it was going to pour—and soon. Buried deep in the dark underbrush, his jaw clenched tight and his neck stiffened at the rumble of thunder. Wouldn't that just put the icing on the cake, though? A thunderstorm while he sat out here waiting for that bitch to finally get home.

Crouched low under the thick mange of bushes that surrounded the apartment building there was no breeze, and the heat had become so stifling under the heavy clown mask that he could almost feel the flesh melting off his face. The smell of rotting leaves and moist dirt overwhelmed the evergreen, and he tried hard not to breathe in through his nose. Something small scurried by his ear, and he forced his mind to stop imagining the different kinds of vermin that might, right now, be crawling on his person, up his sleeves, in his work boots.

He fingered the sharp, jagged blade anxiously with gloved fingertips.

There were no signs of life in the deserted courtyard. All was quiet, but for the sound of the wind blowing through the branches of the lumbering oak trees, and the constant hum and rattle of a dozen or more air conditioners, precariously suspended up above him from their windowsills. Thick, full hedges practically grew over the entire side of the building, and he knew that, even from the apartments above, he could still not be seen. The carpet of weeds and decaying leaves crunched softly under his weight as he pulled himself up and moved slowly through the bushes toward her window.

She had left her blinds open. The glow from the street lamp filtered through the hedges, slicing dim ribbons of light across the bedroom. Inside, all was dark and still. Her bed was unmade and her closet door was open. Shoes—high heels, sandals, sneakers—lined the closet floor. Next to her television, a stuffed-bear collection was displayed on the crowded dresser. Dozens of black marble eyes glinted back at him in the amber slivers of light from the window. The red glow on her alarm clock read 12:33 A.M.

His eyes knew exactly where to look. They quickly scanned down the dresser, and he licked his dry lips. Colored bras and matching lacy panties lay tossed about in the open drawer.

His hand went to his jeans and he felt his hard-on rise back to life. His eyes moved fast to the rocking chair where she had hung her white lace nightie. He closed his eyes and stroked himself faster, recalling in his mind exactly how she had looked last night. Her firm, full tits bouncing up and down while she fucked her boyfriend in that see-through white nightie. Her head thrown back in ecstasy, and her curved, full mouth open wide with pleasure. She was a bad girl, leaving her blinds open. Very bad. His hand moved faster still. Now he envisioned how she would look with those long legs wrapped in nylon thigh-highs and strapped into a pair of the high heels from her closet. And his own hands, locked around their black spikes, hoisting her legs up, up, up in the air and then spreading them wide apart while she screamed. First in fear, and then in pleasure. Her blond mane fanned out under her head on the bed, her arms strapped tight to the headboard.

The lacy crotch of her pretty pink panties and her thick blond bush, exposed right by his mouth. *Yum-yum!* He moaned loudly in his head and his breath hissed as it escaped through the tiny slit in the center of his contorted red smile. He stopped himself before he climaxed and opened his eyes again. Her bedroom door stood ajar, and he could see that the rest of the apartment was dark and empty. He sank back down to his spot under the evergreens. Sweat rolled down his face, and the latex suctioned fast to the skin. Thunder rumbled again, and he felt his cock slowly shrivel back down inside his pants.

She was supposed to have been home hours ago. Every single Wednesday night she gets home no later then 10:45 P.M. But tonight, *tonight*, of all nights, she's late. He bit down hard on his lower lip, re-opening the cut he had chewed on an hour earlier, tasting the salty blood that flooded his mouth. He fought back the almost overwhelming urge to scream.

Goddamn mother-fucking bitch! He could not help but be disappointed. He had been so excited, *so thrilled*, just counting off the minutes. At 10:45 she would walk right past him, only steps away, in her tight gym clothes. The lights would go on above him, and he would rise slowly to the window. She would purposely leave the blinds open, and he would watch. Watch as she pulled her sweaty T-shirt over her head and slid her tight shorts over her naked thighs. Watch as she would get herself ready for bed. *Ready for him!*

Like a giddy schoolboy on his first date, he had giggled to himself merrily in the bushes. *How far will we go tonight, my dear? First base? Second? All the way?* But those initial, exciting minutes had ticked by and here he still was, two hours later—squatting like a vagrant with unspeakable vermin crawling all over him, probably breeding in his ears. The anticipation that had fueled him, that had fed the fantasy, was now gone. His disappointment had slowly turned into anger, an anger that had grown more intense with each passing minute. He clenched his teeth hard and his breath hissed. No, siree, he was not excited anymore. He was not thrilled. He was beyond annoyed.

He sat chewing his lip in the dark for what seemed like another hour, but really was only a matter of minutes. Lightning lit the sky and the thunder rumbled even louder and he knew then that it was time to go. Grudgingly, he removed his mask, gathered his bag of tricks, and extricated himself from the bushes. He knew that there would be a next time.

Headlights beamed down the dark street just then, and he quickly ducked off the cement pathway back behind the hedges. A sleek silver BMW pulled up fast in front of the complex, double-parking no less than thirty feet from his hiding spot.

Minutes passed like hours, but finally the passenger door opened, and two long and luscious legs, their delicate feet wrapped in high-heeled black patent-leather pumps, swung out. He knew instantly that it was she, and an inexplicable feeling of calm came over him.

It must be fate.

Then the Clown sank back under the evergreens. To wait.

CHAPTER TWO

TIMES SQUARE AND Forty-second Street were still all aglow in neon, bustling with different sorts of life even past midnight on a simple Wednesday. Chloe Larson nervously chewed on a thumbnail and watched out the passenger-side window as the BMW snaked its way through the streets of Manhattan toward Thirty-fourth Street and the Midtown Tunnel.

She knew that she should not have gone out tonight. The tiny, annoying voice inside her head had told her as much all day long, but she hadn't listened, and with less than four weeks to go before the bar exam, she had blown off a night of intense studying for a night of romance and passion. A worthy cause, perhaps, except that the evening hadn't been very romantic in the end, and now she was both miserable and panic stricken, suffering from an overwhelming sense of dread about the exam. Michael continued to rant on about his day from corporate hell, and didn't seem to notice either her misery or her panic, much less her inattention. Or if he did, he didn't seem to care.

Michael Decker was Chloe's boyfriend. Possibly her soon-to-be ex-boyfriend. A high-profile trial attorney, he was on the partner track with the very prestigious Wall Street law firm of White, Hughey & Lombard. They had met there two summers ago when she was hired as Michael's legal intern in the Commercial Litigation Department. She had quickly learned that Michael never took no for an answer when he wanted a yes to his question. The first day on the job he was yelling at her to read her case law more closely, and the next one he was kissing her hot and heavy in the copy room. He was handsome and brilliant and had this romantic mystique about him that Chloe could not explain, and just could not ignore. So she had found a new job, romance had blossomed, and tonight had marked the two-year anniversary of their first real date.

For the past two weeks Chloe had asked, practically begged, Michael if they could celebrate their anniversary date after the bar exam. But instead, he had called her this same afternoon to surprise her with theater tickets for tonight's performance of *The Phantom of the Opera*. Michael knew everyone's weakness, and if he didn't know it, he found it. So when Chloe had first said no, he knew to immediately zero in on the guilt factor—that Irish-Catholic homing device buried deep within her conscience. *We hardly see each other anymore, Chloe. You're always studying. We deserve to spend some time together. We need it, babe, I need it.* Etc., etc., and etc. He finally told her that he'd had to practically steal the tickets from some needy client, and she relented, reluctantly agreeing to meet him in the city. She'd rushed into Manhattan all the while trying to quiet that disconcerting voice in the back of her head that had suddenly begun to shout.

After all that, she had to admit she wasn't even surprised when, ten minutes after curtain call, the elderly usher with the kind face handed her the note that told her Michael was stuck in an emergency meeting and would be late. She should have left right there, right then, but, well . . . she didn't. She watched now out the window as the BMW slid under the East River and the tunnel lights passed by in a dizzying blur of yellow.

Michael had shown up for the final curtain call with a rose in his hand and had begun the familiar litany of excuses before she could slug him. A zillion apologies later he had somehow managed to then guilt her into dinner, and the next thing she knew, they were heading across the street together to

Carmine's and she was left wondering just when and where she had lost her spinal cord. How she hated being Irish-Catholic. The guilt trips were more like pilgrimages.

If the night had only ended there, it would have been on a good note. But over a plate of veal marsala and a bottle of Cristal, Michael had delivered the sucker punch of the evening. She had just begun to relax a little and enjoy the champagne and romantic atmosphere when Michael had pulled out a small box that she instantly knew was not small enough.

"Happy Anniversary." He had smiled softly, a perfect smile, his sexy brown eyes warm in the flickering candlelight. The strolling violinists neared, like shark to chum. "I love you, baby."

Obviously not enough to marry me, she had thought as she stared at the silver-wrapped box with the extra-large white bow, afraid to open it. Afraid to see what wasn't inside.

"Go ahead, open it." He had filled their glasses with more champagne, and his grin had grown more smug. Obviously, he thought that alcohol and jewelry of any sort would surely get him out of the doghouse for being late. Little did he know that at that very moment he was so far from home, he was going to need a map and a survival kit to get back. *Or maybe she was wrong. Maybe he had just put it in a big box to fool her.*

But no. Inside, dangling from a delicate gold chain, was a pendant of two intertwined hearts, connected by a brilliant diamond. It was beautiful. But it wasn't round and it didn't fit on her finger. Mad at herself for thinking that way, she had blinked back hot tears. Before she knew it, he was out of his seat and behind her, moving her long blond hair onto her shoulders and fastening the necklace. He kissed the nape of her neck, obviously mistaking her tears for those of happiness. Or ignoring them. He whispered in her ear, "It looks great on you." Then he had sat back in his seat and ordered tiramisu, which arrived five minutes later with a candle and three singing Italians. The violinists soon got wind of the party downtown and had sauntered over and everyone had sung and strummed "Happy Anniversary" in Italian. She wished she had just stayed home.

The car now moved along the Long Island Expressway toward Queens with Michael still oblivious to her absence from the conversation. It had started to sprinkle outside, and lightning lit the sky. In the side-view mirror Chloe watched the Manhattan skyline shrink smaller and smaller behind Lefrak City and Rego Park, until it almost disappeared from sight. After two years, Michael knew what she wanted, and it *wasn't* a necklace. *Damn him.* She had enough stress in her life with the bar exam that she needed this emotional albatross about as much as she needed a hole in the head.

They approached her exit on the Clearview Expressway and she finally decided that a discussion about their future together—or lack thereof—would just have to wait until after she sat for the bar. The last thing she wanted right now was the heart-wrenching ache of a failed relationship. One stress factor at a time. Still, she hoped her stony silence in the car would send its message.

"It's not just the depo," Michael continued on, seemingly oblivious. "If I have to run to the judge every time I want to ask something as inane as a date of birth and Social Security number, this case is going to get buried in the mountains of sanctions I'm going to ask for."

He pulled off onto Northern Boulevard and stopped at a light. There were no other cars out on the street at this hour. Finally he paused, recognized the sound of silence, and looked over cautiously at Chloe. "Are you okay? You haven't said much at all since we left Carmine's. You're not still mad about my being late, are you? I said I was sorry." He gripped the leather steering wheel with both hands, bracing himself for the fight that hung heavy in the air. His tone was arrogant and defensive. "You know what that firm is like. I just can't get away, and that's the bottom line. The deal depended on me being there."

The silence in the small car was almost deafening. Before she could even respond, he had changed both his tone and the subject. Reaching across the front seat, he traced the heart pendant that rested in the hollow of her throat with his finger. "I had it made special. Do you like it?" His voice was now a sensuous inviting whisper.

No, no, no. She wasn't going to go there. Not tonight. *I refuse to answer, Counselor, on the grounds it may incriminate me.*

"I'm just distracted." She touched her neck and said flatly, "It's beautiful." The hell she was going to let him think that she was just being an emotional bitch who was upset because she didn't get the ring she'd told all her friends and extended family she was expecting. He could take what she said and chew on it for a few days. The light changed and they drove on in silence.

"I know what this is about. I know what you're thinking." He sighed an exaggerated sigh and leaned back in the driver's seat, hitting the palm of his hand hard against the steering wheel. "This is all about the bar exam, isn't it? Jesus, Chloe, you have studied for that test almost nonstop for two months, and I have been really understanding. I really have. I only asked for one night out . . . Just one. I have had this incredibly tough day and all during dinner there has been this, this tension between us. Loosen up, will you? I really, really need you to." He sounded annoyed that he even had to bother having this conversation, and she wanted to slug him again. "Take it from someone who has been there: Stop worrying about the bar exam. You're tops in your class, you've got a terrific job lined up—you'll do fine."

"I'm sorry that my company at dinner did not brighten your tough day, Michael. I really am," she said, the sarcasm chilling her words. "But, let me just say that you must suffer from short-term memory loss. Do you remember that we spent last night together, too? I wouldn't exactly say that I have neglected you. Might I also remind you that I did not even want to celebrate tonight and I told you as much, but you chose to ignore me. Now, as far as having fun goes, I might have been in a better mood if you hadn't been two hours late." Great. In addition to the guilt pangs her stomach was digesting for dessert, her head was beginning to throb. She rubbed her temples.

He pulled the car up in front of her apartment building, looking for a spot.

"You can just let me out here," she said sharply.

He looked stunned and stopped the car, double-parking in front of her complex.

"What? You don't want me to come in tonight?" He sounded hurt, surprised. Good. That made two of them.

"I'm just really tired, Michael, and this conversation is,

well, it's degenerating. And quick. Plus I missed my aerobics class tonight, so I think I'll take the early one in the morning before class."

Silence filled the car. He looked off out his window and she gathered her jacket and purse. "Look, I'm really sorry about tonight, Chloe. I really am. I wanted it to be special and it obviously wasn't, and for that, I apologize. And I'm sorry if you're stressed over the bar exam. I shouldn't have snapped like that." His tone was sincere and much softer. The "sensitive guy" tactic took her slightly by surprise.

Leaning over the car seat, he traced a finger up her neck and over her face. He ran his finger over her cheekbones as she looked down in her lap, fidgeting for the keys in her purse, trying hard to ignore his touch. Burying his hand in her honey-blond hair, he pulled her close and brushed his mouth near her ear. Softly he murmured, "You don't need the gym. Let me work you out."

Michael made her weak. Ever since that day in the copy room. And she could rarely say no to him. Chloe could smell the sweetness of his warm breath, and felt his strong hands tracing farther down the small of her back. In her head she knew she should not put up with his crap, but in her heart, well, that was another story. For crazy reasons she loved him. But tonight—well, tonight was just not going to happen. Even the spineless had their limits. She opened the car door fast and stepped out, catching her breath. When she leaned back in, her tone was one of indifference.

"This is not going to happen, Michael. I'm tempted, but it's already almost one. Marie is picking me up at eight forty-five, and I can't be late again." She slammed the door shut.

He turned off the engine and got out of the driver's side. "Fine, fine. I get it. Some great fucking night this turned out to be," he said sullenly and slammed his door in return. She glared at him, turned on her heel, and marched off across the courtyard toward her lobby.

"Shit, shit, shit," he mumbled and ran after her. He caught up with her on the sidewalk and grabbed her hand. "Stop, just stop. Look, I'm frustrated. I'm also an insensitive clod. I admit it." He looked into her eyes for a sign that it was safe to proceed. Apparently, they still read caution, but when she did not move away he took that as a good sign. "There, I've said it. I'm a jerk and tonight was a mess and it's all my fault. Come on, please, forgive me," he whispered. "Don't end tonight like this." He wrapped his hand behind her neck and pulled her mouth to his. Her full lips tasted sweet.

After a moment she stepped back and touched her hand lightly to her mouth. "Fine. Forgiven. But you're still not spending the night." The words were cool.

She needed to be alone tonight. To think. Past her bedroom, where was this whole thing headed anyway? The streetlights cast deep shadows on the walkway. The wind blew harder and the trees and bushes rustled and stirred around them. A dog barked off in the distance, and the sky rumbled.

Michael looked up. "I think it's going to pour tonight," he said absently, grabbing her limp hand in his. They walked to the front door of the building in silence. On the stoop he smiled and said lightly, "Damn. And here I thought I was so smooth. Sensitivity is supposed to work with you women. The man who's not afraid to cry, show his feelings." He laughed, obviously fishing for a smile in return, then he massaged her hand with his and kissed her gently on the cheek, moving his lips lightly over her face toward her lips. Her eyes were closed, her full mouth slightly parted. "You look so good tonight I just might cry if I can't have you." *If at first you don't succeed . . . try, try again.* His hands moved slowly down the small of her back, over her skirt. She didn't move. "You know, it's not too late to change your mind," he murmured, his fingers moving over her. "I can just go move the car."

His touch was electrifying. Finally, she pulled away and opened the door. Damn it, she was going to make a statement tonight and not even her libido was going to stop her.

"Good night, Michael. I'll talk to you tomorrow."

He looked as if he had been punched in the gut. Or somewhere else.

"Happy Anniversary," he said quietly as she slipped into the foyer door. The glass door closed with a creak.

He walked slowly back to the car, keys in hand. Damn it. He had really screwed things up tonight. He really had. At the car, he watched as Chloe stood at the living room window and waved to him that all was okay inside. She still looked pissed. And then the curtain closed and she was gone. He climbed in the BMW and drove off toward the expressway and back toward Manhattan, thinking about how to get back on her good side. Maybe he'd send her flowers tomorrow. That's it. Long red roses with an apology and an "I love you." That should get him out of the doghouse and back into her bed. With the crackle of thunder sounding closer still and the storm fast moving in, he turned onto the Clearview Expressway, leaving Bayside way behind him.

PENGUIN GROUP (USA) INC.
Online

Your Internet gateway to a virtual environment with
hundreds of entertaining and enlightening books
from Penguin Group (USA) Inc.

*While you're there, get the latest buzz on
the best authors and books around—*

Tom Clancy, Patricia Cornwell, W.E.B. Griffin,
Nora Roberts, William Gibson, Robin Cook,
Brian Jacques, Catherine Coulter, Stephen King,
Ken Follett, Terry McMillan, and many more!

**Penguin Group (USA) Inc. Online is located at
http://www.penguin.com**

PENGUIN GROUP (USA) Inc.
NEWS

Every month you'll get an inside look at our upcom-
ing books and new features on our site. This is an
ongoing effort to provide you with the most
up-to-date information about
our books and authors.

Subscribe to Penguin Group (USA) Inc. News at
http://www.penguin.com/newsletters